BOOKS BY JANE STEEN

The House of Closed Doors Series

The House of Closed Doors

Eternal Deception

The Shadow Palace

The Jewel Cage

The Scott-De Quincy Mysteries

Lady Helena Investigates

Lady Odelia's Secret

W0010450

Dedicated to Bob Steen,
My husband and best friend

THE JEWEL CAGE

JANE STEEN

PART I
1877

1

ABSENT FRIENDS

July 1877

Madame Arlette Belvoix, the head of dressmaking in Rutherford's department store, rarely greeted anyone when she entered a room. She merely waited until the sheer force of her personality impinged upon those present. She never interrupted, creating for herself an opportunity to observe the workers unseen.

This procedure naturally struck terror into the dressmaking staff. Those of us who knew Madame well had developed a defensive reflex, an intuition that alerted us to her silent presence. Without interrupting us, she caused us to interrupt ourselves.

Even I, a senior couturière and partner in Rutherford's—not to mention the wife of its senior partner—was not immune to the chilling effect of Madame's noiseless arrivals. When it came to dressmaking, the small Frenchwoman had absolute power by reason of her genius, and I, like the other partners, submitted to her authority absolutely.

I'd been in fine verbal flow as I discussed my friend Elizabeth Parnell's wedding dress with Magda, one of our best embroiderers. But when my words began to stumble over one another and my concentration wavered, I recognized the symptoms. I looked up and rose to my feet.

"How can I help you, Madame?"

I pulled out a chair for my mentor and nodded at Magda, who had also risen. Magda dipped a tiny curtsey—in Madame's direction, not mine—and glided away toward her work bench.

Madame ignored the proffered seat, and my heart sank a little lower in my chest. She had to tip her head back to gaze at me; the light from the atelier's large windows enhanced the effect of her steel-ball irises, already deepened in hue by the sober navy-blue dress she wore.

"Please do me the honor of stepping into my room, Mrs. Rutherford."

A smile of grandmotherly aspect and an encouraging tilt of her head accompanied the request. Neither smile nor tilt fooled me for an instant. They didn't fool the other women either. The muted hum of conversation sank to a hush. Every worker bent her head to look at her work, and *only* her work.

I followed Madame to the tiny cupboard of a room she had claimed as her own, my mind whirring. Avoiding the books, journals, drawings, and fabric samples that had accumulated since last year's fire, I sat on the hard, narrow chair that occupied the remaining piece of floor. Dismay stole over me, although I couldn't, at that moment, have said why.

Madame seated herself opposite me and rested her elbows on her desk, spreading the fingertips of her small, precise hands and tapping them together. She smiled. "Is Miss Parnell's wedding gown finished? The nuptials are just eight days away, *n'est-ce pas?*"

Did she think I was spending too long on Elizabeth's dress? Or had she seen some flaw I'd missed? I tried to smile back. "I must do another fitting. Miss Parnell has lost flesh."

"Better that than the other way around." Madame's eyes glinted with what was perhaps humor.

There were no flaws in the dress, I would swear by it. I had cut it myself, and in my mind's eye saw every inch of silk damask, every stitch of the embroidery, every flutter of satin as Elizabeth walked up the aisle in her Lake Forest church. It would be magnificent.

Madame made a small noise in her throat. "And it has been only—what? Nine or ten weeks since your own wedding?"

"About that." I glanced down at my left hand, where the rose-gold band Martin had slipped on my finger in May sat against the bright constellation of diamonds with which he'd marked our engagement in April.

"You have much to occupy your mind."

Here was the clue, and I decided to get the worst over. "Have I forgotten something? I have, haven't I? Something important."

"Or *somebody*." Madame raised her eyebrows like a teacher encouraging a rather slow pupil.

A cold weight settled in my chest, and a prickling sensation ran down my spine. I clapped both hands over my mouth.

"Bertha Palmer. Oh, glory." I spoke through my fingers.

Madame nodded. "She came to the store *in person* to inquire after the sketches you promised her. For Friday."

It was now Tuesday. Bertha Palmer was the queen of Chicago society—of all people to let down. But I was a member of Chicago society too, like her the wife of a wealthy merchant. I stiffened my spine and faced Madame squarely.

"Was she very cross?" I detected a trace of sardonic humor in my voice that would not have been there when I arrived in Chicago as an unknown dressmaker.

A little of the humor communicated itself to Madame's

expression, which softened a fraction. "Not very, and not at all after I finished talking to her. We should afford a new bride a little—what is the word?—leeway, especially a bride in your social position. Of course, it is a novel experience for these ladies to purchase gowns designed by someone on whom they pay calls." She waved an expressive hand. "Although why it should be different when a *woman* has a profession . . ."

"It is though." I felt the corners of my mouth turn down. "One lady I call on actually laughed out loud when she learned I would continue to work as a married woman." I could hear her voice in my head: *My dear, how democratic.*

"And yet they have already solicited you to sit on their charitable committees?" This time Madame's smile was genuine.

"Before we put away the wedding presents. I refused, of course. What with the new store still being built, and the new house, Martin's so busy too. I must think of him now, as well as Sarah and Tess—"

"A woman carries many burdens." Madame nodded, a trace of sympathy in her eyes. "*Eh bien*, I suppose I cannot fault your dedication to work since the two of you barely took time for a honeymoon. But you should make sure you do not forget your clients too often, Mrs. Rutherford."

I rubbed my forehead with a hand that was a touch colder than usual. "You're quite right. I'd better go home and send the sketches to Mrs. Palmer at once, with a note of apology. They're on my desk. I was almost finished with them, but I kept worrying about the Lombardis. I've told you about my friends in Kansas, haven't I? I put the drawings aside for a few minutes while I wrote another letter to Catherine, and I believe Martin came in and placed some architect's drawings on top. I remember he wanted to talk to me about the new house."

"The Lombardis—yes, the missionary family of whom you are so fond. You still have not heard from them?" A small frown appeared on Madame's brow.

"No, and I'm dreadfully worried. If it weren't for Elizabeth's wedding, I'd be on my way to Kansas by now. I've received no communication from Catherine Lombardi for weeks—months—even when I wrote to her about our engagement. I've written to her four times since. I last heard from her in March, when she saw in the Chicago papers that the store burned down. Of course, I was ill then." I touched the scar by my ear from where my hair had caught fire. "I waited to write back until I had some good news, but I've had no answer."

"Could she be traveling?" Madame stood up, signaling that our meeting was drawing to an end, and I did the same.

"Perhaps," I said. "If something had . . . happened to her, wouldn't I have received word from Pastor Lombardi or Teddy? I can only hope they're now on their way to Chicago after visiting elsewhere—maybe on the East Coast where their families are. I suppose I imagine that if I write enough letters, one will catch up with them. It's more than a year since Catherine promised to come to Chicago for Lucy's health."

And the events of the last year had held me back from returning to Kansas. Only now, with Martin's ordeal as a suspected murderer and the destruction of the store behind us, were my fears becoming difficult to live with. I regarded Catherine Lombardi as a second mother, and I wanted —*needed*—to be sure she and her family were safe.

I followed the small, plump figure of Madame Belvoix out into the corridor. As always, I felt the constriction of our temporary premises. Quite apart from the salespeople and clerks and maintenance people, we now had over three hundred employees on the dressmaking side. Seamstresses,

7

cutters, toile makers, sewing machine operators, embroiderers, beaders, apprentices: they had shifts at different times, and the work Madame and I had done on simplifying and standardizing our pattern pieces had helped, but the demand for our dresses was immense and our staff growing apace.

We even employed dressmakers to work at night; it was surprising how many of Chicago's wealthy women left important sartorial decisions till the last moment. We could produce a dinner gown in twenty-four hours—*if* the customer was ready to pay an outrageous price, and some were.

The gaslit corridor was overly warm, crammed with people rushing to their destination. Dark-clad shopgirls and male sales staff, clerks in sack coats and striped trousers, smartly dressed couturières and dressmaking assistants, embroiderers in light gray—it made it easier to see dropped needles and threads—and men in overalls jostled past one another with words of greeting, only to be swallowed by rooms or stairwells from which others were emerging. It wouldn't be a moment too soon before the new store was ready.

It wasn't until we were on the staircase and about to part company that a question occurred to me.

"Why didn't you send someone to bring me downstairs when Mrs. Palmer arrived, Madame? I should have made my apologies in person."

Madame halted, fixing me with a severe gaze.

"I will not countenance a partner in this store, a senior couturière, apologizing in front of our customers and staff. That would not do at all. We must protect your dignity, Mrs. Rutherford."

"Good heavens." I blinked. "Well, I owe you my thanks for that."

"A letter to Mrs. Palmer accompanied by your excellent

sketches will be thanks enough. A *prompt* letter," Madame said with a regal air. "And you will kindly ask Mr. Rutherford to make himself available tomorrow at eight o'clock sharp. We must discuss the storage of the seed pearls, semi-precious stones, fine lace, and the like. It is imperative that we can get the dressmaking valuables out of the store next time there is a fire—it has been *most* inconvenient to rebuild my supplies."

"Of course, Madame."

"He will no doubt already be planning for the safekeeping of jewelry, with all the robberies this wicked town seems to suffer lately, but he *must not* neglect my stock."

She resumed her descent to the sales floor, leaving me, as she often did, in some confusion as to who really ran the store that bore my married name.

It was late morning by the time I arrived in Aldine Square, so I wasn't surprised to walk into a quiet house. The designs for Bertha Palmer were sitting on my workroom desk, now visible as Martin had taken away the architect's plans. He too was busy; an observant man, he would normally notice my oversight.

Settling into my chair, I spared a glance at my cutting table, where the stacked pieces of a summer dress I was making for Sarah reproached me for my lack of attention to my daughter's needs. Perhaps if I was *very* good and got the work for Bertha Palmer done quickly, I could treat myself to an hour with Sarah's dress after luncheon? I presumed Tess and Sarah would return for the midday meal. We could eat together, and then maybe Tess would sit and talk to me as I sewed, perhaps help me by doing some basting, just like in the old days when we worked side by side, two friends as close as sisters . . .

I sighed as I pulled out my letter paper and searched for the pen with the best nib. The next hour flew by as I reviewed the sketches, added some finishing touches, and wrote an apologetic—but not groveling—note to Mrs. Palmer. After all, the Potter Palmers weren't so *very* much wealthier than we were, and Madame was right: my dignity mattered too.

Having wrapped sketches and letter in brown paper tied up with string, I became far more cheerful. Especially when I heard the front door open below. Would it be Tess, returning from her outing to the market with our maid, Zofia? Or Sarah, back from her morning's airing in the park with her governess, Miss Baker? I rose to my feet, parcel in hand, my step lightening and the corners of my mouth turning up as I almost ran onto the landing.

But it was neither Tess nor Sarah. Only one inhabitant of the house in Aldine Square took the stairs two at a time. Only one of us had long enough legs and the freedom from skirts that made such a speedy ascent possible. My smile widened into a grin.

"You needn't run—I'm on my way down," I said to the footsteps.

"Are you finished composing your craven apologies to Bertha Palmer?" came the amused voice of my husband from the floor below.

"Nothing craven is contained therein, thank you very much. If Bertha's so eager to wear Lillington designs that she comes to the store in person, she's hardly going to abandon the project. She told me my dresses are almost equal to Worth's—and heaven knows they're cheaper and don't require to be shipped from Paris."

"*Almost* equal?"

Another turn of the stairs brought Martin into view. He had stopped on the landing below, arms crossed as he contemplated my descent. I put an extra sway into my hips just to see the grin light up his face.

A pink line indented my husband's forehead where he'd pushed his silk hat hard onto his head. I deduced he had been riding Gentleman, the gray horse that was his favorite mode of transport. He must have come from the store—from where else would he get the news that I'd returned home? Madame Belvoix might protect me from our customers, but she wouldn't have kept the tale of my lapse from Martin.

"I don't expect to equal Worth—not yet anyway." I put the brown paper parcel down on the console table. "As Madame says, true mastery takes time." Freed of my burden, I moved into the enfolding warmth of two long arms.

"Do you think Mrs. Power could rustle up some food straightaway?" asked Martin after greeting me with a prolonged, and most enjoyable, kiss. "I'm starving."

His stomach agreed with a sort of whine. I laughed and wriggled free of his embrace.

"You'll have to wait until Tess and Sarah get home for luncheon." I patted at my hair, which had become mussed, and picked up my parcel again, sniffing at the air. "I suspect Mrs. Power's baking a meat pie."

"That was my guess too, and that smell's not helping. I feel like a famished wolf." Martin gnashed his teeth in imitation of a hungry beast. I sighed.

"If you simply can't wait five more seconds for food, I'll see if Mrs. Power will spare a moment to put up a plate of cold beef and pickles." I put my foot on the first stair downward. "I need to go down there anyway to give this parcel to Mr. Nutt—he should deliver it by hand."

"O excellent wife, whose value is far greater than a whole heap of rubies." Martin, moving toward his dressing room, blew a kiss at me.

"And never ask Mrs. Power to 'rustle up' food—you

sound like a cowpoke asking for a plate of beans. Wherever do you get such dreadful slang?"

"Blame my ever-expanding frontier business. While I'm eating my pre-luncheon, would you look over the plans of the house with me? I'm considering adding a little annex; I have an idea for a billiard room . . ."

His voice faded away as I moved downstairs, in a hurry to catch Mr. Nutt before he ate. I flipped up my timepiece; surely the discussion about the house wouldn't take *all* the time before luncheon? I needed to talk to Martin about the Lombardis. But I should choose my moment, and men became so testy when they were hungry. Maybe I should return with a *large* plate of beef and pickles.

MARTIN'S ENTHUSIASM FOR OUR NEW HOUSE—A DWELLING which seemed to grow larger every time he reviewed the plans—filled the minutes so neatly that I never had a chance to change the subject before Tess arrived.

Luncheon was a lively affair and took longer than I'd anticipated. Tess and Sarah were delighted to have both of us at home, and it would be unfair to rush back to work. By the time we all left the table, I had to relinquish the cherished dream of an hour's sewing and agree to Martin's proposition that we ride back to the store in the rockaway and "put our noses to the grindstone."

"After all," he pointed out as he handed me into the conveyance, "we haven't done nearly as much work as we should these past few weeks."

He helped me settle into my seat as Mr. Nutt shut the carriage door and climbed up onto the driver's bench, then sat beside me, remarking, "Although if you ask me, we should still be on our honeymoon."

His arm went to steal around my waist, and I batted it away. The rockaway's windows were quite large enough for people to see us. A good-natured laugh and a pinch well below the waist were my reward; once married, I'd soon learned that Martin was familiar with the weak points in a woman's armor of layered fabrics. Satisfied with his victory, my husband angled himself into the corner of the seat and crossed his arms.

"It's outrageous that we barely stopped working long enough to marry," he mused, his eyes on the carriage's painted ceiling. "Of course, not many newlyweds are *both* involved in running a large store—one that has to be rebuilt into the bargain."

"We seem to be busier than almost anyone else I know," I agreed. "In our social set, anyhow. I daresay the members of Tess's family work harder than we do. Still," I raised my eyebrows at my husband, "I was quite content with our three days in the Palmer House's bridal chamber."

"Yes, they were a good three days, weren't they?"

The look Martin gave me sent a wave of warmth through the core of my body, and I blushed. Martin didn't laugh though. He reached out to encircle my fingers in a large, warm hand and bent his head to kiss the inside of my wrist above my glove.

"They were a *very* good three days." I sounded a little out of breath.

"Then you're happy, Nellie?"

"You know I am."

Martin relinquished my hand and crossed his arms again, his eyes on me. There was silence for a few moments while we contemplated each other, close together in the intimate space of the carriage, heedless of the bouncing, rocking motion of our progress toward Michigan Avenue. But eventually Martin shook his head.

"And yet something's on your mind, isn't it?" He raised a finger as I opened my mouth. "Don't deny it. You know I can read you like a book. You have that kind of face. No, don't stare out of the window to avoid me. Besides, you told Madame that you're distracted because you're worried about the Lombardis."

"And she took it upon herself to tell *you*? She has no right."

"I suppose she has the right—or believes she has the right —to concern herself with any matter that affects the work of such an important member of the dressmaking staff."

Martin spoke evenly, but his smile had faded. "As the senior partner, I should be concerned too—but on a personal level, I hate to think of you fretting over something and not telling me. We *are* husband and wife now."

"I've been trying to talk to you about it." I looked down at my laced hands in their fine doeskin gloves. "I intended to broach the subject earlier, but you were so enthusiastic about the house, and then it was luncheon, and then—"

"I thought you told me the Lombardis were traveling. Why are you so worried now?"

"I didn't *know* they were traveling—I *believed* they must be. When I wrote to Catherine to tell her we were to be wed, I was convinced she'd come to Chicago. I even wired her the money for the train fares. When she didn't reply, I almost wondered if I'd offended her." I grimaced. "It was rather a triumphant letter, and you know what Pastor Lombardi says about pride. And it was awfully short notice, and I probably spent half the letter exulting over being made a partner—"

"What, more than about marrying *me*? Do tell, Mrs. Rutherford."

"Oh, hush. And we were so busy, and so happy, and there was all that ruckus over the wedding dress—and now I suppose I feel guilty for not having thought more about the

Lombardis. Especially since I didn't write much to Catherine last year."

"No?"

"Well, given that the love of my life stood accused of murdering his wife"—I saw Martin wince and sent him an anguished half smile of apology—"and I'd become a department store spy to help him, I suppose my retreat into brevity was excusable. Catherine knew about your—about Lucetta, of course. It was all over the Chicago papers for months." I watched my husband make a valiant effort not to flinch this time. "I mostly sent assurances that you were doing as well as could be expected and gave her news of Sarah and Tess."

"Must have been deuced frustrating, with you at the center of such a thrilling situation."

"It wasn't thrilling—it was horrible. Martin, I want to go to Kansas. I need to know what's happened to her."

"Now? With Elizabeth's wedding so close?" A line appeared between Martin's eyebrows.

"Well, no," I conceded. "I wouldn't desert Elizabeth right now. But it's only another week—two, since we've said we'll stay with her parents until the twenty-sixth."

"It's the worst time of year for traveling west. The heat apart from anything else, then there's the malaria in Kansas. Cholera, typhoid, yellow jack—"

"*You'd* travel to Kansas." I felt my face assuming its most stubborn expression.

"On my own or with another man, perhaps." Martin frowned heavily. "And then only if necessary. I wasn't planning to visit the frontier till September or October. Couldn't you wait until then?"

"Would *you* wait?" I was almost shouting now, glad that the carriage was moving again and the noises of the street covered my voice. "No, you wouldn't. I don't intend to take Sarah or Tess. I can travel by myself."

"Don't be ridiculous."

"Why is that ridiculous?" My face was hot. "Because I'm a woman?"

"Because I'd never let you go alone when I'm able to be with you." Martin's face was pale and earnest. "Even if it is inconvenient or dangerous. From now on, we face our dangers together."

"Oh." I drew a deep breath. "Oh, drat you, Martin Rutherford, you always have a way of sending me into a temper and then saying exactly the right thing to cool me down. I'm sorry; you're just trying to be sensible. But Catherine's like a mother to me." I swallowed hard against a lump that had formed in my throat. "She's part of my past."

To my relief, Martin's face lost some of its bleak look—the look I'd seen so often in the year after Lucetta's murder. He reached out to stroke the skin in front of my left ear, where the curved scar was fading from pink to white.

"When it comes to your past, Eleanor Lillington Rutherford, I consider my claim the greatest. I've known you since you were three."

I captured his hand and held it over my scar. His fingers warmed the taut flesh for a few seconds before the carriage jolted, separating us.

"Not during that period of my past." I breathed deep, seeing Kansas again, and then farther back in my memory, the Women's House. "The time I spent at the Poor Farm made me into a woman. And the years at the Eternal Life Seminary made me into the dressmaker I am now. Catherine was part of all that."

"I thought we had resolved to start life anew." Martin spoke lightly, but there was a hint of strain in his voice.

I was silent for a few moments, ordering my thoughts. Martin and I had talked about shedding the past in the intense, intoxicating days between our engagement and marriage, when the world had seemed to shrink to the two of us, so strong was the pull to unite as one. I had imagined then that, after being held in a Chicago jail for a murder he did not commit, Martin might want to sell the burned-over site of the first Rutherford's store and move somewhere else —to New York, perhaps. Or that he might insist on an extended voyage through Europe after our wedding. That he might wish to go someplace where the ghost of Lucetta Rutherford, née Gambarelli, would not drift through his memories in a waft of gardenia perfume and a flash of diamonds. We had enough money to live anywhere we wanted, do anything we wanted; the store was unnecessary in monetary terms.

But that would have meant disrupting Sarah's life again, and a child needed stability. And was it fair to ask Tess to part from her family now that she'd found them? Chicago had become our home.

And then there was the store. Seen as a whole, it *was* necessary to both of us. For me, it provided the stage on which my career would unfold. For Martin, it was something deeper—a visible symbol of his creativity, a proof of his masculinity, an edifice that shouted to the world that he was worthy. A legacy to bequeath to his heirs.

"We could only begin life anew if we were reborn as infants, my darling," I said at last. "And didn't you just point out how important you were in my past? I might miss you the second time around."

It was the right answer, and to my relief lines of laughter creased the skin at the corners of Martin's eyes and mouth. "Practical, as always. But won't you allow that my concerns also have their practical side? It's not just disease. You might be traveling toward disaster. It's true that they've driven the tribes out of Kansas, but it's a big state. And the Indian Wars are constantly in the papers."

It was a sultry July day, but an icy chill washed over me. "Is that what you think?" I twisted round to stare at Martin. "Do you believe the mission has been attacked?"

"It's one explanation."

"There are others?"

Up till that moment, my fears for the Lombardis had amounted to a diffuse worry of the kind that rests upon a fundamental conviction that all would be well. I realized that I'd been counting on the perfectly ordinary explanation that would soon be proffered for Catherine's silence. Martin's words had burst that tiny bubble of reassuring delusion.

"Serious illness." Martin shrugged, unfocused gaze on the ceiling. "A roving band of outlaws—"

He stopped and stared at me, his eyes wide.

"Nellie, I'm so sorry. I was thinking out loud. You've gone quite white. What an idiot I am."

He gathered me to him. I let myself relax into his embrace, heedless of who might see us. His heart thudded steadily below my ear; my own seemed to be jittering in my chest.

"You're giving me more and more reasons to go to Kansas as soon as possible," I said into Martin's lapel.

"Of course I am. I forget my wife rushes toward danger instead of running away from it. But those are my wild imaginings—reality tends to be far more prosaic."

"Not for me." Almost unconsciously, I touched the scar by my ear. "I seem to possess a talent for disaster. So do you, come to that. But I'm grateful for the moments of peril I've lived through, in a way. I've grown because of them. I've found reserves of courage I hadn't dreamed I had."

The dark bulk of the surrounding buildings warned us that we were arriving at the temporary store, and we pulled apart—but not before Martin had planted a swift kiss on my mouth.

"You're pure courage from head to toe, my dear. You've been full of fighting spirit since you were a little girl—it's what I've always loved about you. But listen, would you let me make some inquiries before you go rushing off to Kansas? I could contact the denominational office, set the Pinkerton agency onto finding the Lombardis—there are a dozen different courses of action I could put in motion." He put out a steadying hand as the rockaway slowed. "I should have thought of doing them before. It would make far more sense to gather some facts first, so you'd at least know in which direction to travel."

I nodded, conceding the point, and the tension in his face eased. In another moment, Mr. Nutt was opening the carriage door and Martin was handing me out, smiling as I shook out the folds the journey had put in my slate-blue day dress. The harsh sunlight of a Chicago summer flashed dazzling reflections from any window not shaded by an awning and gleamed on Martin's tall silk hat. The moonstones in his cufflinks and tie pin shone like crystallized tears.

In the few seconds before I smiled at the doorman and preceded Martin into the store, I was aware of people staring. A small, grubby child fingered a runny nose, gawping upward. A man in carpenter's overalls looked pointedly at us, impatient at having to wait for us to pass. A shopgirl in a Field & Leiter's uniform caught my eye and gave me a brief smile, as if in rueful acknowledgment of my good fortune.

I was aware I cut a polished figure in my embroidered silk, sober and yet sumptuous, as befitted a partner in that successful enterprise, the Rutherford's department store. But my heart, at that precise moment, was on the plains of Kansas, where the dirt would be drying to an ochre dust and the grasses ripening fast under the spreading sky.

2

CAGE

*N*otwithstanding my promise to Martin that I would not "rush off" to Kansas and his assurances that he had acted at once to send out Pinkerton agents in search of the Lombardis, I was unable to shake off my restless mood. When a messenger boy came to the atelier three days later to summon me to a partners' meeting, my immediate reaction was one of irritation. Did Martin not realize that we were days away from Elizabeth's wedding and that the finishing details of such a fine nuptial gown took time and concentration?

But I was a partner in the company that owned Rutherford's and must not neglect that duty. I gave a few more instructions to my assistants on readying the dress for the late afternoon fitting I had scheduled with Elizabeth and did my best to arrange my face into an expression of polite interest as I entered Martin's office.

Joe Salazar, our general manager and partner, greeted me as I entered, his narrow visage grave. "There's been another robbery, Nell." He held out a chair for me.

"A seriously injured watchman this time." Martin, who

had briefly risen as I entered, went back to studying the broadsheet that lay on his desk. "At Bermann & Sidewash. And once again they were selective. They only took a half-dozen pieces, but one of them—a tiara—was astoundingly valuable."

"Isn't that where you bought my engagement ring?" I forgot my irritation as I leaned over to peer at the closely printed newspaper article.

"Best jeweler in Chicago, in my opinion." Martin looked up. "Joe put me on to them. Sol Bermann's his—what was it, Joe?"

"Second cousin's brother-in-law," said Joe laconically. "We attend the same temple. I must go visit him in the hospital."

"Was he attacked too?" I asked.

"The shock affected his heart," Martin said. "Joe, why don't you take some time off this afternoon?"

"Once we're done here. Leah's there, of course. You can rely on my wife for visiting the sick." Joe pulled the rolled drawing that Martin had deposited on the table toward him, spreading it out and placing small weights on the corners. "So let's hear about this jewelry vault, Martin. With a time lock?"

"The latest model." Martin looked pleased with himself. "The time lock will mean that we can only open it at set times, you see," he said to me. "Times under our control. At all other hours, it's entirely sealed. Even if a robber kidnapped a partner and forced them to work the combination, they couldn't get in. We can vary the opening times so that the gangs won't know when to plan a raid."

"Is that the topic of this meeting?" I leaned over to peruse the drawing, smiling at Joe as he turned it so I could see better. "It looks like a cage."

"It's a big enough expense that Martin is obliged under

the terms of our partnership to ask for our agreement." Joe grinned. "As I pointed out to him."

"You know very well you're as excited about the idea as I am." Martin tapped the drawing as he pretended to bestow a stern look on the man who was not only our general manager and partner, but our friend. "See here, Nell." Another tap. "It *is* a cage, buried inside a two-foot-thick box of concrete reinforced with steel shavings. A massive door—the room is big too. Far bigger than any safe I can buy. We're just in time to make the addition and still open the store at the end of November."

"Do we need something that enormous?" I asked. "Is that where we'll store the dressmaking valuables?"

Joe shook his head, smiling ruefully. "As if we could make Madame Belvoix agree to a vault that isn't accessible whenever she wishes it. She has negotiated her own small strongroom within the dressmaking department. Near a fire escape."

"So why—?"

"Think about it, Nellie." Martin leaned forward, his eyes alight. "Some of the gowns we sell are worn at the choicest dinners and grandest celebrations in Chicago—in the whole of the Middle West. Why should we not supply the jewels as well? You've listened to Powell McCombs lament the lost opportunity."

I nodded. The head of the Rutherford's jewelry department had often expressed the wish that we might sell articles of higher value.

"McCombs would love the tiara they stole from Bermann & Sidewash." Joe ran a finger down the newspaper article, stopping at the description. "Just imagine this. Diamonds, pearls as big as your thumbnail, *and* sapphires. It would look beautiful in hair like yours, Nell."

"I've never worn a tiara," I mused. "I wouldn't ever want

23

to be the sort of woman who drips with jewels. I'm sure Mama would not have agreed with the excess you see in this town."

"We live in a decadent age." Martin shrugged. "And as a merchant, I intend to make the most of it. So, since those gathered around this table represent a majority of shares, is my outrageous expense approved?"

Joe spread his hands in an expressive gesture. "It makes good business sense to install a vault now rather than later. I vote to approve."

"Mrs. Rutherford?" Martin gave me a sidelong smile.

"If Joe says it's all right, I have no objection." I pushed the newspaper away from me.

"Approved, then." Martin looked pleased. "And Joe can go comfort Sol Bermann. Give him our good wishes, Joe, and tell him I'll call on him when he's feeling better."

I turned from watching Joe leave the room and was surprised by the expression on Martin's face.

"What's wrong?" I asked. "You're staring at that drawing as if it were something dangerous or disgusting."

"Am I?" Martin looked up, his brow clearing. "It takes me that way at times, I suppose. I just wish—" He stopped and took a deep breath. "I wish it didn't have to be a cage."

"Oh." I understood at once. Martin had spent too many weeks looking out from behind bars, accused of his first wife's murder, and the experience had marked him. I rose to my feet and closed the office door carefully before crossing to my husband's side, slipping a hand across his shoulders.

"I'm sorry," I said softly. "I didn't realize the memories were still affecting you. You've been so—well, quiet about it all."

"It doesn't befit a man to shake and tremble over a drawing." Martin smiled up at me. "I must enter the confounded vault to inspect the work, so I'm trying to get used to the idea by degrees." One side of his mouth twitched up, sardonic, self-mocking. "Don't tell anyone that your husband's a coward."

"You're not." The hard hug I gave Martin matched the vehemence in my voice. "Is that why you slept so badly last night? I thought you might be having bad dreams."

"Just the old nonsense about being back in jail." Martin rose to his feet and cupped a hand around one side of my face, stroking the skin under my eyes with his thumb. "I'm sorry I kept you awake. You didn't seem to sleep well either. Your eyes have shadows under them."

"I was worrying about the Lombardis." I sighed. "And to be completely honest, about the notion that you might try to prevent me from traveling alone. I don't like cages any more than you do, Martin."

"Ah. I suppose I deserve that." Martin let go of me, depositing a kiss on my forehead. "Look, I don't *want* to worry about you. I don't want to put you in a box marked 'mine,' even to keep you safe."

"Then don't." I met his gaze with a hard stare. "No one person should have the power to limit another's actions, even if the first person rejoices in the name of 'husband' and the second person is a wife." My restless mood was creeping back, intensified by the growing heaviness of the air as the day's heat built toward a storm.

"You're not just my wife." Martin frowned. "You also have a responsibility to Sarah—and Tess—and—" He stopped, biting his lip.

"And?"

"And any other person who might come into our family."

I turned on my heel, moving toward the window so I

could stare out at the gathering clouds visible between the tall buildings. There it was, then, and not for the first time. Martin had told me, back in Kansas when he had confessed to me that his marriage was a failure, that he dreamed of a son. He had married Lucetta because she claimed to be carrying his child. When she had been murdered, the news that she'd been pregnant with a boy child—another man's baby—had shaken him profoundly. I'd assumed I understood this desperate need of his, but now that I was the person on whom that eventuality depended, it was hard to bear the responsibility for his happiness.

"I'm not a broodmare, Martin. You can't keep me penned up in your stable."

I was trying to maintain a light tone, but I didn't miss the note of bitterness that crept in with the second sentence. I loved Martin with all my heart, but I was learning that being joined in marriage to a man was more complicated than merely loving him. I swallowed hard and tried again.

"Knowing that you're waiting for me to announce that I'm carrying your child makes me feel . . . inadequate. We've only been married two months. I might have conceived Sarah easily, but I can't guarantee—"

"No, no." Martin held up both hands in a defensive gesture. "If anyone should feel inadequate, it should be me."

"That's ridiculous." I turned around to stare at him, my voice high with indignation.

"Yes. Add that to my list of inadequacies." Martin looked sulky.

I stood looking at him for a long moment, the man who had been dear to me, in different ways, since I was a tiny child—and suddenly my lips twitched with the desire to smile.

"This is probably *not* a partners' meeting we should be having in your office." I *did* smile as I watched a variety of emotions flit across his countenance, unguarded in my presence. "And it's maudlin nonsense to think yourself inadequate, whether you sire twenty sons on me or none."

Martin stared at me for a long moment, and then his shoulders slumped. "I'm sorry. I *did* sleep poorly—worrying about the strike in the east and our consignments from Baltimore being delayed, and then it all turned into fretting over *you*, and I gave myself bad dreams. It wasn't the vault that did it."

I walked over to Martin, squeezing his hand hard and kissing him on the cheek, watching his face relax into a rueful smile. "I'm glad to hear it. It's just a room, after all. But listen, I must attend to Elizabeth's gown. There's only an hour and a half till her fitting. Let's continue this discussion at home, where I can demonstrate my belief in your manliness more effectively."

"Nell, your talent as a designer of gowns is astonishing. I've never seen anything I like better than the train on this dress."

Elizabeth Parnell twisted around, looking over her shoulder at her reflection as I angled the cheval glass. The fitting rooms in the temporary store were as bright as we could manage, but we didn't have enough natural light. The storm that had blown in over the last half hour had necessitated lighting the gas, its yellow flare making the ivory silk seem sickly to my eyes. Not that Elizabeth seemed to notice.

"However did you imagine those rosebuds and petals tumbling down the train like that?" Her cornflower-blue eyes shone. "I thought it was the cleverest thing when I saw the sketches, but now that the train's attached to the dress and I can see the full effect, words fail me. It makes me picture the trellis around my parents' summerhouse after a storm."

"That's what inspired me. Although the real credit should go to Magda and Mei Ling." I smiled. "I couldn't do my job nearly so effectively without the superb embroiderers we employ. Now stand still while I pin this. You have to stop losing weight."

It suited her though. Some of the flesh had melted from her waistline and rounded cheeks without an inch disappearing from her well-formed bosom and nicely proportioned hips. She was both elegant and womanly, with the fresh, smooth skin of a country girl but the poise and self-command of a sophisticate.

"There." I put down my pincushion. "David is going to fall over with delight when he sees you. I declare you grow more beautiful every day."

"With anticipation." Elizabeth grinned at her reflection. "I can't wait for the moment when my husband takes me into his arms and—has his way with me." Dimples appeared in her cheeks as she raised her eyebrows in mock censure of her own words. "I can barely eat for thinking about it."

"Don't get too thin, will you? We only have time for one more fitting, and then only if I absolutely must. If I take the dress in much more, it'll spoil the line."

"I'll make a point of eating more cakes this week." Elizabeth loved sweet things. "Just you wait till I've had six children and am as fat as a pie cook. You'll rue the day you ever encouraged me to eat when you're cutting a simply enormous gown for me."

"Not at all." I began to undo hooks, taking care not to disturb the pins. "The larger the dress, the higher the price. Besides, I enjoy dressing generously proportioned ladies. They have presence, and they carry bold colors and patterns so well."

I slipped the wedding gown over a form that stood in one corner of the room while Elizabeth contemplated her reflection. She was a charming sight in her layers of finely stitched petticoats; David was a lucky man indeed. He would have a wife with many personal charms in her youth and a lively personality and sharp, inquiring mind to carry her into the future, fat or thin.

"You're not really intending to have six children, are you?" I interrupted her reverie. "I thought you were rather against them."

"Well, I still have the useful little book my sister gave me." Elizabeth's cheeks dimpled again. "About how to avoid having too many babies. But David is very keen on fatherhood, and our income will support a family. David's promotion was splendid news, and Father is being generous, the dear man."

I raised my eyebrows but said nothing. I'd hoped that Elizabeth's Feminist principles would bolster my own determination to continue working rather than sink in a sea of children and domesticity. Alas, those principles appeared to be wavering in the rosy light of love.

"I look forward to having the—the *presence* of a married woman," Elizabeth mused. "I don't believe society takes unmarried women seriously; we're still girls in the eyes of the world. I envy the way you sweep through this store and people notice you as a *person*, not just as a pretty face."

"You'll be the center of attention on your wedding day."

"Well, yes, but as the 'beautiful bride' and not as someone who *contributes*. Don't you see what I mean?" Elizabeth turned away from the mirror and stepped over to the dress, running a finger over the ivory silk. "All I have to do at the church is not fall over and remember the words I'm supposed to say. I feel sometimes that my role is purely decorative. And much as I love this dress, I admit to a little guilt that it's costing Father so much money, even with the discount you gave him."

"I have to pay my workers."

"It's the workers I'm worried about." Elizabeth turned back toward me, the levity gone out of her voice. "There's so much suffering everywhere. Your Miss Baker says the railroad workers are starving to death, and now they're forced to go on strike. The B&O Railroad has cut wages *three times* this year, imagine that."

Well, it was reassuring to find that thoughts of her wedding day—and night—had not entirely vanquished Elizabeth's social preoccupations. There was a great deal in the newspapers about the current unrest.

"There hasn't been enough work around since '73," I agreed. "And things seem to be getting worse. The Panic made *me* richer, but it ruined so many people."

Including the Lombardis. I glanced out of the high window, where a sudden glare of lightning split the cascade of rain.

"I know it's hard on merchants like you when your goods don't get through, but it's far harder for the workers." Elizabeth's voice returned me to the present. "Five years of hardship—and all the companies do is send in gangs of toughs to break up meetings by force." She crossed to the chair on which I'd placed the clothes she'd arrived in, glancing back guiltily at her wedding ensemble.

"You're paying the wages of several women with that gown, if it soothes your conscience," I said, guessing at her thoughts.

"Seamstresses are so badly paid."

"Not in this store." I stepped forward to help Elizabeth dress. "We expect the best, and we pay well. And the lodging houses we provide are healthy and safe. Madame Belvoix personally inquires into the circumstances of every woman under her care. She constantly pesters Martin over extra payments for doctor's bills and the like."

"That's true." Elizabeth grinned. "You've said it often enough; she will not 'ave 'er ladies falling down with ze 'unger. You know, if she ever says that in front of me, I'm quite certain I'll howl with laughter. I won't be able to help myself."

"Don't you dare." With a quick glance to ensure Elizabeth was fully dressed, I opened the fitting room door and beckoned to my assistants to collect the gown. "Come along, Elizabeth, it's late and I have a family waiting for me. I'll take you to the Palmer House before I go home."

"I'll miss being so far away from Rutherford's when we're living on Twenty-First Street." Elizabeth carefully inserted a jeweled hatpin through the straw hat, decorated with an explosion of ostrich plumes like a small feather duster, that perched atop her thick blond hair.

"But you'll be near me in our new house. *Do* come along —I still have to run upstairs to fetch my things, and I'm afraid the storm's going to circle back around." I nodded a farewell to the assistants. "It'll be pleasant to be far away from noise and streetcars. Imagine being able to hear yourself think when you're walking along the street."

"The hushed and perfumed purlieus of the rich." Elizabeth's voice came from behind me as I hurried toward the back of the store. "At least *your* street will be fragrant with money. We'll be a little less exalted."

3

DONNY

$\mathcal{W}$e headed north on State Street to take Elizabeth to the Palmer House Hotel. So numerous were the horses and assorted vehicles that it took us a full twenty minutes to travel two blocks. I watched as Elizabeth disappeared behind the doors of the ladies' entrance and waited for Mr. Nutt to climb back onto the driver's seat.

The air was redolent of wet dirt and horse dung, its heavy feel promising more storms to come. I was tired, hungry, and quite ready to turn my back on the commercial district. I knew I would arrive late for dinner, and the thought of disappointing Sarah was a weight in my chest.

Another twenty minutes and we were past the temporary store, its doors now firmly closed. We soon entered the unattractive area to the south of the shopping district. After a couple more blocks heading south, the traffic thinned out. I sighed with relief as we picked up speed, but all too soon the carriage slowed again.

From the window, I glimpsed burly men digging a hole in

the road. That would explain the delay. I was trying to see what was happening when the carriage door opened.

"Lookie here! We got a pretty one."

A wave of alcohol fumes swept into my face. A shabbily dressed man was heaving himself through the door, looming over me. Worse, I knew from the way the rockaway was listing to one side that someone else was climbing onto the driver's seat. Was he threatening Mr. Nutt?

"What do you want?" I did my best to sound confident.

"What've you got, sugarplum?" He leered unpleasantly at me.

A second man stuck his head through the door on the other side of the carriage. I had no way of escape. I was being robbed; and I didn't have the faintest idea what to do.

"Here." I only had a few coins in my reticule; they weren't worth risking my life for. I picked the bag up and offered it to the man. He was standing too close, inspecting me as if I were a piece of meat.

"Take your gloves off." He stuffed the bag into his pocket and turned to spit tobacco juice onto the street through the open door. A gobbet landed on the carriage window. The breeze had died down, and it was hot again; the odors of tobacco, drink, and rotting breath filled the small space and made me nauseous.

He would take my engagement and wedding rings. I'd had them for such a short time. I froze, summoning thought.

A shout from above and a violent rocking motion suggested that Mr. Nutt was trying to defend himself and me. I rose to my feet, encouraged.

"Leave us alone!" I screamed the words as loudly as I was able. Surely someone would hear me and come to our aid? My face was on a level with the leering man. I wondered fleetingly if I might push him out of the carriage.

"Now then, sweetheart." The second robber, who I'd

thought was still standing in the road, gripped my clothing firmly and pulled me backward, toward him. I sensed the drop to the street behind my heels. "We ain't going to hurt you."

"Not if you're a good girl." His associate smirked. "Just give me your rings and that pretty pin, quick now."

I kicked out hard at his shins, clinging to the sides of the open door to stop the second lout pulling me out. The man I had kicked grunted and aimed a sharp cuff at my right ear that set my head ringing. The top of my ear grew hot; the second man's hold on my clothing tightened. I was losing my grip on the door. I screamed again.

There was a dull noise of an impact behind me. Suddenly I was free, falling forward. At the same moment, unseen hands grabbed the man who had been in the carriage with me. The next moment he'd been dumped unceremoniously into a puddle.

"Ya took too long this time," said a triumphant Irish voice. "Donny! Grab the other feller."

I turned to see the man in the street shake off my second rescuer and run, slipping on the muddy road before gaining traction.

I lost sight of them both as the carriage rocked perilously and I nearly fell out of the door again. As I threw myself back onto the seat, a huge black-haired laborer came into view, his massive fist clenched around a large stone. He swore fluently as the thief he'd thrown into the puddle scrambled to his feet and made good his retreat. I heard the voice of a third man, presumably the one who'd been on the driver's bench, cursing loudly as they ran off.

"The old guy's hurt, Nick," said a voice on the other side of the carriage. The black-haired man stopped swearing and threw the stone down.

"Hurt bad?" he yelled.

"Not so bad, I don't think," said the second voice. "He fell off the seat."

I flew to the door on that side in time to witness Mr. Nutt being helped to his feet by a tall, very muscular young man, rain-soaked, his trousers drenched in mud to above the knee. I realized he and his companion must be the laborers who had been working on the road.

"You got a cut on your head," said the younger laborer to Mr. Nutt. Indeed, my carriage driver was an alarming sight. Blood ran down one side of his face and his coat was torn at the shoulder. Yet he was upright, and his eyes were focused.

"You all right, Mrs. Rutherford?" he asked.

"I'm fine." I reached out a hand toward him. "Come and sit in here. How badly are you hurt?"

The black-haired Irishman shut the door behind me and ran around to join his friend. He and the younger man helped Mr. Nutt into the rockaway, whereupon our driver dropped untidily into the seat as if his legs had buckled.

"I'm all right—all right—just a little winded," he gasped as I pulled off one of my gloves, screwing it into a wad to press against the wound on his head. With my reticule gone, I had no handkerchief; it was the only thing I could think to do.

"It ain't deep," the younger laborer said reassuringly. He had shut the remaining door and was leaning on the open window, watching my efforts at nursing.

"It's a scratch. I hit the lamp on the way down." Mr. Nutt's voice strengthened as he recovered his breath. "I'll be sore all over tomorrow, is all."

"We saw them play that trick before." The young man pushed a filthy hand through a thick, overgrown, thoroughly wet brush of blond hair and grinned shyly. "The police ain't never on this stretch of the road. We would've went to help quicker, but we was down in the hole. I told Big Nick we'd stop them this time though, and we did." His voice was slow, halting, and somehow familiar.

"Did they get away?" Mr. Nutt asked, pulling out his handkerchief to help me clean up the blood on his face.

"Ran like jackrabbits." Big Nick came back into view behind his friend, grinning in satisfaction and displaying a gap where his front teeth were missing. "Did they take anything from ya, Miss?"

"My reticule with a few coins in it, nothing worse. I can't tell you how grateful I am. I'd like to give you a reward." I had begun to relax, knowing we were safe with the two large men.

"Ah, no reward necessary. We had our bit of fun." Big Nick wiped the moisture from his face and nodded at the younger man. "Or perhaps you could give it to Donny since he's the one who worked out what they was up to. They call him slow, but he's smart enough, if I'm any judge."

I looked hard at the younger laborer. "Don't I know you?"

He wasn't somebody you'd easily forget, being at least six feet four and very broad across the shoulders. His massive chest and arms, covered by a cotton undershirt and crossed by suspenders, bulged with the muscles of a manual laborer, but he had a surprisingly sweet face. It had a low brow under the thick growth of blond hair and a perpetual small frown, as if its owner had to work hard to understand what people were saying. The eyes that stared shyly at me from under thick, fair brows were an attractive dark blue.

The answer to my question was a shrug and a half smile. "I knew a lady with hair like yours once. She sewed shirts for us."

"Donny, of course." In my mind's eye, I pictured him, younger and far less muscular, crying as he held up a shapeless black hat to my window. "You were at the Poor Farm.

My name's Nell, do you remember? Nell Lillington—Rutherford since I married."

"Miss Nell." Donny wiped a huge hand on his undershirt and enveloped the one I had proffered. "You haven't changed much."

"Well, ain't that a nice happenstance." Big Nick put a friendly hand on Donny's shoulder. "But beggin' your pardon, Miss, we got to get back to work. You goin' to be all right to drive the lady home?" he asked Mr. Nutt, who was rising to his feet.

"I'll be fine." Mr. Nutt raked back his hair with one hand and dabbed at the cut on his head, which was still oozing a little blood.

"Your hat's here." Donny opened the carriage door again and put out a hand to help Mr. Nutt descend. "You're pretty brave for an old guy."

I could hear Mr. Nutt expressing his thanks as the young man moved away from the door. Big Nick leaned in closer to me, lowering his voice.

"Didn't want to say it in front of the boy, but he could really use a reward. You don't have to worry none about me —I got a wife and a home—but the kid's got nothin' but the clothes on his back. He's a nice boy, but he's"—Nick made a surreptitious gesture toward his head to indicate Donny's slow wits—"and in the flophouses they take advantage, steal from him and all. I been tryin' to help him get regular work, but it ain't easy."

"I have nothing to give him at present, but if I tell you my address, will you remember it and help Donny find it?"

Big Nick nodded. "He can find his way around. You just tell me where you live, and I'll make sure he comes by."

"I'm thinking of hiring a younger man to sit next to Nutt." Martin finished the last bite of pork chop and put down his fork.

Our dinner had been very late. Martin had ridden for the doctor to attend to Mr. Nutt's injuries before he even considered our own creature comforts. I too had contributed to making our driver comfortable in Mrs. Power's large kitchen armchair. He was probably still there, being fussed over mightily by the cook. He'd declared that the large bandage made him feel like a silly old man.

"Won't it be a little cramped up on that seat?" I asked. "The rockaway's not built for two drivers. And besides, Mr. Nutt's already upset about being overpowered and knocked off his perch. Even after I praised his bravery to the skies in front of Mrs. Power and the doctor."

"He was brave, but he's only one man—and, sprightly as he is for his age, he's over sixty. Supposing that had been a serious attempt at harming you?"

He meant rape, of course. I didn't consider myself an overly imaginative woman, but the memory of being trapped in the small carriage with a dirty, smelly, drunk man on either side of me had also led me to anticipate that possibility. Still—

"It's never happened before, and I don't suppose it will happen again." I half rose to pour more water into Martin's glass. "I've already told you I'll get Mr. Nutt to take Van Buren Street in the future and go south on Michigan Avenue instead of State Street. That'll get us farther away from the saloons. Besides, we're only renting this house for a couple more months. After that, we'll stay at the Palmer House, won't we? It's only a block or two from the temporary store *and* the new one. I don't see the point of a carriage at all, not really, until they finish the new house."

"You'll see the point soon enough when it rains or snows

and it's dark. We'll have a carriage and driver—and a body-guard for you."

"Oh, for heaven's sake. Last year I walked around Chicago unaccompanied. I rode the streetcars. In all weather—at night as well as in the day. I liked it. Why should being married to you change that?"

Martin's mouth set into the rigid line that had appeared as I'd told the tale of our encounter on State Street, and when he spoke his tone was exasperated. "In case you haven't noticed, I'm a prosperous man. As my wife—and being wealthy in your own right," he held up a hand to forestall my interruption, "you are vulnerable to kidnapping. The times are hard and getting harder. There've been a few cases around the country where the wives and even children of rich men have been held for ransom."

"Their children?"

"Yes. I didn't want to frighten you, but now the subject's come up . . . I would prefer that we ask Miss Baker to accompany Sarah when she plays in the gardens here in the square. Once we move, I'm going to think about what other arrangements we could make."

I felt a sensation like a shiver in the middle of my spine. It had never occurred to me that Sarah could be in any kind of danger.

"A large young man is a good deterrent." Martin folded his napkin and pushed back his chair. "Come now, Nellie, it's not that unreasonable, is it? And it will give employment to someone."

I stared, unfocused, at the wall behind Martin for a few moments, my mind racing. "In point of fact, it's not unreasonable," I said eventually.

"Merciful heavens, Mrs. Rutherford, are you on the brink of conceding to my wishes?" Martin drawled with a smug expression on his face.

I scowled. "Not if you smirk like that. But listen, I've had a wonderfully practical idea. Donny."

"Who?"

"The younger of the men who came to my rescue. I told you, remember? He used to be at the Poor Farm. Don't you recall a nice-looking lad greeting us when we arrived that day with Catherine Lombardi? After the Great Fire? When they all thought she was a ghost?"

Martin closed his eyes and wrinkled his brow. "That does stir a memory, now you mention it."

"He's grown into quite the colossus—in a good way. He's very tall and *very* muscular. He's a bit on the slow side, but he's clearly brave—and hardworking too. I remember him as a sweet-natured young man. Probably too sweet-natured for the kind of life he's leading these days, but I'm sure he would fit in well with a household."

"But I could easily hire someone with experience— training—in protecting women and children. Don't you think you're being rather hasty? If he turns up for a reward, I'll happily give him one, but—"

"The point is he wouldn't just theoretically protect me. He actually *has* protected me. From real attackers. Big Nick said it was Donny who figured out the trick those men were working and watched out for the next attack. If that's not proof of his willingness and ability to protect a woman, what is?"

The expression of bafflement on Martin's face gave me a secret moment of happiness as he looked down his beaky nose at the tablecloth. "Huh. That's a hard argument to counter."

"I have to win sometimes." I rose from my seat and lowered myself into Martin's lap, my arms around his neck. "We can at least talk to him if he comes to see us, can't we? If I can concede that a little extra protection—a bar of the cage, if you will—may be necessary on occasion, you could at least let me choose my jailer. After all, Providence sent him. I prefer to believe so than in a fantastic coincidence."

"Hmmm." Martin's arms encircled my waist, and he kissed my neck in a way that flooded my body with warmth. "Are you using your womanly wiles to persuade me? Because it's working. Well, partially at least. I'm beginning to forget what we're talking about."

"Good." I straightened up, reluctantly halting the kissing, and cupped Martin's face with my hands. "Then if Donny comes here, we'll consider offering him a job. I still object on principle to any attempt to curtail my freedom though. Not until you give up yours."

"All right, all right." Martin raised his eyes to the heavens, or at least to the Katzenmeiers' coffered ceiling. "I know when I'm bettered in a negotiation." He kissed my neck again. "But for now, Wife, to bed. Tomorrow's problems can take care of themselves, and tonight . . ." The laughter lines gathered around his mouth. "There may still be some plea-sure in this overlong day—if we don't both fall asleep as soon as our heads touch the pillow."

We didn't.

MARTIN WAS A TALL MAN AND HAD FILLED OUT IN THE shoulders since our days in Victory, but Donny Clark dwarfed him. The young worker appeared even more substantial now that he was standing in our parlor, the muscles of his chest straining against the plaid shirt he'd evidently chosen as his best article of clothing. He'd attempted to clean himself up, but the stale smell of the worst kind of lodgings clung to him. I saw bites on his neck that suggested fleas or bedbugs. He had declined to sit on the

Katzenmeiers' furniture, a show of consideration for which I was thankful. He stood in the center of the carpet, surveying us all with a shy expression.

"I'm sure relieved you're able to see me so early, ma'am and sir. And miss and ma'am." He nodded at Sarah and Tess, who had followed him into the parlor. "Big Nick said if you didn't want to see me, he could still get me on a work crew if I came back quick enough."

"It's certainly early." Martin, who was leaning against the windowsill, grinned. "You're lucky we're early risers."

Tess nodded vigorously. "'By much slothfulness the building decayeth; and through idleness of the hands the house droppeth through.' That means being lazy is a real bad idea," she added helpfully.

"They never let us get up late at the institute," Donny agreed.

"What's the institute?" piped a small voice from the region of my waist.

"Where I used to live." Donny smiled at Sarah. "What they used to call the Poor Farm."

"What's a Poor Farm?"

"We'll talk about it later, darling." I'd have to ask Donny not to talk about the Poor Farm—the Prairie Haven Institute for the Feeble-Minded, as he'd told me it was now called—in front of Sarah. I would tell her about her place of birth one day, but not yet.

"I didn't mean you to give me breakfast either, sir and ma'am, but I'm real grateful. I didn't eat such good food since a long while."

I suppressed a grin. I'd glimpsed Donny in the kitchen eating his way through a huge plate of ham and hotcakes at the rapid, efficient pace of a man who rarely had the luxury of sitting down at a table—and Mrs. Power had whispered to me that it was his second helping.

"You were *really* hungry," Sarah agreed, her eyes glowing. It was she who'd asked Donny if he needed to eat and towed him down to the kitchen, her small hand around two fingers of his, when he'd admitted he did.

Donny hunkered down so he could talk to Sarah more easily. "I was, Miss Sarah. It was a real pleasure having your company for eating. I'm beholden to you for introducing yourself so genteelly, but I knew who you was—you had that pretty hair when you was a baby."

"I guess I'll always have hair this color," Sarah said solemnly. "You can have a lock of it if you like, for saving Mama and Mr. Nutt. Mrs. Power says I can go see Mr. Nutt this afternoon if it's all right with Miss Baker—that's what my governess is called. I made Mr. Nutt a drawing of a horse to make him feel better. How come you knew me when I was a baby?"

"We can only offer you a tiny room over the stables for now. Barely enough space for your bed." Martin spoke quickly, forestalling any reply Donny might make to Sarah's question. Despite his initial difficulty in recalling Donny from our visit to the Poor Farm, he had recognized the young man straightaway. He had greeted him with enthusiasm, pressed several bills into his hand as thanks for his bravery, and made him a firm offer of employment on the strength of half an hour's acquaintance—proving, I thought, that I was not the only impulsive member of our household.

"That's just fine." Donny straightened up, towering over Sarah and Tess. "Does the feller I'm sharing with work nights, then?"

"Mr. Nutt has his own room." Sarah supplied the information, stepping back so she could see Donny's face. "You're going to have *your* own room too. It's my favorite of all the rooms in the stable block because it's very little and cozy. You come to the kitchen to eat. Mr. Nutt sits by the fire with

Mrs. Power in the evenings when it's cold—I guess you can too. It's nice and warm in the kitchen."

The small frown that seemed habitual with Donny deepened, and he stared at Martin for a few moments before his face brightened.

"I get my own *room?*"

"Yes." One corner of Martin's mouth twitched up into a smile at Donny's astonishment. "A dollar a day, three meals, your working clothes—and I'll throw in shirts, socks, a pair of boots, *and*—" he raised his eyebrows at Sarah, who shouted, *"Inexpressibles!"* with glee.

"That's how you should refer to all articles that clothe your nether limbs in polite company," she explained to Donny. "Papa taught me the other day when I made Mr. Mulcahy's face go red because I said—"

"Never mind what you said." Martin intervened to prevent the word Sarah had been about to pronounce—one I'd been surprised to learn she'd picked up—before returning his attention to Donny. "We'll be moving to Calumet Avenue as soon as they finish our new home. There will be a carriage house down the street with living quarters for several men above the stables. Each man will have his own room."

"Jehoshaphat," breathed Donny. "I'm going to be living in a palace."

Tess, who had been following the conversation closely, giggled. "It's not a palace, silly. Martin, could you advance him a day's wages so he can go to the bathhouse? If you don't mind me mentioning that you could do with a wash," she said to the young man.

"Miss Tess, ma'am, you can mention anything you like that would make me more pleasing to present company. It's so downright good to see old friends—and a real treat to know I can be of use to you all. You just tell me where to go and what to do."

45

Tess giggled again, and a rosy blush spread over her cheeks. There was something about the way she was looking at Donny that preoccupied my mind while we discussed a few minor details.

Soon Martin and I said our good-byes; it was high time we left for the store. The sound of a door opening below prompted Sarah to grab Donny by the hand again. Miss Baker had arrived, and clearly introductions were about to take place.

"A good day's work, and it's only half past eight." Martin glanced out of the window at the street below, where Mr. Nutt—still sporting a bandage but patently determined to do his job—was waiting for us on the rockaway. "Get your things. I'll go tell Nutt he's acquired an apprentice."

"Is that how you're going to avoid insulting Mr. Nutt?" I inquired. "Oh well, I don't suppose it matters to him much anyway, given that he'll be working for the Katzenmeiers again pretty soon. I just hope this notion of yours doesn't disrupt our household overmuch."

"Disrupt?" Martin, halfway through the door, halted and turned around. "I don't see why it should. And may I point out that this was *your* notion?"

He left before I had a chance to reply, and I decided to let the matter drop. There was no point in arguing—and I had probably just imagined the look on Tess's face, hadn't I?

4

WEDDING

"*Y*our gentle giant seems to be working out well."

Elizabeth's voice was a little unsteady—from nerves, presumably. After all, it *was* her wedding day. My lady's maid, Alice, who was much better at hair than Mrs. Parnell's young woman, had just put the finishing touches to Elizabeth's coiffure by creating a cascade of smooth, corn-blond ringlets with the curling tongs.

"Yes, he's turning out to be a godsend." I stepped forward to inspect Alice's work, giving her a smile of appreciation. Earlier she had arranged what seemed like an entire garden's worth of tiny ivory silk rosebuds into the top portion of Elizabeth's shining locks while the bride sat, as fresh as the summer morning, in her petticoats. Then, with the longer portions of the hair still loose, we had gone through the painstaking business of helping her don the dress, finally swathing the whole arrangement in a linen sheet for fear of the curling tongs touching the silk. The merriment that had made the morning's work so pleasant was held in abeyance as Alice wielded the tongs, Tess and I observing with bated breath; but Alice's skill was such that not a single hair was scorched, and the linen remained unmarked.

"Every ringlet is perfect," I pronounced. "Now, Tess—oh, thank you." For Tess had already held out the pincushion, anticipating my request.

"I've never known a more willing worker than Donny Clark." I moved around to Elizabeth's front, pincushion in hand, and drew out the two long pins that held the sheet. "He never seems to get tired, and he can turn his hand to a surprising number of tasks." I didn't know if Elizabeth was paying attention, but I'd found that chatter helped her to relax. "Sarah finds all kinds of excuses to talk to him, and Tess has been giving him friendly advice. She's practically adopted him."

"I have not." Tess blushed but smiled at me as we each took one side of the sheet. With Alice's help, we uncovered the vision of loveliness that was Elizabeth Parnell on the last day she would bear her maiden name.

"It's like unwrapping a Christmas present," Tess crowed as I circled the bride, looking for stray threads. "The most beautiful Christmas present I've ever seen. Just the shoes and all will be perfect." She darted off to the box holding Elizabeth's satin slippers.

I watched as Alice drew lace gloves onto the bride's hands, noting the tremor in them. Had I been so nervous on my wedding day?

"I *feel* like a Christmas present. A huge doll for a spoiled child." Elizabeth lifted each foot in turn to allow Tess to slip the shoes over her feet. "Are we on time?"

"Quite on time." I turned to consult the dainty carriage clock that ticked quietly on the mantelpiece of Mrs. Parnell's boudoir. "Your sisters should be here in a moment. Tess and I have just enough time to slip into our dresses. Thank goodness your mother is looking after the flower girls. I couldn't have managed with Sarah here."

"Mother has a real knack for making little ones behave." Elizabeth's pretty lips twitched in a tremulous smile. "She'll make them use the WC before leaving the house and not allow them to do *anything* to put a crease in those lovely dresses, if my memory serves. Goodness, what a *trial* it seemed when I and my sisters were young; and yet we always finished the day proud of ourselves for our exemplary behavior. I don't understand how she does it." Elizabeth took a deep breath. "Do I look all right?"

She looked more than all right. I'd kept the front of the dress relatively simple, with large silk roses holding in place a fall of fine silk damask, a fabric that managed to be summery and yet grand at the same time. Bands of satin ribbon, a froth of lace, and another silk rose brought out the beauty of Elizabeth's finely shaped bosom and emphasized her newly slender waist, while the roses reappeared as smaller flowers and a profusion of embroidered buds on the train. The train ended in three layers of pleated satin that would move like rose petals blown down by a lake breeze as Elizabeth walked.

"Exquisite—even if I say so myself." I grinned. "I was right to look for an ivory white that's just on the edge of cream; it suits your coloring far more than a brighter white. Although, with the roses in your cheeks, I could almost have gotten away with a very pale pink. I'd like to design a pink wedding dress one day."

"Oh, if that dress were pink, I'd want it so bad." Tess clapped her hands together. "I declare I'd break the seventh commandment by thinking of ways to steal it. Nell, this is even more beautiful than *your* wedding dress. I wish I could wear one just like it." She sighed loudly.

"You wouldn't if you knew how much the train weighed."

I finished folding the sheet and put my pincushion where I hoped I'd find it later. "Now, ladies, we have about fifteen minutes to finish making ourselves look splendid. Alice, I'm expecting a miracle of speed."

ALICE ROSE TO THE CHALLENGE, AND WE WERE AT OUR OWN carriage in fourteen minutes. Martin, resplendent in a morning coat of immaculate cut and a pale blue vest, helped us into our seat and settled himself opposite. Mr. Nutt, now recovered from his head wound, was to crown his period of employment with us by appearing in full livery of dark green; beside him sat Donny, similarly attired. Martin, who intended to buy property in Lake Forest, was ensuring we appeared in that town in some style.

He wasn't entirely in a celebratory mood. "I've had three telegrams from Fassbinder," he informed us as soon as Mr. Nutt had set the carriage into smooth motion. "Five hundred men from the Workingmen's Party crossed the river in St. Louis to join the railroad men on strike. The ladies of the city are convinced they're going to be murdered in their beds."

"Is *he* worried there'll be rioting?" I asked. Friedrich Fassbinder, the only partner in Rutherford & Co. not directly involved in the store and not resident in Chicago, was not usually given to panic.

Martin grimaced. "He says they're harmless enough— speeches more than violence—but the speeches are about the working man ruling the country. I don't see President Hayes standing for that. He could send in the troops."

"What do they actually want?" I asked. "I mean, I can understand the unrest. Wages have been falling since '73 for many people, and if I couldn't feed my family, I'd put up a fight. But what, specifically, are they asking for?"

"Depends on who's writing the demands." Martin shrugged. "Many of them just seem to want an eight-hour day and an end to employing children."

"That doesn't make them sound like the brigands the press want us to believe." I observed the sunlight's play on Martin's pale hair and glossy top hat as we drove between the dappled shade cast by the young trees. "And yet they claim that you—*we*—are robber barons, stealing what should be theirs."

"I'm hardly a robber baron." Martin's eyes narrowed. "I'm one of the more generous employers, as you well know. And I can't count the number of times I've worked far longer than ten hours in a day. Besides, the more extreme among them demand that the railroads and telegraph be nationalized—isn't that stealing from the men who worked hard to create them? They're hand in glove with the Communists, whose main aim is to take what isn't theirs."

"I suppose so. But imagine what it must feel like to see all this." I indicated the carriage and the spacious street with its large houses and neatly trimmed gardens. "You must admit we're more fortunate than most."

"You're right, Nell." Tess nodded. "If we have two coats and our neighbor has none, we should give him a coat."

"I might have known you'd come up with that Bible verse." I smiled at my friend. "It always makes me feel so guilty."

"We give money to the poor though." Tess frowned.

"We do. If we gave away everything we had, we'd deprive ourselves of the power to do good. Or am I just making excuses for myself? I don't understand what it is to be really hungry. None of us do."

"And you never will." Martin reached forward to clasp my hand, squeezing it gently. "You realize, don't you, that this provides me with yet another reason to insist you don't go rushing off to Kansas before we've heard something concrete? You can't avoid passing through St. Louis."

"But we have to find out what's happened to the Lombardis," said Tess. I'd confided my worries to her in the end and was glad; she'd stoutly promised to go with me to Kansas should the need arise.

"We do." I looked at Martin. "You said the denominational office was worse than useless."

"It's a scandal that they can remain so sanguine when one of their missionary families hasn't been heard from for months." The storm clouds gathered in Martin's eyes. "I'm putting my hope in the Pinkertons."

"How long do you think it will take to get some news?" My attention was on the road ahead; we were almost at the church.

Martin was also alert to our imminent arrival. He twisted round to consult briefly with Mr. Nutt about the best place to stop and then unlatched the landau's door, holding it closed as the carriage halted.

"Any day now," was his eventual reply. "I've told the Pinkerton bureau where to find me. I can't think we'll need to wait much longer."

Had the wait felt as long to him as it did to me? At that moment, the Lombardi mission seemed infinitely distant from this leafy, nicely ordered little town with its smart churches and well-dressed, well-fed people. It was hardly possible that the same sun would shine down out of the same blue sky, or that the Pinkerton agents could be heading toward us, bearing news of—what?

But there was Sarah, standing in front of Mrs. Parnell with Elizabeth's niece Eudora, who, like Sarah, was six years old. Both children were still clean and tidy, and both of them were waving at us with big smiles on their faces. I waved back, my spirits lifting.

"Let's put our worries aside for a few hours, shall we?" Martin had descended from the high landau without anyone's assistance and was pulling down the steps as Donny came to help. I grinned; in his eagerness to get his women-folk where they needed to be, he was forgetting his desire to look dignified in front of the Lake Forest townspeople.

"Elizabeth was extremely nervous when I left her," I remarked as I stepped out of the carriage, my hand in Martin's.

"I don't know why." Martin let go of me and offered a hand to Tess. "Were we nervous at our wedding? David was as white as a sheet last night when the fellows were trying to ply him with whiskey. I hope they didn't succeed—supposing he's sick?"

WE NEEDN'T HAVE WORRIED. DAVID FLETCHER WAS SOBER AND serene as he said his vows; and Elizabeth, Feminist as she claimed to be, promised to obey her husband without the slightest catch in her soft, clear voice.

"A splendid wedding," was Mrs. Parnell's verdict as she watched her youngest daughter—surrounded by her siblings, their families and children, and various generations of Fletchers—trying to talk to everyone at once and almost succeeding. "Perhaps I like it best because it's my last, Mrs. Rutherford. I have seen all of my children married from this church. Elizabeth is quite the prettiest, particularly in that absolutely marvelous dress. When the happy couple returns from their tour of the Great Lakes, I will arrange for them to visit a photographer's studio and be immortalized in their wedding clothes. I understand it's the modern thing to do, although my husband finds the notion very vulgar."

"It's a shame she has to change into a traveling dress

later." Tess's eyes were on the bride too. "I wouldn't want to get on a boat just after I got married. I'd want to stay in my dress for as long as I could, even if it meant being up till midnight. Being a bride is the most wonderful thing there is."

"You know, Miss O'Dugan, I can't agree with you." Mrs. Parnell's bright blue gaze sharpened. "When I was a young woman, we didn't make nearly so much fuss over weddings. Everything important comes *after* the ceremony; I believe that our society is losing sight of that crucial reality. It's the marriage that's the true turning point in our lives, not the wedding. I tell all my children so. Elizabeth, of course, calls it 'Mother's little lecture,' but then I have always allowed her to speak too freely. Of all my children, she is the one who reminds me the most of myself."

"I suppose being married would be nice too." Tess's brow was creased in a frown. "I hadn't really thought about that part. Isn't it difficult?"

Mrs. Parnell burst out laughing, and I joined in—not at Tess's naïveté, of course, but at the peculiar aptness of her question. Tess, never one to see a slight where none was intended, laughed too.

"It is, in my opinion, the second most difficult task that falls to our lot," Mrs. Parnell pronounced. "The first, alas, is when those we love die; but the good Lord is kind enough to soothe our grief as the years pass. When it comes to marriage, the challenges change almost daily, but they are always there. We do not live in a novel, which inevitably ends with a happy couple and declines to follow them into the future. Except," she held up a finger in reflection, "for the second volume of *Little Women*. Yet although I believe Miss Alcott to be a most worthy person, I find her somewhat saccharine, and besides—she has never married."

"Where is Mother?" Elizabeth's voice cut across our conversation, and in a moment the bride had joined us and flung her arms around her mother's neck. "I haven't had one second to hug you, you excellent parent. I waylaid Father right after the ceremony, but I might have known you'd be somewhere on the fringe of the crowd, giving Nell your opinions of the bride's and groom's performances. Did I do splendidly?"

We all joined in with congratulations and reiterations of our opinion that there had never been a better wedding. Out of the corner of my eye, I saw Martin holding on firmly to Sarah with one hand and Eudora with another. Should I rescue him? But there was so much hilarity in his countenance that I deduced he was enjoying himself and continued chatting with Elizabeth. Her earlier nervousness had given way to such a degree of animation that she was a joy to watch. I saw David Fletcher gazing at her with an expression that combined love, amusement, and admiration to such a degree that I did not hold any qualms about their honeymoon.

"Of course, the best is yet to come," I heard Elizabeth say. "After all," she rounded her eyes into an expression of the utmost candor, "I have been to Europe, but I've *never* seen Detroit. I'm looking forward to our lake voyage immensely. So many quiet days when we will have almost *nothing* to do."

Mrs. Parnell took her remark at face value and began chatting about the glories of Mackinac Island and the Niagara Falls, while I avoided catching my friend's eye and fought the temptation to kick her in the shins. Only Elizabeth could allude to her forthcoming honeymoon with such delicate use of the *double entendre* and get away with it.

"And I will be enjoying myself just as much," said Mrs. Parnell in all innocence. "After all, we will have Mr. and Mrs. Rutherford, Sarah, and Miss O'Dugan all to ourselves. Their presence will get us nicely over the *difficult* moment of seeing our last chick fly the nest."

5

LOSS

*T*he news of the strike that had distracted Martin from the Fletchers' wedding was no better by Monday.

"They're having guns delivered to police stations in Chicago." Martin, his face grave, laid the most recently opened telegram on the Parnells' breakfast table, on top of a pile of letters and newspapers.

Mrs. Parnell, at the other end of the table, was deep in her own correspondence. "Ah!" she remarked, not having heard Martin. "The *Alpena* has altered its itinerary and will avoid Detroit." She looked up. "Guns?"

"The militia has been told to prepare itself for riots." He pushed his fingers through his hair and glanced at me. "I must go back, Nellie. I know Joe has the matter in hand, but I *should* be there. They had better not damage the new store, or I won't be responsible for my actions."

"Is that letter from Elizabeth?" I asked Mrs. Parnell since it seemed more polite to respond to my hostess first.

"No, from the shipping office." Mrs. Parnell's sharp blue eyes lifted once more, dancing with amusement. "I don't imagine Elizabeth sat down to write to me on the first day or two of her honeymoon tour."

I caught Martin's eye, and we both grinned. I'd hinted to him about Elizabeth's impatience for her wedded life to begin. I hoped that a large cabin in a paddle steamer would be a congenial setting and the weather on the Great Lakes would be free of the violent storms that swept over the water even in summer.

"The *Alpena* will avoid the larger cities altogether, in case of violence, and instead call in at some 'charming' smaller ports." Mrs. Parnell shook her head. "I find it a great shame that these—these *socialistic* elements of society should so disrupt the lives of ordinary people, don't you?" She looked at Martin. "It would be a terrible pity to cut short your stay, but I understand that, for a man, business comes first."

"I should go back with you," I said to Martin.

"No," he replied with emphasis at the same time Mrs. Parnell exclaimed, "Not at all! The women and children must remain here; there will be no rioting in Lake Forest, I'm sure." She turned her head to look through the open window, through which we could see Tess and Sarah taking a turn in the garden with Miss Baker. Sarah's governess had rejoined us the previous afternoon, full of news about the angry mood in Chicago, now sweltering in the summer heat. Sunday had been a day of meetings, and many were calling for a general strike to bring the country to a halt until the employers raised wages.

"Nell, my dear." Mrs. Parnell stared earnestly at me as she folded her letter. "You surely see the sense of staying here until this moment of trial has passed. I suppose Mr. Rutherford must go to Chicago—I can't imagine my own husband altering his routine one whit—but there's no reason to involve the womenfolk."

"I'm grateful for your hospitality." Martin gave Mrs.

Parnell a brief smile as he rifled among his papers. Finding the sheet he was seeking, he flipped open his notebook and wrote a few lines before looking at Mrs. Parnell again. "Joe Salazar—our general manager, you remember—has sent his wife and children to visit with friends in Door County. He maintains that nothing will happen in their part of Chicago, but he doesn't want to take any risks."

"Sarah and Tess—and Miss Baker, of course—can stay here with my blessing, for as long as Mrs. Parnell will have them." I glared at Martin. "I'm not going to be the only partner in the store—apart from Mr. Fassbinder—who's not present during this crisis. Why should being a woman make a difference?"

"Fassbinder is complaining about being excluded from the fun." Martin laid his hand on a piece of paper closely written over in Mr. Fassbinder's quaint European script. "But he concedes he has plenty to do establishing temporary quarters away from St. Louis and ensuring it's business as usual in the frontier stores. He's having his daughters and their children stay with him while his sons-in-law guard the buildings in St. Louis."

"You see?" Mrs. Parnell said to me.

"We're reinforcing the fencing around the new store and hiring extra men to protect it," Martin informed us. "Joe's already obtained boards for the windows of the temporary store, and many of the male staff volunteered to patrol for fires all night." He pinched the bridge of his nose. "The real nightmare is supply. It might be possible to get shipments from the East Coast without using the railroads—I've written letters—but our silks come from San Francisco, and that's two thousand miles away." He sighed, moving the various sheets of paper around with one hand. "Madame Belvoix has much to say on the subject of silks."

"Is *she* leaving Chicago?" I asked, hearing the edge in my voice.

Martin huffed. "As if I were able to persuade her. She's having a bed made up in one of the women's dormitories—"

He stopped as both Mrs. Parnell and I cried out, she in dismay and I in triumph.

"I fear you just talked yourself into losing the argument," Mrs. Parnell groaned.

"He most definitely has." I grinned at my husband, who had thrown himself back in his chair. "So I too will stay at the store. What about the other women?"

Martin ground his teeth. "Those who wish to are staying," he admitted. "Several of the younger women's families asked Joe to allow the women home for the duration of the troubles, and of course he's agreed. But we've welcomed those who've expressed a desire to stay and help. They will receive an extra dollar or two in their pay packets. The women who go home will be on half pay, except for embroiderers who take work with them."

"Ha." I felt smug. "You don't have a leg to stand on, Husband dear. You can't apply the principle of sending the women away selectively. Volunteers are staying—and I'm a volunteer."

"She's got a point." Mrs. Parnell reached for the coffeepot that a maid had just brought in along with fresh cups. "But I hope you'll be sensible and reserve a suite at the Palmer House. You'll need somewhere to go when you're tired of camping in the store."

"Already done." Martin gave me a sidelong smile. "A suite fit for a married couple. I don't suppose I ever truly imagined I'd get away with leaving you here."

THE NEXT DAY WE WERE BOTH BACK IN CHICAGO—AND BACK at work.

"Oh good." I barely glanced at Martin before writing "July 23rd" at the top of the sheet of paper on which I had just executed a sketch. Despite the currents of panic and rumor that buffeted the store with every new arrival of a customer or merchant, the atelier was working as busily as ever, even without its full complement of seamstresses. I had plenty to do and was busy doing it. Martin, faced with a dearth of customers on the sales floor, was spending most of his time meeting with the other merchants and making plans. I was happy to see him return from his latest meeting, and, given his deep understanding of his own trade, I was never reticent about seeking his opinion on my designs.

"Tell me what you think about crimson satin bows here, on the back of the dress." I indicated their position on the sketch. "And at the back of the cuffs. If we line them with gold satin to match the flowers . . . I've been getting telegrams all day from my customers, if you can believe it. These disturbances have created a few new social occasions."

I looked up, realizing that an odd silence and tension was hanging around Martin like a cloud. My heart sank a little.

"Don't tell me it's a fire. Not like in Pittsburgh." I rose to my feet, my pulse racing. Fire was our greatest dread, and in Pittsburgh the mobs had decided to drive off the military by setting the railroad depots on fire. There were depots immediately to the north and south of the Chicago business district. Every merchant knew how vulnerable our stores were to fire. Martin and I knew it personally.

But Martin's only answer was to shut the door behind him. It wasn't until I heard the key turn in the lock that my alarm turned to a black knot of dread. When my husband put a gentle arm around my shoulder and cupped my cheek with the other hand, the dread formed itself into a sharp spike that pierced my heart.

"It's not the strike, is it?"

"No." Martin closed his eyes for a second and then, looking me full in the face, drew a deep breath. But I perceived what was coming.

"It's the Lombardis. You've heard. Oh, not all of them. Please don't say it's all of them."

I had the strangest sensation I was in bed having a nightmare I'd had before, and I knew what Martin's response would be. He was going to say, "All of them," wasn't he? I couldn't feel my feet.

"Not all of them."

"N—not?" I stared at him. Was I hearing right?

"Not all of them," Martin repeated. "At least the Pinkertons don't think so." Martin's hand moved down to my waist, steadying me. "Teddy and Thea are not . . . there. The mission is deserted except . . . except for three graves. I'm so sorry, my darling."

Both of his arms were around me now, gathering me close to him, his lips brushing my forehead.

"Catherine?" The question emerged in a whimper, and I felt Martin swallow hard.

"Catherine, the pastor, and Lucy." His voice strengthened, as if once the worst of the news was over, he could tell the rest easily. "Their resting places were marked with their names and dates on boards. Somebody had buried them with care. I can't help suspecting that was Teddy's work—at least I hope so. That would mean he's alive and strong."

"Catherine, the pastor, and Lucy," I whispered into Martin's waistcoat. If I could just turn time back ten minutes —five—to when I still assumed I was mistaken, worrying too much. If only I could turn it back—how long?—and not be so consumed by my own selfish concerns. If I had insisted, really insisted, that they left Kansas . . . might it not have worked? But I'd never had the right to insist.

The image of the dates written on those far-off boards emerged from the swirl of despair. "When?" I asked.

"The beginning of June."

Seven weeks? Eight? Not long after our wedding. If I could just make time go back eight weeks . . . To think I had been so happy and so absorbed in my life, when they . . .

"Pastor Lombardi went first." Martin's words broke into my horrified reflections. "Then Lucy passed, then Catherine. One of the Pinkertons rode day and night to break the news to me in person. The others went in search of the missing children. They won't give up until they find them."

"It wasn't Indians, was it? Or bandits?" Was that my voice? "Oh God, Martin, were they beaten or tortured or . . . ? Lucy was thirteen. Only thirteen."

And with that terrifying picture, the tears fell, scalding my cheek as they made their way downward to soak into Martin's jacket. A great sob shook me, and then another. How had I not *known*? Catherine was my second mother . . .

Martin waited, still and silent with his arms tight around me, until the worst of my tears was over. Then he loosened his grip and held me a little away from him, fishing in his pocket for a clean handkerchief.

"I'm sure it wasn't anything like that, Nell." He shook the linen out and wiped my cheeks. "They didn't all die at once, and Teddy—probably Teddy—buried them. It's unlikely to have been an attack. Perhaps the Kansas malaria, but I guess it's more likely to have been an epidemic. Something bad enough to make everyone else leave the mission. Or maybe they sent everyone away. You know what they are—were —like."

"Yes." Martin's common sense was steadying me, and the visions of horrific, violent death were fading from my imagination. I commandeered the handkerchief and used it more effectively, blotting my eyes and blowing my streaming nose while I thought. "Catherine and her husband would have sent everyone away if they hoped it would save them from catching the illness. Teddy would stay no matter what, the dear brave boy. And Thea—yes, I imagine Thea would have gone." I wiped away a fresh rush of tears. "That would mean they're separated."

"And Teddy's first concern after he buried his mother would be to ensure Thea was all right. They may be anywhere, Nellie."

"Anywhere," I echoed. I sniffed one last time and looked up at my husband.

"I'll be all right." I straightened up. "The first shock is over. I can grieve for Catherine later—all my life—but we need to find her children. They may be in Wichita. Or Springwood—have you sent someone to the Eternal Life Seminary? Teddy wanted to apply for a place there one day once his parents no longer needed him at the mission. It would be an obvious place of refuge. I should write to Dr. Spedding."

"It hadn't occurred to me to tell the Pinkertons about the seminary." Martin's eyes lost their focus on me. "You're right, but let me telegraph Dr. Spedding instead. There was a telegraph office in Springwood, if I recall."

"They may have headed east too, or they may be trying to get there. Their parents were from New York."

"Wherever they are, they won't find traveling simple at present. It's likely that every railroad from the East Coast to the West is shut down, and the strike's affecting the steamboats. I hope they have a horse at least."

"Teddy might travel on foot, but you have a point. If Thea were with him, he wouldn't make her walk." I frowned. "But why didn't they wire us? They can't possibly think they can manage by themselves."

Seeing that I had recovered my composure, Martin unlocked the door. "Teddy's a man," was his next remark. "Old enough to work and look after both of them. He might not even be planning to seek help. His father liked to stand on his own two feet, and Teddy resembles him."

"Teddy's only seventeen. Thea's not fifteen yet. Even if you're right, we must find them and offer our help and support. I owe that to Catherine. They must come and live with us."

Martin looked at me a little curiously. "I'm not sure we should go that far. Help, yes; money, as much as they want. We can supply all their needs until they're back on their feet. But they're too old for mothering."

"I wasn't when Catherine treated me so kindly. When she held my hand as I gave birth to Sarah because Mama wasn't there. I was seventeen—"

"But you'd had a gentle upbringing. These two were obliged to take on responsibilities you'd never have dreamed of at that age. Thea's been teaching school and keeping house since she was very young, and Teddy's been doing hard physical work. You can't judge their needs by your own."

"Every child needs a mother."

"You say that, but you were inordinately fond of yours. I worry you'd be taking on too much. Out of guilt."

"Guilt?" I blinked; my eyes were sore and my head pounding.

"Guilt that you didn't solve the Lombardis' problems. That you couldn't convince Catherine to act against her husband's wishes."

"I never tried—" I stopped short as a sudden wave of emotion threatened a return of tears.

"I'm sorry." Martin's face registered dismay. "I'm a brute, lecturing you at a moment like this." He kissed me gently on the lips. "I'll go to the Pinkerton bureau straightaway and give you some time to yourself." He hesitated. "Don't forget that they all had faith in a better place than this life, and now they're there. Comfort yourself with the assurance that they are free from illness or pain, my darling. May they rest in peace."

And then he was gone, leaving me to stare at the walls of my room as if I no longer recognized it. The sketches and notes on which I'd been working lay in a disordered heap, the smart day dress that had so absorbed me just half an hour before now a matter of little interest.

"Oh, Catherine," I whispered. "Yes, you must rest in peace now. I'm sorry I didn't try hard enough to help you. I'm sorry I put my needs before yours and let you down."

Just as I'd let down my own mother—of whom, Martin was right, I'd been inordinately fond. I'd let her down by bearing a child out of wedlock; by refusing to utter Jack Venton's name and solve the problem with a hasty wedding; by putting my own desire for freedom over the morally correct course of action.

Well, I would have no more mothers. I didn't deserve them. But we would find those children, and I would do everything in my power to further their interests. Such was now my duty.

6

STRIKE

I spent the night alternately weeping for Catherine, the pastor, and Lucy and worrying about Teddy and Thea. I had finally fallen asleep when Martin rose at four, fretting over his stores old and new, and woke me up. By the time the working day drew to its close, we were both exhausted.

"They're asking for a lot." I tried to put aside the headache that had dogged me all day and concentrate on the sheet of paper Martin had given me. "Text of the Addresses of the Chicago Workingmen's Party" was set in heavy type at the top.

"A great deal but demanded with commendable brevity. It's smart of them to ensure it fits on one page." Martin jerked the window closed and resumed his seat on the corner of his desk.

"I had a letter from Miss Baker," I said. "Sarah and Tess are well. Miss Baker says that although she knows we'd let her have time off to come to Chicago, she realizes she's left it too late for the trains. She won't countenance putting Mr.

Nutt or Donny in danger to drive her here as they are working men too."

"And so am I." Martin stretched, yawning. "Do you think I could demand an eight-hour day?"

"I could just see you walking away from a three o'clock meeting with Madame because you'd been at the store since seven." I felt a faint grin tug at the corners of my mouth. "But you're not being oppressed by the robber barons."

"I *am* a robber baron, or so you tell me the world believes." Martin yawned again. "I happen to sympathize with the idea of an eight-hour shift in some circumstances, as you very well know."

"And as some of our women have cause to thank you for." I patted the bony knee nearest to me. "I'm more in favor of *that* demand than of the government taking possession of the railroads and telegraph lines."

"Morgan and the Vanderbilts and their ilk would soon set up companies producing flying machines to compete with their former businesses, and then we'd have strikes of the flying machine workers. They could drop grenades on us from great heights." Martin mimed the action he was describing.

A rap on the door of Martin's office prevented our conversation from proceeding, and just as well—we were both too tired to talk sensibly. Joe Salazar entered, his tall hat in his hand.

"And there you have it," he announced. "All railroads officially closed. I hoped the Chicago and North Western would hold out at least. This is now an open strike." He placed his hat on Martin's desk. "It's like an oven in here. Why don't you open a window?"

"I thought it would be better to roast than breathe the Chicago air. But anything to oblige." Martin got down from his perch to push up the lower half of the sash. I wrinkled my nose at the stink that was blowing toward us from the stockyards.

"I possess one of those announcements," Joe replied as I tried to pass him my piece of paper. "They won't get anywhere. The way to change is through the ballot box, not violence. Not in *this* country at least."

"The violence won't come from the railroad men either." Martin resumed his seat and took the sheet from me, folding it and stashing it in his pocketbook. "As Mayor Heath has noted, they're not the ones to fear. It's the toughs, the deadbeats, and the loafers who'll pick a fight with anyone that we should worry about. Although the inflammatory language the strikers are using will get some of the younger men riled up. It's easy enough to accept you could die fighting when you're young." He nodded at Joe. "You know that better than I do."

"You're plenty ready to fight, if it comes to saving your store." Joe reached over to punch Martin on the shoulder. "And my army experience won't amount to much when we're barricaded behind the shop windows." He grinned. "My army rifle might though."

"And I have my hunting guns." Martin nodded. "A few of the other men have brought guns from home. If anyone threatens my store or the people in it—damn it, Joe, I wish we'd insisted on sending the women home."

"The women won't go, from what they've told me," I pointed out. "And we'll open the store tomorrow morning, won't we? After all, we have the state troops just around the corner to protect us."

"Maybe." Martin glanced at the window, then stood up, reaching for his jacket. "Come on, the two of you. Let's check the fire precautions again and then shut the shop." He adjusted the black band on his sleeve; both of us were wearing black for the Lombardis, and my mourning dress made me feel even hotter. "I'd like to see the shutters closed. If the saloons and taprooms are indeed closing at six, the streets may get a little rowdy this evening. Chicago men don't appreciate going thirsty."

"Oh, and Nell?" Joe put a hand on my arm as I rose to leave. "Happy birthday." To my surprise, he lifted my right hand to his lips and kissed it, retaining his grip to admire the large peridot that now sparkled on my middle finger. "I'm glad Martin found a moment to give the ring to you—and I'm glad you're wearing it despite being in mourning."

"It seemed churlish to refuse to wear my rings," I admitted. "Especially when they're so new."

"These might have to wait for later." Joe grinned as I opened the small box he presented to me and exclaimed in wonder at the exquisite earbobs nestled on the velvet lining.

"I'm afraid so; I can't cover *these* with black gloves." I held up one earring so that the elongated teardrop peridot caught the light. "They're ridiculously extravagant, Joe, but thank you from the bottom of my heart."

"Not as costly as you imagine." Joe raised his eyebrows comically at me. "I drove a hard bargain—this is one of the jewelers we're trying to inveigle into an exclusive arrangement. You wait till you see some of the work he's done when we begin selling his pieces in the new store."

"He's extremely good." I squinted at the gorgeous filigree mount.

"He's a genuine artist. Rutherford's is going to become as well known for its jewels as for its gowns."

"*If* it's not burned to the ground while its principals indulge in chatter." Martin was pointedly holding the door open. "You'd almost think we weren't in the middle of civil disorder."

THE STORE OPENED THE NEXT MORNING, BUT IT WAS A BRIEF attempt at normalcy.

"We'll close at noon." Martin spoke into my ear as I leaned over the cutting table in the atelier, checking the positioning of some pattern pieces. "You must let the women know; there isn't room on these premises for me to make a proper announcement to everyone at once, so I've decided we'll do this quietly and without fuss. Make sure they understand that if they've changed their minds and want to go home, we'll provide an escort."

"None of them will leave. They've all made that clear." I straightened up and tipped my head back to look at Martin's face. "Even with the store closed, we can keep working. Why are we closing anyway?"

"The banks are at a standstill. 'Short at both ends and in the middle' is how they put it. Our takings have been so low in the last couple of days that we're starting to run out of change. People are deserting the streets."

"Is there any danger?" I asked.

Martin shrugged. "They say there are as many as twenty mobs. At the moment, they're visiting the industrial parts of the city, threatening or arguing the men into striking and joining the crowd."

"Well, I suppose that with the store closed we could bring the buckets of water and sand down onto the sales floor in case of fire."

"Indeed. And we'll spend the afternoon ensuring that as much stock as possible is secured out of harm's way."

The women near us were blatantly listening by now, and those in the farther corners of the workroom had stopped what they were doing and turned their faces toward us. I looked around at the pieces laid out on the cutting tables, the dress forms with half-finished work, the embroidered panels. So much effort, and so easily damaged—that night in February the flames had devoured almost all our hard toil.

"Please fetch Madame," I instructed one of the nearby seamstresses. She nodded and hurried off toward the door.

"We'll take care of things here," I assured Martin. "I don't intend to lose a stitch of this work if I can help it."

"I HAVE TO GO TO A MEETING," MARTIN ANNOUNCED ALMOST as soon as he'd finished his last bite of luncheon.

We were eating in the basement refectory with the rest of the staff, "to encourage the troops," as Martin put it. The steamy dampness, the loud talk, the clatter of heels on tiled floors, and the pervasive smell of cooked vegetables were powerful reminders of my brief career as a shopgirl, except that there was no line of employees waiting for the next lunch shift. We were down to about a hundred souls, all of us wondering what the coming hours might bring; but spirits were high and appetites good, and the remaining personnel would have plenty to keep them occupied.

"*Another* meeting?" I asked. Martin had spent much of the last two days talking to his fellow merchants along State Street.

"This is big, from the sound of it. A grand mass gathering of businessmen at three thirty." Martin patted the region of his breast pocket, and I heard the rustle of paper—more telegrams. "I'll take Joe."

"Men only, I suppose. Does the term 'businessmen' include women?" As discreetly as I could, I pulled a wry face at my husband.

"I'll take you too, if you want—but you'll have every man in the place staring at you."

"No, I won't insist." I wiped my mouth with my napkin. "I

don't resent being left out of these meetings, partner or not. You are the senior partner, and besides—this is all about organizing safety guards and the like, isn't it?"

"Oh, there'll be a lot of speeches, and then we'll pass a resolution and issue a declaration and all the rest." Martin came around the table to pull out my chair as I rose. "It's essentially political; the point is to show that the merchants are on the side of law and order and support the authorities. There was too much talk in Pittsburgh about sympathy for the plight of the working men, and it's believed that encouraged the communists."

"Do you think it did?"

"No, I've told you that mobs attract troublemakers. That's the problem with strikes—but I'll concede that they do draw attention. They make people think. They make *me* think. I wonder if it might be more productive to hire more employees to work shorter hours."

"Start by sending yourself home after eight hours," I suggested, squeezing the arm under which I'd passed my hand.

"*That's* the pot calling the kettle black." The arm squeezed back. "I'll probably have to meet with the State Street men after the bigger meeting too. You may not see me till midnight."

7

HEROES

I didn't see Martin till the next day. Waiting for him, I had spent the night in the store with the other women; by midmorning, having had a note from him that he was at the Palmer House Hotel, I went in search of my errant spouse.

"Martin?"

I pushed open the door to our suite as quietly as I could and stepped onto the soft Turkey carpet, my heels sinking deliciously into the thick pile. Our suite contained only a parlor, a dressing room, and a bedroom, and I didn't see my husband in the parlor. A gentle snore and a movement in the room beyond reassured me that my guess as to his where-abouts had been correct.

Martin lay sprawled across the bed, dressed in the clothes he'd worn yesterday. He had taken off his boots but was otherwise completely clothed, right down to jacket, cravat, and tiepin. His pale hair was mussed, every item of clothing bore creases, and there was dirt under his fingernails, but his chin was smoothly shaven and eminently kissable. So I kissed it. And his cheek, when the first kiss produced no effect.

"What? What's happening?"

"I couldn't leave it any longer." I sat on the bed, comparing its luxurious springiness with the much harder one I had occupied in the women's dormitory. "Your note said you were getting a shave and a change of clothes, but that was four hours ago."

"Four—oh, for heaven's sake. Why didn't someone from the hotel wake me?"

Martin heaved himself up and retrieved his watch from his vest pocket. "It's stopped." He blinked stupidly at the golden object.

"You didn't *ask* anyone from the hotel to wake you," I pointed out. "I'm glad of it. You can't patrol all night and work all day."

"Is the store all right?"

"Do you think I'd be so calm if it weren't? The men have been rounding up the delivery drays, as you asked. Madame's getting a little agitated about not having the silks for the Van Studdert trousseau, but we've completed several rather complicated gowns ahead of time. Where we've been lacking a fabric, we've substituted something more costly if we can, so our customers should be delighted."

"Huh." Martin lay down on the bed again, staring at the ornate woodwork of the canopy. His stomach rumbled.

"I'll order you some food if you get in the bath," I said in response to the gastric noises. "It'll be ready by the time you're clean."

"I haven't got time for a bath or a meal." Martin pulled himself up anew.

"You *need* a bath." I sniffed delicately to drive my point home. "And eating will take you ten extra minutes. There's nothing for you at the store except correspondence—and listen, I have some excellent news."

I plucked a telegram out of my reticule. "I've been opening your personal telegrams, for which I make no apology. This is why I couldn't wait one more minute."

Martin rose and half staggered to the window, slipping on the polished wood in his stockinged feet as he stepped off the rug. He stared at the paper in his hand, attempting to focus his sleep-fogged brain on the words.

"It's from Dr. Spedding at the seminary," I said helpfully.

"I can see that." Martin yawned. "Is he saying Teddy was there, or were both of them there? Why didn't he contact us weeks ago?"

"Why should he?" The excitement I had felt when I'd opened the telegram earlier in the morning bubbled up in me again. "I left just after he arrived—he probably didn't realize I was such friends with the Lombardis."

"True. 'Am told you seek Edward Lombardi. Here briefly. Left heading west.' West?"

"In the wrong direction," I remarked. "It would have been nice of Dr. Spedding to give us more information, but my guess is that Teddy was still on his own. I've wired the seminary—I wanted to make sure Dr. Spedding knows to tell him to contact us if he comes back."

"That's wonderful news, in any event." Martin shucked off his jacket and threw it over a chair, then tensed in the act of removing his tiepin as a huge shout sounded from somewhere in the direction of the lake.

"Don't worry. It's just people cheering the troops," I reassured him. "More regulars from the frontier—all veteran Indian fighters. They're quartering them in the Exposition Building and the park."

"Write a note to Joe," Martin called from inside the bathroom. "Tell him those drays need to be ready to leave at a moment's notice."

"Why?" I pressed the bell near the fireplace to summon a page. "What will you do with them?"

"Transport police officers, most likely. They don't have enough vehicles to get to where the trouble is—when it starts."

BY MIDAFTERNOON, THE ONLY PEOPLE LEFT IN THE STORE WERE the women and the elderly men.

"I hate having to wait like this," I said to Madame.

"Men have the easiest part of a battle." My mentor's crown of gray hair wobbled as she nodded emphatically.

"Where do you think they are?" I shaded my eyes against the sunlight. I had spent an eternity gazing to the south; I felt I would be able to recall every detail of the street for years to come.

"We will not find out until they return."

Martin's arrival at the store had been swiftly followed by the call he'd expected, and all the younger men had left with him to drive the police reinforcements down to the viaduct. The rest of us had tried to work but had soon abandoned the attempt.

We had spent the day living on rumor. The workers had thrown stones; in retaliation, the police officers had wounded some strikers with rifle fire. A mob had torn a horsecar apart. Colonel King had brought two companies of regulars down La Salle Street with Spencer rifles. Sometimes I thought I heard shouts to the far south, but it was hard to tell. Sometimes the distant crack of a rifle pricked the air. I often heard cheers to the west of us, which must be the

78

crowds saluting the Indian Wars veterans arriving to reinforce the troops already in the city.

There always seemed to be people, singly or in small groups, dashing back and forth on State Street in search of information or excitement, even if the normal throng of shoppers was absent. With the presence of the soldiers ensuring their safety, the remaining Rutherford's staff had straggled out onto the sidewalk to see what was happening, abandoning their defensive posts behind the shuttered windows.

It seemed an age—two ages—before a gentleman in shirtsleeves, sans hat, coat, or gloves, brought us some news. I recognized him as one Mr. McTigue, the proprietor of a pleasant nearby store that sold perfumes, soaps, and hair oils. Our seamstresses quickly surrounded him.

"They're quite all right, ladies." Mr. McTigue, finding himself mobbed by women, puffed up his chest. "They just can't get back till the police officers no longer have a use for them. Right now, they're busy taking the wounded to the hospitals." He caught sight of me standing by the store's front entrance. "Mr. Rutherford's just dandy, ma'am." He put his hand to his head to tip his hat to me and then looked around, puzzled, for the lost article.

"No wounded?" I shouted so he could hear me above the buzz of voices.

"We were safely behind the cavalry." Mr. McTigue's teeth showed beneath his abundant mustache. "Ma'am, you should've seen them." He made his way through the crowd in my direction. "Swords drawn, riding at a gallop—I swear at a gallop—toward the rabble. All their accoutrements flashing and jingling like sleigh bells on a Christmas morning, and those horses—" He let out a long whistle. "Just in time too." He coughed hoarsely before continuing. "The police were going to get murdered for sure. The mob chased them all the way from the Halsted Viaduct clear up to Fifteenth Street soon as they ran out of bullets."

He coughed again, turning aside politely to spit into the street. "I must've swallowed a half pound of dust. I figured there wasn't much else I could do, and Mrs. McTigue must be having a fit of the vapors by now. She's of a nervous disposition."

He hurried off, followed by our shouts of thanks for his information, and I resumed waiting. Now I was sure Martin was unhurt, I was impatient to see him—but it was half past four before the Rutherford's wagons rounded the corner from Van Buren Street. The horses moved at a walk, their heads sagging; the men too looked subdued, their faces flushed from the day's heat. They were begrimed from head to toe with dust and less acceptable substances, including what seemed to be brownish smears of blood. None of them showed any obvious signs of injury.

Our drays appeared empty except for the Rutherford's men; the ones in the back stood as they approached and waved tiredly. The wagons themselves were filthy, the yellow paintwork of their wheels and trim almost hidden by dirt.

Martin sat on the fifth dray, driving the horses; he was in the same flushed and dirty condition as the rest of the men. He too was hatless, his coat abandoned next to him, his collar gone.

"Goodness, you're dirty." I had an absurd impulse to climb aboard the wagon and hug him tight, but it didn't seem proper for a partner to give in to a fit of hysterics. "Where's Joe?"

Martin's answer was to twist around and look into the body of the dray.

"Ha. Asleep. Joe!"

Laughter sounded from above me as two of the men pulled a tousled Joe Salazar to his feet. Martin jumped down from the driver's seat and went to the head of the huge draft horse, running his hand over the animal's downy nose and wise, patient face.

"We need to get the horses back to the stables," he said over his shoulder to me as I approached. "I won't be back for at least another hour, Nellie."

Something in his tone of voice checked my movement toward him and prevented any display of affection or relief. Joe, his chin and cheeks stippled with sprouting black hairs, joined us beside the horse, which snorted and jerked its head up and down until Martin calmed it with a few soft words.

"Bad?" I asked my husband.

"They shot at the crowd." Martin's eyes were on the animal, his jaw so rigid that the words emerged with difficulty. "The police reinforcements we took to the scene shot at the working men. As soon as the rioters saw the cavalry and the fresh contingent of police, they turned to run—and the lawmen fired at their backs." Martin scuffed at the dust of the street with the toe of his boot. "The cavalry mostly held off—they threatened with their swords, but they didn't try to cut anyone down. But the police . . ." He shook his head.

"Their blood was up," Joe said quietly to me. "They'd seen their own men being chased by the mob—within inches of being torn apart, I think, when we arrived. Some fired shots, and the police officers who'd been running from the rioters turned back around and laid about them with their clubs, hitting anyone they could reach."

"They weren't all men, those so-called rioters." Martin pushed a dirty hand into hair dimmed by a layer of dust and looked at me at last. "There were women, boys . . ." He let his hand drop. "I know there were toughs and troublemakers in the crowd, but I think most of them were just regular people caught up in the heat of the moment."

"Fighting is like that." Joe gave Martin's shoulder a gentle thump.

"I understand, but it sticks in my craw all the same." Martin rested his head against the horse's neck for a second, then straightened his shoulders. "Come on, Joe, let's get the men organized to take the horses home. These beauties need food and rest."

"And so do you," I pointed out. "Do you realize you're the heroes of the hour? The merchants of Chicago have taken their stand against lawlessness."

"I'm not so sure we shouldn't have fed them instead of helping the police, now that it's all over." Martin shrugged one shoulder. "But I'll argue the point later—I've got a lot to think about. We'd better go, Nellie."

"I'm coming with you." I looked around to where a handful of the men were clambering upward, settling in their seats. "And after we're done at the stables, the three of us are going back to the Palmer House. Baths for you two, and food for all. We don't know how long this unrest will last, so we'd better be prepared."

8

NEGOTIATIONS

*W*ith the city full of troops, we could reopen Rutherford's the next day, which was Friday. Customers were few, although they had increased by Saturday afternoon. Our seamstresses also returned to the store, and by the time we closed in the evening, even Madame was satisfied with the volume of work produced. We all looked forward to our Sunday rest with unusual appreciation.

"'*The city authorities having dispersed all lawlessness in the city, and law and order being restored, I now urge and request all business men and employers generally to resume work, and give as much employment to their workmen as possible.'*"

Martin laid down the notice from which he'd been reading and crossed his arms. Outside the window of our Palmer House suite, we could hear the normal noises of State Street on a rainy Sunday. The cooler temperature was bliss; the peace after the rioting even more so.

"I detect a note of sympathy in that last phrase of the mayor's," I said. "He's right—what people need is work."

"And the railroad men got none of what they asked for."

Martin shifted uneasily on the settee. "I figured Hayes wouldn't stand for mob rule in Chicago—not after what happened in Pittsburgh and St. Louis—but I'm not happy at the way we arrived at this so-called peace. You put enough troops in any city and the people will act peaceful just to save their skins, but they have resolved nothing."

"They prevented mob rule." I rose, crossing the rug to settle down by my husband. "You took the side you had to take. I don't see how you could have done otherwise."

"I don't either." Martin sighed as he slipped one arm along the back of the settee, inviting me to nestle into him. "But I'm starting to consider how I could do differently in the future."

"An eight-hour day? Madame won't like it. She's annoyed that most of our ladies only work ten hours."

"Eight hours for everyone. Obviously, we must arrange for shifts at different times, but no employee will need to choose between shorter hours and losing their job. Clerks, shop girls, couturières, carpenters—any extra hours worked at one-and-a-half times' the usual rate, so that the department heads won't be tempted to persuade their employees to work longer shifts."

"Good heavens, Mr. Rutherford, that's practically socialism." I closed my eyes, enjoying the smoothness of Martin's fine wool jacket under my cheek, the warmth and the solidity of him. "Just don't break the news to Madame until we're back at full production, will you? All the Chinese silks are several days late, and that consignment of Irish linen has vanished into thin air. Madame keeps lamenting that we have almost nothing new for our fall and winter commissions."

"Hmmm." I could feel Martin's body relaxing, the two of us molding together like warm wax. "I keep excellent records, so I will be able to tell all of us—the partners *and* Madame—how much money, if any, my newfound socialism is costing us. Although, I've been working out the numbers in my head, and I think we'll be more profitable. People spread a day's tasks to fit into the hours at their disposal, you know. I suspect they'll do just as much work in eight hours as in ten. We'll hire more people to make up the shortfall—and the more people we employ, the more profit we generate."

"It's an outlandish notion, but I trust in your business sense." I yawned. "Goodness, don't let me fall asleep. I must still write to Sarah, Tess, and Miss Baker. They need to know that we're all unharmed, and that I'll be traveling down to Lake Forest on Wednesday."

"Do you think they'll mind if we all move in here instead of going back to Aldine Square? We need to remove our belongings from the house the second week of August anyway."

"I'll break the news." I changed my position so that my head was more comfortable. "And it'll be easier to put Thea and Teddy up here than at Aldine Square. When we find them."

"WHAT HAVE YOU DONE?" I MARCHED INTO MARTIN'S OFFICE and closed the door firmly. "I asked you not to mention an eight-hour day to Madame until the atelier had settled down again."

"He didn't." Joe appeared from the adjoining small room where Martin's private safe resided.

"*I didn't,*" Martin said indignantly, rising automatically to his feet. "And kindly don't rush into this room and begin talking about matters strictly between the three of us without checking there's nobody else here."

"I shut the door," I began and then thought better of it.

"I'm sorry. You're quite right; it was wrong of me. It's a good thing you took Joe into your confidence."

"It is," Joe said drily. "Given the explosively political nature of such an innovation. I've persuaded Martin to keep quiet about it until we've settled into the new store." He put a stack of bound ledgers on Martin's desk. "We're about to start working out how we can estimate the effectiveness of the change in financial terms. I've warned Martin already; if it doesn't work, it will be hard to reverse our position."

"It's a risk." Martin looked pleased at the idea. "But it's going to work, you'll see."

"But Madame *knows*." I was determined not to let Martin divert the conversation. "She said something to me that made it clear she not only knows, she's talked to you about it."

"She guessed." Martin frowned. "I'm not sure how. That woman is a force of nature. She appears to have a strongly developed intuition for anything that might affect her precious atelier. *My* atelier. *Our* atelier." He grinned. "She completely rattled me. She swept into this office at seven thirty a.m., shut the door and proceeded to negotiate with me."

"Negotiate? Is she determined not to allow it to happen?" I asked.

"She's prepared to let it happen," Martin said. "*If* I make a concession."

"Martin's notion has given her a bargaining chip." Joe's eyes danced. "Out with it, Martin—what's the old lady up to?"

"House models." Martin grimaced as Joe let out an "Ah!" and thumped the desk. "Yes, I know you're in favor too."

"I think they're an excellent idea, and most in keeping with the times. Worth uses models." Joe wagged a finger to emphasize his point.

"Worth is in Paris," Martin said, his tone exasperated. "This is Chicago. People are a degree more straitlaced."

"I don't understand. We already use models to show off our work." I frowned. "It makes little sense to put a dress on someone it hasn't been made for, but I've often called ladies in from millinery to model a hat. Or I've placed a cape on one of our assistants' shoulders to show it off. And we have dresses displayed on forms throughout the store."

"It sells the hats, doesn't it, Nell, to let the customers see them from all angles?" Joe's saturnine face was alight with interest. "In Paris, the more important dressmakers are copying Worth, using women to display gowns in the same way as you'd demonstrate a hat by putting it on a real woman."

"I know—I *do* read the fashion journals, Joe." I smiled at his enthusiasm. "But our clients are our best publicity. Women tell their friends who made their dress."

"And you're one of our finest models yourself." Martin smiled at me. "I'm a lucky man to have such an elegant wife. But Madame wants to do much more. She wishes to employ attractive young ladies *specifically* for the purpose of showing the dresses."

"What kind of woman would do that?" I mused. "Parading up and down in front of other women—"

"In front of their husbands too." Joe raised his eyebrows. "If necessary. You've seen how some men want to see the investment they're making before they buy. Although I think it's insulting not to give your wife a dress allowance and let her get on with it."

"There are definitely some people in Chicago who would find *that* shocking," I said. "Men standing around watching as young women parade by—"

"The ladies at the pinnacle of society won't be shocked," Martin said. "The ones who've already traveled to Paris and seen how things are done there will consider us advanced, and where those ladies lead, others will follow." He shrugged. "Madame insisted that since we're going to turn the trade on its ear with our eight-hour shifts, we may as well surprise them with house models into the bargain. Ten women to begin with, she says."

"They'll have to be pretty, of course." Joe crossed his arms, thinking. "And move well. Perhaps women who would rather not be on the stage, but are proficient in dancing?"

"Why don't we hire ordinary women?" I asked. "Why do they have to be more attractive than the others? Dresses are for real women."

"We are not selling the dress." Martin produced a creditable imitation of Madame's accent. "We are selling the dream of beauty."

"You're sold on the idea," I said to him accusingly.

"It's another risk—and, yes, I am ready to take it," said Martin. "Less than a week ago I was whipping up the horses to follow a cavalry charge, not knowing in the least what would happen to me and not caring. I didn't like the outcome, as you saw, but I liked the sensation of that moment." His expression turned serious. "That's how I felt when I first decided to build this store. It was a challenge, and somehow the idea of not one but two challenges makes life seem full of possibilities. A sign, perhaps, that I've finally put the events of last year behind me."

"Very well." I crossed to the door. "I defer to you gentlemen, as always, when it comes to sales decisions. I suggest we all talk about this further once I've been to fetch Sarah and Tess."

9

LIKES

"Mama! Look at the toy horse Mr. Parnell gave me. He said it was his when he was a little boy. Isn't that nice? Are we really going to live in the hotel again? May I order ice cream after dinner every day? Isn't it hot? Why is August so hot? Are you still sad about the Lombardis? I remembered Lucy last night and cried awful hard. Where do you suppose Teddy is? Did people throw stones at the store? Mrs. Parnell said people throw stones at windows sometimes when there's a riot. She said sometimes storekeepers nail boards across their windows. Did you and Papa do that? Mrs. Parnell said they should send those lawless ruffians to prison for a long, long time. And Miss Baker said Mrs. Parnell is prejudiced. I think that means she's mad at the workers—oh! She said I shouldn't repeat that to anyone, but now I guess I've told you, so you won't tell, will you? Have you seen Donny?"

"Donny's helping Mr. Nutt with the trunks Tess has already packed." Sensibly answering only the last question, I bent to pick Sarah up. Then I decided she was getting rather heavy and sat down on the bed instead, pulling my daughter up onto my lap. "We're staying at the hotel till the new house is ready. That should be in November—three months from now."

"September, October, November." Sarah punctuated each word by placing a finger on the pleats that trimmed the collar of my mourning gown. "Is that in the winter? Will there be snow?"

"There might be. Papa's hoping we'll be in our new home in plenty of time to get it ready for Thanksgiving."

"And then the new store will open, and there'll be a big Christmas tree. Will we have a big Christmas tree in our new house?"

"Oh yes, there's lots of room."

"Will Donny live in our new house?" Sarah ran her forefinger over the jet buttons on my bodice.

"He'll live in the stables just down the block. Mr. Nutt will have a room there for a little while too until the new driver and stable hands are settled in and our new carriage is finished."

"Isn't Donny going to be a driver too? Mr. Nutt's been teaching him while we've been here. What will he do?"

"Donny will drive sometimes, and sometimes he'll sit next to the driver to keep him company." *And keep us safe,* but I wouldn't say that. "At other times, he'll look after the horses and carriage and do any other work we find for him. You've seen how good he is at all the practical jobs." I smiled. "Don't worry, sweetheart, we'll find plenty of jobs for him. He's such a good worker, and we like him."

"Tess likes him too." Sarah's jade-green eyes seemed to glow as she gave me a direct look that somehow conveyed significance.

"Of course she does. I expect you've had fun visiting all over, haven't you?"

"Yes, lots of fun. But Mama, Tess *likes* Donny. Courting

kind of likes." Sarah put a hand in front of her mouth and mimed a suppressed giggle. "She wants to hold hands with him."

I felt uneasy. "You're far too young to be thinking about romance, Sarah." I stroked the ringlets of bright copper hair that shone against my black dress. Sarah was the sharp, noticing kind of child, and she spent much too much time in adult company. "You know you mustn't gossip about Tess and Donny with anyone, don't you?"

"Thou shalt not go up and down as a talebearer among thy people," Sarah intoned solemnly. "Tess just taught me that. She showed me where it says so in her Bible. That was because I told a little tale about a big boy who lives in the house opposite. About how he got whipped for looking up his cousin's skirt. Oops." This time Sarah put *both* hands over her mouth, as if to stop any more gossip leaking out.

I sighed. "Then you understand you're not to gossip about Tess and Donny? Even to Miss Baker. Tess might well like Donny in the way you say, but he might not be interested in her. I've seen no sign of him liking her in a courting sort of way."

I almost added, *Have you?* But wouldn't that be encouraging Sarah to gossip? Sometimes being a mother felt like walking through a forest full of traps.

"Tess says he's shy of girls."

"He might well be, at that. And isn't he younger than Tess?"

"Only three years." Sarah held up three fingers to illustrate the point. "His birthday is three days after Tess's, and three is Tess's favorite number now. Oh, Mama! Are we going to celebrate your birthday? Tess and I have made something for you."

"When we're all together at the Palmer House, we'll order a little cake for the four of us."

"And ice cream?"

"And ice cream." I hugged Sarah to me. With all the time spent outdoors riding the Parnells' pony, she was becoming lithe and whip-strong, a creature of iron and flame, like my father. She had his love of learning and innate curiosity—I remembered my Papa as always reading books—but the hard core of determination, and the daintiness that hid it, were Mama's. All I saw of John Harvey Venton in her were the crisp waves in her hair, her eyes, and the shape of her face. But those were unmistakable.

"I didn't really gossip about Tess to *you*, did I, Mama?" Sarah's voice was muffled against my dress, but when she pulled away her expression was anxious. "I didn't mean to. I don't believe it's gossip if somebody tells somebody else about somebody else because they're worried about somebody else."

I mentally worked my way through the "somebodies" for a moment and frowned.

"Why are you worried? Are you afraid Tess will leave us if she wants to marry?" I had to admit that idea worried me too. "If it ever came to that, darling, I promise Papa and I would make very sure Tess was well looked after."

"I don't *think* I'm worried about Tess getting married, not really." The center of Sarah's smooth forehead wrinkled. "It's just that—well, isn't Donny a kind of servant?"

"An employee," I said quickly. "He's a working man, just like Papa. Papa was fortunate to get a good start in life—he inherited Grandmama Rutherford's business. Otherwise he would have started with nothing, as Donny has."

Sarah blinked hard. "But we're rich and Donny isn't. He only has the wages Papa gives him, doesn't he?"

"He has wages, yes. And a place to sleep and food and clothes that we buy for him. He earns those things by working hard for us."

"But Tess is a rich lady. And she sits and drinks tea with all the other rich ladies, doesn't she? The ones who come to see you and the ones you and Tess go to visit."

"Yes."

"Sooo . . ." Sarah frowned. "Won't the other rich ladies say Tess shouldn't like Donny because he shovels Gentleman's muck out of the stable? They're always talking about finding a 'suitable' husband for young ladies. Wouldn't that mean one who doesn't shovel muck?"

"Oh, heavens." I put my head in my hands. "How is it you even come up with these things at six years old? And what does it matter what the 'rich ladies' think?"

"Nearly six and a half, Mama. It *does* matter. It matters what the rich ladies think of you if you take tea with them." Her rosebud lips trembled slightly.

"Oh, Sarah." I cupped her small face in my hands, kissing the tiny wrinkles on her forehead. "This is about your 'bad word,' isn't it?"

"A little bit." Sarah sniffed. "I don't want the rich ladies to look down on Tessie for marrying a—well, Donny doesn't even know where he comes from, does he? He doesn't have a real last name. His last name is Clark because somebody left him at a priest's house in Clark Street."

Bastard. That was Sarah's 'bad word'—the one Thea Lombardi had taught her when she was only three years old, and she'd never forgotten it. Why hadn't I spoken Jack Venton's name out loud to my mother and stepfather? But if I'd married Jack, I'd have lost Martin. And we were so happy . . . my selfish heart would not have wanted it any other way, but my selfish actions had left a scar across the heart of the child who had been the first genuine love of my adult life.

"Listen, darling." I kissed Sarah again. "There's a long path to walk between liking someone in a courting sort of way and getting married. It probably won't even happen, but if it does, any rich lady who says anything against Donny won't be allowed into our house. Most of the rich ladies' husbands and fathers got their hands dirty once. We'll stare them in the face and not fret about their opinions, won't we?"

But that was easier said than done. We'd built our lives in Chicago on the untruth that I'd been a widow when I married Martin—and some 'rich ladies' suspected the lie. Perhaps Sarah was right to be so worried about what Chicago society thought.

I waited almost a month to tell Martin about what Sarah had said. I decided to observe Tess and Donny for a few days first and then forgot to talk to Martin because both Sarah and Miss Baker fell ill with the mumps at the same time as Tess took to her bed with a bad cold. Two weeks of confinement and worry had tried my temper, my crotchety behavior had tried Martin's temper, and we had a tendency to find ourselves out of sorts with one another. I might, perhaps, have found a better moment to broach the subject of Tess and Donny than the day Martin had asked me to visit the new house, now receiving its decorative touches.

"So what you're in fact saying," Martin pointed out after listening to my concerns, "is that you'd far rather Tess gave up her happiness to secure yours by ensuring our household arrangements never change."

He swiped impatiently at the sleeve of his jacket, which was covered in fine sawdust. The sound of hammers, saws, and planes from the adjacent hallway shielded us from listening ears, but we were talking quietly, having retreated to the bay window of our future front parlor to get away from as much of the noise of the workmen as possible.

"I neither said that nor meant any such thing," I

responded with indignation. "Of course I want Tess to be happy."

"But with the right man, not the wrong one."

"It's not as if we know what Donny's feelings are. I was trying to gauge them when everyone fell ill. He admires Tess, certainly. He thinks she's very clever—and given that she takes every opportunity to engage him in talk, I agree with him."

Martin smirked, and a stab of annoyance made me grit my teeth. "She'd manage him all right if they married," he said. "And I get the impression he has no idea she has some money. He doesn't seem to spend much on himself in any case."

"No, of course there's no suspicion of self-interest on Donny's side. It's cynical of you even to mention it."

"I suppose I am cynical." Martin ran a finger over the yet unpolished marquetry pattern in the wood paneling. "But I'm not the one who's objecting to a hypothetical marriage based on class distinction."

"I am *not*—oh, stop being provoking. These last two weeks have been bad enough; at least you've been able to go to the store. You haven't spent your nights with a feverish, fidgety child."

"That's rather unfair. It was you who insisted I take another room, precisely so I *could* get some sleep and do my work. I wouldn't have minded getting up at night for Sarah." His face softened a little. "Don't you remember that when I first met you, *you* had the mumps? Gave them to me too, although at least I didn't get nearly as sick as you did. It was the first time I saw how brave you were—three years old and your cheeks swollen like a pumpkin, but still insisting you were 'in excellent health.'"

I crossed my arms, refusing to be mollified. "Be that as it may, I *did* have a lot of broken nights, and I *was* confined to our suite. And still no word of Teddy and Thea. I feel like all Creation is conspiring against any attempt I want to make to find them. I don't mind telling you that the last two weeks have tried my nerves."

"You hardly have to tell me that." Martin chucked me under the chin as if I were once more that three-year-old child. "You've been as irritable as I don't know what. I can't imagine why I married someone who turns into a shrew if she's not allowed to work her fingers to the bone producing gowns."

I looked up into clear gray eyes that reflected the even light of the cloudy sky outside.

"And I don't know why I married someone who says such infuriating things." But I was unable to stop the corners of my mouth from twitching up, momentarily delighted to see Martin's answering grin. "I'm just worried about how awkward the situation might become. I've had too much time to reflect, I suppose—it's never good for me."

"How very observant of you," Martin drawled, widening his eyes at me. "I must ensure in the future that you have no time to think at all. Exactly which awkward situations has your underemployed brain invented?"

"We may have to discharge Donny if he rejects Tess and makes her unhappy."

Martin shrugged. "I could find him another situation if it comes to that."

"Or she might embarrass him by expressing her feelings, and then *he'd* be unhappy. Tess is so . . . *forthright* about such matters. She'll probably walk right up to him and propose marriage."

"She might, at that."

"It's not funny—don't grin like a baboon."

"Again, the solution would be to find Donny another situation. I might give him a job driving for Rutherford's, with a little training. Or he could work in the company's stables. He's good with horses."

"I suppose so." I pouted. "But the notion of either of them being unhappy just—"

"Sticks in your craw?"

"If you must put it so vulgarly, yes."

"You can't make everyone happy, Nellie."

"I can try." I shot back the retort with considerable force —and then wondered why Martin's remark had stung so much. Yet he remained silent, so I continued. "On the way to Lake Forest, I worked out a lovely little scheme whereby I was going to buy Tess a small carriage of her own, a landaulet or something like it, and have Donny drive her. We can't go on arranging our days around Tess needing to visit the Back of the Yards. Besides, our stables are simply enormous. Like this house." I gestured toward the hallway behind the door, which was so big we could have held a dance in it.

"The stables are no bigger than those of any other house in this district," Martin said a little sulkily.

The size of our house was another tiny bone of contention between us. It was decidedly more modest than the palatial edifice Martin had built for Lucetta; it was a family home rather than a building meant for show or lavish entertaining. But it was undeniably large—larger than we had agreed upon before our wedding. Among other things, it made me wonder how many children Martin intended me to bear, and that implication also didn't improve my temper.

"Don't worry." I rolled my eyes but kept my head turned toward the street, where a double line of twelve-foot trees hinted at a future avenue. "I've resolved to say no more on the subject. We can hardly shrink it all back down again."

"Hmph." Martin seemed about to say more but thought better of it and changed the topic. "Perhaps we should give

Tess a landaulet as a Christmas present? I could go see the carriage maker."

"Yes, but the point is I thought I'd found a specific role for Donny to perform when he's not acting as my bodyguard. Now I fear I'd be throwing them together for hours at a time, giving Tess a chance to—to press her advances on him."

I narrowed my eyes at Martin, over whose face a grin was once more attempting to spread. He took a deep breath.

"As I said, you can't solve everyone's problems for them. Sometimes you just have to let the circumstances play out and be ready to offer a shoulder to cry on if things go wrong."

"It's all right for you to say that. Yours won't be the cried-on shoulder." I sniffed. "And there's another thing: Sarah's worried about the social consequences to our family if Tess marries our coachman or bodyguard or handyman, or whatever Donny is."

"Social consequences?" Martin frowned. "The fellows in our set would laugh and congratulate Donny on making an excellent match."

"Perhaps, but their wives wouldn't. You know we're considered . . . eccentric enough already."

Martin's eyes darkened. "Tainted by scandal, you mean. On both sides."

"And justified on mine. Sarah won't be six years old forever. I can't shelter her behind Miss Baker all her life. Eventually, she'll need lessons in art, music, drawing, dancing, deportment, all the rest—and she'll need to pursue those activities alongside other children. She needs to get to know the people who'll be in her own social set as she grows up."

"Didn't you hate the kind of childhood you're proposing to inflict on our daughter?" Martin went to lean on the window frame but then remembered the sawdust and straightened up, crossing his arms.

"*I'm* inflicting it on her? Since we live in the smartest district in Chicago, we must at least try to behave like our neighbors. I'll admit that hadn't occurred to me before I married you."

"And it's too late now." Martin's face was grave.

"I told you, I'm resolved to do what is best for all of us. Naturally, I won't force Sarah to do anything she doesn't want to do. But she's already far more interested in acquiring the social graces than I ever was. She likes to be correct in her behavior." I swallowed hard. "As she grows, we'll face a dilemma. We could continue to isolate her—or we could take the risk of plowing forward. The risk that the circumstances of her birth might be raised. The risk I've taken all her life."

"You're being inconsistent, my darling." Martin uncrossed his arms, touching my cheek gently. "If we're prepared to take risks for Sarah's sake, we have to be prepared for the risk of Tess incurring the disapproval of a few hidebound society matrons. I say we take the risk."

"I believe that's more or less what I told Sarah," I admitted.

"That's my Nell."

Martin leaned forward with the clear intention of kissing me, but then he stopped, and I saw his expression change.

"What on earth are you doing here?"

I turned away from the window to see Joe Salazar hovering in the open doorway, a letter in his hand.

"This arrived for you at the store." He crossed the room and handed the envelope to Martin.

"As urgent as that?"

"I was certain you'd want it straightaway. It wasn't marked personal, so I opened it."

Martin pulled out the sheet of paper, turning it so he could see the signature—and froze.

"What?" I asked.

Martin gave the note to me. "The news you've been waiting for."

"Oh!" I didn't look up till I had read the whole thing and stared for a few moments at Teddy's signature as if I needed to be quite sure it was real.

"They're at a boardinghouse on Washington Street, a few blocks west of Union Park." My worries had evaporated, replaced by a sudden rush of joy. "Both of them. Teddy says they arrived two days ago. The denominational office helped find them a place to stay."

"Indeed?" Martin raised his eyebrows. "And there I was slandering those people as useless."

I ignored him, my eyes on Teddy's letter again.

"He says they'll be out all day looking for work but will be back every evening at six for dinner and all afternoon on Sundays, and would we care to call? *Would* we?"

I looked at Martin, feeling my face flush with the pure relief and excitement of the news. "Of course we'll go there tonight."

1 0
MAN AND WOMAN

I returned to the store elated. Martin appeared a little more subdued. But that evening as we headed westward, our carriage bouncing over a variety of road surfaces, I too was beset by apprehension.

"She wasn't an easy child, was she?" Martin's words broke into my thoughts as I stared out of the window at the straggling rows of houses interspersed with cheaply built shops and saloons.

"I should say not." I watched a passing horsecar; we were still on Madison Street. "I often felt that only her mother's and father's authority held her in check."

"As far as authority's concerned, that point's clear." Martin's tone was dry, decisive. "Teddy is the man of the family now, and Thea has to obey him."

I rose to the bait immediately. I was tired—we both were —and now that we were on our way, our eagerness to reunite with the Lombardi children seemed to be transforming itself into a state of irritation with the situation and each other.

"Really?" I looked down my nose at my husband. "And supposing Thea doesn't agree with Teddy's decisions?"

Martin blinked. "Then she has to obey him anyway. A woman should obey the head of her family."

"I don't always obey you."

"You almost never *obey* me." A sarcastic edge crept into Martin's voice. "The best I can hope for is that you take my advice."

"Because I'm a reasonable person."

"I'll grant you that. Most of the time." Martin folded his arms. "Young ladies of fifteen are generally not so reasonable, especially the ones who were difficult children. As I have cause to remember in your case."

Sometimes it was extremely provoking to have as one's spouse a man who remembered one as a child. I became immediately determined to argue Thea's side.

"She's lost her mother and father. Such a tragedy may have caused a more tender woman to emerge." I felt I was making a noble concession to Martin's erroneous views on the female gender. "Even the toughest bud may reveal a beautiful blossom." I thought that sounded rather fine.

Martin snorted rudely. "Stuff and nonsense. Beautiful blossom indeed. She'll be a gawky, obstreperous hayseed after all those years in that out-of-the-way corner of Kansas. Teddy's going to have his hands full until she's old enough to be married."

There are few things more offensive to a wife's ears than to be told by her husband that she's talking stuff and nonsense. This further proof of Martin's error gave free rein to my tongue, where perhaps I should have curbed it.

"Well, that's a fine thing to say. It sounds to me like you and Teddy between you are going to create a cage for the poor child, with the only door leading to the marital state.

Any woman of spirit would do anything in her power to subvert such an imprisonment, as you should know."

Some part of me regretted that remark as soon as it passed my lips, but I was too indignant to care. We both knew I referred to Lucetta's romantic entanglements. Dark flashes of color appeared on Martin's cheekbones.

"We had better not talk if we cannot be civil to one another," he said in his iciest manner.

"You would certainly be better off silent if you're going to behave like an absolute and utter . . . *man*."

I pursed my lips and stared resolutely out of the window, determined to say no more. Beside me, my putative lord and master froze into a reproachful immobility that cooled the late summer air by several degrees.

We kept up these attitudes until we reached our destination. The boardinghouse to which Teddy had directed us stood in a row of clapboard houses, fairly recently built but of cheap construction. The street opposite had unbuilt gaps like missing teeth. From the smell and the activity, we had arrived at that part of the city where the horsecar company and various other transportation concerns stabled their horses. The waning sun made the buildings glow pleasantly, but I didn't imagine the area would be fit for young people to return to after dark.

A strong fragrance of cabbage met us as the door opened. We had arranged our faces into more amenable expressions than either of us wished to show each other, and our first sight of the pleasant Polish woman who greeted us galvanized both of us into polite cordiality. The landlady, Mrs. Nowak, evidently expected us, and ushered us in with many smiles and remarks about the pleasure of making our acquaintance.

The house gave every sign of respectability despite its unprepossessing surroundings. Any space on the walls of the narrow hallway held a picture of a Catholic saint, surrounding a statue of Jesus exposing his heart above a dish of what I supposed must be holy water.

We had clearly arrived after the dinner hour. Through an open door, we saw a dining room where several men and two women lingered over the cleared tablecloth, reading journals or playing chess, conversing and laughing with each other as they did so. The convivial, homey scene relieved some of my anxiety.

I needed to pull my black skirts in to pass more easily up the stairs. As instructed by the landlady, I kept heading upward. Behind me, Martin remained silent, his tread steady and even.

As we neared the top of the building, a door opened. A skylight illuminated Teddy's sandy hair. A genial smile split his long face, so like his father's, but his round gray eyes were not those of the boy he'd been. A stillness hung about him, a new sense of sobriety and determination. He had grown as tall as Martin and had to duck his head to clear the low doorway as he backed up a little, making room for us.

"The first truly friendly faces I've seen since we arrived," he said, shaking my hand vigorously. "You're a sight for sore eyes, Mrs.—confound it, I've been telling myself all day not to call you Mrs. Lillington, and there I was, just about to say it. Mrs. *Rutherford*, to be sure. And Mr. Rutherford, sir, it's good to meet you again. I was real happy to get the news about your marriage."

"*Really* happy," came a voice from behind a blanket nailed across the middle of the room. "Your grammar is terrible, Teddy. And what's so wonderful about his marriage? Mr. Rutherford lost his wife—his *first* wife."

Disapproval flitted across Teddy's face, but a rueful grin quickly followed. "She's been through a lot. You must pardon her . . . outspokenness," he said in an undertone.

He motioned us both into the small room. We only saw one side of it, of course; it contained a simple iron bedstead, a plain wooden chair on which sat a worn Bible, and a washstand. Shelves and hooks took up every available space on the whitewashed walls. A very few possessions, startling in their meagerness, were ranged about the room. The three of us, standing close together, occupied most of the remaining floor space.

"Are you going to come out, Thea?" Teddy spoke with a note of dry authority I hadn't heard before. "You can't sit there all day waiting to make an entrance. Your audience is ready."

"You are quite ridiculous." But a slim hand pushed aside the blanket, and Thea Lombardi emerged.

Martin had expected a hayseed; we saw a tall and graceful flower. Thea would be fifteen by now, but she could have passed for eighteen or even twenty. In a word, she was beautiful. There was no other way to describe the effect of her large, brilliant hazel eyes, fringed by lashes so long they almost didn't look real. A cascade of glossy dark auburn hair, falling to her waist in soft waves, set off her perfectly regular features and clear, pale skin.

I heard Martin make a small, quickly stifled noise of appreciation, and I experienced a stab of annoyance—but he *was* a man, after all. The meager skylight set into the ceiling above Teddy's bed showed a red sunset sky; the crimson rays seemed to gather in the ringlets that terminated each section of Thea's hair as if the light itself was enamored of her beauty. She stood taller than her late mother, her figure perfectly modeled, her simple calico dress enhancing her firm breasts and tiny waist and hinting at the length of her legs. In the plain setting of the impoverished room, she shone like a ruby dropped in the dust.

Martin had ended up closest to Thea. He held out his hands to grasp hers.

"I'm so sorry about the loss of your parents and sister." His voice bore a wealth of sincerity. "You and Teddy have been through more than children—young people—your age should be expected to bear. We'll do everything we can to help you. We're hoping you'll make your home with us here in Chicago."

Thea had practically ignored Martin in Kansas, devoting most of her admiring looks to Lucetta. Now she smiled graciously at him, and my senses prickled. Her teeth were white, small, and even, like Catherine's, but where Catherine's smile had been open, frank, and generous, Thea's smile seemed that of a woman who already understood that beauty could be transformed into power.

"You're so very kind." She gazed intently at Martin's face. "I was so sorry to learn of your wife's passing."

For a second, we all appeared to be frozen into our positions like characters in a tableau, but then Teddy moved, picking up the Bible from the chair and swiping his hand over the seat. "Please take this seat, Mrs. Rutherford. We're a little cramped at the moment. Still, I'm grateful to have a place to stay."

"Even if it's a little too Catholic." Thea was still looking at Martin. "I'm surprised Teddy hasn't already lectured the other boarders on the evils of idolatry."

Teddy's stern expression made him look even more like his father. "Mrs. Nowak is a good landlady, and I'm beholden to the denomination for arranging accommodation for us at such short notice. A godly woman is a jewel, even if she's a papist."

"Don't try to sound like Pa." At last, Thea turned away from Martin to scowl at her brother. The expression dissipated the illusion of elegant womanhood, and I glimpsed the hayseed; she was, after all, very young.

"I don't have a chair on my side of the room, or I'd be happy to offer it to you," Thea said to Martin in a tone that managed to convey her martyrdom in relinquishing the room's only seat.

"I'm fine standing." Martin, his face unreadable, assisted Thea to sit on Teddy's bed with as much ceremony as if he'd been in a Prairie Avenue drawing room and then took up a position in front of the dividing blanket. Teddy lounged against the doorjamb, his hands in his pockets.

"You'll want to know what happened," he said to me.

"You don't have to—" I began, but Thea interrupted me by rising to her feet.

"I'll go see if Mrs. Nowak has any of those little pastry things she makes. We should offer our guests something."

She was out of the door in a second, so fast that Teddy had to flatten himself to the wall to get out of her way. Yes, a child, I thought, and one who rather lacked the social graces—what had Catherine been thinking, to neglect that part of her education?

It was growing dark. Teddy lit the small lamp that appeared to be the room's only source of light. The three of us remained silent; I couldn't see Martin's face.

"She doesn't want to learn about their deathbeds," Teddy said eventually. "I've tried to tell her, but she won't listen. I wish she would. It's a comfort to me to know that they faced death with the assurance of God's nearness, and I'm sure she'd benefit from hearing about their final moments."

"She's only fifteen, Teddy." I experienced a moment of sympathy for the girl who was so clearly afraid to mourn. "Was she not there, then?"

Teddy shook his head. "Mr. McIlvaine—he's a trader from Wichita who spends most of his time on the trail—came to the mission just after Prudence died. You remember Prudence, who cooked for us? She stayed to nurse Mamma when she—Mamma, I mean—took the diphtheria."

Dismay flooded my chest. At least it hadn't been Indians or bandits, but diphtheria, by all accounts, was a terribly hard illness. The image of them all fighting the dread disease to their final defeat, choking and struggling to breathe, made me curl my hands into fists on my lap.

Teddy turned the lamp's dial so that the flame flared a little brighter, looking away from me. "Mamma was the first to get sick. She probably took it from a half-breed woman and her son who lived in a soddy on the Holmgren homestead, on the run from somebody, as Mamma believed. She didn't seem so bad at the start. She begged Mr. McIlvaine to take all three of us away, but Lucy and I wouldn't go."

"Of course you wouldn't," I murmured under my breath. And then out loud, as another thought struck me: "So Mr. McIlvaine took Thea? On their own?"

Teddy turned to look at me, and a spark of amusement lit his round gray eyes. "You needn't worry on that score, ma'am. Old Bill McIlvaine's sixty-five if he's a day and lost the bottom part of one leg years ago on account of a cattle stampede. He's as safe as houses. He took Thea to his sister's homestead, fifty miles to the northwest. Then I got sick, and Pa a day later, and Lucy the day after that, even though we'd kept her well away from the sick people. Mamma was able to nurse us, ill as she was. The workers started leaving once the news spread around that we were all infected. The last two men disappeared after they buried Prudence."

"Cowards." Martin's comment was voiced almost at a whisper.

"Yes, sir, I guess they were." Teddy's mouth twisted. "After all Pa and Mamma did for them. Well, that was us left to ourselves."

"No doctors? No neighbors?" Martin sounded incredulous. "Surely everyone helps each other out there?"

"They do, sir, but sometimes it's just in God's hands." Teddy sounded so much older than seventeen. "The Holmgrens were our nearest neighbors, but they fell sick too, on account of the half-breed woman. I went there once I was well and found Mr. and Mrs. Holmgren had made it through, but they lost their daughter. The half-breed woman and her son died too. Old Dr. Stanmore died of an apoplexy last year, and Dr. Munro was fifty miles away, tending to a man at one of the mines that's still working. I didn't stay sick for long. My neck swelled up like a bullfrog, and I thought I'd never eat again, but I could stand and help Mamma once the fever passed."

"And your father?" I asked. He had been such a strong man.

"Pa didn't last three days." Teddy looked down at his boots. "It's strange how these things go. He went down like a tree under the ax—died in Mamma's arms."

"Poor Catherine." I glanced at Martin, and our ridiculous bickering suddenly made no sense.

"The next day Mamma took a bad turn, and she took to her bed and never got out of it. A good thing too—that way she didn't see Lucy's eyes." For the first time, I sensed from his voice that Teddy was holding back tears, and my own throat tightened. "She'd have been blind if she'd lived."

Martin shifted his position to place a hand on Teddy's shoulder, but the young man took a deep breath and gathered his strength. "Mamma kept asking after Lucy, and I'd say she was all right. I reckoned God would forgive me that lie. I didn't tell her when Lucy died either. By that time, Mamma was raving, and she thought Mr. McIlvaine had taken both girls, so I let it be. Mamma passed in her sleep a few hours later. I thank God I was there to watch the people I loved pass into heavenly bliss."

A long moment of silence followed Teddy's words. The young man had his eyes closed, his lips moving in prayer. I closed mine too—but I could summon up no words of prayer. All I pictured in the darkness was Catherine, but the image was mixed up with my own mother's deathbed. Catherine hadn't been much older than Mama—forty, perhaps.

I opened my eyes and wiped away a tear as footsteps sounded on the stairs. Martin and Teddy moved to allow Thea to enter the room. There was a black scowl on the young girl's beautiful face, as if she'd heard Teddy's last remark, but her features rearranged themselves into a pleasant mask as she offered first me, then Martin, a plate of small pastry squares folded over a filling of apricot jam.

I barely registered that I was eating something, but I had to admit the small ceremony of hospitality helped to dissipate the atmosphere of grief that hung around us. And Teddy was right—there was a strange comfort in knowing the facts, distressing as they had been. My imagination had supplied worse.

"Are you still living in Aldine Square?" Thea put the plate carefully on the bed, there being nowhere else, and smiled at Martin. "Mamma described your house to me from Mrs. Rutherford's letters. She wanted to come to Chicago, as I'm sure you know, but Pa insisted we hold on just a little longer and not split up the family. He wanted her to wait till they'd found someone to take the mission and given him a new post." She looked significantly at Teddy, almost accusingly, and I wondered if my offer had caused a rift in the family. I bit my lip.

"Pa didn't want charity." Teddy, having eaten the pastry his sister had left, dusted the crumbs off his hands in a way that made Thea narrow her eyes—at his vulgarity, I supposed. "They argued over it—and my parents didn't argue as a rule. Pa said that with God's help our family would pull together, and it was part of God's plan that the denomination would find him a position in Chicago."

"And Mamma said it wasn't God's plan, it was Pa's plan." Derision sharpened Thea's voice. "She said people who talk about God's plan for their lives are sometimes just covering up their own pride and stubbornness."

I winced and looked at Martin. His expression was stern, unreadable; he was looking into Thea's face, which was lifted up toward his as she spoke.

"She shouldn't have let you hear that." Teddy's open, honest countenance flushed. "She only said that because she was mad at Pa. And angry at God, I think. Because of Lucy's long illness. Our poor little girl suffered so, even before the diphtheria came. I don't reckon she was ever strong enough for the plains."

"Lucy. Always Lucy." Thea looked down at her hands, balled into fists clutching at the cotton of her dress, and carefully straightened them out, folding them primly. Before Teddy could reprimand her—I could see he wanted to—she smiled tremulously at Martin.

"If you let us stay at Aldine Square for a little while, Mr. Rutherford, I'd be grateful. I'm so tired of poverty. Aldine Square sounded so nice the way Mamma told me about it— like Paradise." She glanced at me from the corner of her eyes, as if I was the snake in that Paradise.

"It's hardly that." My ears pricked up at the note of forced joviality in Martin's voice. "In any case, we've moved out of Aldine Square now. We're staying at the Palmer House while our new home is being built."

"The Palmer House?" An expression of shock spread over Thea's face. "Isn't that the grandest hotel in Chicago?"

I thought it was time I played some part in the conversation. "The Grand Pacific would probably contest that title." I smiled at Martin, but his eyes didn't meet mine. "The Palmer House is certainly comfortable."

Teddy cleared his throat. "If it's all right with you, ma'am and sir, I'll decline your kind offer. But I'll be real happy if you would look after Thea for a while till I find my feet."

"I don't need looking after." Thea's eyes narrowed.

Teddy ignored her. "I found work today at the horsecar stables. I guess with Thea gone for a while, I could get another man to share this room. Then I'll save up till I can afford better."

"You're included in our offer of help." Martin nodded approvingly at Teddy. "But I applaud you for wanting to stand on your own two feet. Perhaps you'll allow me to make you a gift of clothing, in your parents' memory—and some books if you want to study in the evenings. Do you still want to be a pastor?"

"More than anything in the world." Teddy looked wistful. "I want to work with the poor, like Pa did. I can't see anything more noble than doing God's work."

"Then when the time comes, you must apply to me for a loan to help you." He held up a hand to forestall Teddy's protests. "I'm an investor, and I know a good risk when I see one. We will put any help you need on a business footing."

He turned again to Thea, reaching out to take her small hand into his large one. "As for you, Miss Thea, consider yourself our guest at the Palmer House. I'll arrange for us to move into a larger suite tomorrow so you have your own room, as a young lady should, and you can come to us in the afternoon."

11

RESPONSIBILITY

"*T*hat went well." Martin settled himself into his accustomed position in the rockaway.

"Do you think so?" I leaned back wearily. We hadn't stayed much longer; it was dark, and neither of us liked leaving the rockaway outside for too long. Mr. Nutt, who had benefited from Mrs. Nowak's hospitality, shut the door with vigor. We felt the carriage sway as he hoisted himself up into the driver's seat.

"They're both safe, and Teddy even has a job. Aren't you pleased?" Martin reached over me to pull down the blind on my side and then did the same on his side.

"I suppose I ought to be." I closed my eyes, trying to will away the headache building in the middle of my skull. We would have to talk to the hotel manager when we arrived, and the next morning would be all bustle and chaos as we moved to new apartments. Why had Martin asked Thea to come to us so soon?

"And yet you're not happy, are you?" Martin's voice sounded from the dark of the carriage.

I waited a few seconds before replying. "Not entirely."

113

"I suspected your enthusiasm for taking Catherine's place had waned rather suddenly. When you saw Thea, wasn't it?"

"I wouldn't call it enthusiasm. Determination is nearer the mark." I pinched the bridge of my nose. "I'm just—well, now that I've seen her, I'm daunted by the sheer responsibility of looking after her."

"As she pointed out, she doesn't need looking after. Consider her a guest—a temporary guest."

"That's not what I—oh well." I slumped in my seat, the constant jolting of the carriage annoying me more than usual. "It won't help if she's going to flirt with every male personage in her vicinity."

Martin had been burrowing himself into the seat corner to give himself as much room as possible for his long legs, but now he sat up straight.

"You mean *me*?"

"Who else?"

"Well, of all the—" In the darkness, I almost detected the heat from the flush that would no doubt be decorating Martin's cheekbones. "I hope you're not implying that I was —I am *not* that sort of man, Nellie. She's a child."

"Who can do an excellent imitation of a remarkably beautiful woman."

The frozen tone returned to Martin's voice. "If you are harboring any shred of belief that you can't trust me with her, you had better say so at once."

"Oh, I'm not implying any such thing." I fumbled for Martin's arm in the darkness, squeezing it hard. "In fact, I'm hoping she was batting her eyelashes at you because she considers you a safe target. And she was probably wishing she would rile me up into the bargain—which she did. That remark about the loss of your wife stung."

To my further annoyance, Martin chuckled. "Yes, that was a well-placed shot if I ever saw one. But listen, Nellie, aren't you extrapolating a rather elaborate theory based on very little evidence? She might be correctly behaved in wider society—and if she is a flirt, we will just have to curb her."

"Hmph."

"Does your startlingly lucid insight into Miss Thea's behavior stem from your own experience?" I sensed Martin shift in his seat and turn toward me. "I remember a young lady who was a consummate flirt at that age. Never with me, oddly enough."

I ignored that last remark. "That's precisely what worries me the most," I admitted as realization dawned. "Look what happened to *me*."

"Perhaps we could marry her off."

"At fifteen?"

"Wasn't your Mama looking for suitors for you when you weren't much older than that?"

"Yes, but with a view to an engagement when I was at least eighteen, and a long engagement, at that." I sighed. "I imagine she calculated that having a good, steady boy in my sights would make me less heedless. I must have been a dreadful disappointment to her."

"We might offer to pay for a school for Thea," Martin mused. "A finishing establishment for young ladies or some such place."

"She could do with some polish. She's a little countrified; I didn't believe so at first, but there's something about her accent . . . When you consider how refined Catherine was, I'm surprised more of that refinement didn't rub off on Thea."

"She might resent the suggestion of a school. Wouldn't you?"

"Probably. By fifteen, I was convinced I was quite done with education. And Thea's been teaching school at the mission. I'm the last person to want to put Thea in a cage of any kind, Martin."

"Especially the marital cage." Martin's tone was light, but there was an edge to it.

"If Thea wants to marry a suitable party, I'll dance at her wedding," I said with emphasis. "After all, it's the usual thing." I ignored Martin's snort of derision. "But until that time, I just want to find out how I—we—can make her happy. I don't think she had a great deal of happiness in Kansas."

"On that point, we're in agreement." Martin clicked his tongue. "You know, I liked Roderick Lombardi, but his insistence on following his calling as a missionary in the wilds of Kansas now seems unreasonable to me. Especially sticking it out after he lost his money in '73 and not insisting that the denomination make up the shortfall between his income and outgoings. When a man's duty to his calling overrides his duty of care to his family, maybe he needs to think carefully about whether he's on the right path."

"He'd have called it his duty to God, and to him his vocation took precedence over everything else. Wouldn't it be the same if he were a soldier? And up till Lucy showed signs of not thriving in Kansas, I'm sure Catherine agreed with him."

"I daresay she did, but they were wrong." Martin's voice had a note of anger. "If a child of mine were wasting away, I would move anywhere, do anything—"

"And even if you were unable to leave, you would let me go away with her."

"I'm glad you realize that."

"So even though you insist Thea must obey Teddy, you concede that a man owes it to his womenfolk to not frustrate their wishes." I began to relax at last.

"I—blast it, Nell, you rely far too much on my reasonableness. Most men wouldn't let you twist them around like this."

"That's why I like you."

"Like?"

"Love you." I adjusted my position so that my shoulder was leaning against Martin's. His arm slid over both of my shoulders, warm and reassuring and sweet after our day of disagreement.

"But surely a girl her age should have someone in authority over her," Martin said rather sleepily after we'd jolted along another block.

"Now *you're* being inconsistent." All the irritation was gone from my voice.

"Not at all. I still say that Teddy should and will make the decisions regarding Thea, whatever role we play."

"If you insist." I was too tired to argue further. "But he won't find it easy."

"Why is Thea going to have a prettier hairbrush than mine?" Sarah, pale and thin and still a little swollen on the left side of her face from her attack of mumps, ran a finger over the mother-of-pearl hairbrush back, which was set with small flowers of abalone.

I sighed. The morning had been trying. Even with a bevy of hotel servants to hand, moving to a new suite was hard work of the kind I didn't like. A fractious child whose governess was absent, recovering from her own illness, was no help. I had arranged a few days before for Alice to have the day off, and Tess was still under the weather, so I had told her to rest and done all of our packing.

I had attempted to relieve the tension with a brief trip to the store to buy some things for Thea—but had denied myself the pleasure of looking in on the atelier, and that made me a little depressed. I wanted to return to my working life with a keen longing that surprised me. My fingers itched to embark on a new sketch, but I had no time.

"Thea is a young lady." I unwrapped the matching mirror and comb. "And she is our guest. It's important that we make her feel welcome."

"Why does she have to be our guest?"

"Because she's lost her mother and her father and her sister. Teddy needs to work and can't spend his days chaperoning her. It's ungracious to question a guest's arrival, Sarah."

"We have to show her Christian charity, Sary." Tess uttered this pronouncement placidly enough but then spoiled the effect by muttering, "Although why the Lord tests us so is a mystery to me."

Sarah didn't fail to catch that remark. She shot Tess a conspiratorial grin.

"Why can't Teddy stay too?" she asked. "I like Teddy much better."

"You've asked that question several times now. I hope I won't hear it again." I removed a dark blue parasol from its brown paper wrapping. "Teddy declined our offer of a room at the hotel, as he'd rather not be beholden to us. It's appropriate that a man should insist on his independence. Do you think I made the right choice with this parasol, Tess? I didn't want to buy anything too childish."

"Thea's only just fifteen, Nell." Tess surveyed my purchase. "It's pretty though."

"She's old enough to put her hair up like a lady." I stared critically at a selection of hair combs, wondering if Thea had ever put her hair up. I had probably erred on the side of suitability for an older girl, but I knew how I'd have wanted to be treated at fifteen.

"Thea won't try to teach me my lessons, will she?" Sarah fiddled with the hand mirror, holding it up to see her face. "I don't want her to."

"Of course not. Miss Baker will be back in a day or two. Thea's not coming here to work." I placed the combs inside one of the dresser drawers. "Please don't tell me you have any ideas about Thea's station in life being lower than ours. I told you, she's our guest."

"Her station?" Sarah giggled, but there was a certain lack of mirth in her giggle. "Like a train station?"

"You know perfectly well what I mean." I struggled to find some patience. Sarah would surely be better behaved once she was fully recovered.

"Yes, Sary, you're a little too fond of telling people where they belong these days." Tess's tone was tart. Sarah had made one or two little remarks about Donny lately—remarks that had not pleased Tess. Sarah, of course, was incapable of tact at her age; but she was also highly intelligent, and her comments could be extremely well placed. We would have to curb her tendency to speak out to her elders. Perhaps I should have a talk with Miss Baker. If only Miss Baker were here to take Sarah into her room for a while . . .

"All *aboard*!"

Sarah waved Thea's new mirror wildly above her head in imitation of a train guard. Tess and I, seeing the danger, exclaimed at the same time.

"Sarah, you're going to—"

"Be careful—"

And then the inevitable happened. The mirror's handle slipped out of Sarah's hand and the trinket flew across the room, straight at the marble fireplace. There was a sharp crack and a tinkling noise.

"Oh." Sarah stared at the broken mother-of-pearl surrounded by silvery shards.

I took a deep breath. "Kindly go to your room," I said as steadily as I could manage. "Now."

"I didn't mean to do it, Mama—"

"Now means now, Sarah Amelia Rutherford."

Sarah's small lower lip pushed out as far as she could make it go—it was a little puckered by the swollen side of her face. But even that reminder of her recent illness would not soften the maternal heart, and she knew it. She carefully smoothed her skirts and exited with as much dignity as she was able to muster—but quickly, and with one eye on me.

"That's seven years' bad luck," said Tess in a lugubrious tone of voice.

"Doesn't the church teach us that superstition is ungodly?" I inquired acidly as I crossed the room to press the button that would summon a femme de chambre. This was one task I couldn't do myself since we had no dustpan and brush. "Anyway, I can get another from the store."

1 2

GUEST

*B*y late afternoon, Tess, Sarah, and I were waiting in the Palmer House's rotunda under the watchful eyes of its costly classical statues. I had arranged for Mr. Nutt to collect the young people and bring them to the hotel to save them the trouble of taking the horsecar with Thea's luggage.

Beside me, Sarah hopped from one foot to the other with impatience, commenting loudly on the ladies and gentlemen who passed in and out of the doors. The scene was a constant parade of Chicago's most affluent residents and visitors, the lobby all bustle and cheerfulness as the doormen greeted the guests and called for hired and private carriages outside. I had frequently replied to nods, smiles, and greetings from people we knew.

"Moderate your voice, please." I rested a warning hand on Sarah's bright hair. She had just pointed out—far too loudly —that one tall, portly gentleman in a dark gray suit and red waistcoat looked like a robin. Several individuals in our vicinity swiveled their heads around to stare at the man, and a boy in short trousers bellowed "Wo-o-o-o-o-orms!" as his exasperated mother dragged him through the doorway.

"Beg pardon, Mama." Sarah giggled as she observed the lad being berated by his parent and smiled broadly at a group of adults who were also laughing at the fun.

"Oh, there's Teddy!" Sarah forgot the robin and also forgot to moderate her voice. "Teddy! Teddy!"

It was indeed Teddy passing through the entrance, preceded by Thea. My heart sank. The doorman had almost not let them in, I rather thought. He had turned to stare at them, but they had, after all, arrived in a private carriage. I could see Mr. Nutt arranging for Thea's luggage—a pitifully small case—to be brought up to our rooms.

I cursed Martin inwardly. Why didn't he give us more time to think? And then I cursed myself—I was a dressmaker, for heaven's sake. I should have thought about what Thea would wear. I should have insisted I take an extra two or three days to get some dresses run up for her.

She had done her best. She'd somehow contrived to have a day dress dyed over black—of course, she'd need to wear mourning in public. Her boots had been carefully cleaned. Her magnificent hair cascaded down from under a hat that was entirely wrong for her, but at least it was black—I supposed she had borrowed it from somebody at the boardinghouse. The hair and the beautiful face under it brought admiring looks from all the men in the lobby, but the mamas and daughters gave Thea sidelong glances and spoke to each other in low voices.

Thea stared straight ahead and walked rapidly toward us. Behind her, Teddy, a black armband around the sleeve of his rusty sack coat and with what appeared to be his father's broad-brimmed hat on his head, looked far more at ease than she did.

"Are they poor, Mama?"

Mercifully, Sarah's whisper was not a loud one this time.

"They look like poor people," she continued. "Thea's dress—"

I raised a hasty finger to still her words. *"Not—a—word—about—her—dress,"* I hissed from between gritted teeth with such vehemence that Sarah's eyes bulged in astonishment and she gave a tiny, mute nod. Tess said nothing, but there was sympathy in her expression as she gazed at the two Lombardi children.

We had withdrawn some yards back from the entrance at the time of the robin incident, so I began moving forward. Sarah, not easily diverted from the important business of showing off, skipped ahead of me.

"How do you do." Sarah made a polite curtsey, pronouncing the words in her best imitation of Miss Baker's English accent. She was wearing one of her best dresses, a pale blue plaid with a tarlatan underskirt that rustled as she moved, and the curtsey was designed to show it off to perfect advantage. She'd been practicing all morning.

"Welcome to the Palmer House," Sarah continued in her "society" voice. "It's been so long since we last met." And then, in her own natural voice, "Teddy! Look at my *face*. Did you ever see such a thing?" She pointed to the swollen side of her jaw and grinned, enhancing the lopsided effect.

"What's wrong with you?" One side of Thea's own face lifted in an expression that was half disgust, half fear.

"I got the mumps." Sarah grabbed Teddy's free hand and craned her head to smile up at him. "It's all right, I'm not infeshuss anymore. The doctor said so."

"In-fec-tious." Thea looked down at Sarah with the faintest of sneers on her pink lips. "And for your elucidation, the diphtheria that killed my parents *and* my little sister also

123

produces a swelling of the face. You're not being particularly tactful."

"Thea, she's a little kid." Teddy hunkered down to smile into Sarah's eyes. "It's a fine disfiguration you're sporting there—temporary, of course. My own throat swelled right up when I got the diphtheria, and I looked far worse than you do. That's a highfalutin dress."

"Thank you." Sarah let go of Teddy's hand to execute a twirl, holding her arms up like a ballerina. "Are you coming up to see Thea's room? Mama bought her some nice things."

She darted off in the direction of the steam elevator. With no word to me, Thea followed quickly; her color was high, her expression thunderous. Tess, whom Thea had also ignored and who now looked decidedly less sympathetic, took her place behind her while Teddy and I stayed in the rear.

"I almost thought she wouldn't come," Teddy said into my ear. "Fussed like crazy about her dress."

"I'm so sorry I didn't think of that," I said. "There's no point in my pretending I don't know what you mean. It's a terrible ordeal for a girl that age to stand out in a crowd."

"She outgrew just about everything she had this year." Teddy watched his sister's ramrod-stiff back. "Mamma was despairing over finding something for her to wear."

I sighed. "Why didn't your mother write me? Pride is all very well, but it would have been nothing at all for me to get some clothes run up and sent to Kansas. It's what I *do*."

Teddy shrugged. "I reckon by the end of last year Mamma was just so sore about Pa refusing to leave that she was willing things to get worse. Like if it was bad enough, he'd see sense." His expression was glum. "It's real sad that Thea couldn't have had a few nice things. She always likes to be the biggest toad in the puddle, and she had downright lost face in front of the other girls before the epidemic. The McIlvaines would have liked to help when she stayed with them, but they're as poor as church mice."

Sarah waited until we had stepped into the elevator, then spoke to the car operator. "Fifth floor, please, Norman. See, our friend from Kansas is here to stay."

Norman, a weedy young man with a dark fuzz of incipient mustache, blushed furiously and ducked his head at Thea. She stuck her nose in the air, her own cheeks flushing anew with angry color.

By the time we emerged into the hushed, gaslit corridor, with its deep carpeting, ornate tin ceiling, and framed prints of chaste classical subjects, the atmosphere surrounding our small group was far from cordial. Even Sarah's chatter had fallen silent. She watched Thea with a serious look in her jade-green eyes.

When we reached our suite, Sarah's exuberance returned in her haste to seize the role of hostess. She ran ahead of us and flung open the main door. "Welcome to your new abode."

"You'll stay and have dinner with us, won't you, Teddy?" Like me, he had halted in the middle of the parlor as Sarah pointed to the various doors, describing the features and attractions of the rooms for Thea's benefit. "Martin will be home soon. We can ring for the food to be brought up here if Thea's sensitive about appearing in the dining room. I don't suppose she has anything to wear for dinner."

"We haven't been to many dinners lately." Teddy's tone was dry.

"You realize that if I'd had any idea things had gotten so bad—"

"I know." He smiled at me, nodding. "Please don't blame yourself, ma'am."

"I'll take her to the store tomorrow for a fitting. My ladies can run her up a mourning dress in half a day to begin with, and then we'll outfit her with everything she needs to hold her head up in Chicago. And I won't listen to any objections."

"I'm grateful to you." Teddy's brow furrowed. "I find it hard to be dependent on your kindness—I figure I have something of my Pa in me—but I'm willing to swallow my pride for Thea's sake."

"You're a credit to both of your parents." I coughed against a sudden hoarseness in my throat. "I'll do my best for her, Teddy."

We turned as Sarah threw open a door with a loud shout of, "Ladies and gentlemen, our main attraction!"

"Is that Thea's room?" Teddy asked Sarah encouragingly.

"It sure is. Come and see. Did Mama ask you to stay for dinner? You *have* to." She pouted just the tiniest bit. "You may even have wine. It's French from France. Papa will order it for you if you want it."

Teddy grinned. "It's aqua pumpaginis for me, Miss Sarah. My folks never held with intoxicating beverages."

"Aqua *what?*"

"Pump water, sweetheart. Best thing a body can swallow."

"It's bad manners to show off," Thea informed Sarah as she walked into the room. She reached the point where she could see her reflection in the cheval glass I'd had placed near the window and stopped, staring at herself for a few moments before turning toward me without speaking. It was a magnificent dumb show, conveying a wealth of emotions with one flash of her splendid hazel eyes.

"Teddy agrees that I can take you to the store tomorrow," I hastened to tell her. "For clothes."

The long lashes swept down in acknowledgment. "I would hate to make you look bad in front of your fine friends." And then, as if it had been forced out of her: "I didn't realize you lived like this."

"Our house in Aldine Square was a little less—lavish." I sounded defensive. "Mr. Palmer loves ornamentation."

"Well." Thea looked at the bed piled high with soft pillows, a down comforter, and a beautifully embroidered counterpane I'd found for her in preference to the Palmer House's version, which I'd thought too staid. Her face was now quite white. "May I please be left on my own for a while?"

"Come on, Teddy." Sarah's joy in displaying our hospitality to Thea had deflated. "Let's go sit with Tess for a spell."

I did my best to keep up a cheerful demeanor as we gathered around the empty fireplace in the parlor, but I kept glancing toward the closed door that led to Thea's room. I had fulfilled my duty to Catherine—but just how much trouble was this new responsibility about to bring down on the heads of all those I held dear to my heart?

"We'll have this run up for you by this afternoon." I handed Thea the rapid sketch I'd made while two assistants were measuring her. "It's based on standard pattern pieces, and for a little decoration I've added the ribbon fob, which we'll pin with a silver clasp. Do you have it, Miss Chocomowski?"

"Right here, Mrs. Rutherford." Miss Chocomowski, a rather shy girl but an excellent and promising apprentice, blushed as she handed me two boxes. "Mr. McCombs picked out the little brooch to match it."

"How kind of him," I said, opening the second box. Thea had her arms in the air as the two ladies passed the tape measure around her tiny waist, so I merely tipped the boxes toward her. "They're pretty, aren't they?"

Thea stared at the matching set of pins, small flowers on

an incised background. "It's been a long time since I wore any jewelry."

"Don't you have any from Kansas?"

"None worth keeping." She looked as if she were about to say more but then remembered the assistants and reddened.

"When you're done," I told my ladies, "please make a copy and take it to Miss O'Regan. Tell her we need a complete set of all the necessaries—corsets, combinations, stockings, nightclothes, and everything else a young lady might require. The petticoats with black ribbons for mourning, of course."

I seated myself again, watching in silence as the ladies finished the measurements and helped Thea back into her shabby black dress.

"We'll have you dressed from the skin out by the end of the day. The boots will take a little longer, of course." I watched the young girl's face for a moment. "We're quite used to ladies coming from the frontier or newly come into wealth or working girls who have saved for a special ensemble. You mustn't think all our customers are wealthy." I smiled. "We will dress anyone who can afford to pay us. Some young ladies bring us a little money every week till they have enough—we enjoy surprising them by showing them we can stretch their dollars farther than they imagined."

Thea nodded. She had been quiet since her arrival at the hotel; she had eaten with us and then retired to her room again. I had arranged with her to come to the store early.

"I think coffee and a pastry would be in order, don't you?" I consulted my timepiece. "We've been hard at work for two hours, and neither of us had breakfast. We don't have a restaurant in this temporary store, but I can send down to the staff canteen for something—let's eat in my room as a treat."

Thea looked at me from under her eyelashes. "Are you ashamed of being seen with me?"

"You must know I'm not." I felt my shoulders slump in dismay. "I just understand what it's like to be in a new place and not feel you belong. We came straight from Kansas to the Palmer House—I'd been a working seamstress, and suddenly I was a lady of leisure, and I didn't entirely enjoy it. You've had responsibilities and hardships, and now you're torn away from everything you've known and thrown on what must seem like our charity."

"*Seem* like?" The derision in Thea's tone spoke volumes.

"I don't see it that way. I view it as repayment of a debt to your mother—for everything she did for me." I took a deep breath before continuing. "At the Poor Farm. She was gracious and kind at a time when I had no reason to expect grace and kindness."

"Yes, my mother was a saint. As was my father. That's what everyone said." Thea stood up. "I think some coffee would be nice."

"Who are those women?" Thea flicked a finger toward a line of young ladies assembled at one end of the large room we were traversing.

"Ah." I felt a surge of interest. "Those must be the house models Madame hired." I stopped to scrutinize them from a distance. "I've been away, you understand, because of Sarah having the mumps, so I haven't met them yet. I see she's had dresses made up for them." The ladies were, from what I could observe from our vantage point, all handsome but of various types—tall and petite, dark and fair, softly rounded and willowy. I presumed Madame had selected the dresses. The choice was clever, showing the main lines of the fall offerings in day and evening wear. I was beginning to see the point of the scheme.

"They work here?" It was the first time I'd seen Thea interested in something since we'd arrived at the store.

"It's an innovation based on the House of Worth in Paris," I explained. "As well as displaying our dresses on dress forms on the sales floor, we will employ living models so that the gowns can be shown in movement. I presume they're waiting there to start rehearsals. Madame says we are selling the dream of beauty, so they must learn to move like—what was it she said? Feathers, I think it was. No—swansdown. I pity them."

"Why?" Seeing that the models were beginning to notice us, Thea moved toward the door, and I followed.

"Well, for having to parade up and down all day pretending to be swansdown. It sounds like hard work to me."

Thea turned toward me, and something like a smile curved her lips. "It's hard work to lift or clean or chop or darn or hoe. How can it be hard to be paid to walk around in nice clothes? To not even speak? To be not there, not yourself, just a dream in somebody else's head?"

"To wait around for hours until called for, to be told where to go and what to do." I laughed. "If you really want an easy life, I suppose you could do what the Prairie Avenue girls do."

"And what's that?"

"Be pretty, sing and draw well, speak nicely, and have perfect manners—and wait for a handsome young gentleman to propose to them. Or at least one with money."

"But then you have to be married."

I raised my eyebrows. "And you're not interested in the married state?"

"You have to do what your husband says—and wants."

Thea pursed her lips prettily. "And go where he goes. And bear his children."

"And you don't want that." I looked at Thea with renewed interest.

"I don't want to find myself trapped anyplace I don't want to be. Never again."

13

THE JEWEL BOX

*E*lizabeth Fletcher met Thea when she and David went with us to the theater to celebrate their return from their honeymoon tour.

"She really is awfully pretty." Elizabeth's bright blue eyes fixed on Thea, to whom I had introduced her five minutes earlier. We had just entered the small auditorium of the Jewel Box Theater; Thea's face, so often sullen, brightened as she studied the plum-colored velvet of the curtain, lit by a row of footlights.

"She's awfully hard to please." I lowered my voice so that only Elizabeth would understand. "I hesitated over bringing her because she's in mourning, but I was desperate to find something she might be interested in. Nothing's worked so far."

"I declare she's interested now." Elizabeth watched as Martin helped Thea into her seat. "Quite an inspiration of Tess's to come to this new theater. And I'm so happy you asked us to accompany you."

"I wanted to see you." I squeezed my friend's arm. "You seem well—marriage suits you, then?"

"Goose, you know it does. And I can detect the indelicate inference behind your carefully chosen words. *It* suits me just fine."

"*I'm* indelicate? What a confession." I gave Elizabeth the tiniest poke with my fan. "Let's stick to subjects suitable for polite company. How do you like housekeeping?"

"Oh, Mother has taught me how to handle servants. The ones she hired for us are well-behaved. I seem to have little to do except look pretty for David. Which reminds me: I need some new gowns. That long bodice is so flattering. I declare Miss Thea looks much older than fifteen—when she remembers not to scowl or hunch her shoulders. I can almost hear Mother hissing 'deportment' at me at that age. You must cure her of that before you put her in a lower-cut gown."

"Yes, it's as well the deep décolleté of our mothers' youth isn't modish right now."

I gazed at Thea, admiring my handiwork. In the days since her arrival, I'd provided her with two more dresses, including the evening gown she wore. Because of her youth, I'd lightened her mourning a little by adding small white frills to the heavily pleated cuffs that fell just below her elbow and to the deep, narrow V of the neckline. A short train gave the gown added dignity. Thea wore long white gloves and carried a white fan bordered in black ribbon. Alice had arranged her hair into a becomingly modest mass of shining auburn, tied with a broad band of black velvet.

"Where's Tess?" I looked around for my friend. "I must tell her what an excellent idea this was. Some ladies we call on told her about this theater."

"She's over there with David." Elizabeth agitated her fan. "I've been told about the Jewel Box too. Apparently, it's quite the latest thing, and considered most cultured and respectable—for Chicago anyway. But there's a rumor about—"

A gong sounded somewhere in the vicinity to warn us to take our seats. I took my place next to Martin and smiled at Tess, whose pink gown made a pleasing contrast to my gray silk. Tess still wore mourning for Catherine in the daytime but refused my offer to make her a dark evening dress, saying dull colors aged her.

"You see, Nell, I do have good ideas." Tess looked pleased with herself. "Young girls need treats, don't they?"

"I suppose they do."

"The Prairie Avenue ladies said Mr. Canavan is a treat for the eyes." Tess showed me where the name "Victor Canavan" was emblazoned across the bill of entertainment. "But he's a most pure soul because he comes from Europe, and they're much more *refined* there."

I doubted that, but I let the comment ride and settled myself back into my seat, grateful for the disappearance of the wretched bustle that used to make sitting such an awkward business.

The play's title was *The Catch*. Unlike the general practice in so many Chicago theaters, no singing acts, performing dogs, or acrobats preceded the main attraction. In addition, the tickets cost more than usual so that the audience mostly comprised the best society of Chicago. I even glimpsed one or two matrons known to disapprove of theatrical entertainments.

The play was as airy as spun sugar, a confection of brilliant epigrams and humorous coincidences. It told the story of a young man pursued by half-a-dozen young women, all of them beauties, with a view to matrimony. Complication built upon complication, the man evading all the young ladies' attempts to capture his heart until eventually—and by a series of clever twists—the young ladies met, realized they had all experienced the same lack of success, and found sympathy and friendship in their lamentations. At this point, the young man arrived, explained he had felt unable to bestow his heart on any of the ladies because he'd been affianced to a lady in another city, but she had jilted him, and he was now able to declare his choice.

The young man, of course, was Victor Canavan, the actor whose name featured so prominently on the bill of entertainment. He had also written the play and was the manager of the theater. It didn't take me long to realize he'd given himself most of the best lines, the rest of the good ones falling to a tall, blond, rather doll-like actress listed as Miss Paulina Dardenne. She, naturally, was Mr. Canavan's ultimate choice, although why he should settle on the most vapid example of womanhood on the stage perplexed me. I said so to Elizabeth as the last of the applause faded away and the gaslights in the auditorium flared to life.

"Because she was the sweetest and most admiring among them all, I suppose." Elizabeth grinned up at her new husband. "Men love women who adore them without question."

"If I wanted slavish adoration, I would acquire a dog." David Fletcher tucked Elizabeth's hand under his arm with the pleasantly decided air that I had always liked about him. "I much preferred the women with opinions."

"They were all so beautiful." Tess's small teeth showed in an eager smile. "And everyone loved the play, didn't they? People laughed so. I laughed and laughed when he said he wished he could divide himself into six and marry each one, but—what did he say, Nell?"

"Something along the lines that no woman of worth would ever be satisfied with one-sixth of a man's attention since no woman is ever satisfied with even seven-sixths," I said. "I'm probably getting it wrong."

"He said it funnier," Tess agreed. "He really was very funny, wasn't he? Clever funny, I mean."

"Did you like the play, Miss Lombardi?" David, finding Thea standing next to him, addressed himself to her politely. "Did it compare well to others you have seen?"

"We didn't have such things in the wilds of Kansas." Thea's tone was quite neutral. I was glad it was David who had asked her opinion, as she generally responded more kindly to men and saved the sharp edge of her tongue for her female acquaintances. "Besides, my father didn't approve of theatrical entertainments. So I can make no comparisons. I can only say that I could have happily left this real world behind and stepped into that artificial one."

"Is that a fact?" David, as was his wont, treated Thea's words with serious gravity. "It was certainly artificial. Such a beautiful room could hardly exist in real life. Perhaps the Silk Room at the old Rutherford's store came close."

"Ah, my new store will outdo even that fine creation." Martin didn't resist the lure of such a compliment. "Joe is a master at setting a stage too—you'll see. But I have to admit I've never seen so harmonious a background. It was cleverly done, wasn't it, Nell?"

"I'll admit I was studying the colors. I liked the way they used a restrained palette for the room and had all the young ladies in dresses of similar design, but each in a bright hue. The dresses weren't well designed, but there was a clever concept behind them. They made me imagine gemstones on a necklace in that scene when they were all spread out across the stage."

"The jewels in the Jewel Box." Martin moved toward the lobby. "With the hero in black velvet in the center, only the color of his cravat giving the clue as to which lady he would choose."

"I spotted that too." Elizabeth looked pleased. "And such a

handsome man." Catching her husband's swift glance, she included all the female contingent of our party in a sweeping gesture of inquiry. "Well, isn't he?"

"He's beautiful," Tess sighed.

"You can't call a man beautiful," Thea said sharply. I imagined for a moment she was going to expand further on Tess's error, but to my relief she continued: "He *is* handsome though. It's so nice to see men dressed in fine clothes." She smiled at Martin, batting her long eyelashes. "And I include present company in that remark."

With that sally, she turned and walked with stately steps toward the lobby. I had the distinct impression that she imagined herself on a stage.

"You didn't find him handsome, did you, Nell?" Martin turned to me. "His hair is far too long."

"I believe that's supposed to be artistic. I read something about it in one of my journals." I had already decided that I absolutely refused to be bothered by Thea's attempts at flirting with my husband.

"Put him in buckskins and he'd be a frontiersman." Martin rolled his eyes. "One who hadn't seen a barber for weeks."

"Not with that exquisitely shaven chin." I laughed at the exclamations of protest that Martin's words had forced from Elizabeth and Tess. "It's no good, Martin, you won't persuade the ladies to think anything less of him."

"Hmph." But Martin shrugged and smiled good-naturedly at me as we entered the lobby. Victor Canavan was, I supposed, superficially handsome—broad-shouldered, narrow-waisted, tall, with regular features. But weren't those the typical attributes of a successful leading man? I had not been particularly struck by him.

A squeak from Tess, quickly muffled, was followed by a

tug on my free arm as we stepped into the lobby. Disengaging myself from Martin, I turned toward my friend.

"He's *here*." Tess's best attempt at a whisper was loud enough for all of us. "Over there!"

I followed the direction of her finger and saw Mr. Canavan at the center of an adoring crowd. He was standing, I presumed, on a small platform built for the purpose, as his head and shoulders were quite visible. Beside him, in a similarly elevated position, stood Miss Dardenne, who on stage had been the fortunate recipient of Mr. Canavan's eventual devotion. The faces of both actors showed traces of the hasty removal of stage cosmetics, but they did not fare too badly in ordinary gaslight. Mr. Canavan was animated, responding to the questions and remarks of his public in a way that appeared to delight them; Miss Dardenne's expression, by contrast, remained somewhat impassive without any real spark in her large china-blue eyes.

Up close, Mr. Canavan's appearance was arresting.

"He *is* a striking man," I breathed into Elizabeth's ear. "Such strong features. Made for the stage, wouldn't you say?"

"Quite overwhelming, close up." Elizabeth turned toward me so we would not be seen whispering at each other like schoolgirls. "I don't mean he's unnatural-looking, of course— 'artificial' might be a better word. But my goodness, he does draw the eyes." She pulled me a little to one side; the rest of our party was caught up in the general movement toward the actor. "Miss Dardenne's his mistress, you know."

"She is? Rather insipid, in my opinion."

"You've said that already. I was trying to tell you earlier— there's a rumor that he arranges parties for the more exalted patrons of his theater late at night. Where they can spend more time with the actresses."

I raised my eyebrows. "In an immoral sense?"

"I have no idea. Aren't all actresses supposed to be immoral?"

"Miss Dardenne doesn't appear as if she has the wit to be immoral."

"Isn't that Thea whose hand he's kissing? Come on, we should get closer."

Elizabeth skillfully worked her way through the bystanders to Victor Canavan, who was indeed holding Thea's hand. Our guest was gazing up at him, not with the expression she used for Martin, but with the serious concentration one might expend on a perfectly executed painting.

"I think I'm too young to be called beautiful," she was saying.

"My dear lady, youth is always beautiful." The actor's voice was more intimate than the ringing instrument he had employed on stage, but the English accent—underlain with something else, a slight hint of a different origin—was no less pleasing to listen to. "It is the first freshness of life that never returns, and we who have eyes for beauty are drawn to it as a flower to the sun." He smiled, his wide, mobile mouth parting to show white teeth. "And yet I swear I have been ungenerous with my compliment. You are exquisite; one of nature's finest works. A setting must be found and the gem polished—but the potential is there for a masterwork."

"Oh, really." I turned back to Elizabeth, annoyed. "He'll turn her head, and she's vain enough already."

"Yes, I've noticed how much she likes mirrors." Elizabeth had a wonderful talent for breathing words so that nobody else could hear them except for their intended recipient. "Still, is there any harm in it? Look how thrilled she is."

She was correct. There was no real outward change in Thea's demeanor, but she seemed somehow to glow.

"I suppose you're right." I felt myself soften. "The child

has had little enough excitement in the last few years. Perhaps this will help her feel more at home in Chicago."

"That's the spirit. Oh, look at Tess—I think she will burst."

Mr. Canavan had bent down to salute Tess with a kiss on the forehead, murmuring, "Thank you, little lady." I hadn't heard what Tess had said—but I wondered if she had, despite Thea's admonitions, applied the word "beautiful" to Mr. Canavan's person in his presence.

14

MANNERS

"*The cats!*"

The door to our suite flew open, and Thea had barely entered the parlor before the cry burst from her. Beside me, Sarah flinched and moved a little closer.

"What's wrong, Thea?" I tried to keep my tone as even as possible, but the sound of Thea's voice had set my heart racing. I was beginning to dread her homecomings, and this time she had returned much earlier than I'd expected.

"Everything." Thea plunked her reticule down on a low piece of furniture near the door and pulled the hatpin out of her straw hat. "I *hate* this stupid town." Having removed the hat, she shoved the hatpin back into it with such force that I was sure she would ruin it. No doubt that would provide cause for complaint tomorrow.

"I thought you were getting on with the Misses Thuringer."

"Oh, they behaved nicely enough in front of *you*."

Thea's expression was one I was coming to know well and dreaded. Haughty anger, wounded feelings, discontent; it was a mixture of all of those. If I spoke to her, I would make things worse, no doubt, but to ignore the pain she was so clearly experiencing would be ignoble of me.

"And the other young people? What about that boy, Jeremiah? He seemed rather nice."

"He's a prig. And those fat-bottomed coarse girls played up to him from the moment we arrived at the park." Thea affected a simpering expression. "Oh, do show us how you can run, Jeremiah!" She continued in falsetto. "You must be so good at lawn tennis. Do you play lawn tennis, Miss Lombardi? Oh, you must—it's divine and so good for the figure. Do you play croquet? Oh, I suppose there wasn't much call for it in Kansas."

Her imitation of the Thuringer twins was accurate enough that a grin tugged at the corners of my mouth, but I suppressed it ruthlessly.

"Maybe they were trying to find something you could do together," Sarah suggested. Her hand stole around my arm.

"Maybe little girls shouldn't have so many opinions," Thea said, and Sarah's hand clung tighter.

"Thea, please don't speak to Sarah like that," I said softly.

"Like what?" Thea picked up her hat and marched into her room before I could formulate a reply. She didn't quite slam the door, but she didn't shut it as quietly as a lady should.

"I may have opinions, mayn't I, Mama?" Sarah asked, her voice barely above a whisper.

"Yes, you may." I bit the inside of my lip to stop myself saying more. And then I bit it a little harder to stop myself from getting up, opening Thea's door, and telling her exactly what I thought of her behavior.

A soft knock sounded at the main door. With a sigh, I rose to answer it. I had been so looking forward to this Sunday afternoon—a chance to spend some time alone with my family. Perhaps, I had imagined, Thea would find something in common with the Thuringer girls, who were the daughters of a Joliet merchant and seemed reasonably free from airs and graces. When Mrs. Thuringer had invited Thea on an outing to the park, I had agreed with gratitude and some apprehension. Thea had been invited out before by three other families from church on three distinct occasions —and not only had she never been asked back, all my efforts to reciprocate the favor had been declined with protestations of another engagement.

I accepted the small blue envelope from the page and opened it with the silver paper knife we kept for such purposes.

"What does it say, Mama?" With Thea in her room, Sarah was recovering some of her spirits.

"Oh, it's merely a note from Mrs. Thuringer thanking us for Thea's company." I folded up the letter and put it in my pocket. At that moment, I knew just how a horse felt when a burr worked itself under its saddle. The words on the paper would irritate and vex me for hours to come, as much as I mentally bucked and kicked or pretended that they were not there. Mrs. Thuringer had been polite in her hope that Thea had arrived back at the Palmer House safely but had made it quite clear I should not entertain any hopes of a second invitation. I anticipated another night with little sleep as I racked my brain for someone of my acquaintance who could not only manage Thea but make her happy. I had tried hard, but she simply didn't respond well to me.

"When's Tess coming home, Mama? She's been staying out awful late." The corners of Sarah's rosebud mouth drooped.

I fixed a smile on my face. "She's merely trying to take advantage of the light evenings before fall comes to see as much of her family as she can. But Papa will be back soon, and we can go for our own little walk, can't we?"

"With Thea?"

I put a hand on Sarah's wavy hair. "I must ask her along, darling. She's our guest."

"Perhaps she won't want to go because she went for a walk already." Sarah's face lit up with hope.

"Perhaps." I looked toward Thea's closed door and then at the clock on the mantelpiece. Sunday afternoon suddenly seemed dreadfully long.

TESS APPEARED IN A LOW MOOD WHEN SHE ARRIVED HOME, BUT the hour was late, and I put her subdued answers to my questions down to tiredness. The dawning of Monday morning did not brighten her countenance, however.

"Is something wrong?" I eventually asked. "You seem rather depressed in spirits. Was your visit not a good one?"

Tess made a face at her oatmeal. "Where's Sary?" she asked instead of answering my question.

"She's gone for a walk in the park with Donny. It's such a lovely morning, and she seemed so full of energy that I planned to take her out, and then Donny turned up because he'd been talking with Martin about—something." I bit my lip; the subject under discussion had been the landaulet, about which Tess was still unaware. "He took her for an outing, as they'd both already had breakfast and he knew I was waiting for you. He seemed as excited about going to the park as she was."

"That's nice." But Tess spoke listlessly, pushing her oatmeal around her bowl instead of covering it with sugar the way she usually did.

I sighed, looking about me at the men and women— mostly women—who were, like us, partaking of breakfast in the echoing space of the Palmer House's dining room. The smell of coffee wafted on the air, competing with the sweet aromas of baked goods and the salty tang of the kippers being consumed by a large, florid man who sat alone three tables from us, a copy of the *Chicago Tribune* propped up on his coffeepot.

"I'm getting rather tired of hotel meals, aren't you?" I watched Tess while pretending to be absorbed in the movements of the waiters. "I'll be glad when we move."

"Mmmm." Tess dumped her spoon into her oatmeal and sat back.

"Would you prefer a pastry?" Giving up on my own breakfast, I put out a tentative hand, laying my long fingers on Tess's short ones. "There is something wrong, isn't there? Won't you tell me what it is? While there's just two of us?"

Tess's spectacles reflected the morning light from the windows as she looked up at me. "I *didn't* have a good visit." Her small lower lip protruded. "I told Mary there was a young man I liked, and she told Aileen, and Aileen told me I had no business liking young men, being feebleminded as I am."

"Aileen said *that?*" I could hear the shock in my voice. "That's hardly sisterly."

"Then she asked if the young man was like me, and I said he wasn't a bit because he's much taller and stronger, and then she put on her cross voice and said of course she meant was he feebleminded too, and I said I didn't think he was at all feebleminded, but then she went *on* and *on* and got me all confused, and I said I'd known him at the Poor Farm, and then she said that meant he was an imbecile, and did he *look* like me, and—" Tess stopped, her lips trembling, and fished into a pocket for a handkerchief to stem the large tears that had caught in the rim of her spectacles. "What does she mean, does he look like me? Why should he look like me?"

"Oh dear." I understood what Aileen meant. I had seen

Tess's almond eyes, short stature, round face, and fine, straight hair repeated on other men and women, at the Poor Farm but also on the streets of Chicago. I realized some of those individuals could not even talk and had never met another with Tess's fine attributes of character and intelligence. She was no genius and needed help with many things, but she was shrewd, loyal, observant, and kind. As was Donny. If I'd had doubts about him at any point—and I didn't believe I had—they were subsumed in the hot wave of anger that swept over me when I reflected on how Aileen was ready to reject the young man without even knowing him.

"Aileen should be ashamed to say such words to her own sister." I leaned forward to put a hand on Tess's shoulder. "Why should you not want the same things as most women do? As for you being feebleminded, well, she must be soft in the head herself to think so."

To my relief, Tess's small teeth showed in a faint grin. She sniffed and turned to the side to blow her nose and wipe her eyes.

"You're so funny, Nell," she said when she turned back to me, but her expression became somber again. "Do you think Donny doesn't like me because I look—like I do? Like an *imbecile?*" The last word came out in a hoarse whisper.

"I *don't* think he doesn't like you." I frowned. "When I said I'd noticed no sign of romantic attachment, I didn't mean he doesn't appreciate you as a friend."

"He probably only wants to be romantic with pretty girls." The despair on Tess's face was so theatrical that it might have been comical in other circumstances. "He's so handsome, and I'm plain."

"You are *not* plain." I did my best to smile at the dear face opposite me, the dearest woman I had ever known apart from my adored Mama. Yes, there were lines on Tess's face that were not on mine, even though she was only three years older. She appeared older than her twenty-seven years, it was true. But nobody who loved her would call her plain. "You have the sweetest face, and everyone smiles when they look at you—including Donny."

Tess's lips curled in a tremulous answering smile, and then she straightened in her chair. I turned to see Sarah proceeding toward us at the fastest pace she could manage and not disobey the frequently repeated instruction that children must not run indoors. She was towing Donny by two fingers of his left hand. The young man was wearing a decent enough jacket and trousers that his intrusion into the hallowed precincts of the Palmer House dining room did not cause anyone to frown; in his right hand, he clutched his cap.

"Good morning, my best Tess!" Sarah let go of Donny's fingers to run around the table and salute our friend with a hearty kiss. "I wish you'd been awake to come with us. We saw an organ-grinder with a real live monkey, but he said he'd bite me if I put my hand out—I *think* he meant the monkey would bite me, not himself—and we saw a man in *such* funny clothes selling very long sausages, and an old man slipped on something nasty and sat down in it and said something very rude." She grinned at me. "Good morning *again*, Mama." She looked up at Donny with the air of an actor giving another player a cue.

"Good morning, Mrs. Rutherford," Donny said shyly, the beautiful smile spreading across his face. He turned to Tess. "Good morning, Miss O'Dugan. I hope I find you both well."

Tess's face fell, just a fraction. We were usually "Miss Nell" and "Miss Tess" to Donny, and his sudden formality had not escaped either of us.

I noticed Sarah nod at Donny, and my eyes narrowed. But she was speaking again.

"Won't you come upstairs with me?" she said to Donny

and wrinkled her nose. "I have to go upstairs. Thea may be awake by now."

An expression of alarm crossed Donny's face. "I can't, Miss Sarah. I have to run to the stable and fetch Mr. Capell. I'm probably already late." He looked apologetically at me—of course, he needed to fetch the carriage for me as I was due at the store. Alphonse Capell was the name of our new driver. He turned back to Tess, putting his cap back on his head and taking it off again. "I wish you a good day, Miss O'Dugan."

"*Hasn't* he got nice manners?" said Sarah as she watched Donny's tall, broad back disappear from view.

"He's certainly a tad more formal than he was," I observed. "Did you have something to do with the change?"

Sarah's face assumed a self-conscious expression. "Well, I *did* say that you and Tess are rich ladies and he ought to call you by your last names." She looked at me from under her straight copper eyebrows. "I was just trying to be proper."

"I'm going upstairs, Thea or no Thea." Tess's mouth set in a grim line with a hint of lower lip as she rose to her feet. "I hope Miss Baker arrives soon."

"Sarah Amelia Rutherford—" I began as soon as Tess disappeared out of sight.

"Mama, I really, *really* have to use the ladies' retiring room." Sarah bounced on her toes to emphasize the point. "And I don't want to go upstairs on my own because of Thea —and I guess now Tess is cross with me. It'd better be the one over there." And she vanished before I could question her further. She knew I wouldn't stop her; she was as familiar with the public areas of the hotel as with our own parlor and despite Martin's fears about kidnappers had asserted her right to visit the ladies' room on her own, like a big girl—when it suited her.

"Poor Tess." I massaged my temples, whispering the

words under my breath and trying not to let my emotions show on my face in this busy, all-too-public space. Between my friend's lovesickness, Sarah's ongoing campaign to emphasize the social distance between Tess and Donny, and Thea's overall unpleasantness, I might as well have said "poor me." But at least I had my work to escape into.

15

BREAKAGE

*T*he worse the situation with Thea became, the more I focused on my profession. When Martin came to find me one evening in October, I was so deep in my work that the store might have caught fire again and I wouldn't have noticed.

"Is it really that late?"

I looked up at the clock that hung on the wall of my office.

"The clock has no reason to lie to you." Martin grinned, seating himself on a corner of my worktable. "You've been busy." He indicated the pile of sketches in front of me.

"Three ball gowns, five evening dresses, a fur-trimmed paletot, a silk day ensemble, three wool ditto. And a riding habit—isn't it good that Mrs. Karak has entrusted that to us? So many ladies insist on a tailor. Everything a newly wealthy young bride needs for a prolonged stay in Boston."

"Be that as it may, it *is* very late." Martin looked meaningfully at the clock. "Your husband is here to escort you home. I thought we could walk since we won't get many chances once winter sets in."

I felt a now familiar brush of dread and unease. "Do we have to go home?" Once I'd stacked the drawings, I stretched my arms across my desk and laid my cheek against the fine wool of my sleeve. A faint groan escaped my lips.

"Sarah will want to play the piano piece she's been learning for us. We can't disappoint her." Martin bent to plant a kiss on the top of my hair, kneading my shoulders with his long fingers. "Come along, O cowardly one."

"I'm not sure I can bear another evening." I lifted my head and rested it on my fist, looking up at Martin again. "I don't suppose I'm ever going to do anything Thea approves of."

"Girls of that age can be difficult. And you can't leave Sarah and Tess alone with—"

"Oh no, I'd never do that." I shook my head vehemently, rising to my feet. "Tess will be with Billy, remember?" Tess's brother Billy regularly came to the Palmer House to eat dinner *tête-à-tête* with his sister. "I asked Alice to give Thea a lesson on how best to do her hair by herself—for the day she might need such a skill. How to use the hair ornaments I bought for her once she's out of mourning. That kind of thing. I asked her to keep her busy while Miss Baker ate her dinner downstairs—she's staying the night at the hotel. Miss Baker, that is."

"Ah, appealing to Thea's feminine vanity—how clever of you. She can spend even more time looking in mirrors."

"It's all right for you." I hid a yawn behind my hand, glancing once more at the clock. "She saves all her smiles and wiles for *you*."

"And I've told you, I'm entirely impervious to them."

"I do realize that." I stood on tiptoe to kiss Martin. "But with Thea, nothing you do is wrong and everything I do is wrong. Yet I've tried so hard."

"It's a pity she didn't take to the piano lessons." Martin

took my cape from its hook and settled it over my shoulders. "Or the drawing classes."

"And when I suggested lessons in deportment, she practically bit my head off. I wasn't trying to criticize."

"I know. And to think she'd only just been complaining about how her years in Kansas had made her into a country bumpkin. You'd imagine she'd be eager to improve herself."

I turned to the small mirror beside the clock, inserting a hatpin through my hat and into my thick hair. "I'd be happy with just everyday good manners."

"Well, at least she thanked you for the dresses."

"Grudgingly, and only because Teddy made much of what he insists on calling our 'ceaseless generosity.' He reckons we're making her too grand for her lot in life, you know."

"And you agree?" Martin tilted his head to one side, watching me as I ensured my hat was at the right angle.

"I don't see how I could offer Thea any less than I would offer Sarah, if she were the same age."

"But she's not Sarah. Teddy's right, in a way—Thea's in rather a false position. We have plunged her into the life of the idle rich, but she's not one of them."

"*I'm* not idle. And I suggested we talk to Mrs. Parnell about serving in the soup kitchen or teaching poor children their ABCs. Many of the women you're pleased to call 'idle' spend hours at a time helping the less fortunate."

"I stand corrected. I suppose Thea didn't agree to that either."

"Of course not. She declared herself quite done with lice and dirt."

"But she finds it hard to be a pupil again after being the teacher, doesn't she?"

"She seems to find everything wearisome apart from her own appearance. There, at least, I have succeeded. I swear she spends four hours a day looking in the mirror." I turned

away from my own reflection and passed through the door Martin opened for me.

"Well, I wish she'd use it to better effect." Martin offered me his arm. "I can't abide that dreadful, haughty expression she adopts in public. She appears to believe it makes her look more beautiful—but let me tell you, Nellie, as a young man I'd have run a mile from that face. I *did* run a mile from that face. You only got through my defenses because you were so much younger than me, and for a long time I never saw you that way. And you didn't care a fig about how you looked or what men thought about you." Martin grinned. "In a funny way, you still don't—you're one of the best-dressed women in Chicago but also one of the least vain."

"I'm glad I was never as obnoxious as Thea." I couldn't resist a smirk at Martin's compliment.

"Oh, you were. Just differently."

And with that the conversation turned, and I thought no more about Thea. Until we arrived at the Palmer House.

WE HEARD THE CRYING AS SOON AS WE STEPPED OUT OF THE elevator. Martin and I looked at one another and hastened our steps. Sarah didn't cry often—and she certainly didn't usually howl at the top of her lungs. My heart was beating far faster than usual as I opened the door to our suite of rooms.

"Mama!"

I grunted as Sarah's wiry little body collided with my legs, her arms wrapping around them with the strength of a limpet. In the brief glimpse I'd had of her, I'd seen a bright pink, tearful, but apparently uninjured face, and the fierceness of her grasp reassured me she was not hurt.

I looked around the parlor. One of the glass coverings of the large gasolier that hung from the middle of the ceiling lay on the parquet near the wall, smashed to pieces. How on earth did it get over there? The uncovered gas jet flared noisily, casting a bright, harsh light on the damage. To one side of the debris stood Miss Baker, her eyes wide, trying to control her breathing.

"What happened here?" Martin turned to Miss Baker.

The Englishwoman took a couple more deep breaths before she spoke. "There has been an—an unfortunate occurrence. With Miss Lombardi."

"Is she hurt?" I asked as I prized Sarah's arms loose. I gathered her to me, picking her up and crossing to the settee so I could settle her on my lap and rummage in my pockets for a handkerchief. Her sobs were subsiding into little hiccups, but she was trembling.

"Miss Lombardi is—nobody is hurt." I realized Miss Baker was quivering too.

"But Sarah is badly frightened." Martin frowned as he looked at our daughter. "Just tell me what happened, as calmly as you can. Is Miss Lombardi in her room?"

"She . . . ran . . . away." Sarah forced the words out between gasps and then burst into a fresh flood of tears and wails. I cuddled her close to me, making shushing noises to soothe her.

"You must have just missed her," Miss Baker said. "She —she—"

"She threw the gasolier cover at you, didn't she?" Martin was looking at the wall above the area of floor where the broken glass lay.

"She did." The governess sounded as if she'd like to burst into tears herself. "Missed me by an inch." Straightening her back, she summoned up a tremulous smile. "So I don't believe she was really aiming at me. I'm sure her aim is excellent."

"She didn't pull the cover off, did she?" I looked up at the gasolier. "It's too high—and it would have been very hot."

"It fell off," Miss Baker said. "When she slammed her door."

"Ah." I tried to imagine just how hard Thea had slammed the door.

"But it was still hot when she threw it; I felt the heat of it as it passed me." Miss Baker was recovering her poise. "Fortunately, I had the sense to turn away from the wall. It was odd—everything seemed to slow down."

"I've had that happen." I applied a handkerchief to Sarah's face, remembering a river in Illinois. I forbore from pointing out in front of Sarah that Miss Baker could easily have been cut by flying glass—either of them might have been badly injured. How could Thea have done such a thing? "Were you having words?"

"She'd said some very nasty things to Sarah."

"She called me the bad word," Sarah sobbed.

The governess immediately came to kneel by me, stroking her small charge's bright hair in a fashion that endeared her to me enormously.

"I've told you, haven't I, Sarah, that words don't make you bad?" she said. "That when people use them against you, they're the unfortunate ones? Because they are unable to follow the example of our Lord."

"Yes." Sarah sat up a little straighter to look at Miss Baker, nodding.

"And the circumstances of your birth do not make you bad either." She looked up at me. "Or your mother."

"Thank you." I swallowed the lump in my throat.

"I've seen many women in similar straits," the governess said as she leaned forward to kiss Sarah on the forehead. "And none of them bad."

She got to her feet and seated herself in an armchair,

twisting her hands together to calm herself. How did she know? I wondered. But it didn't matter. Everybody seemed to guess my secret in the end.

"We had better go search for Thea as soon as Sarah and Miss Baker have recovered." Martin's voice was grim. "Chicago's a big place."

16

SEARCH

"For all we know, she may have remained in the Palmer House." Martin grasped my hand, mutely urging me to sit down beside him on a street-corner bench.

"But we looked there first."

"She may have hidden from us. Or perhaps she went back there after we left." Martin stared glumly down at our linked hands. "We've been running around uselessly for an hour and a half, and I don't see how we're going to find her." His stomach gave a huge growl. "We're both tired and hungry and thirsty, and we've only covered a few blocks."

"I'm not exactly hungry." I stared at the people passing us, noting their curious glances at the sight of two well-dressed individuals sitting on a street bench holding hands. "I'm empty. I believe food would turn my stomach."

"You're lucky." Martin's belly whined again. It had grown dark, and a chilly breeze was whipping up a few fallen leaves that had somehow found their way into the treeless, feature-less street where we had halted. In the gaslight, they reminded me of scurrying rats—they made a sinister rustling sound, audible above the muted conversations of workers tramping home.

"You're right." I stood up, letting go of Martin's hand. "This is pointless."

"What would you like to do?" Martin tipped his face up to me. The pale yellow light made his skin appear sickly under his hat and threw the shadow of his beaky nose across his chin. He looked tired and drawn with worry.

"I don't know." I hung my head, closing my eyes, letting the tiredness overwhelm me. "I can't think. You decide."

Martin rose to his feet. "Then we'll return to the hotel first to see if Thea has gone back there. And we'll eat a sandwich or something—you must eat, Nellie." His stomach sounded again, and he grinned. "And I will not be responsible for my actions if I can't get some food soon. Why is it that the streets are always full of people selling food when you don't want it, and they all disappear when you do?"

"We're in the wrong part of the city, I suppose. I expect we can find you some roast chestnuts or something once we're south of the river again." I felt a stab of irritation. "Why are you always hungry?"

Martin laid a hand on his lean belly. "Roast chestnuts." The longing in his tone would have made me laugh in other circumstances. "Will you carry me if I faint?"

My voice broke. "How can you possibly make jokes when Thea may have been—may be—" I sniffed hard.

"She's far too sensible to have fallen prey to thugs or—or whatever you're imagining." Martin seized my hand again and began walking fast, so I forgot my imminent tears in the effort to keep up. "This is what we'll do. We'll eat—yes, you too—and then we'll go to the Harrison Street precinct to see if the police might help. I'll remind them I drove a cart full of police officers during the riots." He sounded much too cheerful for the circumstances. "We'll find her.

And then you'll need to restrain me from giving her a thrashing."

"You'll never do that."

"No, I have that in common with the Lombardis. Do you suppose this is what it's really like to be a parent? Of an older child, that is. Sarah's too small to be any trouble—yet." His pace slowed. "Poor little Sarah. To be reminded of—well, of her birth in such a vindictive way."

"Yes. And I don't suppose that'll be the last time unless we do something about Thea." I stopped, forcing Martin to halt. "But what are we going to do?"

"Perhaps I should buy a small house for her and Teddy."

"That's hardly fair on Teddy—and he'd never accept it."

"He would if I begged him to take Thea off our hands. I'll get down on my knees if necessary." Martin frowned and began walking again. "You don't think she could have gone to the boardinghouse to find Teddy, do you? Perhaps she might solve all our problems by moving back to Mrs. Nowak's."

"It's possible." Hope surged in me as I set off in my husband's wake. "Martin, it's only three blocks to Randolph Street. Couldn't we take the horsecar west? To the board-inghouse?"

Martin shook his head. "No point in alarming Teddy unduly if she's not there. We'll stick to my plan." He turned to look at my face and relented. "And then we'll get Nutt to drive us out to Mrs. Nowak's, even if it's midnight."

I fell silent—partly because Martin was walking so fast that talking was rather an effort. I breathed deeply as we approached Lake Street, then stopped.

"Martin!"

"Do you see her?" Martin looked wildly round him.

"No, over there. The Jewel Box."

The lights of the theater had caught my attention. A performance had clearly ended a short time before—a few carriages were still there to take the last of the audience home.

"It's the only place I can recall Thea having been to that's still open," I pointed out. "She might have been there—it won't do any harm to inquire. And they will surely let me use the ladies' retiring room," I added hopefully.

Martin gave a short laugh. "Very well. And I'll see if the doorman can whistle up a cab for us. I've had quite enough of wearing out my shoe leather."

It seemed strange to be walking into an almost-empty theater. But both doorman and cloakroom attendant listened to our story with a sympathetic ear. They had been too busy; they would not notice one young lady among the crowds. But if we would like to wait, they would inquire of the management. It was the supper hour, and everyone else was upstairs, so it would not take long.

The retiring room was empty, so I was soon done. I was grateful that we hadn't arrived at the Jewel Box a little earlier. We might have encountered acquaintances, and I didn't want to have to explain our evening's adventure.

I breathed in the delicious smell of coffee as I made my way back toward the lobby. The fragrant aroma, along with the scent of roast chicken, came from the top of a low flight of stairs that led off the corridor I was in. My stomach decided that it might, after all, be interested in food, and I sighed.

"But I want to stay here with you."

I stopped short. It had been just the briefest burst of sound, a moment of clarity against the muffled hum of voices and occasional laughter that had formed the background to my visit to the ladies' room. That hum, I supposed, represented the actors and staff of the Jewel Box at their supper. But that particular voice, half obscured as it was, was familiar. I turned and hurried toward the stairs.

There was no door at the top of the staircase, just another corridor. Light showed from under two of the doors farther along the passage, and most of the noise was coming from the farthest room, but the voice I had detected had been closer and clearer. Yes, the first door was ajar. I listened, certain I had not been imagining what I'd heard but suddenly reluctant to enter, to take up the burden of responsibility once again.

"My dear Miss Lombardi." I'd been right. The voice that was speaking was unmistakably that of Victor Canavan. "I must return you to your guardians as soon as you've finished eating. You must see that coming here is most irregular—at your age."

"They're not my guardians."

"Your hosts, then. You said they were the people who accompanied you to the theater the first time we met. I remember that moment so well. Such beauty is hard to forget." There was amusement in his voice. "Such freshness— believe me, with a little training and practice I am sure you would be an asset to our small establishment, and I thank you for offering your services to us. But your hosts would complain to the city authorities if you stayed here, and I would get into no end of trouble. You don't want that, do you? It would be easier if you were a foundling off the streets, and even then I'd hesitate. But a young lady like you —of good family, I am sure."

"We were good once." There was suppressed rage in Thea's voice. "But my mother and father ruined everything— they took it all away from me." There was a pause, and the clink of a coffee cup. "Now they're dead and there's only my brother. I'm *almost* a foundling."

"But not quite. What would your brother say to your coming here?"

"Oh, he'd make a tremendous fuss. He's like my pa—

pretty straitlaced about dancing and entertainment and anything that's fun."

"Well, then. You wouldn't want to get me into trouble, would you? I adore children—and you are still half a child, it's no use pouting at me—but I am not the kind of man who should look after a young lady like yourself. You must eat up and let me find someone to accompany you back to where you belong. I'd take you myself, but I only have forty-five minutes before I'm required on stage."

I decided I'd listened long enough. I retreated a little way toward the stairs and then approached the door again, making as much noise as possible. I knocked smartly.

"Enter." The voice was indifferent—Canavan clearly didn't mind being found alone with Thea. I opened the door and confronted the young lady, whose mouth positively hung open at the sight of me.

"How on earth did you—" She glared at Canavan. "Did you send somebody to tell them?"

Victor Canavan had risen to his feet, his expression one of surprise but not of alarm. His face was still painted with cosmetics, giving him an odd, artificial appearance, although he didn't need much in the way of enhancement to his thick dark eyebrows and well-marked lips, or the large, straight nose that gave his countenance an arresting manliness.

"My dear young lady, you didn't even tell me their names. I could not have fetched them." His voice hung somewhere between hilarity and astonishment as he addressed me. "You find me at a disadvantage, madam. What a peculiar evening this is turning out to be. We have met, I remember, but I do not know your name, and I cannot account for your presence."

It was time to take matters in hand. "Eleanor Rutherford." I held out a hand to the actor. "I found you by the merest chance. We came to inquire if they had seen Miss Lombardi here, and I heard her voice."

"Not the Eleanor Rutherford of the department store? The couturière?" He grasped my hand and held it for a long moment, looking into my eyes.

"The same." I darted a glance at Thea that was not as forbearing as I would have liked. "Miss Lombardi is our guest."

Mr. Canavan raised his eyes to the ceiling, let go of my hand, and clapped his palms together. "A perfect rain of fortunate coincidences." He smiled at me, and I almost smiled back—there was something irresistible about the man, an air of confidence and gaiety and assurance and ease that few men possessed. "I was planning to come to your store to commission some gowns for my ladies."

"Your ladies?" Did he keep a harem?

"My actresses. I don't like my seamstress. One cannot sell a dream with such dresses."

"Then I'm sorry to meet in such circumstances." I regarded Thea severely and spoke directly to her. "You can't take up any more of Mr. Canavan's time. I can't force you to return to the hotel with us, but it's either that or we take you to Teddy. You can't wander the streets. The police will make the worst assumptions."

"You won't be too harsh on the young lady, will you?" Mr. Canavan said. "Youth is a season of excessive emotion, as I'm sure you remember."

"She threw a glass gasolier cover at my daughter's governess," I said as steadily as I was able.

"She told me. It was foolish of her—not the least because she's burned her lovely hands." Mr. Canavan gestured toward Thea, and I realized her palms were bandaged. "We have applied soothing ointments. Don't worry, it's just blisters."

I closed my eyes for a second. I was utterly exhausted,

starving, and drained of all emotion except an overwhelming sense of relief that we had found Thea and this endless day might come to a close. "I won't punish her."

"You are a generous soul." Mr. Canavan put his fingertips on Thea's shoulders, steering her toward me. "And if you're a very good girl," he informed her, "I will arrange for you to attend the dress rehearsal of our new piece. You'll like it—it's called *The Parrot*, and it's very funny."

Thea swept past me without looking at me, and I turned to Mr. Canavan. "Thank you for taking care of her."

"Not at all." His expression changed, softening beneath the thick greasepaint. "Miss Lombardi told me she is fifteen and has recently lost her parents, and I felt a bond between us. Circumstances were very hard for me at fifteen—harder than you can imagine. Friends of the family helped me to forge a new life amid the ashes of the old. Let's say I am repaying a debt."

"So am I." I held out my hand to shake his. "To her mother."

"Then we are allies." To my surprise, he lifted my hand to his lips, kissing it gently. "I look forward to meeting you again—in more businesslike circumstances."

"I HOPE MISS BAKER DIDN'T GET TO BED TOO LATE," I murmured to Martin as he closed the door of our Palmer House parlor. "And I hope Tess is all right."

"She'd have had a wonderful supper with Billy, and I doubt Miss Baker would tell her about the business with Thea. Talking of whom—she's in her room, I presume?"

Martin had left me and Thea to return to our suite while he arranged for food to be sent up. I was by now so tired that I barely had the energy to move my legs and would have gone straight to bed myself if Martin hadn't insisted I eat too.

"Yes, she didn't want anything to eat." I yawned, trying to get comfortable in my armchair and wishing I could undress and go to bed. "I imagine she's under the covers by now." I glanced at the door, under which a narrow strip of light showed. "But not asleep—her lamp's still on."

"Good." Martin headed toward the door in question.

"Oh no, darling." I threw out a hand to stop my husband. "You're not going to—can't we do this tomorrow?"

"No," Martin said curtly. He knocked, not as quietly as I would have liked.

"But Sarah and Tess—"

"I don't care." Martin knocked again.

"What do you want?" Thea's voice, none too friendly, sounded from within.

"I'd like to talk to you." Martin's tone was the sort that did not brook argument. It always worked far more efficiently with Sarah than any remonstrations on my part.

There was silence. Thea had been nicer to Martin than to any of us, and I wondered if she was weighing the alternatives of withstanding the oncoming lecture—knowing his bark to be far worse than his bite—or refusing to talk to him and breaking the one relationship she seemed eager to cultivate.

I had my answer when the door opened. Thea had donned a salmon-pink Japanese kimono I had chosen for her out of a gorgeous shipment from San Francisco; it hung open over her pintucked and ruffled nightdress, from beneath which peeked satin slippers of deep plum. Her hair cascaded over her shoulders almost to her waist, each section ending in a twist of pretty curls. From the way she was running her fingers through one side of her locks, I surmised that she had been braiding them for bed but had decided to present us with a less childlike image of herself. Against the paleness of her face, her thickly lashed eyes looked huge. Her delicately tinted lips were arranged into a neutrally pleasant expression.

But she didn't know Martin's moods as I did—had not seen my husband when he was deprived of food for too long after a truly exasperating day. I would not intervene, I decided. I curled my fingers around the plush velvet armrests of my chair and waited.

"That is the last time you *ever* speak to my daughter about the subject you broached." Martin's voice was quiet, but it held an edge of steel.

Thea's mouth straightened into an entirely different expression, but she held her nerve. "She's not your daughter."

If she'd been a man, Martin would have hit her; I saw that from the curling of his fist. Thea was very fortunate that Martin would never lay a finger on a woman. "She is my daughter in the eyes of the law." The fingers straightened and clenched again. "I have adopted her, and she is my daughter in my eyes and in every sense of the word. You will not speak to her in that way again. You will not attack any member of my household—family or staff." His back was rigid. "You will speak to my wife with courtesy and gratitude for her generosity. You will remember that she was the one who urged me to take you in."

"But *you* offered me a home." A little dismay crept into Thea's expression.

"I did, but I would have left you to your own devices had Nell not so wanted to help you. I was of the opinion that Teddy could look after you perfectly well by yourself."

"I don't *need* looking after." The child showed from behind the woman's façade. "I had to look after *everybody* else and *everything* else at the mission—Lucy and the house and those snot-nosed, lice-ridden brats those women kept bringing to us to teach. Women who didn't have a husband, and half of them never had one in their lives. Women that Mamma should have turned away, except she was too busy being a saint." She glared at me; I realized that only Martin's glowering presence kept her from saying, "Women like her," but the thought was plain on her face.

"Never mind that." Martin's voice became harsher. "Your actions today show that you not only need looking after, you need correction. That man Canavan is a stranger to us, and he might have been *anything* but the gentleman he showed himself to be this evening. Although even then he might not have been a gentleman if you'd stayed much longer. Don't you understand?" Martin's voice rose in exasperation. "I suppose your mother never warned you."

"About men?" Thea laughed. "Or about the things women and men do? Do you think I didn't see things and hear things out there in that coarse, ugly country? And you needn't worry about my wanting to do those things with anyone. I'm not ending up like *her*." This time she did directly address the words to me, spitting the last one out with bitter vehemence.

"You will *not*—" Martin roared, taking a step forward.

"Martin, please." I was at his side in an instant, not even knowing how I'd gotten there so fast. I sank my fingers into the cloth of his jacket, but the anger that had propelled him forward was held in check, and he stopped. I could feel his arm trembling.

"She's right." I looked up into the darkness in Martin's eyes and then at Thea, who had held her ground. "I don't understand why she hates me so much, but I can at least be an example to her of where wrongdoing leads. I was a foolish girl who didn't think about what I was doing," I said to Thea. "I wronged myself and others, including Sarah. I've repented ever since—and never done such a thing again. You're right to despise me, but it's not Sarah's fault. How can you hate such a little girl so?"

"Because she's had *everything*. Your little princess." Thea's face was perfectly white. "*You've* had everything, and you don't deserve it. And we lived like paupers and darned and scraped and never had enough to eat because Pa was always giving our food to some dirty half-breed—" She stopped, sucking in a deep, ragged breath.

"I would have happily shared my money with your family," I said as steadily as I could. "I offered your parents help more than once."

Thea let out a sound like a half-smothered scream, and at last I saw the tears come to her eyes. "Just a little longer. Just a little longer. That's all they ever said when I begged to leave —to go home. We're stronger together as a family, they said. But it wasn't true." Tears slid down her smooth cheeks and ran into her gritted teeth. "We were the laughingstock of the whole stupid territory with its stupid farms and silly, dough-faced girls with enormous arms and fat bottoms."

She ran into her bedroom, throwing herself onto the bed and pulling a pillow over her head. I shook my head at Martin, mutely begging him to stay outside, and followed her in.

"I'm so sorry." I bent down so she could hear me. "I know what it's like to lose your parents when you're young—and I lost a little brother too when he was born. I understand that you hurt, but time will help you. I'll help you, however I can. I want to be a friend to you, Thea—and I want to help you honor your parents' memory."

The pillow lifted, and a pair of bloodshot eyes stared at me from behind a screen of shining auburn hair. The lashes were wet and stuck together, looking even darker and longer than usual.

"I don't want to honor their memory. I hate them."

"You know that's not true." I put out a hand to stroke the beautiful hair. "You can't hate your parents."

"Oh yes, you can." Thea's voice was raw and hoarse. "When they take everything away from you. I had a happy life, a pleasant home, Nonna to take care of us, and they took it all away. I had friends, and I lost all of them. We were something, and now I'm nothing—just a nobody who doesn't belong here. I had a sister—I didn't hate her." She snuffled. "She was always sweet to me, however cross I got. But I was losing her every day because she was going to die out there. I begged them to take us home. And now they're dead, and all I'm left with is you, and I won't like you however nice you try to be. Mamma loved stupid fallen women like you more than she loved us. She was as hateful as Pa because they thought being saints was more important than *us*."

"Oh, Thea." I sat on the bed and put an arm around her trembling shoulders. "I'm so, so sorry." There were tears in my voice. "It breaks my heart to see you like this. But I promise you, I won't desert you however cross you get with me. I know you think right now that you'll never be happy again, but you will find happiness." I caressed her shoulder. "Whatever I can do for you, I will do. I swear it."

Thea moved, and for a moment I thought I was going to be able to gather her into my arms. But with a swift movement she twisted away from me, so quickly that she left some strands of long, silky hair in my fingers. She retreated as far away as she could and aimed a kick at me with one small foot.

"Go away. Just go away. If you want to make me happy, just do that. Leave me alone. *You're. Not. My. Mother.*"

173

17

INSPIRATION

"*S*he can't possibly stay, you know." Martin shucked off his jacket and threw it onto a chair before turning to close the door of our bedroom.

My back stiffened, but I waited for the door to close before I turned toward my husband. We'd eaten in silence, all too aware of the muffled sound of Thea's sobbing before she eventually continued her preparations to go to bed.

"How can we send her away?" Exhaustion roughened my voice. "I just promised her I won't desert her. It will get better."

"But she's tearing our family apart." Martin took off his collar and massaged his neck where a faint red line showed. "How can we allow her to destroy our peace and happiness?"

I was silent as I reached for my buttonhook and sat down to remove my boots. Martin would have to help me take off my dress—we generally found this procedure most gratifying, but we were both too tired to derive pleasure from it after the emotions of the day. I could hear him removing his shoes, sock garters, and socks as I concentrated on my own task, allowing myself a little time to think. Martin was right, of course—Thea was destroying the harmony of our household. We had made a mistake in inviting her to stay; but how would we rectify it?

"Perhaps she'll be happier once we're in our new home," I said once I'd finished taking off my boots and had reached up to remove my garters and roll my stockings down my legs. "She'll have more space. It must be hard living so close to people who are almost strangers to her."

But I wasn't convinced by what I was saying, and my tone reflected my doubts. I straightened up to see Martin laying his cufflinks, watch, tiepin, and the contents of his pockets on the dressing table and caught the wry look that said he had little hope of improvement either.

"I forgot to tell you," Martin said as he pulled me to my feet, ready to help with the various strings, buttons, lacings, and layers of fabric that lay beneath my day dress. "There's been another burglary. At Field & Leiter's—they broke in through the wall and blew the lock off the safe. The principal item stolen was a ruby necklace ordered for Mrs. Robson De Luca. They were keeping it for her until she returned from London next month."

His eyes narrowed in reflection, and he paused in the act of undoing my bodice, fingering the faint stubble on his chin. "I'm going to take Marshall Field out for lunch and ask him some questions. He rarely deals in such expensive jewelry, and I find it odd that a burglary happened just when he was storing such a piece. I want to tell him about my vault too."

"You might regret your plans to sell better jewelry." I hid an enormous yawn behind my hand.

"Ah, but I have a safe room." Martin gave me a tired grin. "What are *you* doing tomorrow?"

"I will be making lists. We're moving to a new house in less than a month and moving the atelier to the new store shortly after, and I simply must start organizing. And if we're to hold a Thanksgiving dinner—with a new staff—I can't leave anything to chance, not even for the simple affair I have in mind. Maybe I could involve Thea in the planning."

"You never give up, do you?" Martin kissed both of my cheeks, then my mouth.

"I'm not given to despair." I turned my face into his shoulder to hide another yawn. "I will find a solution to the problem of Thea."

"I'VE HAD AN IDEA," I ANNOUNCED WHEN MARTIN CAME TO MY office late the next afternoon. "Let's start walking—we promised Sarah we'd be home early, and after yesterday she must be anxious. I'll tell you once we're in the street."

Five minutes later, we were heading north toward the Palmer House. The light was already fading, and there was a distinct nip in the air.

"I always enjoy being alone with you." Martin drew my arm a little farther through his.

"If you call this 'alone,' you are a true citizen of Chicago." I surveyed the crowded sidewalk, from which people were spilling out onto the pavement. "Listen, I'm dying to get your opinion of my idea for Thea. I started off by remembering myself seven years ago. I concede I wasn't perhaps the best-behaved of young women."

"You were a paragon of politeness and good temper compared with Miss Lombardi."

"Don't interrupt and stop grinning like that. What, in the end, was the making of me?"

Martin frowned, slowing his steps as he tried to puzzle out my riddle. "Sarah?" He lowered his voice. "The Poor Farm?"

"You're partly right, but not in the way you're thinking.

The Poor Farm was a salutary experience, and Sarah changed my life—but I had begun to change before Sarah was born."

"How?"

"The work. It was having work to do that changed me, Martin. I went from being a spoiled girl to having genuine responsibilities—work that I liked."

"But Thea hated having to work at the mission, didn't she? And she didn't want to do volunteer work when you suggested it."

"I don't think she hated the actual work as much as she makes out. In fact, when I saw her at the mission, she seemed to enjoy being in charge. Biggest toad in the puddle, as Teddy said. And she was always a hard worker, even as a child. Good with her needle too." I raised my eyebrows at Martin. "Do you see what I'm aiming at?"

"It almost sounds like you're going to offer her a job." Martin steered me around some horse apples as we crossed Adams Street.

"Precisely."

"But you saved her from having to look for employment by deciding she would move in with us." Martin looked even more puzzled.

"And I concede I was wrong," I admitted. "At least I imagined she would love living as we do, and in many ways she does. She doesn't like the Palmer House as much as I'd hoped, but that's because she imagines the other guests are looking down on her."

"Whereas in fact they're gawping at her for her pretty face and fine clothes. When she comes out of mourning, she'll be the loveliest young lady in the entire place." Martin winked at me. "Except you."

"Flatterer. It's true that Thea doesn't seem to mind wearing pretty clothes, but she's finding it hard to settle down into society. She's had too many years out in the wilds of Kansas while the other girls have had gossip and piano lessons."

"And giving her employment would solve this?"

"It's worth asking her if it might. We will lose nothing by asking, and this is the ideal time since we're hiring more people for the new store. Including very young ladies as apprentices."

Martin, who had been watching the carriages on State Street, decided the opportune moment to cross had come and grasped my elbow. We moved as rapidly as we were able across the wide street toward the cliff-like façade of the Palmer House.

"Just consider," I pointed out once we were back on the sidewalk, "with Thea's looks, she could easily become a shop-girl. She's neat and clean and speaks well. We must try her out in a few departments—"

"You're building castles in the air." Martin made a dismissive gesture. "She'll never agree to it. I still reckon we should offer to send her to a young ladies' finishing academy somewhere out east."

"Well, we'll put that idea to her as an alternative. That will make it seem less like we want to send her away."

"Brace yourself if you want to talk to her." Martin made a pantomime of squaring his shoulders as we headed toward the entrance door. "Either she'll throw something again or she'll show polite interest and you'll faint from surprise. But I don't think you have a hope of success."

"There's no harm in trying." The thought of taking action had put a spring in my step.

"There's no harm in shooting an arrow into the air above an empty field either." Martin shivered as a gust of wind hit us, and he towed me through the door, smiling a greeting to the doorman. "You have a faint chance of hitting the right blade of grass."

18
FOREVER MORE

"*N*o." Teddy half rose from his chair as Thea finished speaking.

"That wasn't what we agreed." Martin was also staring at Thea. "We offered you a position as an apprentice, nothing more."

"But I want to be a house model." Thea held Teddy's gaze, her tone one of utmost reasonableness, but my eyes narrowed. She was making mischief, I was sure.

To Martin's complete astonishment—and mine, if I were to be honest—Thea had not met my proposal of employment with derision. She had listened carefully and asked some rather intelligent questions about the work involved. Our stipulation that we must consult Teddy before we made any change produced a black scowl, but she had agreed.

Now we sat in the parlor at the Palmer House, engaged in negotiations, and I was wondering what Thea was up to.

"You don't even know what a house model is," Thea said to Teddy.

"It's like an artist's model, isn't it?" Teddy looked at me, radiating disapproval.

"You see, you have no idea." Thea's grin was faintly malevolent. "I'm quite surprised you've even heard of artist's models, Teddy."

"It's not a bit like an art model," I said hastily. "House models wear clothes. The clothes I design, in fact. The point is to show the gowns to potential customers more effectively. It's done in the House of Worth and a few other dressmakers' establishments in Paris. It's perfectly respectable."

"And we are *not* proposing to employ Thea as a house model." Martin gave Thea a severe look. "She's far too young, and that work requires training in dancing, deportment, and so on."

"I knew it wasn't respectable." Teddy glowered. "Pa would have fifty fits if I let her dance around in front of people like a saloon girl."

"But Teddy," I remonstrated, "if Thea continued to live with us, she'd have to attend a dance occasionally. It's how young people get acquainted with one another."

"How do you know what a saloon girl does, Teddy?" Thea's eyes were bright with malicious mischief. I was beginning to wonder if she'd agreed to consider our offer just so she could provoke Teddy.

"I've spoken to soiled doves in Kansas." Teddy's cheeks flamed crimson. "I've tried to get them to see the error of their ways."

"Error?" Thea's face hardened. "What's so stupid about taking money out of the pockets of men who don't deserve to have it? We all listened to the cowpokes—weeks on the trail earning money, and then they'd spend all of it on whiskey and girls. The girls were the smarter ones."

"How can you call them smart?" Teddy's face was now entirely red. "Those girls were always in some man's power. They got sick, and they got beat up, and they got landed with some man's by-blow—" He stopped, chewing at the inside of his cheek. By his glance at me, I could tell he was thinking of Sarah.

Martin used the pause to regain control of the conversation. "We did offer an alternative plan to Thea. A finishing school for young ladies—out east, probably." He looked down at his fingers for a second before engaging Teddy's gaze. "But that would involve dancing too. I'm sorry if you consider we're being a bad influence."

"I don't wish to go to a finishing school," Thea stated flatly. "I'm done with school, and the girls will be silly and spoiled."

"She doesn't get on too well with the daughters of our acquaintants," I said to her brother. "It's hard for her to find common ground with girls who've not experienced hardship and hard work. In our store, she would work as a junior—an apprentice—with other young ladies who have shown some talent or aptitude. They're from modest families and need to earn a living, but they are a cut above the other girls their age. Like Thea, they're intelligent and well-spoken. Becoming an apprentice is the first step on a path upward. Dressmaking is a respectable trade, and one of the few employments where a young woman can gain some refinement and acquire skills she can use after marriage. And if Thea wants to be a shopgirl instead of a dressmaker, she will learn poise and address."

"She needs to learn how to keep house." Teddy folded his arms.

"I *know* how to keep house," Thea flashed back, spots of color appearing on her cheeks. "What do you imagine I was doing when I wasn't teaching school? What I *need* is to learn to fit somewhere in this city *you* brought us to."

"But you're proposing to fit in as a clothes-horse—"

"Oh, Teddy." Thea gave a deep sigh, and to my surprise she smiled. "You're so easy to tease. I realize I can't be a house model. But wouldn't you let me be an apprentice? Just think, I will earn money I can put by."

I was immediately on the alert. What was the child up to? She had switched in an instant from provoking rudeness to sweet reasonableness, playing Teddy like a fish on a line. At her age, I too imagined I could bend the world to suit me, but had I been this good at manipulating others?

"Well . . ." Teddy appeared to soften. I realized that Thea's strategy was carefully reckoned—first to anger her brother, then to appear to make a huge concession to his wishes. She must really want the job we'd offered her.

"She'll still live with you, won't she?" Teddy looked at me.

"I'd much rather live in the residence." Thea smiled at Teddy again. "No offense to Mr. and Mrs. Rutherford, of course, but perhaps I can make friends better if I live with the other girls."

"We have more than one residence for single women now." Martin smiled encouragingly at Teddy. "I've already told Thea how strictly run this one is—it's for the youngest girls. She might wish she were at that school."

"Morning and evening prayers, of course, and mandatory attendance at a church of the girls' choice," I added. "The girls must only go out in pairs or more, and they all have to be back in the residence by sunset. Any infringement of the rules results in dismissal from Rutherford's. And absolutely no gentleman visitors."

"It's a system we set up after the fire, when we didn't have space in the temporary store for dormitories." Martin grinned. "It's worked so well that we only have two dormitories in the new store for special circumstances. It does no harm that all the properties I've bought are in good locations and are an excellent investment."

"We have so many young men and women working for us now that it's practical," I said. "Most of our ladies have their own homes, but there are always a few of the young ones who'd rather be in a residence with all their meals and laundry provided. We find a good housekeeper for each house, and they pretty much run themselves."

"You see? I'll be safe and happy." Thea rose, picking up the coffeepot that sat in the middle of the table. "Would you like some more coffee, Teddy?"

"I'M STILL NOT QUITE SURE HOW THEA GOT TEDDY TO AGREE. I was convinced at one point that he'd insist she be locked in a convent."

I ran my fingers through the curls that cascaded down over my shoulders and yawned behind my hand. We had retired early, fatigued from the strain of the meeting with Teddy. Martin was settled in an armchair in our bedroom, the light from the gas jet above him gleaming on the dark red silk of his paisley dressing gown as he perused a closely printed column in the *Chicago Tribune*.

He looked up at me and smiled. "I would suggest that marriage would be Teddy's idea of a suitable mode of confinement, but then you might get all prickly again."

"I refuse to be prickly tonight." I sank into the depths of the matching armchair with a sigh of relief, comfortable in my nightgown and wrapper. "Somehow we've snatched victory from the jaws of defeat—am I saying that right? At least Thea has. I'm quite proud of her for not gloating. She seemed almost subdued at dinner, didn't she?" I slipped my feet out of my slippers and drew them up onto the seat of the chair, looping my arms around my legs and burying my forehead in the silk of my wrapper. My hair fell forward in a heavy mass, smelling of lemon and herbs from the oil Alice combed through it.

"We're the biggest winners of all, if you ask me." My husband's voice rose above the sound of my own breath. I heard him stand and felt his fingers comb through my thick tangle of curls. "Just imagine being able to come home to smiles instead of tears and black looks. I'm not a praying man as a general rule, but I just sent a request upward that Thea be *very* happy in the residence."

I uncurled myself and leaned back, blinking at him. "I prayed fervently while I was bathing," I admitted with a grin.

"And now we can move into our own new home in peace. You're a genius, Nellie. I can't wait till we're curled up together on our own Chesterfield settee in front of our own fire."

He stopped playing with my hair and stroked my face. "I want it to be a happy home, Nellie. For Tess and Sarah too, but especially for you. You've had far too much to do lately, and there are dark shadows under your eyes. You don't have to feel under an obligation to hold a Thanksgiving dinner."

"But I *want* to, and besides, all I have to do is plan the meal and instruct the servants." I put a hand on Martin's. "Just a small dinner for a few friends, a token of the peace and harmony that will reign between us."

"Forever more." Martin's warm fingers curled around mine.

"Forever more." I closed my eyes, which were indeed weary. *Let it be so*, I whispered in my heart. *If only Thea could be happy.*

19

ROBBER BARONS

*T*hea moved to the residence the following Wednesday; two weeks later, we were in our new house on Calumet Avenue.

"The thing I like about Thanksgiving is that you don't need to give presents to anyone." Tess was pulling open the drawers of one of the three sideboards that graced our new dining room and shutting them again. She frowned. "Nell, I can't find anything."

"Alice might know. Oh no—I expect we have to ask Mrs. Hartfield now." Our new house contained a new house-keeper, a dignified, reserved Connecticut woman who, according to Martin, had come highly recommended.

I crossed to the sideboard where Tess stood and ran a hand over the gleaming wood. "I suppose we don't *need* to know where anything is."

Tess looked up at me, dismay on her face. "We're awful grand now, aren't we, Nell?"

"We are, rather." My reflection stared at me from the mirror over the sideboard, pale-faced and blue-eyed. I put an arm around my friend's shoulders and smiled at our mirror-selves. "We can still be *us* though. We needn't put on airs and graces because we have a large residence. This is what Martin considers suitable for his family, and I'm determined to love it."

"Aileen says such a house is a wicked extravagance." Tess turned away from our reflection and crossed to another sideboard. Aileen had been all smiles when we'd invited Tess's family to see our home, but I might have known she wouldn't spare Tess the benefit of her opinions even if she knew that Tess would repeat them to me.

"Da says that if it's honestly come by, wealth is no sin, and we should rejoice in the good fortune God has meted out to us." Tess opened another drawer. "I reminded Aileen of what Jesus said in the seventh chapter of the book of Matthew about not judging others, and Aileen said Martin is a robber baron who drinks French brandy while the workers are starving. I said that Martin doesn't drink brandy and—oh! Here are some knives and forks, but they're not the pretty new silver ones."

"Those are probably in the silver safe." I closed my eyes for a second, thanking Providence that Tess's family had declined our invitation to Thanksgiving dinner.

"We have a silver safe?" Tess turned to look at me, her eyes round. "Like the big safe Martin has in his office?"

"Well, no, it's a sort of large pantry with a big lock on the door. I'll get Mrs. Hartfield to show it to you."

"We need an entire *room* for our flatware?"

"And the punch bowls and the tea service and coffee service and finger bowls and sugar baskets and ice cream dishes and every imaginable kind of knife, fork, or spoon." I pulled out one of the dining chairs and sat down, gazing up at the polished mahogany beams that crisscrossed the ceiling. "And more other items than I could count. Martin had it all sent from Tiffany in New York."

"Is that where the coffeepot disappeared to?" Tess asked. "I wondered about that. Nell, this house is very confusing."

"We'll get used to it." I pulled a list from my pocket and contemplated it. "Compared to Martin and Lucetta's house on Prairie Avenue, this one's quite restrained. Aileen should have seen *that* house."

"What does restrained mean?" Tess asked.

"Not too big or extravagant. The Prairie Avenue building has seventeen different kinds of marble, I've heard. Of course I was only there once, and I didn't pay overmuch attention to the marble."

"I do like my room." Tess sat down too and clapped her hands at the notion of the pink-and-white bower that was now her domain. "When Martin uncovered my eyes and I saw it, I thought I would faint. My own bathroom *and* a sitting room! Aileen says it's too big for one person, but I love it. Billy says it's grand and I should be proud of it, so I should. Is Donny going to sit next to me at the Thanksgiving dinner?" She looked pointedly at my list.

I bit my lip. "Donny says he's eating downstairs with Alphonse Capell and the other household staff."

"But he's not a servant." Tess raised her chin and glared at me.

"He's not a family member either, and he seems to think his place is downstairs. He does work for us, after all."

"Who else is coming?"

I looked down at my list, which did not have Donny's name on it. "Apart from the four of us, there's Joe and Leah Salazar and their three children, Madame Belvoix—I'm surprised she accepted—Elizabeth and David, and Mr. and Mrs. Parnell because their other children aren't able to join them in Lake Forest this year." I surveyed the twenty chairs ranged around the dining table, counting people in my head. "Oh, and Thea and Teddy, of course."

Tess's glare intensified. "But Thea and Madame and Mr. Salazar work for you. Why are *they* invited and Donny is not?"

A dull ache somewhere over my right cheekbone hinted at the beginning of a headache. The new store was to open on the twentieth of November, a mere week away, and Martin was so busy he was barely at home. Right now, I would have welcomed his presence.

I drew a deep breath. "Joe Salazar is a partner, Tess, not an employee. And yes, theoretically Madame Belvoix is an employee, but Martin would make her a partner tomorrow if she'd let him. She prefers to stay exactly where she is. And as for Thea, we took her in to live with us—"

I stopped, feeling the foundation of my argument crumble under my feet.

"We took *Donny* in too." Tess slapped the shining surface of the table in triumph.

"Well, yes, we did," I conceded.

"So why should it make a difference that Thea works in the store and Donny works in the house?" Tess stuck her short nose in the air. "I say he should come to our dinner, so Sary and Aileen and goodness knows who else who wants to stick their nose in my business can be quiet. I'm going to tell him he *must* come."

COMPLICATIONS

I looked around the table at my assembled guests. We had just finished giving thanks; as merchants, we did not neglect to thank God for His care of the owners and staff at Field & Leiter's. While I had been busy arranging our Thanksgiving dinner, changing the seating plan to include an extra guest, Field's had been burning. Martin had spent that day riding up and down State Street "like Paul Revere," as Joe told it, helping to organize the transfer of all the rescued goods to the Exposition Building. He put all the Rutherford's drays and any staff he could spare at Marshall Field's service, as did other merchants; no lives were lost and a great deal of merchandise saved. Martin and I suffered only a recurrence of bad dreams on my part and a short delay in the atelier's move to our own new premises.

Now Leah Salazar's delicious pumpkin soup, fragrant with a hint of spice, was placed in front of the diners by our new maids and the tall young men Martin had hired to help with this large gathering. Their feet made no noise on our dining room's deep carpet as they walked; the opening and closing of doors toward the back of the house let escape the scents of delicate white fish and roast turkey. Our new silver gleamed as our guests raised their spoons, and soon murmurs of appreciation and the beginnings of conversations mingled with the sounds of a splendid feast well begun. One high, clear voice rose above all the rest.

"What should I call you?"

Thea smiled sweetly across the table at Donny, her smile widening a fraction as the young man blushed.

"I only know you as Donny," she continued, tipping her head to one side in an encouraging manner. "That was all very well when you were carrying my trunk or opening the carriage door, but it doesn't seem right to call you by your first name when we're dining at the same table, Mr.—?"

I groaned inwardly. Seating Donny had been a conundrum: not close to Sarah because she was equally prone to calling attention to Donny's social status, not too near Tess so she couldn't make eyes at him. So I had placed him by Mr. Parnell; Elizabeth's parents were easygoing and democratic despite their wealth, and I could count on them to be kind to the young man. But I had also placed Thea down at that end of the table, away from Teddy and close to the Parnells and Madame so she had no opportunity to boss the children about. Clearly, I had made a tactical error.

I saw Donny's lips move.

"I'm so sorry, I didn't hear that," Thea said. "Would you speak a little louder, please?" Her own voice was audible to all present.

"Donny Clark, like Clark Street," Donny said loudly. "I was called Clark because I was left at a house in Clark Street when I was a baby. A priest's house. I went to find it when I came to Chicago, but it burned down in the big fire."

"Somebody left you?" Thea's expression was one of polite interest. "You mean you were a foundling? How interesting. Is that why you were at the Poor Farm?"

"What's a Poor Farm?" asked little Eli Salazar, who sat between his mother and Madame on my right.

"A place where they put the poor and feebleminded, unwed mothers, and other unfortunates," Thea explained to the small boy, smiling graciously. "My dear late mother was once the Matron of the Women's House at the Prairie Haven Poor Farm—which is now the Prairie Haven Institute for the FeebleMinded, isn't it, Mr. Clark?"

"That's right." Donny's expression brightened at the introduction of a topic he understood. He'd been rather lost in the flow of talk before the prayers. We had covered the Indian Wars, Custer's funeral, and a speaking machine invented in New Jersey.

Donny straightened up a little, tugging at the plain yellow waistcoat I had ordered to cover his considerable breadth of chest. I had decided against full evening dress for the dinner; knowing Mr. Parnell disliked a starched shirtfront and wing collar gave me an excellent excuse to declare the occasion a family meal and allow Donny to appear in a cutaway coat, smart striped trousers, and low-heeled boots.

"I don't remember the Poor Farm well," Thea continued. "But I was only a child when we left for Kansas. Mamma used to bring us to the Poor Farm at Christmas and Easter, and we'd give gifts to the inmates. How long did you live there, Mr. Clark?"

Donny looked blank. "A long time," he answered at last. "I don't remember. All my life, maybe." He smiled his beautiful, shy smile. "I remember your mother, Miss Lo—" He stopped in confusion, clearly unable to recall Thea's surname. Since Sarah's lesson, he was trying not to call her "Miss Thea."

"Lombardi." Thea brought a tiny, lace-trimmed handker-chief to the corner of her eye. "Poor, dear Mamma."

I couldn't help glancing at Teddy and saw the corners of his mouth tuck in. I had watched his solemn yet tranquil face during the first part of our celebration; Martin had begun the prayers and expressions of thanksgiving, and Teddy had ended them. The sincerity in his round gray eyes had been touching as he'd spoken of his absent parents and sister, thanked God for sparing his life and Thea's, and paid a charming tribute to Martin and me for our role in helping the two of them find their feet in Chicago. Thea had been quite silent, staring at a spot somewhere in the middle of the table with an expression that hid her feelings. She was a picture of quiet splendor in her black silk gown, the sprig of jasmine in her glossy auburn hair scenting the surrounding air.

"Your mother was a real nice lady, I remember." Donny beamed. "I didn't see her much, but she always smiled and waved at us men and said nice things to us when we were outside working on the farm."

"She was ever gracious." Thea frowned. "But why did you leave the institute, Mr. Clark? Has it changed to a great degree?"

"They didn't let us do good work like they used to." Donny scratched at his chin, from which the wisps of fuzz that were all he seemed capable of growing had been shaven. "They acted like we was good for nothing but the easy work, the stuff they used to give to the old men and the real slow ones. I wanted real work, so I lit out and headed for Chicago." His eyes shone as he looked down the table at me. "And then I met Miss Nell—Mrs. Rutherford, that is. Sorry, ma'am." His gaze returned to Thea. "Was you one of the little girls we saw at Christmas?"

Thea nodded. "The other girl was my sister, Lucy." The handkerchief came into use again. "She died in Kansas with my mother and father."

Naturally, this remark elicited all kinds of expressions of sympathy from the diners. Eight-year-old Eli left his place to offer the flower his mother had tucked in his lapel to Thea. He craned his head when he returned to his seat to reassure himself with the sight of his own sisters, who with motherly kindness were helping Sarah to some butter. Madame Belvoix said nothing, her small, plump hands laced beneath her chin as she watched Donny pat Thea's hand clumsily. Tess looked glum as she observed the two of them. Fortunately, Sarah was too busy enjoying the presence of the Salazar children, whom she liked, to apply her usual powers of observation.

"But I won't spoil this lovely occasion with sadness." Thea kept a brave smile on her face as she nodded her thanks to Mr. Parnell, who had taken over from Donny in patting her hand and offering words of condolence. "I have such beautiful memories of our time in Prairie Haven. Nonna looking after us at home, Pa in his church, and Mamma doing such wonderful work for the unfortunate inmates at the Poor Farm. It's so strange after all these years to think there are *six* of us at the table who have close ties with that place. How small the world is."

The floor swayed under my feet as tiny frowns appeared on our adult guests' faces, manifestly due to the effort of working out who those six people might be. I heard a tiny "Ah" escape Madame Belvoix's lips, just the tiniest breath of sound, and Elizabeth raised her eyebrows at me. Well, I thought, this moment had been rushing toward me since the day I invited Thea into our home. I would not be a coward—although I was craven enough to be grateful that Sarah was chattering to the Salazar girls.

"Yes, Tess and I were inmates." I smiled as I lifted my spoon. "I worked as a seamstress. I'm most thankful for that time in my life, not least because I found the sister of my heart in Tess."

Thea's beautiful hazel eyes glowed. "And Sarah—"

"Ah, the reminiscences of our younger days." Madame's throaty French accent cut across Thea's words. "How wonderful my own recollections of my youth in Alsace—its mountains, its rivers, its vineyards!" She took a dainty spoonful of soup in a way that somehow barely interrupted her speech. "The happy memory of my arrival in Paris, my apprenticeship at Gagelin—and above all, Worth. Ah, the dear empress was such a sight to see in her splendid gowns, never the same one twice and all of her ladies almost as magnificent. They laugh at the crinoline now, Mrs. Fletcher," she lifted a finger playfully as she addressed Elizabeth, "but I can tell you that in those dresses the women floated like thistledown."

"Oh, I'm not so young that I can't remember Mother in gowns she could hardly get through the doorway," Elizabeth laughed.

The conversation became animated. There was nothing people, particularly females, liked more than poking fun at, or defending, outdated fashions; even the men were soon drawn into the web of words. Which, I realized, was entirely controlled by Madame, who directed the succession of topics with such adroitness that I had little to do to fulfill my role as hostess.

Above all, Thea did not get another chance to introduce the topic of Sarah's birth. If she made any attempt to steer the flow of talk toward any subject other than the most anodyne, Madame swiftly cut her off—without ever seeming to, and oddly enough without producing any of those barbs of sugarcoated prickliness with which Thea generally reacted to not getting her own way. In a word, Madame *managed* her—and our Thanksgiving dinner proceeded swimmingly.

"Well!"

It was the day after Thanksgiving. Elizabeth Fletcher lowered herself with her accustomed straight-backed poise onto my settee, blue eyes alight and a mischievous smile on her face.

I sat down too. I had a good idea what thoughts were behind that "Well!" but the smile reassured me. As had the warm thanks, the perhaps more fervent than usual presses of the hand from the Parnells and Salazars, and David Fletcher's cheerful farewell the night before. If Thea had thought to ruin me socially, she had not picked the right circle to begin with. She left in the same hired carriage as Madame, a fact which did much to calm Martin's temper.

"Well?" I asked in response, trying not to sound defensive.

"That was a most interesting Thanksgiving, Nell. I've come to thank you in person; *so* much nicer than a note, and besides, I haven't talked to you in private for *ages*. And you'll show me all around your splendid home, won't you? It's so elegant and yet comfortable at the same time. Mother and Father couldn't stop exclaiming over how nice it is. It was wonderful to see people from such different walks of life at the table too—far less boring than the usual talk about the same old people, the same old clubs, the same old parties. Father said he hadn't enjoyed himself so well in a month of Sundays."

"Because of the interesting revelation?" I asked. "That was a bit of a disaster, wasn't it?"

"It might have been had you reacted otherwise, but you did just the right thing—and Madame Belvoix was magnificent."

"She was, rather. I wish she'd been able to stop Thea *before* the cat popped its head out of the bag though."

"Father said Thea should be thrashed. Martin almost looked ready to do the deed—you weren't close enough to see, I suppose. It was fortunate for everyone's sake that Madame intervened."

We interrupted our conversation as Beatrice, one of our new housemaids, arrived with tea and *petits fours*. To my surprise, Elizabeth declined the sweet cakes and didn't even put sugar in her tea.

"You were all quite magnificent," I said with a sigh when I'd taken a few sips of the hot brew. "I don't deserve such friends."

"Don't be silly—of course you do. Besides, I already knew about Sarah, Mother guessed a long time ago, Father is imperturbable where such things are concerned—he'd have to cut half his male acquaintances if he cared—and David, bless him, said he'd always liked you and Martin and he wouldn't stop liking you because a malicious little girl told tales." Dimples appeared in her cheeks. "I hope one day you'll tell me about the Poor Farm though. What an adventure!"

"I must make sure I never invite Thea to a dinner where the Prairie Avenue set are present," I said ruefully. "I can just imagine all the 'rich ladies,' as Tess calls them, snubbing me and refusing to purchase my dresses."

"Then you'd just have to sell your gowns to those women who *would* buy them, and to the deuce with the rest. I don't think it'd be long before they'd be back anyway. What woman puts morality above wearing the best-cut clothes in Chicago?"

"Martin said something similar last night." The memory brought a faint smile to my face. "And I can't see myself inviting that set to dinner, anyhow. Martin is adamant I shouldn't have to do much entertaining unless I want to."

"Except for us, I hope?" Elizabeth grinned at me. "And do invite the Salazars again. What an intelligent woman Mrs. Salazar is, so witty and well-read. It's a shame she'll never get a chance to shine in society, at least outside Jewish circles."

"Yes, a crying shame. Joe is becoming a wealthy man, yet none of the clubs or societies Martin belongs to will have him because he's a Jew."

"And they're a charming family—such beautiful, well-behaved children. I wondered whether it was a good idea to have the children at the table with us instead of in the nursery, but you've won me over. I must do the same." Elizabeth's cheeks, already a delicate rose-pink, deepened in color by a shade.

The self-conscious expression on my friend's face put me on the *qui vive*. I felt a queer, sinking feeling in the pit of my stomach but hid it to the best of my ability.

"You look as if you're dying to tell me something," I said. "Are you—?"

"In an interesting condition, yes." Elizabeth placed a hand on her belly, a protective and oddly touching gesture. "Already. Mother was *aching* to drop a hint or two, only I made her promise not to. And you won't tell anyone except Martin, will you? David and I want to keep the news between us and our closest friends for a little longer."

"Thank you for counting us among your closest friends." I rose from my chair to give Elizabeth a hug. "I'm delighted for you. If you're happy, that is—and you are, aren't you, despite all your earlier protestations?"

"I am." Elizabeth shrugged. "David was *so* thrilled, and, well, babies *are* rather sweet."

I shook my head in mock dismay. "A great loss to the Feminist cause."

"Nonsense—I'm still a Feminist. Children make no difference to a man's opinions. Why should being a mother change those of a woman?"

I laughed. "I won't think up a rebuttal. It's probably bad for the baby to argue. When is the happy event?"

"April." Elizabeth blushed again. "Yes, nine months after the honeymoon. Far too soon, but it's all my fault."

"In what way? It does take two." I sat down and picked up the teapot, stealing a quick glance at Elizabeth's figure. Yes, her bodice was tight at the front where her breasts had increased a little in size. If I hadn't been worrying about the Thanksgiving dinner, I would have spotted that sooner. A dressmaker always does.

"It's my fault for not insisting we take precautions. All of Frances's wonderful sisterly advice up in smoke." Elizabeth sighed, but her eyes shone bright blue from a rosy face. "To be honest, I was having too much fun."

"Merciful heavens, Mrs. Fletcher, another shocking admission." I made my tone as playful as possible. "Our husbands would have conniptions if they heard us."

"Or love us all the more."

We continued in a similar vein, soon helpless with laughter as we surveyed the joys and annoyances of the married state. And yet—I was dismayed at the pangs of emotion that passed through me, unbidden and unwelcome, every time I allowed my busy chatter to still a little so I could truly listen to what Elizabeth was saying.

The pangs were not for me. No, they originated in knowing that, sooner or later, I would have to tell Martin that the Fletchers had conceived a child before their honeymoon was even over, while we—

Why, I wondered as I watched Elizabeth's animated face, a smile concealing my inner turmoil, was life so complicated?

21

SHOPGIRL

I arrived at the store the next day knowing exactly what my first task was. I found Arlette Belvoix in her new office, a neat square chamber with a wide north-facing window. It was larger than any room I had yet seen her inhabit, with two walls lined with shelves from floor to ceiling. Yet the stacked crates into which she was peering with thoughtful eyes suggested it would soon be as over-crowded as her former lairs.

"Sixes and sevens." Madame looked up at me, tapping the crate with a shining fingernail. "That is how you say it, no? I am at sixes and sevens, thanks to that most unfortunate fire at Field & Leiter's. I have lost valuable time."

"You've given them so much help with organizing their dress goods. Does it matter if we're set back a few days? At least it wasn't *our* fire."

"Ha." Madame barked a short, mirthless laugh. "We are the lucky ones this time. In confidence, I have heard that Field's have lost nine hundred thousand dollars' worth of merchandise."

"Martin told me that too. Perhaps two hundred thousand

dollars' worth saved, and they are already back in business. If I can help with your unpacking—"

"*Merci bien*, but no." A brief gleam of amusement crept into Madame's steel-ball eyes.

"I'll admit I was hoping you'd say that." I sighed with relief. "I've had quite enough of moving. I came to thank you, in fact. For coming to my rescue on Thursday." I hesitated. "Did you . . . talk to Thea?"

"I think it may be a little time before she tries that trick again." Madame smiled a small, tight smile, but then she shook her head. "But she is a liability for you, Mrs. Rutherford. A—how do you say? A millstone around your neck. She makes you worry, and worry is not a good thing for a young woman like you. You have sufficient responsibilities."

"I can't abandon her." I fiddled with one of the smooth ringlets Alice had created that morning to cascade over my shoulder as a change from my usual piled-up hairstyle.

"You *will* not abandon her. You *could*." Madame sighed. "*Eh bien*, one day when she is old enough, she will abandon *you*. And I do not know whether she does you more harm now or whether she will be more dangerous in the future."

"Dangerous?" I raised my eyebrows.

"Just so. And yet," Madame shrugged, "she has considerable potential in our trade. I will wait a few days more, and then we shall speak of her again."

"So she's giving satisfaction as an apprentice?"

"She learns very fast. She will not do for the dressmaking side, in my opinion."

"No? I remember her being good with her needle as a child."

"She wants a larger stage. She already asks to work as a shopgirl." Madame paused before looking back up at me. "When we had our little talk, I suggested that it was a position where one had to exercise great discretion. One had to learn to keep one's thoughts to oneself."

"Really?" I tried to imagine Thea keeping her tongue behind her teeth but failed.

"Hmmm." Madame's eyes gleamed. "I believe she has the inner discipline to heed my advice, *if* she wants preferment badly enough. This is a struggle I might allow her to win—but only if she plays by my rules."

"So, Mrs. Rutherford." Madame appeared as if from nowhere some days later, Thea in her wake. "The time has come to talk about this young lady."

She had found me gazing out of the atelier window, woolgathering as a dress took shape in my mind. Light flooded the huge room; we were a dizzying six stories high, our new store being two floors higher than the old, and we soared above the adjacent buildings to take full advantage of even this weak winter daylight. Behind me, the atelier murmured with quiet purpose, the soft creak of scissors cutting through fine cloth making itself heard above a muted buzz of foreign tongues, the half-whispered conversations of the embroiderers seated a few feet away from where I stood.

I loved the sounds of the atelier, and I loved its huge windows. It soothed my soul, somehow, to stand there and contemplate the vast December sky, a pool of pale blue above the jumble of brick, iron, and glass below us. Columns of smoke rose vertically into the still air. I could almost feel the city of Chicago breathing, working, working, striving to thread the tentacles of its commerce across America, across the globe. It was the lifeblood of trade, the great force Martin understood how to manipulate, creating money with the same apparent ease with which I created beauty.

I let my fanciful thoughts go, turning to gaze at the young woman who stood at Madame's side, her eyelids lowered in an attitude of respectful submission. It was false submission, I was sure, but it was enough. Madame had proposed a challenge, and Thea had taken it.

I had to admire the child. Her willfulness subdued under the discipline Madame had imposed, Thea's whole being was transformed; she had at last achieved that indefinable quality called poise. She didn't fidget or shift her feet, but neither did she look stiff or uncomfortable. She held herself in perfect balance, like an athlete, with a fluid confidence that belied her age.

Nor had her weeks in the residence resulted in any of the untidiness young girls were sometimes prone to when left to their own devices. Her hands were linked in front of her, their nails cut short and neatly kept. Her hair was dressed in a modest but becoming style, her collar and cuffs were spotless, her dress well brushed and free from wrinkles. She had listened attentively as Madame spoke and then angled her head deferentially toward me to catch my reply.

"What do you have in mind?" I knew already, but Madame was the ultimate authority when it came to the apprentices, and I always deferred to her.

"Christmas approaches." Madame glanced up at the sea of blue outside our windows. "The sales floor becomes more busy while the atelier becomes quieter." She nodded in the grandmotherly way that fooled nobody who knew her well. "Mr. Salazar asks me for girls with good English, trained in our ways and presentable, and I have selected a dozen, including Miss Lombardi. She does not have the passion for the dressmaker's art that would cause me to reserve her for special training."

I nodded. "Are you still eager to be a shop junior, Thea?" I asked her. "It won't be very interesting, I'm afraid, but one has to start somewhere. Sorting ribbons, sweeping up, handing things to the older shopgirls, cleaning the glass counters with newspaper and vinegar." My words brought back memories, and I grinned. "Remind me to tell you one day about my experience at Gambarelli's."

The smooth eyelids lifted; the brilliant hazel eyes met my gaze, alive with light but entirely emotionless.

"I'd like to try working on the sales floor, if you please, Mrs. Rutherford. I'm eager for preferment. I understand I must do more menial tasks until I've earned some seniority. Some girls at the residence say I have an eye for luxury goods. Jewelry and such."

"Where you work doesn't depend on me or Madame— that's up to the department heads." I smiled, but Thea did not reciprocate. "Juniors go where they're most needed, and I believe they try to give them some variety to see where they do best."

"*Bien.*" Madame nodded. "We will make a sales uniform for you, Miss Lombardi, and we will inform you where to report. You may return to your work."

Thea bobbed a small curtsey and turned to go, but not before I'd glimpsed a momentary expression that somehow didn't look nearly as submissive as the polite mask she'd schooled her face into. Madame and I watched as the young woman walked away from us, her back arrow-straight and the clear light from the windows sparking flashes of red fire from her auburn hair.

"Is she really giving satisfaction?" I asked.

Madame pursed her small mouth. "That child is deep. I sense there is a great deal of anger in her. But she is most intelligent, and it has not taken her long to learn that we do not brook slyness or insolence. She has taught herself to keep her feelings locked away and her tongue still, and that will take her far. Above all, I believe it is important to her that she stay at Rutherford's rather than return to being a guest in your home. Curious, *n'est-ce pas?*"

"Not really. She had a great deal of autonomy in Kansas, and I'm certain that to be a dependent in someone else's household, however luxurious, is irksome to her. I sympathize—I was not fond of my stepfather, as Thea is not fond of me, and when he sent me to the Poor Farm, I reveled in no longer being under his authority." I shrugged. "Even if it meant I was under the authority of others, Thea's mother included."

"You consider your experience has given you an especial insight into the girl's struggle to find her own way." Madame's eyes were thoughtful as she gazed up at me.

"I do. I've always liked the notion that I was my own woman. Haven't you?"

"Oh yes. Yes indeed." And for a moment I thought I saw past sufferings flit across Madame's visage as she looked beyond me to the crystalline heavens.

"I feel—if it isn't too conceited—that I was inspired when I suggested Thea work here." I watched a skein of geese cross the sky in the far distance, wings flapping vigorously as they spread out into their characteristic V. "It's solved so many problems."

"We must hope, then, that it does not create new ones."

NICE THINGS

I invited Teddy and Thea to join us for Christmas, as part of the family. Things went quite well until after dinner.

"But how can you make a voice go into a machine and come out again?" Tess was asking.

We were sitting around the table enjoying nuts, oranges, cheese, and sweetmeats. Tess had listened to Martin's explanation of the invention called the phonograph with great attention but had clearly not grasped the principle behind it. Truth be told, neither had I. I put down the nutcracker and waited for Martin's reply.

Martin ran a hand through his hair and thought for a moment. "Well, let's see if this makes sense. Have you ever noticed that when there's a really loud sound nearby, you can feel the air move?"

Tess screwed up her mouth in disbelief. "Sound is sound, Martin. It doesn't—" Her face brightened. "Yes, it does! When I saved Nell from that nasty Mr. Poulton and fired the rifle, it made a very loud sound near my ear and the air *did* move. I remember."

"Bang!" Sarah, overexcited after too much food and a surfeit of Christmas, shouted so loud that the air probably moved quite fast. Tess jumped, and Thea scowled.

"Children should be seen and not heard," she pronounced "They definitely shouldn't shout."

"I was making a rifle noise." Sarah, reassured by the presence of so many adults—and knowing she no longer risked being alone with Thea—glanced sideways at the older girl as she slid down from her chair and headed for Teddy. "*I* could shoot a rifle too. Teddy, can you teach me how?"

"Perhaps when you're older." Teddy allowed Sarah to scramble up into his lap. "Right now, you're too small to hold a gun."

"I bet I could." Sarah wiggled her feet in their patent-leather bow shoes.

"Young ladies shouldn't talk about betting," Thea said.

"You just said I'm a child." Sarah's eyes narrowed.

"Sound causes a vibration, you see," Martin continued, recapturing Tess's attention. "Mr. Edison realized he was able to use that vibration to make a needle move, scoring a pattern on a sheet of tinfoil. He worked out a way of turning that pattern back into sound, do you see? So when he said 'Mary had a little lamb' into the device, he was able to reproduce the sound of his voice several times before the tinfoil became too scratched."

"Mary had a little LAMB, its fleece was WHITE as snow, and EVERYwhere that MARY went, the LAMB was SURE to GO." Sarah spoke in the loudest voice she could summon, putting a great deal of singsong emphasis on some words. "When we have a house in Lake Forest, Papa, may I have a sheep? As well as a pony? They have sheep in South Park, and they keep the grass nice and short, so a sheep's a really useful thing."

"Why don't you ask for an entire menagerie while you're at it?" Thea asked. "And a carriage like Tess's?"

We had all walked down to the stable block after church, and Thea had been unable to banish the resentment from her carefully schooled face as she'd stood watching Martin's demonstration of Tess's new landaulet. Donny had proudly led out the horse purchased to pull the carriage, and Thea had not missed the opportunity to make some acid-sweet remarks designed to draw everyone's attention to Donny's status, or rather the lack thereof, in our household. I had seen Sarah observing her.

Now Sarah simply gave Thea another sidelong glance as she launched herself from Teddy's lap—causing him to wince as her shoes made contact with his shins—and ran to Martin.

"*May* I have a carriage, Papa? Just a little one, so I could learn to drive?"

"Ask me again when you're older," Martin laughed. "Tess needs to visit her family, which is a different matter from buying you a carriage merely so you can ride round and round a field. Now go sit down and behave. You're being too loud." He gave her a tiny push on the back of her blue silk dress.

"Is the phonograph a toy, Papa?" Sarah asked as she resumed her seat.

"Do you want one of those as well?" But Thea's remark was generally ignored as Teddy rose to fetch the journal containing the etching of Mr. Edison's invention, which, to my mind, looked more like a collection of spare machine parts than anything useful.

"You might call it a toy for rich men." Teddy scrutinized the numbered diagram. "I'd be happier if some of the money and time they put into inventing new gimcracks were—"

"—given to the poor." Thea finished her brother's sentence with a roll of her eyes. "You sound exactly like Pa."

"I'm proud to sound like Pa." Teddy sat down rather stiffly. "Don't jeer at who our parents were. Our father always chose the way that was *right*."

"I think Thea's unhappy because your Mama and Papa aren't here for Christmas," Sarah said to Teddy. She had commandeered a handful of hazelnuts and was busy arranging them in a straight line.

"Hush, Sarah." I put out a hand toward my daughter, who smiled and said prettily, "Yes, Mama." But we were too late.

"I'm unhappy about that too," Teddy replied to the company at large. The tips of his ears had flushed a rosy red. "But there's only one of us behaving like an ornery mule and riling everyone up about any subject that's raised at what's supposed to be a pleasant family dinner."

"Well, I like that." In contrast to Teddy, Thea had grown somewhat paler. "I'm not allowed to speak my mind when everybody else does? May I remind you I have just the same right to opinions as *you*."

"May I remind *you* I'm the head of our family, and a man."

"Man?" Thea gave a short laugh.

From the look on Teddy's face, Thea's jeer was the final straw. He was not given to outbursts of temper, but at that moment there was a remarkably intense expression in his round gray eyes. "Man enough to assert my authority over you," he said in a low voice. "Man enough to correct you when you are being rude to our hosts. Man enough, if I have to, to take you out of Rutherford's and make you stay at home, where a woman should be. Maybe it's time I took my place as the man of this family. You need someone to disabuse you of your highfalutin ideas about your own importance."

Thea's face grew a shade paler, and I looked at Martin in dismay. I certainly didn't want to sanction a family row at our dinner table, but we could only stop it by treating the two of them like children, and that was distasteful to me. What was more, Teddy's exasperation was understandable, but his remark about a woman's place being in the home was one I did not agree with. Unable to think of the right thing to say, I kept silent.

"I'm earning enough now that I can afford two rooms and a sitting room in the house of one of my friends," Teddy said to Martin and me. "Mr. Hezekiah Galloway and his wife are fine people. Mrs. Galloway runs a boardinghouse Pa would be right happy to see. Mr. Galloway is a stonemason, a lay preacher, and an impressive speaker in the cause of temperance and the suppression of gambling and low entertainments of all kinds. Thea could help Mrs. Galloway in the house in return for a cheaper rent. There's always plenty of cooking and cleaning to do."

"And her employment?" I asked, my dismay increasing. "Thea may be young, but she's a hard worker and knows how to behave at the store." I resisted the urge to show my annoyance that the child wouldn't behave *outside* the store. "She might rise high in a few years, and it's my belief she wants to be there. Why would you take that away from her?"

"Because my family is extremely fond of taking *everything* away from me." Thea spoke through a clenched jaw, her magnificent hazel eyes blazing in a white face.

"A woman belongs at home." Teddy was now clearly determined to say something he'd been thinking for some time, and heedless of the consequences. "Her house and children are Thea's proper domain, when the time comes for me to find her a suitable husband. Until that day, she should learn the skills she'll need for later on."

"I don't need to learn *anything* about keeping house. Mama made sure—" Thea bit off her words, making a visible effort to control herself, and to my surprise Tess interrupted.

"I don't think the Lord means *every* woman to spend all

her time cooking and cleaning." She looked straight at Teddy, her expression earnest. "It says in Genesis: 'And the Lord God said, It is not good that the man should be alone; I will make him an help meet for him.' He didn't say He was making a cook. Mrs. Lombardi once said to me that man and woman were one flesh and one bone and should work together side by side, as one person. Like Nell and Martin do. Martin doesn't clean or cook, and I don't see why Nell should either." She turned to me and smiled. "It took me a long time to figure that out, Nell."

"Teddy, please don't take Thea out of Rutherford's." My body was rigid with the need to convince Teddy that he was wrong, but I refused to begin the argument again. "And let's not argue on Christmas day."

"Peace on earth and goodwill to all men." Sarah had been quite silent, watching with stunned horror the storm she had caused to rain down on all of us by her boisterous behavior. Now she spoke into the tiny interval of silence in a small, frightened voice. "I didn't mean to make you cross, Teddy."

"You haven't, darling." Teddy had the grace to look a little ashamed of himself. "I apologize to the entire company. Including my sister." He shook his head. "I guess I'm finding it hard to be Pa after all. He wouldn't have used harsh words against Thea, however downright provoking she was. I let my heart speak; I've said more than I should."

"I know you're trying to act in Thea's best interests," I said. "I understand how painful this year has been for both of you. But Thea has at last found something to do that she likes, and she's doing it well and giving no trouble. Surely that's better than seeing her rebellious and miserable in a boardinghouse. You don't mean to make her wretched, do you?"

"We give each other nice things, Teddy, remember?" Tess spoke as soon as I stopped to draw breath. "We don't give our children stones or serpents or scorpions. I don't like Thea very much—well, I don't, Nell, I'm just trying to be truthful and you needn't flap your hand at me like that—but I think cleaning house is kind of a scorpion thing for her."

Martin reached for the bowl of nuts and offered them to Teddy. "If you'll take the advice of an older man, Teddy, a girl Thea's age is too young to be lectured on her womanly duty. Give her a little freedom while we're still able to exert some authority over her, won't you? She's obeying the rules of the residence just fine. She'll become more womanly in time."

Thea had listened attentively to our exchange, her face now suffused with warmer color. To my surprise, her small white teeth suddenly showed in a charming smile, directed at her brother.

"I forgive you, Teddy. And you'll see that I'm far better off at Rutherford's, really I am. I'll save money out of my wages so we're beholden to nobody, not even your Mrs. Galloway, just how you like it. You won't have to worry about looking after me because I'm so well looked after already. It's what Pa and Mamma would have wanted."

Teddy stared down at the tablecloth with a sigh. "Seems like you're all determined to convince me." He looked up, directly at me. "You've been kinder to Thea than her behavior warrants, and I'm in your debt for trying so hard. For your sake, I'm prepared to keep my own counsel for a while longer."

PART II
1878

23

DILIGENT IDLENESS

arch 1878

"What are you smiling at?" my husband asked.

I turned to see Martin behind me, enjoying the warmth emanating from his person as he moved close and placed a hand on my shoulder. Although it was early March and the sun was shining, the snow lay in an even blanket on all untrodden ground, pitted here and there as it melted under the force of the sun's rays. Cold radiated from the window out of which I was looking; icicles dripped large blots of clear water onto the stone sill outside, making small splashes on the glass.

"I'm smiling at Tess," I answered Martin, reaching for his fingers. "She looks so dignified."

Martin's breath was hot on the side of my head as he leaned forward to watch our friend descend from her very own landaulet. We had had an extra step made, but she still had to cling hard to Donny's outstretched hand, hampered as she was by her ruffled day dress and fashionably long, buttoned coat with its deep fur trim. She accomplished the maneuver with a straight back, and we watched the single plume atop her small, neat hat bob as she turned to reach out to Sarah.

"Sarah's going to get her feet wet again." I sighed. Sarah jumped from the top step to the dry street and then ran straight into the melting snow, heading for the snowman she and Martin had built the day before. It was also melting, and the old top hat it wore was sliding down its round head, which had lost an eye.

"We'd better go down." Martin kissed my temple and turned toward the stairs. I followed more slowly, yawning. I had taken advantage of the quiet Sunday afternoon to do what I almost never did, lie down after luncheon on the chaise longue in my boudoir while Martin made himself comfortable in an armchair. Lulled by the soft rustling of Martin's newspaper and the distant sounds of the trains making their way along the shoreline, I had drifted off to sleep in the blissful calm.

We reached the bottom of the stairs just as the front door opened.

"I fixed Mr. Snowbanks, Papa." Sarah brought the fresh smell of snow with her from the outdoors, and her fingers were bright pink and dreadfully cold as she seized my hand. I shivered.

"Your feet are wet." I watched as Sarah pulled at the bow of ribbon tied under her chin and handed me her hat.

"I know." Sarah took the button hook I gave her and began working on her smart black patent-leather pumps. Her thin legs—grown suddenly longer in the last month— were comical in their black-and-white striped stockings.

"Where are your galoshes?"

"I don't know."

"Seven and a half is old enough to remember to put galoshes on before you go in the snow."

"It was only for a moment, Mama." Sarah wriggled her feet, now free of their boots, as she started on the buttons of her double-breasted coat. "Goodness, what a lot of buttons."

"May I help?" I asked my daughter as I helped Tess remove her coat.

"No, thank you, Mama." Independence was Sarah's watchword; commendable, of course, but I couldn't suppress a brief pang of loss at every indication that my child was growing up away from me.

"I'm going straight to the library to toast my feet in front of the fire." Sarah handed me her coat; independence did not yet stretch to hanging up her clothes. "Miss Baker says you should never sit around with wet feet." She lifted one foot, put a finger on the wet wool, and then, noticing the damp print on the wooden floor, ran around experimentally for a few seconds. Nodding with satisfaction at the resulting pattern, she dashed off to the library, Martin in her wake.

I lingered with Tess in our spacious hallway, which still smelled faintly of sawdust, putting Sarah's coat away and placing the damp boots near the stairs. We expected our servants to take their Sabbath rest as much as possible, so nobody had come to disturb our peace. When another yawn stole over me, I let it come, stretching my arms over my head.

"You're tired, Nell." Tess stood still while I unpinned her hat.

"I had a nap. You look a little weary yourself. Was Aileen difficult?"

"She guessed Donny was the young man I told them about."

Tess came to me, and I put an arm around her shoulders. She felt good—warm and solid and reassuring—and I silently thanked God for sending me this friend and stalwart ally.

"I suppose that's for the best, isn't it?" I said. "Did she

offer an opinion on him? They must have seen him a few times by now."

"Oh yes, I introduced him the first time he drove me, and of course Ma and Da insist that he step into the parlor for a drop of tea and a bite of cake each time he comes. They can always find a boy to hold the horse for a short while and keep the alley rats off till he gets back."

"How nice."

"Yes, I'm glad they met him. It's harder to rail against people when you're acquainted with them, isn't it?"

"Sometimes." I tightened my grip on my friend's shoulder. "So what about Aileen?"

"I don't really know." Tess turned a puzzled face up to me. "She's polite enough to him, but she *watches* him—like a cat watches a mouse, I guess."

"Perhaps she's trying to figure out if he likes you back."

Tess wrinkled her short nose. "If she figures it out, do you think she could tell *me*?"

I laughed. We reached the library and made our way around the huge double desk in the center of the room to sit on the Chesterfield settee. Martin, ensconced in an armchair, lowered his journal for a moment to smile at me. Sarah—sitting at a sensible distance from the fire since she had already singed her stockings on more than one occasion—twisted round to greet us anew with a wide grin, exposing gaps where two of her incisor teeth had fallen out.

"We're going to have a telephone! Papa says."

I groaned as I lowered myself onto the leather seat. "Oh, for heaven's sake. Still, I might have known it would happen." I looked at Martin. "Must we have one in the house as well as at the store?"

Martin opened his eyes wide, their gray irises reflecting tiny glimmers of flame from the fire. "How else am I going to speak to Joe whenever I want to?" He leaned forward, the journal dangling from his fingers. "Just think, we'll be able to talk to our people directly, without having to send messages back and forth. This far from the store, that's a godsend."

"Or the work of the devil."

I sniffed faintly, leaning into the settee's curved back and once more thanking Providence for the disappearance of the bustle. My house dress, cut in one smooth line—the princess line, as it was called—was the most comfortable item of day dress I had worn since I had come to Chicago. I closed my eyes, listening to Martin explain the telephone again to Tess with interruptions from Sarah, who seemed to have absorbed a great deal of information about the new machine.

"Are you sleeping, Mama?" I sensed a weight on the settee beside me and opened my eyes to find Sarah's face close to mine.

"If I was, I'm certainly not now." I gathered her to me, rubbing her feet as I did so. They were very warm and almost dry. There seemed to be fewer and fewer occasions nowadays when I could hold Sarah in my arms; she was changing fast, acquiring new interests daily. Even her face was altering, growing longer, strong bone emerging from the soft roundness of early childhood.

"You look tired." Sarah touched a careful fingertip to the skin under my eyes, one after the other. "Your eyes are sort of different. Not just today, all the time now."

"It's merely the winter." I smiled. "Soon it'll be spring, and we won't be getting up in the dark. I always feel so much better when I wake up to daylight. That cough I had in January didn't help either." I stroked Sarah's crisply waved hair as she settled her head under my chin. "And last year was such a hard one—bad news everywhere—wars with the Indians, the withdrawal of the troops from the South, all the hardship in the country. And for us, the strike, the Lombardi family—Thea . . ." I let my voice trail off, kissing Sarah's forehead. Days of calm like this were all the sweeter for the memory of Thea's sour looks and slamming doors.

"Not to mention moving to a new store and a new home." Martin spoke fondly, but there was a small frown between his eyebrows.

"Other people did most of the work when we moved," I laughed, trying very hard *not* to look tired. I wanted to erase the frown on Martin's face; I wanted Sarah to see my smiles and not my weariness. But I *was* weary. The sore throat that had started on the second of January had become a hacking cough by mid-month, and although I was now well in body, I seemed to be a little low in spirits. Winter was dragging on forever, even though snow in March was not at all unusual, and I could not reasonably expect the return of the warm weather until the end of April. I was both restless and all too often exhausted.

And yet I had nothing to complain of. Thea was doing well as a sales floor junior; I sometimes saw her as I crossed the floor, and she would respond to my greeting with a polite nod. The report from the residence in which she lived was that she was reserved but not unfriendly toward the other girls and had found two or three girls to walk out with on her afternoon off. Martin regularly invited her to our house on Sundays, but she had only accepted the invitation once since Christmas. I was optimistically inclined to view this transformation as a minor miracle, even though Elizabeth, now ripe and round with the imminent arrival of her first child, had a tendency to mutter darkly about still waters running deep. Tess was no less skeptical, and Madame said nothing at all.

I yawned again, gazing at the flames that were licking the sides of the fresh log Martin had put on the fire. Tess, who had repaired to her favorite armchair to study her Bible, took advantage of the moment of quiet to read out loud, as she loved to do. I recognized the passage from Ecclesiastes:

"He hath made every thing beautiful in his time: also he hath set the world in their heart, so that no man can find out the work that God maketh from the beginning to the end. I know that there is no good in them, but for a man to rejoice, and to do good in his life. And also that every man should eat and drink, and enjoy the good of all his labor, it is the gift of God."

Tess put the ribbon back in its place and smiled at me as Sarah slid down from the settee. Sarah wriggled herself into the corner of one of the window seats, a position from which she could see Martin's journal. He was now reading about electricity; he was, truth be told, a little put out that Wanamaker's in Philadelphia were installing electric lighting and was determined to have a telephone before they did. I was clearly going to have to reconcile myself to the infernal machine, which rang a bell to signal a "call." It would probably be even more of a disturbance than the stock ticker that chattered away at intervals in Martin's office.

The sun had vanished in one of Chicago's rapid changes of weather, and clouds had gathered. Through the window behind Sarah, I could see sparse snowflakes falling, slowly at first but gradually becoming a fine, fast torrent that whispered against the windowpane. I had always connected the snow with my father's death, but that fear was gone; now I imagined him sitting in the window seat smiling at the granddaughter he had never known and felt a smile curve my own lips.

Thoughts drifted through my head—the two rows of buttons on the highly modish dress I had cut the day before for a girl not much older than Thea but already showing promise as a society belle; the choice of menus for the next week; and above all a memory of Elizabeth, the softened contours of her face in late pregnancy and the inward-looking smile that had appeared on it as she smoothed a hand over her belly. I had been turning the pages of *Peterson's Magazine* to show her a warm winter coat which, we both agreed, could easily be adapted to a maternal condition. "For next time," she had said. "It's too close to my confinement now. Or perhaps you'll be next to have a baby?"

But that wasn't why I was tired. I was certain I wasn't with child. Elizabeth's baby appeared before me, clad in a princess-line dress with two rows of buttons, and I was fitting it for a fur-trimmed winter coat as sleep took me into its arms.

EVIDENTLY, MY LOWERED STATE OF HEALTH HAD ALSO BEEN noticed at the store.

"You are tired, Mrs. Rutherford."

I lifted pencil from paper and looked up at Madame Belvoix, who had appeared at my side.

"Was I yawning?"

In answer, Madame sat on the empty chair next to my desk and tugged out the papers below the design on which I was working. I'd been sketching out ideas for the summer: long, sinuous silhouettes of dresses that followed the curve of waist and hip seamlessly before flaring out into a train. Not the princess line this time; these were formal, sophisticated gowns for dinner parties and outings to the theater.

"Good." Madame leafed through the papers, running a finger down the notes I had made at the side. Once she approved such designs, which were never drawn with a specific customer in mind, we employed artists to make up drawings to use on the sales floor. Our couturières could alter details of the dresses to suit the customer. Although I involved myself with the choice of fabrics and trimmings in many cases, it was quite possible for a Lillington design to be achieved without the high cost of my own presence.

"Thank you," I said in reply to Madame's praise. But her next words threw cold water over my complacency.

"Good, but not up to your usual standard."

I was taken aback. "They're not?"

"It is fortunate that your usual standard is so high." Madame favored me with one of her fleeting smiles. "So these are still good. Our customers will like them. But they are not brilliant. They are not *inspired*."

I leaned my head on my hand, gazing at the drawings Madame had replaced on my table. She was right, of course.

"I'll start again."

"The result will be the same. You are tired. Too much new house, too much new husband, too much new Rutherford's department store. Too much *incident* in your life. You've had many changes in the past twelve months, have you not?"

"You know I have." My hand went to my hair, looking for a loose curl I could make even looser. "And it's almost April and still snowing." I sighed. "Christmas is so far behind, but spring is so far ahead."

"And you work so very hard. So does Mr. Rutherford. The two of you never stop." Now there was a sympathetic gleam in Madame's eyes, but not *too* sympathetic. For her, hard work was the normal condition of life.

I puffed out a brief laugh. "That's true. Heavens, it's almost a year since we married, and we've had just a few days off here and there."

"As I pointed out to Mr. Rutherford this morning. He was worried that you were looking fatigued. *Naturellement*, it took a woman to explain the solution to him."

"Which is?"

"I will tell you something you need to understand."

Madame's hand descended on my arm, patting it in a regular rhythm to emphasize her words. "You are a creative artist. Art must be *fed*."

I raised my eyebrows. "I don't think of myself as an artist. I'm a dressmaker."

"You do not think what you do is art?" Madame's hand left my arm, and she tapped the side of her own head with one small finger. "Your dresses come from *here*. And *here*." She laid a hand on her bosom. "And for a very long time you have been starving both head and heart. When you do not give them room to expand, your ideas get smaller."

"But I read the journals—I talk to you and the other couturières—" I stammered in my haste to defend myself.

"It is not enough." Madame's eyes shone steel gray as she gazed at me. "The shadows under your eyes say it is not enough." She waved a hand over my summer dress designs. "*These* say it is not enough. You must learn to live for your art. And Mr. Rutherford worries about your health, and worry will make him tired also."

"Yes." I remembered the drawn, lined look of Martin's face two years before when we had not yet found Lucetta's killer. Mama always said that there was a worrier in every couple, and Martin was ours.

"Very well. For Martin's sake, I will do anything you say." I looked hard at the little Frenchwoman. "What's your remedy? I can tell there's one brewing in your mind."

"*Paris!*" Madame clasped her hands together into a tight knot and pointed that knot toward me.

"Paris?" I sat up straight, suddenly not at all tired. "You mean we should travel to Europe? When?"

"June, I think," Madame said judicially. "Too early and the Exposition will have an unfinished air. I do not believe it will be ready according to schedule. These things rarely are."

"The Exposition? Oh, you mean I—we—should go to

Paris for the Universal Exhibition? I read about it in the newspaper."

"*Hélas*, Mr. Rutherford does not believe we can spare the two of you for more than three months. Otherwise, I would send you to Rome and Florence in October. Rome especially is not healthy in the summer months. Paris is dreadful in August, but Mr. Rutherford agrees that the coast of Normandy is most salubrious. I will arrange for you to meet some people of fashion and intelligence. France is not as it was under the Empire, of course, but there is much worth seeing."

"You've already spoken with Martin about the voyage?" Surprise made my voice waver.

Madame sniffed. "As I have said, he is concerned." She waved a hand. "For your health and spirits, of course, not your work." Her eyes gleamed. "But I see potential for greatness—ah, do not look so surprised—and it is my task to nurture it. You need a, how do you say it, *furlough*. A long one. A furlough with a purpose. You must fill your head with beauty and novelty, and your work will improve."

"I daresay it will." A grin spread over my face at the thought of that beauty and novelty. Paris! Even if it would clearly be our duty to attend a great exhibition.

"You may continue to send us drawings as you wish, if you are inspired to do so." Madame smiled graciously. "But it is not absolutely necessary. Your watchword must be diligent idleness."

"I think I can accomplish that." I could sense the excitement building in my chest, a warm buzzing.

"And, of course, Worth will instruct you on how to make the most of those idle hours."

My heart jumped, and I felt a vein pulsing in my neck. *Worth!* Madame Belvoix had talked before of sending me to her old friend, the most exalted of Parisian dressmakers. We sometimes purchased his designs to make up in the store, and I had studied them carefully. Worth's gowns graced the forms of many a wealthy Chicago lady of my acquaintance, and acquiring a Worth dress was a sign of real wealth and elegance.

"But that is for the summer. For now, you need more rest." Madame tipped her head to one side, looking at me.

"I intend to visit Mrs. Fletcher a great deal once her baby is born. She expects her confinement soon. Will that do? They say a change is as good as a rest." I grinned at Madame, my head still full of Paris and Worth.

"A baby is a commonplace object, of little artistic interest." Madame waved a dismissive hand. "But at least you will not be able to work with one in the room."

24
TRAVEL PLANS

"She's a funny-looking little thing." Elizabeth Fletcher gazed into the eyes of her newborn daughter. "But the monthly nurse says she's a fine, healthy baby. David's delighted. He doesn't mind a bit that our first-born is a girl."

"Aren't you delighted?" I reached out to take little Mabel from Elizabeth's arms, settling her so I could scrutinize her tiny face. "And she's not at all funny looking. That's what newborn babies look like. I declare she looks somewhat like you."

"*I* think she looks like my great-uncle Josiah." Elizabeth sighed. "Perhaps I'm lacking in maternal instinct. Or I'm simply bad-tempered from turning into a frump."

"You're quite beautiful for a woman who gave birth last night. Your figure will return. You're merely tired and a little overwhelmed, I imagine. That's natural."

"That's more or less what Mother said. She told Nurse not to overindulge me—and then she dashed out to buy me what she referred to as 'nourishing but dainty' food to tempt my appetite."

"After sending a note instructing me to call this morning and buck you up." I grinned at the baby who had half opened one eye.

"Mother sat up all night with me," Elizabeth continued. "And supervised my breakfast and then disappeared for half an hour and *then* returned fresh as a daisy to tell me you were coming and she was going out. David gave her the *biggest* hug before he went to the bank—her face turned quite pink."

"Your mother's a force of nature. And it's my opinion that you take after her, even if you don't want to hear it."

"Heaven forbid." Elizabeth yawned. The baby in my arms squirmed, agitating her tiny legs as her face flushed and paled in response to some internal process. I watched, fascinated and charmed, but prey to a thousand conflicting emotions.

"What a strange expression," Elizabeth remarked, and I looked up to see her bright blue eyes studying me. "Are you experiencing a rush of maternal yearning?"

It took me a few moments to formulate a reply. "I feel guilty, I think," I said at last.

"For not presenting Martin with a son and heir in the first year of marriage?" Elizabeth's fair eyebrows arched.

"For being so . . . well . . . *ambivalent* about the prospect of becoming a mother again." I smiled, but the smile died quickly. "At least with you, I can admit it. Of course, I realize children are part and parcel of marriage—"

"And you love Sarah very much," Elizabeth said softly.

"I do. I never return home without a sense of excitement that the two of us will be together soon. Part of me longs for the day when I can announce the imminent arrival of a brother or sister for her and see her face light up with joy—and Martin's, especially Martin's. And yet I dread it as well."

"I believe I can guess why." Elizabeth held out her arms to receive the baby, who had started to squawk, from me. "I'm getting an inkling of the sheer disruption inherent in motherhood. This little one seems to need me every moment, even with a hired nurse around." She kissed her daughter's reddening face. "Don't pay any attention to your cross mother, will you? It's just . . . well, it's hard to be so much in *demand*." The fond smile she gave her baby was reassuring though, and I laughed.

"You haven't even started. She's a little person, you understand, with her own wants and needs. I know what I'm letting myself in for . . . and I'm torn enough between all the roles I play. Dressmaker, partner at Rutherford's, Martin's wife, Sarah's mother, Tess's friend . . . And there's Thea, of course. Have you ever seen those Chinamen who spin plates on sticks and constantly rush from one to the other to stop them from falling? I'm worried that a new baby will bring something else crashing to the ground. It seems much more difficult, somehow, than when I merely had myself to consider."

"And you're worried most of all that what will crash will be one of the two roles you mentioned first," Elizabeth said drily. "Dressmaker and partner at Rutherford's. The roles that are your heart and soul."

I was aware of my face growing red. "Madame says I'm a creative artist and must learn to live for my art."

"If she says so, it's undoubtedly true." Elizabeth made shushing noises at her crimson-faced baby. "Oh dear—Nell, would you please ring the bell for the nurse?"

"Perhaps I should go." I crossed the room to press the button.

"She'll probably make you." Elizabeth grimaced. "You see, I can't even have a conversation."

"Nor will you be able to for a while. Sometimes I suspect I live too much for my work, Elizabeth. I couldn't even summon up the energy to furnish our house—Martin made most of the decisions." I hesitated, then plowed on. "Sometimes I see the house as yet another burden I have to carry."

"Yes, it's dreadful being outrageously rich, isn't it?" Elizabeth dimpled at me, straightening up against her pillows as the door opened. "Oh, Nurse, there you are. Do you think she's all right? After all, I've spent *hours* with her attached to me."

"She's just hungry, waiting for your milk to come in." The nurse, a large, efficient-faced woman, looked down her long nose at me. "You'll have to leave soon, Madam. But I'll take Baby for a few minutes and try to settle her."

She scooped the squalling infant into her arms, silencing her by inserting her little finger into the round red mouth. "Baby and I will return soon, Mrs. Fletcher. We must see to your needs as well."

Elizabeth made a face at the closing door. "Heavens, what a termagant. Or do I mean ptarmigan? She tells me when to use the water closet."

"I'm fairly sure a ptarmigan is a bird. But she's right: you need rest and food. I'm sure your mother will be back soon."

"I suppose so." Elizabeth settled herself more comfortably against the cushions. "But listen, about our conversation the last time we talked, while I was still my own woman." She rolled her eyes. "David's quite adamant we can't come with you to Europe."

"I suppose that was too much to hope for."

"He says we can't afford it ourselves, and although he knows Martin would pay for the whole thing, that's not how he intends to live his life. I will have to be content with spending the summer months in Lake Forest. David didn't even want me to impose on Mother and Father's hospitality for that long—he says Father was quite generous enough over our house and my dress allowance—but Mother simply *insists* that Chicago isn't safe for Mabel in the hot weather."

"She's probably right."

"Yes, drat her, she usually is. Of course, what she really wants is to dote."

"And why shouldn't she?"

"You're far too often on Mother's side." Elizabeth pouted a little, but then her dimples returned. "Oh, but *Paris*, Nell! I will give you a long list of shops to visit."

"I'm beginning to wonder how much time I'll have for buying things. Martin plans on us visiting the exhibition several times—although I will draw the line at looking at machines. Or perhaps I'll go see the flying machine—how can you make a machine fly? Madame insists I see what seems like all the works of art in Paris. She's already given me a list of certain things I *must* see and read before I keep my appointment with Mr. Worth. I must not approach him in ignorance, she says. It's like being a schoolgirl again—and I never did like school that much."

"On the subject of school, is Miss Baker going with you?"

"Yes, although she won't be with us all the time. We'll be in London for the last two weeks, so she will leave us to visit her family in the north and meet us in Liverpool for the return sailing."

"London." Elizabeth grinned. "I haven't been there for years. And I've *never* been to the Normandy coast. You'll have to stay with me for a week to tell me *all* about it."

"I'm rather hoping that absence will make me homesick for Calumet Avenue and that I won't want to go anywhere else." I detected a wistful note in my voice. "That it feels like my home once I come back."

"Is Tess going with you?"

"Ye-e-e-e-e-s." I let my voice reflect my doubts. "But only because Sarah begged her. She has her own reasons for being reluctant, as you know; or at least one reason."

"Your nice Mr. Clark." Elizabeth's smile lit up her bright blue eyes.

"The very same. Teddy's coming too. Not Alice; she gets seasick, so I must hire a maid in London and France if I need one."

"And Miss Lombardi?"

"Mercifully Thea declined our offer."

Elizabeth made a face. "I'm happy for you. Although she's a fool to pass up the chance to visit Europe. Why on earth did you even invite them?"

"Because I was convinced I had to." I set my mouth in a firm line; my invitation to Thea had been a bone of contention between Martin and me. "Teddy was most enthusiastic, but not for Paris. He has his own reasons for wanting to go to Europe and very decided views about the voyage. He begged Martin to buy him a second-class ticket rather than the first-class one we offered, and he's refused any other help. He's been corresponding with some people in England who've set up what they call 'home missions' for the poor, and he's received an invitation to spend the summer working and traveling with them. He wasn't going to go—he couldn't afford it, of course, and would never have approached Martin to ask for money— but he's interpreted our invitation as a sign from God."

"A strange sign when you refuse to keep company with the people who are inviting you." Elizabeth's eyes were wide. "Do you mean to say you agreed to let him go second class?"

I shrugged. "Why not? If it's what he wants." I smiled, remembering the joy on Teddy's face. "He was so delighted at the idea of spending the summer doing pastoral work—you know, Elizabeth, I hadn't realized how much he must miss working alongside his father. He's always quiet about his parents. Stoical is the word, I suppose."

"It all sounds rather dull. The poor are everywhere, and I imagine they're much the same in England as in America. When you go to Europe, you go for the culture—the beauty of the cities—and the *clothes*." Elizabeth twitched down the coverlet and passed a hand over her middle, looking glum.

"Your midriff won't be like that for long." I stood as my ears registered the approaching sound of a screaming newborn. "Now, you must get back to motherhood and I to my store. I'll come again tomorrow, and in a few days we'll start discussing some new dresses. That will cheer you up."

"Nell!" Tess's face brightened as she turned toward her sitting-room door in response to my knock. "How is Elizabeth? What does the baby look like?"

"Elizabeth's well, and I'm sure Mrs. Parnell will let you and Sarah visit soon. The baby—well, she's a baby. Two arms, two legs, facial features all in the right place, and the correct number of digits."

Tess's small teeth showed as she burst into a laugh. "You're funny, Nell. Is she pretty? What's her name?"

"Mabel, and of course she's as beautiful as any newborn can be. It'll be a few days before she stops looking so red and creased. But I'm quite sure her eyes are going to be exactly like Elizabeth's."

Tess clapped her hands. "Mabel! That's so pretty. I will buy her a pink bonnet, and when she's bigger, I'll play peek-a-boo with her just like I did with Sary. Are you going to eat luncheon with us?"

I looked at my timepiece. "I suppose I could. What are you doing?"

Tess turned back to the beautiful little desk Martin had found for her, indicating a small book.

"I'm looking at the book Martin writes in to show how rich I am."

I had never seen the book, so I peered over Tess's shoulder to look at Martin's neat handwriting. "Has he been doing this for long?"

"Since last summer. He said it would be a good idea if I understood my money. Only I don't understand, not really, but on Sunday afternoons when you're out for a walk with Sary and Martin's looking at the household books with me, he gets out his notebook and copies things into *my* book. I asked him if I'm rich, and he said that 'rich' means different things to different people, but in the eyes of most ordinary people I'm a wealthy woman."

Based on the figure at the bottom of the page, Tess could be described as wealthy by many people's standards. From the modest amount she'd earned at the seminary, Martin had gradually built a nest egg for her. It helped that we never spent her income; we gave her pin money each week, and as we'd opened accounts at all the shops she liked, we simply paid the bills as they were sent in. Tess didn't understand money at all, but she could add figures and enjoyed looking at them. I loved Martin all the more for understanding my friend so well.

"Just think, all this came originally from your hard work." I bent down to lay my cheek against Tess's, the wire of her spectacles pressing against the scar near my ear. "You should be proud. Were you planning to spend some of it?"

"I'm going to buy Donny a ticket for the *Germanic*," said Tess firmly. "I want him to come with us."

Mama had once told me that "improving each shining

hour" sometimes meant waiting for the right opportunity to do the right thing at the right time. It was time to talk to Tess. I crossed the room to fetch one of her dainty chairs so I could sit next to her.

"Why is it important to you that Donny come with us?" I asked. I knew the answer, of course, but I needed to hear it from Tess.

"Because he's my friend." Tess's eyes, magnified a little by her spectacles, were resolute.

"So you intend him to travel as a friend, and not as a—"

"If you're going to say *servant*, I'll be cross." Tess assumed the fiercest expression she could manage.

"I've never called him a servant. But you have to admit he's hardly used to traveling in first class. How do you imagine Donny will feel, sitting at dinner with the likes of the Vanderbilts and the Morgans? I'm nervous enough about that as it is, and I know you are too. And *we're* used to society by now."

"Donny sat with the likes of the Parnells at Thanksgiving," Tess said defensively, then blushed. "He looked so nice."

"But—have you even talked to Donny about this idea of yours? Or are you just going to spring the surprise on him? He didn't much like being told he had to have his Thanksgiving dinner upstairs."

Tess looked confused. "I guess I hadn't thought about that yet."

"That's what worries me, sweetheart." I smoothed a fine wisp of hair that waved around her ear. "I would be happy to keep company with Donny, but this has to be his decision as well as yours. And it's a big decision, isn't it? Martin's the only one among us who won't find the crossing hard, socially speaking—well, except Sarah. She's lucky she's too young to sit at dinner."

"I wish I didn't have to," said Tess in a small voice. "But I guess I'm not a servant or a child either, so I have to be brave, and I can pray to the Lord to help me." She frowned. "Will the rich people be mean to Donny?"

"I hope they'll be far too well-bred." I smiled at her fondly. "And we'd always be there with you. But the point is you haven't asked Donny for his opinion—and as far as the world's concerned, he's your driver. Must he pretend to be something else before he's ready? Has he given you any sign that he's as sweet on you as you are on him?"

"What sort of sign?"

"Well, has he tried to hold your hand? Or kiss you? Has he said any sweet nothings to you?"

"What are sweet nothings?"

I tried to recall things Martin had said to me when we were alone, and for a moment I felt the warmth of our bed, his arms around me. My mood lightened a fraction.

"That you're beautiful. That he can't live without you. Compliments on your eyes, your hair, your—"

I stopped, aware I was blushing. Martin was occasionally quite effusive with his sweet nothings. "Well, compliments," I finished.

Tess thought for a moment. "He says I'm real smart."

"Does he say it in the way a friend does, or in a lover-like way?"

Tess thought again. "Is a lover-like way like when Martin asked you to be his wife and went down on one knee? Like when the two of you kiss and all that when you think nobody's looking?"

I wanted to ask what "all that" was but didn't dare. "Yes, like that."

Tess shook her head. "I guess Donny says nice things in a friendly-like way."

I cleared my throat and held out my hand to my friend.

She put her small hand into mine, her short, stubby fingers curling round my longer ones in complete trust.

"Donny's a delightful man," I began, "and it's possible that love might grow between you in time. But I have seen no real signs of romantic interest on his part, and it's not fair to him if you act as if there are such feelings between you. Paying for a trip to Europe is the action of far more than just a friend. If you insist he come, I don't suppose I can stop you—I couldn't stop you inviting him to the Thanksgiving dinner, after all. You're part of our family and we respect your wishes. But how is Donny going to live for all those weeks? Will you feed and clothe him? Or ask us to pay? We would, of course—you know Martin would." I smiled. "But will you insist he accompany you to every dinner and trip to the theater and the Universal Exhibition and everything? Make him talk to all the people we meet? How do you imagine that'll make him feel?"

A tiny frown puckered the skin between Tess's almond eyes. "Like a doll," she intoned at last. "Or a pet dog. Or a child. Like the way people who don't know me treat me sometimes."

I kissed the small hand that lay in mine. "Tess, there would be nobody more delighted than I if love were to blossom between the two of you. Real, lasting love. It would thrill me to see you settled in a home of your own—although I'd miss you terribly, and so would Sarah." I looked into the dear face of my best friend and remembered how heartbroken I'd been a year before when Tess considered moving in with her sister Mary. "Heaven knows, you deserve every kind of happiness God might see fit to shower upon you."

Tess blinked. "I *am* happy, Nell." Her gaze turned inward, and she frowned. "Mostly." Her frown deepened. "I was very happy until I saw Donny, and now I feel different. Why is that?"

"Because romantic love isn't always a comfortable sensation." I remembered my emotions when I realized I'd fallen
in love with Martin, in those days a married man. "Sometimes it's easy, but often it's not. What I'm trying to say is . . .
I don't think Donny's ready to woo and win a woman yet. I
imagine he still sees you as a friend, or even perhaps as a
grand lady. You've gone far beyond the Tess of the Poor
Farm." My words faltered. "We have all gone far beyond the
Poor Farm."

"I want Donny to love me the way Martin loves you." It
dismayed me to see Tess's lower lip tremble. "And I'm not at
all sure I like being a grand lady, Nell." She looked around at
her beautiful sitting room, and a fat tear caught in the rim of
her spectacles. "I mean, I *like* being rich and living in a pretty
house. But it's difficult being rich too. I liked it when we
were in Kansas."

"I know what you mean." I gathered Tess to me, small and
soft and warm in my arms, and rested my cheek on her fine
hair. "When I accepted Martin, I didn't dream about traveling to Europe in the company of the Vanderbilts and
Morgans." A tiny convulsion of mirth shook me, and I
hugged Tess tighter. "I'm sorry, I shouldn't laugh—but it *is*
laughable, in a way. From disgrace to wealth. It's like one of
those novels you like to read."

Tess sniffed. I loosened my grip as she fumbled in her
pocket for a handkerchief. "At least you're elegant and look
like you belong in a ballroom, Nell."

"Even if the ladies think I'm eccentric because I'm a
working woman?" I tried to smile. "But listen, darling. I
didn't ask for love—it just came. Could you be patient a little
longer? And if you're adamant we should take Donny to
Europe with us—in whatever capacity—don't you think we
should at least ask his opinion first?"

Tess replaced her spectacles on her nose. "Can we do it after luncheon?"

I looked at my timepiece again and sighed, seeing the afternoon's work recede from me like a retreating tide. But I knew when I absolutely had to put friendship first.

"Of course." I rose, smiling as cheerfully as I could. "Let's walk down to the stables after we've eaten."

25

JEALOUSY

*O*ur stable and coach house were not part of the main house, as Martin had bought a separate piece of land after deciding he wanted a larger residence and garden. They were on a stub of Twenty-Second Street, near the railroad but screened from it by a high wall topped by spikes to keep out intruders. An icy wind blew off the lake even now that it was April.

We found Donny filling a bucket with water from the pump. Our driver, Capell, who was washing the tail of Martin's horse, Gentleman, called a polite greeting as we entered the yard. The horse, a friendly beast, turned its head to see the visitors and blew through its nostrils, nudging Capell with its noble nose.

A giggle alerted me to a young woman standing behind Donny. She was tall, dark-haired and dark-eyed, with muscular arms and a freckled countenance; the work-roughened hands and the scarf tied tightly around her curls, along with her manner of dress, suggested to me she worked in the laundry we had passed on the way to the stables.

"Who's that?" She placed a hand on Donny's arm somewhat familiarly, calling his attention to us. "The horse seems to like them." She smiled at us in a bold but not unfriendly fashion, revealing good teeth. "Hello, ladies."

Donny let go of the pump handle, his shy smile stealing over his face. "Good afternoon, Mrs. Rutherford. Good afternoon, Miss O'Dugan." Clearly, Sarah's lessons in correct address had continued.

"Ah, you've got such nice manners." The girl cast a fond gaze at Donny and then inspected us, inscrutable dark eyes roving over our smart walking dresses. "You ladies better mind the horse apples with them nice boots. You friends of the place too?"

"The owners," I said briefly, fiddling with the buttons on my butter-soft doeskin gloves. "How do you do?"

"Yes, I work for them, Annie." Donny wiped his hands on his trousers.

She didn't seem impressed. "Pleased to meet you, I'm sure." Her gaze flicked to Tess. "Are you the little lady he drives in his carriage?" Her cheerful smile lit up her face again as she looked back at Donny. "All smart in his uniform. I s'pose I do some of your washing, ladies—although I guess your maid does most of it."

Of course—I had always known that our rougher linen went to a laundry, but this was the first time I'd had to concern myself with such details since we'd moved to Chicago. Another sign of my elevated social status, I supposed. I nodded, not quite knowing what to say. "Thank you" seemed the best response.

"Oh, you're welcome." Annie's smile widened. "I do the menservants' laundry too."

Donny blushed, and Annie threw back her head in laughter, exposing her long white neck.

"Ain't it sweet how he gets all bashful about his combinations? Well, it's made my day to meet you ladies." She stood on tiptoe to give Donny a swift peck on the cheek, which caused him to blush even more. "Be a good boy now," she said to him. "I got to get back or Ma O'Shaughnessy will fine me a nickel."

She tugged the plaid shawl over her shoulders and walked out of the yard at a leisurely pace, waving a cheerful farewell to the stable hands who were emerging from the tack room. It was all very friendly; I gathered that Annie was a regular visitor.

"May we talk with you, Donny?" I asked, dismissing the laundrywoman from my mind. "Perhaps we could go inside where it's warmer."

"Sure, there's a fire in the tack room."

Donny led the way into the room, where a small fire was burning in the grate. He offered us two of the straight-backed wooden chairs before seating himself. The smells of horse, leather, saddle soap, brass polish, and oil melded together in a pleasing harmony that made me think of Martin when he returned from a day off hunting, fishing, or riding with his merchant friends.

"Tess has a . . . proposition," I began when it became clear that Tess was waiting on me to speak. I turned to her. "Don't you want to ask him yourself?"

"You do it." Tess blushed, but it was an uncomfortable blush rather than the rosy glow that usually graced her countenance when Donny was around.

"Very well," I said. "Donny, Tess has a notion—in short, she'd like you to accompany us to Europe. As a first-class passenger, you understand. Would you like that?"

Donny's eyes widened. "No, ma'am." He shook his head vehemently. "I'm not getting on no boat."

"It's a big ship, not a boat." Tess sounded a little offended. "Martin says it's like a great floating hotel with dining rooms and a gymnasium and even a library. You'd get your own room and everything."

Donny shook his head again. "What would I want to go on a big ship for? I belong here." He looked around at the gleaming saddles mounted on the walls. "Mr. Capell says he's going to teach me to drive two horses, and once I'm steady with two horses I can try a four-in-hand one day. I like it here. I got a room all to myself and good food, and I can work hard all day. And nobody steals my money, and I don't got critters in my clothes no more."

"I'm so glad you're happy here," I said. His smile in response lit mine, but Tess's face was the picture of dismay. I knew I had to try harder. "I think the point is," I said, "that as our friend you don't have to work hard. Tess thinks we got off on the wrong foot by employing you instead of—well, instead of just inviting you into our home. Like we did with Miss Lombardi."

Donny broke into a guffaw. "I'm not a smart man, Miss Nell—Mrs. Rutherford—but even I know you can't pick a pebble up off the road and shine it into a diamond," he said when he'd finished laughing. "Miss Lombardi, now she's different. She's genteel, a young lady. But I'm a working man, and it's right that you gave me a job to do. I couldn't live without working hard, and I'm proud to work for you and Mr. Rutherford and to drive Miss O'Dugan here. So this is where I stay as long as you got use for me. But I thank you kindly for the thought."

It was the longest speech I'd heard Donny make. I hardly dared look at Tess.

"Would you accept if you traveled second-class as our driver or bodyguard, or whatever role you wish?" I said. "We're going to Paris and London. Wouldn't you like to see those places?"

Donny crossed his arms over his massive chest, shaking

his head again. "No, ma'am. If you make me go, I guess I have to go, but if I can choose—"

"You can choose." Tess spoke in a small voice.

"Of course you can choose to go or stay if you wish," I confirmed.

"Then I'll stay right here, ma'am. I'm Donny Clark of Clark Street, Chicago, and Chicago is where I choose to stay."

"It's because of that Annie." Tess barely waited until we were outside the stable yard to say what was on her mind.

"I'm sure it's not, Tess."

"But supposing I come back from France and he's married *her*?" Tess's voice rose to a wail. "Then I'd lose him forever." She took off her spectacles to scrub at her face with her handkerchief. "I wish I hadn't promised Sary I'll go."

"You won't make his heart grow fonder by insisting on sticking by his side, will you?" I pointed out. "If he likes you at all in a romantic way, he won't marry someone else when you're gone."

"Martin did." Tess sniffed loudly.

My steps faltered to a stop. "Well, Martin—but he—he—he made a mistake." I had to admit she made an excellent point.

"And if that man hadn't stuck a knife into the first Mrs. Rutherford, Martin would be lost to you for always and always."

I felt my shoulders slump. "Yes," I said. "He would." I reached out a hand toward Tess. "I don't have any answers left. I'm sorry."

Tess sighed. "You were right, though; I can't make Donny do things he doesn't want to do. It wouldn't be fair."

"Yes, he's very much his own man, isn't he? I admire his determination to be true to himself. Many men in his position would have conceded anything just to keep their job."

A tremulous smile spread across Tess's face as she looked up at me.

"He's a good man, Nell."

"Worthy of your love," I agreed.

We walked on in silence until we were on Calumet Avenue, and then Tess spoke again.

"I don't like feeling this way. I'm all uncomfortable inside. I'm thinking unkind things about Annie."

"And you didn't even know she existed this morning," I observed.

In a couple more minutes, we arrived at the house. Tess was silent once more as we mounted the shallow steps to the front door. She said no more until we were inside and had shed our outer clothing into Mrs. Hartfield's arms.

"I'm going to my room," she said at last.

"Would you like me to stay with you?"

To my surprise, a smile—almost carefree—spread across my friend's round face.

"You go to the store, Nell. I'm going to pray. Mrs. Lombardi always said we should take all our troubles to God, so I'm going to pray and pray to Him to make me brave about going to Europe and about Donny. And to make me stop thinking unkind things." She patted my hand. "If you don't have any answers left, then I guess praying is all I can do."

26

BAUBLES

"*Good* afternoon, Mrs. Rutherford," said my husband when I finally arrived at work.

I grinned at Martin, who was resplendent in his working uniform of morning coat and silk cravat. I had found him on the sales floor with his notebook in his hand, talking to Powell McCombs, the head of the jewelry department.

"I'm aware it's three thirty, thank you," I said. "You needn't be so pointed."

"No criticism was implied," he lied. "How is Baby Fletcher?"

I had almost forgotten about my visit to Elizabeth, truth be told. "Her name is Mabel, and she looks healthy. Elizabeth needs cheering up, though—I'll have to visit often until we go to Europe." I smiled at Mr. McCombs. "I'm sorry to interrupt your conversation."

"Actually, you should see this." Martin turned to Mr. McCombs. "Could you get that pin out again?"

Within a few moments, we were all inspecting a large oval pin of quite astonishing beauty. "That must be a sapphire," I said, taking the object from Martin's hand and holding it up to the light to view the large blue cabochon stone in the center. "And are the table-cut stones emeralds? If they are, that's a far more expensive piece than we usually sell."

Martin and Mr. McCombs exchanged a look, and the older man spoke first. "Not for much longer, ma'am. This is by a Chicago designer—a woman—and I've found more artists of similar quality."

"The pendant's an emerald too, but more natural." Martin indicated the large green stone that dangled from the base of the pin. "The artist has traveled in Europe a great deal—you can detect the Renaissance influence in the enamel base." His eyes shone clear gray in the light from the windows. "We're already developing a reputation for affordable jewelry to go with our dresses—now we want to do the same for our wealthiest clients. Give them something truly special."

"I'm confident I can sell a piece like this in a week or two," Mr. McCombs said. "Especially with the help of the dressmaking department." His eyes, a soft brown, twinkled at me but then took on the alertness that stole over any salesman when a potential customer drew near. "I observe you are interested in this exquisite piece, sir," he said to a spot just behind me. "Are you looking for a gift for your lady wife, perhaps?"

"I don't have a lady wife," said a deep, familiar voice, and I turned to find Victor Canavan looming above me with a benevolent smile on his well-shaped lips. "In fact, I've been hoping for a word with Mrs. Rutherford. But it *is* very beautiful. May I see?"

Martin, who had possession of the brooch, handed it to Mr. Canavan. The latter surprised all of us by taking a small brass object out of a vest pocket and folding back the covers to reveal a little magnifying glass—a jeweler's loupe, perhaps —which he used to scrutinize the pin in every detail.

"I note you are a connoisseur, sir," Mr. McCombs said, a sale still clearly on his mind.

Mr. Canavan smiled, handing the piece back to Martin. "I like jewels as I like all beautiful things. That's why I called my theater the Jewel Box. Mrs. Rutherford, could I trouble you for a brief consultation?"

I acceded and led the way to a chamber that adjoined the suite of vast rooms where we displayed our fabrics. Decorated with heavily carved woodwork and blue tiles, hung with gasoliers and sparsely furnished with large tables and comfortable chairs, it was where the couturières brought customers who had asked for specific advice. Here we could find a little peace to talk, perhaps display sketches or send for fabrics, and determine the customer's wishes before inviting them up to the various sanctums and fitting rooms on the second and third floors.

"Please sit down." I indicated a chair next to a free table and then smiled as Mr. Canavan hastened to pull out a chair for me first. There was nothing wrong with his manners. "This is about your costumes, I suppose?" I wanted to add, *I hope you won't find us too expensive*, but in the course of my dressmaking career I had learned to bite my tongue when it came to discussing prices. Until the customer wanted to discuss them, of course.

I was a little disconcerted, therefore, when Mr. Canavan linked his long white fingers together and said, "I do want to assure you, dear lady, that I am not about to ask for credit. I will pay cash for your work."

"I wasn't going to—" but I flushed a little, and Mr. Canavan noticed. He laughed.

"Did you think I was reading your mind? Not at all. I'm simply used to the assumption that a theater manager, particularly an actor-manager, must needs be teetering on the brink of bankruptcy. I assure you I manage my affairs well, and my credit is excellent. I will supply you with a letter from my bankers."

"That won't be necessary."

"But it should be. After all, you barely know me—I'm not even in the city directory as yet. And I'm going to ask you for quite a lot. Not just in terms of quantity; I will be a demanding customer. Dresses for the stage should be well made and easy to move in, as well as being delightful to the eye since they have to go through a lot of wear and tear. My ladies are in despair with the rags they are currently wearing. I will save money in repairs; and if you recall, my theater is small, and the audience is close. We cannot rely on distance to render our mends and patches invisible."

"And do you want me to design everything?"

"Design and cut. I hear you are a superb cutter. I presume your *atélier* will do the rest." He pronounced the French word with what sounded to me like a perfect accent. There was something quaintly British, I realized, in the way he spoke when not on stage.

"I must warn you, I will be away for much of the summer," I said. "But if you give me a commission now, I can promise you the work can start within the month—if you don't mind my not being there for the finishing. Usually, I would supervise the final touches."

He nodded. "I realize you are no mere employee, dear lady. We will manage splendidly. May I give you some initial instructions?"

"Of course." I stood, and he did the same. "My sketch-books and so on are upstairs. Would you like to start now?"

I SPENT MUCH OF THE FOLLOWING TWO WEEKS VISITING
Elizabeth and the rest of the time drawing sketches. Some
were for Mr. Canavan, others for my friend; as she became
accustomed to motherhood, I started to imagine dresses for
her that reflected her new status in subtle ways while
retaining the freshness suited to a recent bride. I arrived one
morning with a portfolio in my hand and waited while Elizabeth settled her daughter to sleep.

"*Now* we can talk."

Elizabeth put a finger to her lips as she led me away from
the cradle. Little Mabel, already filling out in the cheeks, was
a pretty sight. Her small red mouth moved in a sucking
motion and her fingers stretched then relaxed, curling into
her palms as sleep took her farther into its embrace. I had to
smile; despite my own ambivalence about more children, the
sight of Mabel reminded me of the pleasurable moments of
Sarah's infancy, the sweet, soft touch of my baby's skin
against my lips.

Elizabeth brought me back to the present by gently
grasping my shoulder to draw me out of the nursery. She left
the door ajar; we tiptoed down the stairs to the parlor where
Elizabeth shut the door firmly.

"Nurse will hear her if she cries." She snorted. "*When* she
cries."

"Oh, hush." I was quite used to Elizabeth's pretense at
diffidence. "You have a sweet, healthy baby who sleeps well
and feeds well. Don't pretend you don't adore her. And you
look wonderful."

"Thanks to your visits." Elizabeth passed an arm through
mine as we settled on the sofa. "Mother declares I barely
needed her."

"Nonsense. Besides, it's done me good to come here so
often. Madame's right; I *have* been feeling a little jaded by the
pressures and responsibilities that have fallen to my lot." I

looked around the small but cheerful room with its Japanese prints and light yellow curtains. "Coming to a home where the only *work* is represented by a baby is no end refreshing to me at the moment."

"Are you so averse to work you can't bear to show me the sketches you brought?" Elizabeth's dimples showed. "I was looking forward to them as the highlight of your visit."

In reply, I handed her my portfolio, watching as she untied the cloth ribbons.

"Oh, Nell." Elizabeth looked up, her eyes bright. "I can hardly bear to wait for my next quarter's dress allowance."

"We can measure you just before we leave for Europe—I generally find that about six weeks after the birth is the best time. Then we can start on the dresses as soon as you tell us to."

"But these gowns are just mine, Nell." Elizabeth's expression was avid. "What about the costumes for the play? I asked you to bring those."

"And how would you think if I showed *your* sketches to everyone in Chicago?" I waved a hand over the drawings. "You pay for exclusivity. So does Mr. Canavan."

"How *horribly* like a businesswoman you sound." Elizabeth pouted prettily.

"The benefit of increasing experience." I shrugged, grinning at my friend's sulk. "And having a Chicago merchant for a husband. I *am* allowed to tell you the name of the play: *A Summer Frolic*. And I can hint to you that the dresses match the title. In fact, my efforts on Mr. Canavan's behalf partly inspired your sketches, so if the play's a success, you will be the most fashionable woman in Chicago."

As I *was* a businesswoman, I forbore to inform Elizabeth that I had reduced my prices to Victor Canavan in exchange for a full-page advertisement in the bill of entertainment.

"Now listen," I said as Elizabeth continued to study the sketches, "I have a favor to ask you."

"Anything." Elizabeth's eyes were blue pools as she examined a frivolous confection of broderie anglaise and pin-striped cotton, trimmed with lace and pink bows that swooped across the underskirts like a gathering of butterflies on a white flower.

"Would you keep an eye on Thea while we're away?"

Elizabeth turned her head to look at me. "Are you worried about her?"

"No-o-o-o-o, but it won't hurt to be a little vigilant. After all, Teddy will be away too."

"Hmmm. What do you want to know?"

"Mostly, I suppose, if she has any visitors at the store or if there are any rumors about her. Madame has assured me she will keep her eyes and ears open, but it would be nice if there were someone else who had an excuse to visit the sales floor."

"Well, I certainly do." Elizabeth's countenance brightened. "Now that I'm no longer as round as a balloon, I can simply *haunt* Rutherford's. There are the fittings, of course, and I will need a new hat or two." She patted her thick corn-colored hair. "I can think of a thousand excuses to spend time in your store. In which department does Thea work?"

"In costume jewelry, although Mr. McCombs has occasionally asked for her. Somehow she's wormed her way into his good graces. She has quite a knack for sales, you understand, and all jewelry looks marvelous on her. She has lovely coloring and a certain poise—she's stopped rounding her shoulders and hanging her head."

"Well, thank heaven for that. She has the potential to be quite beautiful."

"Yes, and she's a hard worker. She appears to be using her skill at manipulating people for the purpose of selling our goods, which is something of a relief."

"When you say visitors, do you mean she may have a gentleman follower? Or two?"

"I certainly hope not—she's not sixteen till June. But she's a pretty girl and no doubt has attracted attention. I owe it to Catherine to be a little vigilant."

"I'll do my best to follow in your footsteps as a department store spy." Elizabeth nudged me with her elbow. "And what's it like working with Mr. Canavan? Do you thrill to his deep and resonant voice? Does his handsome face make your heart beat faster?"

"And I a bride of just one year? Not in the least. In fact, he's easy to work with. Polite and reserved—never talks anything but business."

"How disappointing."

"He seems genuinely interested in what I offer on the dressmaking side." I frowned, thinking back over my conversation with the actor. "Come to think of it, he talked quite a lot about art; I would surmise that he's spent a great deal of time in France and Italy, especially Italy. He seems very knowledgeable on such subjects. But he said nothing about himself."

"And was what he said interesting?"

"Some of it went rather above my head," I admitted. "But he sent me a book afterward—about the Renaissance, by an Englishman called Pater—and said I should read it before I go to Europe. I'm trying, but it's dreadfully hard going. I don't really care about what beauty means to me or to anyone else; I simply like to create something beautiful *because* it's beautiful, and I like making a woman feel the joy of owning an ensemble that enhances her own charm. There's beauty in even the plainest woman, you know."

"I know that you see it, and that's enough for me." Elizabeth grinned. "How amusing, Nell—you, the most reluctant of students, forced to study for the sake of the art you already execute quite superbly."

"Madame Belvoix is very pleased that I'm reading the dratted book," I confessed. "She keeps talking to me about enriching my talents, whatever that means. I'm becoming somewhat nervous about meeting the great Worth—what if he also expects me to be some sort of expert in the arts? I thought I was an excellent dressmaker, but people like that make me doubt my own abilities. Supposing he decides I'm not good enough to bother with?"

"He won't, not if you're recommended by Madame." Elizabeth patted my hand. "And you're not being sent to him as an expert, are you? You're being sent there to learn."

I could feel the anxiety building within me, a sensation I had had frequently in the last two weeks.

"I just don't know if I'm ready. It's only, what, two months? No time at all when you consider how much I have to do to ensure we're all ready to leave."

"You have servants. You'll manage." Elizabeth's eyes gleamed. "You're like an actress who thinks she's nervous about going on stage but will be magnificent as soon as she steps on the boards. The only way you'll find out how you can perform for the great Worth is to do it."

27

CROSSING

*T*he weeks to our departure flew by. They seemed to go quicker than the voyage itself, which was somewhat monotonous. We did not see Teddy at mealtimes, but he often visited us on the deck of the ship so he could talk to us and play with Sarah, of whom he was fond. I did not get a chance to speak with him alone until we had almost traversed the Atlantic.

"Are you sure you won't stay with us for a little while?" I asked him. "Not even to see London?"

I wasn't certain Teddy had heard me at first. He had taken off his wide-brimmed hat to prevent it from being swept away by the salt-laden breeze that tugged at my own hat, firmly pinned to my hair as it was, and threatened my coiffure. Below us, green-gray waves ran past in endless repetition, varied only by their caps of white; above us, the vast sky performed its ever-changing variations on clouds and sun. It was a scene to which I was all too accustomed after several days at sea. I suspected that Teddy too was straining his eyes for a sight of the coast of Ireland, which, we had been assured, was not too far over the horizon.

"It reminds me a little of Kansas, in the oddest way." Teddy turned to lean his back against the railing of the promenade deck, dragging his gaze away from the restless sea. "That sense of endless space and freedom and the sky spread above us like God, watching and protecting."

"I hope He *is* protecting us." I looked up into the young man's solemn face. "You're right, this ocean gives me the same impression that the plains did—that we're infinitely small and frail." I glanced over to where light streamed down through a rift in the clouds, turning the waves a lighter green. "It makes all human effort seem futile—although Martin would say that we've conquered the sea."

Teddy snorted softly, his eyes also on the faraway shaft of sunlight. "Conquered, is it? But if it makes us feel better to entertain such illusions . . . We can only do what we can with the work in front of us and try to leave the world a little better than we found it."

Now he looked directly at me. "You understand I can't stay with you. It's mighty kind of you to want to give me a vacation, and I must seem like an ungrateful guest to you, but I would have been uncomfortable traveling in first class and staying in big hotels with you. It's hard to explain, but I just don't believe I belong there."

"You're not the first young man I've heard that from." I was thinking of Donny, of course. "You know your own mind."

"I'm grateful for your understanding and your generosity, really I am." Teddy smiled hesitantly. "I'll see the sights of Europe right enough, in my own way, and at the time the Lord thinks is appropriate. I wouldn't have come, but I felt so pulled to Europe I couldn't help it. I can sense Pa inside me, urging me on to do some good work and give my spiritual muscles some exercise for a change."

He jerked his head in the direction of the wide staircase

leading down to the Grand Saloon. "You must pardon my directness, Mrs. Rutherford, but those people there are empty—sounding brasses, a thing that makes a noise in the wind but has no substance. It's been just a week and I'm plumb tired of the sight of them—no offense meant, of course." He looked down at his boots. "I guess I'm as rude as Thea, saying such things."

"You're trying to tell me the truth. I suppose neither of you are cut out for society after all those years on the plains."

"I suppose I'm not." He hesitated. "In some ways, it was just as much a shock to me as it was to Thea to find you so rich. The store, the Palmer House, the carriages, the clothes —it was as if I left you in Kansas as an ordinary woman and found you in Chicago as someone entirely new. Only Sarah's the same—when she forgets to show off." He grinned, and I couldn't help smiling in response.

"You've changed too; you wouldn't have been so ready to judge two years ago," I pointed out. "I wish you'd spend more time with these people you're so eager to condemn. Many of them do a lot of good; some of them are considerable philanthropists; and quite a few of the women are involved in charitable work and would have listened to you with interest."

Teddy looked at me for a long moment before he spoke, his round gray eyes solemn. Then the corners of his lips twitched just a little, and he beat his hat gently with his left hand.

"But they're not *my* people. I often get the impression we live in different universes, you and I." He returned his gaze to the shifting, watery horizon. "Not that I blame you for being worldly, nor Mr. Rutherford. You're good folk in your way, and I'm certain you love God and seek to do His will as far as your understanding of it goes—but you're not godly, not in the way the people I'm drawn to are. Not like Mamma and Pa."

"I'm not the woman you'd prefer to step into your mother's place where Thea's concerned." I smiled briefly to let Teddy know I didn't resent the implications of his words.

"To be honest, I'm not sure if even Mamma and Pa could have curbed Thea, so I don't blame you for falling short. She's built an iron shell around her heart, and God will need to perform a miracle to melt it."

"But your mother would have tried?"

"She would, and perhaps Thea would have hated her for it." He moved one hand impatiently, gesturing toward the sky. "We'll never know. But you—forgive my frankness—you'll let your own excellent intentions regarding Thea get in the way of doing any *real* good."

"Are my intentions so terrible? I want Thea to be respectable; of course I do. More respectable than I was." I was aware a flush stained my cheeks, but I stared steadily at Teddy. "Not that I did anything worse than many a young man has done—make a foolish, impulsive mistake—except I had to pay for my error."

"What you call respectability isn't godliness. God's standards are different," said Teddy softly.

"God's standards are too often what men tell us they are," I snapped back with a swiftness that surprised me. "I sinned once, yes, but then I sinned no more—not in that way, in any case. I had to practice deception for Sarah's sake because decent society would not allow me to be truthful and still live within its bounds. I repented, and isn't that what you want? I hope not to give Thea any cause to need such repentance. I may not be your mother, but I will do my best for her."

"You will find her a rich husband."

"If that's what she wants. Or an ambitious one, or a kind one, but one who makes her happy—if such a thing can be achieved." I frowned up at Teddy. "And only *if* that's what she wants, when she's older, and *if* she wants our help. She may want to work. Some of our department heads are single women who have never wanted marriage." I shrugged. "Perhaps *that's* what Thea wants. Would you object?"

Teddy sighed, looking downward again. "I keep thinking about what Miss O'Dugan said about not giving the people we love snakes or scorpions for gifts. My heart is divided in twain, truth be told. I want my sister to be happy—if anything can make her happy, which sometimes I doubt—but I want her to make my parents proud too." He splayed long, bony fingers, the raw hand of a very young man, over his chest. "I want to do right by her, but I can't grasp what *right* is. I've always liked you, Mrs. Rutherford, and I was downright knocked over with gratitude when you promised to help us, but I'm unsure if I made the right choice after all."

Sympathy engulfed me as I looked at the young man—so very young and so keen to take up burdens of care and worry that were better suited to one twice his age. He was insulting me, if I cared to bristle at the insult—but I didn't. I smiled instead.

"Neither do I. After all, I'm only six years older than you. Don't forget that. But can't you trust my sincerity? Or Martin's at least?"

We both jumped as the ship's horn sounded, a massive wave of noise that startled a large group of seagulls from the roof of the deck house where the Ladies' Saloon was situated. From somewhere below us, a cheer arose, men's voices, followed by laughter and speech raised in a hubbub of comment.

"I wonder if that signifies land?" I stared at the horizon, one hand shielding my eyes from the diffuse glare of a half-hidden sun. "I can't see anything."

"We will soon. The seagulls mean land is near, I think. We'll see the coast of England—and then Liverpool, where we'll part ways." Teddy smiled suddenly, a genial expression that made him look like his father. "I will miss you, you know. I hope we separate as friends."

"Always." I held out my hand to Teddy, who grasped it briefly. "Sarah will be sad when you leave," I said. "She's so fond of you."

"And I of her. But we've had some pleasant talks this last week."

"Yes, you have. And thank you for playing with her on deck—watching you and Martin explain the rules of baseball to her and Miss Baker had me in stitches."

"She understands I have to work in England," Teddy said. "She talked about your work too—your studies under Mr. Worth—as if it was the most normal and expected thing on earth."

I shrugged. "When she was smaller, I had to toil to earn our living, like any woman does when she doesn't have a man to support her. She's more intrigued by Mr. Worth being a man in a woman's world—now *that* might be eye-opening to all of us."

28

NEW IDEAS

"*T*urn, please, madame." Worth smiled his tired smile. "I beg your pardon for addressing you so brusquely, but I wish to see every detail of your gown. Arlette Belvoix wrote to me about you at length, and I am intrigued."

I turned, aware of the drag of the gray ottoman skirt with its short, ruffled train. I had worn this ensemble because of the difficulty of draping the heavy silk and cotton cloth with its pronounced ribbing. I was sure I had cut it exceptionally well. The light would make the sheen of the gray fabric move like the waves on the sea, accentuated by the slight iridescence of the silk I had used for the ruffles. The black satin bodice, cut long in the cuirass style to descend in points below the hips, was heavily embroidered in grays, sea greens, and blues, with touches of mauve to pick up the multihued effect of the ruffles; a deep border of Indian silk added yet more richness. I had intended to wear a much lighter dress that day, but I was finding Paris cold for June. I didn't want to appear before the great Worth all pinched and chilly.

He was unprepossessing in his person, this Napoleon of

dressmakers. An ordinary-looking man of medium height and around fifty years of age, he would have disappeared into any crowd if it weren't for his outlandish mode of dress. He wore a flowing gown of almost Oriental appearance over a matching vest, a floppy cravat, and an equally limp velvet cap on his head. The cap, I rather imagined, was to hide a balding pate—but his mustache was thick and dark, and from beneath it came a rapid flow of British-accented syllables as he commented on every aspect of the gown I wore. He spoke in the efficient undertone of a man accustomed to working with women amid the overblown luxury of gilded carving and velvet draperies.

"Now bend, as if you are petting a small dog—yes, reach down. Straighten, and then walk on a little, turning to left and right as if you are greeting acquaintances."

I did as he asked, trying not to grin as my gaze met Martin's. My husband was reclining on a sofa ornamented with far too much gilt metal, his legs stretched out in front of him and his arms crossed. He said nothing, but his eyes were busy. I sensed him noting every detail of the room and was sure his impressions would be transferred to his notebook as soon as he had the chance.

I performed a few more movements at Worth's request until finally the designer beckoned me to approach him.

"You cut well, and you understand fabrics. And I hear that you have a good eye for what will suit a woman when you meet her. So Madame Arlette wishes me to spend an hour or two with you and pass on my secrets? They are no secrets at all, really. We will look at my prints and photographs and talk about the paintings you have seen, and you will tell me what details you notice and how you might bring them into a gown. You will show me your sketchbooks, and perhaps I'll borrow your secrets too. That's how it works, isn't it?" A puff of air blew out the thick mustache to indicate amusement.

"That's why I started selling my designs to other houses. They copied them anyway. We must cultivate originality, Mrs. Rutherford, if we are to be leaders, and I will show you the trick of it, for Arlette Belvoix's sake."

"I'm grateful—" I began.

"Bah! Don't be. My price is high; I will dress you as I wish, not as *you* wish. Having your own dresses made will teach you much, of course, and I will allow you to be privy to the process."

I turned to Martin in astonishment. Fool as I was, I hadn't once considered the possibility of purchasing Worth's dressmaking for myself. For one thing, I was used to dressing myself out of my own resources, and for another—well, I suppose I had been too nervous about meeting the man to actually *think*.

Martin's eyes crinkled in amusement at my expression, and then he turned to Worth. "Twenty?" he asked. "To start with anyway. I have to dress the rest of my family as well . . . and purchase some more trunks for the return voyage." His fair eyebrows rose toward his hairline, mocking me, and it was to me he next spoke. "I wouldn't be much of a robber baron if I didn't bring myself and my womenfolk back to America dressed from the skin out in the best Paris has to offer. You especially—I want the whole of Prairie Avenue to see you fresh from Paris."

I had the sense to hold my tongue but loosened it again when Martin had taken his leave of Worth and I was walking him to the door. Apparently, my measurements had to be taken before Worth and I continued my lessons.

"*Twenty* dresses?"

Martin cast a quick glance around the vestibule before answering. "Goose, did you really imagine he would instruct you for nothing? You're being allowed privileges normally reserved for royalty—or famous actresses. What you'll learn will pay for the dresses *and* the voyage to Europe and every blessed thing we buy. *And* raising Madame's salary beyond its already outrageous height." He gave me a swift kiss on the lips and stuck his hat on his head. "Don't forget to include some light and frothy summer gowns. Even this part of the world gets warm sometimes in the summer. There's your escort—my, one of the young Messieurs Worth again. How dreadfully *French* his sons are."

Martin headed rapidly in the direction of the doorway as I turned to smile at the young man advancing toward me. My nervousness had dissipated—true, I was struggling to remember the little French that Grandmama had taught me, and I was no doubt about to be made to feel like a complete novice, but I, Nell Lillington of Victory, Illinois, was in Paris with an unmatchable opportunity to improve my skills. And improve them I would.

"You walk as if you're barely touching the ground," remarked Martin a few days later as he escorted me along the corridors of the Grand Hôtel du Louvre. "I can't tell you how happy I am to see that worried, tired expression on your face replaced by interest and enthusiasm."

"I'm beginning to understand why Mrs. Parnell is always lamenting Chicago's lack of culture." I took a firmer grip on Martin's arm; the carpet was so deep I could have been walking on sand. "Look at what Paris offers compared to us, even without the Exhibition. And *that's* the most astonishing spectacle I've ever seen."

"Astonishing is too small a word." Martin was grinning like a boy; I wasn't the only one who'd found a new sense of enthusiasm. "The electric light—imagine being Sarah, born to such an era! And the flying machine."

"Which flew for about a minute," I remarked drily. "And we only have their assurance for that."

"And what about the latest sewing machines? American, of course, but we probably wouldn't have seen them for months. I must write to Singer. And if that statue of *Liberty Enlightening the World* ever gets to America, we should visit it."

"Tess and Sarah would insist. Do you realize Tess now has fifteen souvenirs with pictures of it?" I nodded my thanks at the uniformed boy who had just opened a door for us. "We'll need ten more trunks—none of us seem able to stop buying things."

A babble of voices met us as we paused at the top of the grand staircase. I could not distinguish words, so I listened to the sounds; the women's voices created tiny peaks of high notes amid the bass drone of the men, like so many birds chirping in the breeze. The bright colors of dinner dresses clashed and swirled among the black-suited men—like birds again, but in opposition to nature's habit of making the males brighter than the females.

Martin leaned against the banister, signaling his desire to delay our descent into the crowd, and inspected me with a slow sweep of his gaze. I couldn't help smiling; a new dress always brought a smile to a woman's face, and *this* dress was by Worth.

"You're glowing like a sunset." Martin's expression told me all I needed to hear. "I like you in those bright colors."

"I'd never have dared put this dress near my hair." I smoothed down the rich brocade of my dinner gown, deep orange flowers on a magenta background trimmed with antique lace and pale gold ribbon. "I've always preferred subtle hues because of my hair color, but studying those paintings—well, I've never seen so much red hair in my life, and so often next to pink, red, or orange. The Old Masters must have liked redheaded women."

"They have good taste. Seeing you alight like this makes me want to take you back to bed, but I suppose we *must* have dinner."

"Tess and Sarah must be down there somewhere," I said, leaning forward to get a better view and trying to ignore the surreptitious caress on my lower limbs, quite discernible through my narrow skirt. "We must have an early night. I want to spend the morning in the Louvre. *You* can take Tess and Sarah to the Exhibition again. It's most tiresome trying to observe and sketch when there are people *yawning* behind me."

"I only yawned *twice.*" Martin grinned sheepishly as I turned back to him. "But of course I'll take them. I want to spend an hour or two in the fabric halls and visit the Japanese and Chinese exhibits. Will you join us after luncheon? Sarah is wild to try the balloon ascent again."

"I'll stay with Tess on the ground and wave. You know she won't go up."

"I'm not against an early night." Martin spoke quietly as he moved past me, then touched my arm and waved to indicate that he'd spotted Sarah and Tess.

I waved in my turn, easily locating Sarah by her hair. Which was startlingly like the color of my dress, I mused as we moved forward. But all thought was suspended as I clutched the stair rail with one hand and Martin's arm with the other; negotiating steps needed great concentration when you had more than a yard of train to your dress, especially if you desired to move with elegance.

"I could stay here forever." Martin smiled sideways at me. "But we must travel to the coast and meet Madame's fashionable and intelligent friends, I suppose."

"They'll be interesting." I relaxed my grip as we reached

the bottom of the stairs, holding out a hand to Sarah, who had been wriggling her way through the crowd. I spotted Miss Baker's dark-clad form close behind, attracting little attention from the bright, fashionable guests. Tess, bringing up the rear, looked self-conscious, a little flustered. "I've noticed that every introduction Madame has arranged has had some benefit to the store behind it. So many people who seem to know everyone it is necessary to know. I sometimes wonder who Arlette Belvoix really is."

Absorbing as it was, our stay in Paris seemed to roll by with the speed of an advancing train. And it was in a train that we left the graceful city, doing as the French did in summer and seeking the cool of the seaside. It was not until then that Tess expressed the feeling I had seen growing in her looks, in the way she stood, somehow even in the way she breathed.

"I'm longing to be home again."

Tess looked up and sideways at me; the movement necessitated bending her neck rather far back because of her fashionable hat. We were promenading by the shore at Deauville and therefore dressed in our utmost best, which for both of us meant Worth.

One thing I had discovered about the French was that clothes truly *mattered* to them in a way they did not to Americans in general. Even the lowest Parisian *midinette*, as they called the shopgirls and seamstresses, seemed to spend an inordinate amount of effort on her toilette. The merest outing was an opportunity—not to be missed by any woman —to show herself at her best. We had risen to the occasion for our afternoon of sea air; my walking gown used stripes and lace in a startling combination that I was aching to try out myself, while Tess's dress was an eye-catching deep red with matching roses on her hat.

"You know *why* I wish I were home, Nell," Tess said after a brief hesitation.

"Of course I do. You want to see Donny again."

"I wish he could write better. Then he could write me back." We had all, including Sarah, enjoyed sending "letter cards," an ingenious innovation, from the Universal Exhibition. Tess had sent three to Donny.

"It would take weeks for any letter to reach you, especially since we keep moving from place to place. You'll just have to be patient, Tess."

I slowed my steps, realizing I had begun to walk a little too fast for my friend. The sea breeze—which lived up to its reputation for freshness, although I was not fond of the seaweed smell—tugged at my splendid hat, in black velvet to match my dress but feathered and ribboned in bright colors I would not have worn before Paris.

In the distance, I could spot Sarah running along the broad, sandy beach on which large waves were breaking in a monotonous fashion that was somehow quite mesmerizing. At least to me, who had never seen the sea before this summer, they were large waves. Our current hosts had laughed when I had commented on them, explaining that the sea was positively gentle this year and pointing out the huge banks of pebbles that storms had deposited in recent winters. Martin had made some remark about the height of the waves during a storm on the Atlantic but had fallen silent when he'd seen my face. He knew I was already nervous about setting off across the ocean in September. I'd never realized how *big* it was until our journey over, and America seemed a dreadfully long way off.

To our left rose buildings, set well back from the promenade but so large they formed an inescapable reminder of the delights of a modern resort. Grand hotels, a casino, a gallery of shops, and the huge, fanciful villas of the wealthy gave plenty of scope for the acquisitive and the merely curious. Yet the town was not crowded despite the splendid weather. The day before, our hostess—a delightful Frenchwoman married to an Austrian banker—had echoed the lament I had so often heard, "You should have seen it under the Empire." She had said it in her excellent English, but her words had been caught by an artist trying to capture the children at play on the August beach. He had relayed it in French to the various men standing around him; some of them spat quite disgustingly on the sand to show what they thought of the Empire. I gathered that France was now a republic, which seemed a far better way to proceed.

"It's mostly Donny," said Tess after a few moments of silence. "But I'd like to be back in America too, just because it's home. I can't understand anything people say here—and I'm *sure* they're talking about me."

I forbore from pointing out that people talked about Tess behind her back in America too and simply gave the hand that held my arm a sympathetic squeeze. I knew what she meant. She was a familiar enough sight in the stores along State Street and in our neighborhood that her arrival would elicit smiles and greetings from those who were acquainted with her. Here she was a stranger, and people were not always kind to strangers.

"The Von Friedensbergs think you're wonderful, and that's all that counts." I smiled down at her. "All the people Madame Belvoix introduced us to have liked you, including Mr. Worth. He was far merrier with you than he was with me."

"He *was* funny." Tess smiled. "But he's English, and I like English people almost as much as Americans, even if they can't speak our language properly. I miss Chicago, Nell. Don't you?"

"I miss . . . the store," I admitted. "Now, you see, you're laughing at me, and I suppose I deserve it for pining after work. But you've seen all the sketches I've done; I have so many new ideas that my head must be twice as large as when we left Chicago. I've sent the best to Madame, of course, and I hope she'll have turned at least some of them into gowns by the time we return."

"Martin's right. You're a hopeless case." Tess tried to purse her lips into a reproving expression, but it turned into a broad grin. "At least *he* knows how to enjoy himself without working. I don't suppose he'll leave that equestrian club until the evening." She waved her free hand toward the buildings in the distance; in one of them, presumably, Martin was talking horses. "Or he'll watch the horses racing or go for a ride or a long, *long* walk."

"While we teeter along a promenade." I sighed. Sometimes I envied Martin, and even Sarah, who had taken off her shoes and stockings to splash in the shallows. Miss Baker's slight, boyish figure was so close to the water that I wondered if she too was paddling. We all sea-bathed most mornings, but it involved such a rigmarole of struggling with hooks and eyes in a dark wooden hut that I occasionally wondered if it were worth the effort.

"Will you want to come to Europe again?" Tess asked suddenly, stopping so I too had to halt. She led the way to a green-painted bench before I had the time to answer, seating herself with a satisfied smile. "That's better. Look at Sary and Miss Baker! Mrs. Parnell says Miss Baker runs around like a hoyden, but Miss Baker says she'll be dignified when she's old. She told me she grew up in the country and climbed *lots* of trees."

"I don't imagine for a moment Martin will be satisfied

with just this one voyage." I shaded my eyes with my hand, squinting at the bright sea and trying to discern all the different colors in it. "Wouldn't it be nice to visit Italy? And Martin tells me the Alps are quite spectacular. I suppose it would be good for Sarah too, to see a little more of the world." I looked at Tess. "But don't worry, I'm never going to propose moving here or anything like that. I'm quite astonished by all the Americans we've met who say they're never going back to our country; what on earth do they imagine is wrong with it?"

Tess frowned. "I don't think I like traveling, not all that much. It's very hard to always see new things all the time. I'm glad I've seen Europe, but I don't want to cross the ocean again. I'm going to tell Sary I'm happier at home."

"I'm sure she knows already." I patted Tess's gloved hand —even our gloves were new from Paris. Elizabeth was going to be green with envy. "She told me you were homesick."

"She's very clever." Tess's eyes, magnified by her spectacles, were moist. "All I really want is a nice fire to sit by, a cozy chair, and people I love around me. I've thought very hard about how much I'd miss you if you went traveling without me, but perhaps I could invite Billy to stay and keep me company—if I had nobody else."

The downward turn of her lips told me more than she said. I was beginning to realize she was trying to come to terms with Donny's apparent lack of interest, but no amount of effort could make her less miserable.

"We won't travel often," I promised. "For one thing, Martin and I don't like being away from the store. And if you stay at home, we'll have all the more reason to hurry back, won't we? But Madame was right—I needed some diligent idleness. What I've seen in the last few weeks seems to have lit a fire inside me." I shrugged, my eyes on the tumbling waves. "I want . . . *something*. I'm not sure what it is. Not money; we have too much already. Nor fame." I laughed. "Could you imagine me wearing ridiculous clothes like Mr. Worth with my clients groveling for five minutes of my time?"

"Perhaps you want a store of your own," Tess suggested. "With Lillington & Co. over the door. Only you're Rutherford now." Her brow wrinkled. "But your dresses are Lillington dresses. From Rutherford's store. That's very strange."

"It's an idea." I looked up at the seagulls circling overhead, my mind busy. "But no, I don't think I want my own store. Certainly not a department store." And one day I would be the head of dressmaking at Rutherford's anyway—that was Madame's obvious intention. By that time, I hoped, I would have achieved what Madame called "true mastery."

"That's it." I smiled at Tess. "I want to be at the absolute top of my profession. An acknowledged expert. Like Madame."

"Does Madame ever *make* dresses?" Tess asked. "I've often wondered."

I blinked at her, surprised. "No more than Worth does, I imagine. She makes other people do the work, which gives her plenty of time to walk around and terrify the dressmaking staff." I frowned. "Come to think of it, perhaps she makes her own gowns at home occasionally. I've definitely seen her in confections I'm sure have never passed through our atelier."

"You don't make dresses anymore either." Tess looked down at her rose-red walking dress, kicking her small feet out experimentally so that the vertical pleats at the bottom of the underskirt spread themselves and then returned perfectly to where they were supposed to be. "You never finished Sary's dress, and I expect she's too big for it now."

I felt instantly guilty because Tess was entirely correct.

My feet had barely touched the ground for more than a year —far longer, in fact. Was it two years since Tess and I had sat companionably sewing together? I realized that because I hadn't been sewing, neither had Tess. When we had moved to the Palmer House, Sarah's summer dress had been packed in a box. It was probably still in that box, somewhere in the attic or the basement or wherever such things were stored in our grand new house. We had lived there for the best part of a year, yet I could not have told anyone what exactly was in the cupboards and closets.

"Supposing—supposing I took the whole of every Wednesday off instead of working in the morning and rushing home to make and receive calls?" I asked, after a few moments in which my mind raced and thrashed and somehow suddenly found itself in an entirely new place. "After all, we'll have that dratted telephone thing if Martin or anyone else absolutely *must* talk to me. We could sit and sew together all morning, have luncheon, and then change for making our calls."

Tess beamed, but the smile was as brief as a glimpse of sun through cloud. "Would you be doing that just for me, or for yourself?" she asked after a few moments' silence.

I hesitated, but I had to be truthful. "Well—partly for myself. I'm sure that's the wrong answer, but if Madame's right and I have to feed the artist in me, those peaceful times will help. I've realized most of my ideas come to me when I'm *not* working—or at least not surrounded by people and letters to write and things to sign." I sighed. "I'm sorry if that hurts your feelings, Tess. I'm sure you'd like me to be a better companion."

To my surprise, Tess seized my hand in hers and kissed it, laughing. "That's the *right* answer, silly. And if you can do something just for yourself, I can be a little selfish too. I don't want to pay calls, Nell. I'll come down and visit with some of the ladies when they come to our house—the ones I like—but I don't want to dress up and go out unless I feel like it. I've been doing it for your sake, but it's the least favorite thing I do." She turned her grasp on my hand into a handshake, grinning. "Like Martin says, do we have a deal, Mrs. Rutherford?"

"Good heavens." I stared at my friend. "I declare you just maneuvered me into a good many concessions."

"I don't know what maneuvered means," Tess said artlessly—but there was a gleam in her eyes that contradicted that assertion. "Don't you think it's time we went back to Villa Rosa? Sary will need a good wash, and we don't want to be late for tea."

RETURN

"As soon as we dock, I'm going to the White Star Line office for our mail." Martin grinned as he took off his hat in salute to a group of cheering men on a small packet steamer far below the deck on which we stood.

Ships and boats of all kinds thronged the harbor. Across the water was New York, its mass of buildings punctuated here and there by church steeples. Ahead of us was a green park dominated by the Emigrant Landing Depot, where we would stop first.

"It'll be busy, of course, so you needn't come with me. I'll see the four of you onto the hotel omnibus beforehand and make my own way later. I'll probably look up a couple of business acquaintances."

I winced and put a hand to my ear; Martin had spoken directly into it in rather a loud voice.

"Leaving me to make all the arrangements at the hotel, I suppose." I aimed a surreptitious poke at my husband's lean midriff and got a kiss on the cheek in return.

"Nonsense. It's the same suite at the Fifth Avenue, the same femme de chambre and everything. Stop pretending you can't cope. All a man has to do is to sit around and watch, and where's the fun in that? I've spent the crossing writing telegrams while you've been playing with Sarah, talking to Tess, and making sketches. An afternoon's freedom from the womenfolk is all I ask."

"Hmph."

But my pretended indignation was forgotten as I darted forward, not for the first time, to prevent Sarah from trying to climb the deck railing. Miss Baker did the same. We grinned at each other as our hands landed on Sarah's skinny shoulders at the same moment.

"But I want to see the poor people." Sarah looked over her shoulder at us.

"*Emigrants.*" Miss Baker firmly captured Sarah's hand and settled her straw boater back on her head. "They're not there as entertainment for little rich girls, Sarah."

"You'll see them when they put the gangways down." I added. "And then we're going to the Ladies' Saloon, or somewhere where there's some shade. It'll be at least an hour before we reach Pier Forty-Five." I put up my parasol with a snap; the scar by my ear was beginning to sting as it always did when I got too much sun.

A shudder ran through the ship, and an increase in shouting suggested the process of docking was taking place. The air smelled of salt and soot and people; there was very little breeze. Perhaps being at the hotel wouldn't be so bad. I would give the chambermaids instructions and then all the *womenfolk* could go find some refreshment in a nice cool parlor.

I didn't expect much mail as we'd received a large packet of letters when we'd arrived at the *Germanic*. Two from Elizabeth, mostly about baby Mabel; one from Teddy to inform us he was in Ireland and would prefer to defer his return to Chicago until the end of winter. Much correspondence for

Martin, all business; several notes from female acquaintances for me; and letters for Tess from various family members. Our normal life, waiting to envelop us once we set foot on American soil.

There had also been a dutiful but brief reply from Thea to the letter I had sent her. In between news of Mabel, Elizabeth had informed me that Thea had spent the summer working hard and had had a very smart dress made at cost in the store. She spent most of her working life in the jewelry department. This report had been corroborated by Madame, who had mentioned in one of her letters that Thea was doing nicely.

I closed my parasol and moved under the large black umbrella that Martin had opened above his own head. Miss Baker had one as well. A number of umbrellas had spread like mushrooms on the promenade deck as we watched the constant stream of people below us, herded by officials toward the imposing round building. Imagine them all having been on the ship, I thought, and we'd barely even seen them.

"All right?" Martin put out his free hand and drew me as close as our hats allowed.

"Too hot."

"Chicago will seem hotter, no doubt."

"Ah, but it's home, and that makes all the difference." A thrill ran through me as I anticipated seeing familiar streets and buildings again. "And I have such plans."

MARTIN DIDN'T ARRIVE AT THE HOTEL UNTIL NEARLY dinnertime. By then we were all cool and refreshed and comfortable in our surroundings, even Tess, who declared herself delighted to be back in an *American* hotel. Sarah had been at her most restful, passing the hours after luncheon reading *What Katy Did*, with some help from her grown-ups when she had difficulty with a word. She stopped many times to discuss the actions and words of the children in the book. I experienced a queer, aching sensation as I watched my child grapple with the notion of having brothers and sisters and friends and cousins and spending time in the company of children rather than adults. If I'd married Cousin Jack, we'd probably have six children by now, and Sarah would be the oldest, just like the Katy of the novel. But perhaps I'd have died, like Katy's mother; and I would have to be married to Jack if I didn't die. I was sure I wouldn't be as happy with Jack as I was with Martin.

Martin's arrival ended my reverie. His hot and dusty appearance and the strong smell of other men's cigar smoke clinging to his person made me glad I'd been relegated to the womanly, domestic role of settling into the Fifth Avenue. He drank coffee as he listened to Sarah's minute description of every feature of the hotel—which he knew well, having stayed there often—and sorted the letters into piles. Two for Tess, two for Miss Baker, three for me, and at least a dozen for Martin. This ceremony over, my lord and master declared he would have to wash and change quickly. He headed for our suite in the confident expectation that everything would be arranged just as he liked it.

Twenty minutes later, I put my head around the bathroom door, a prey to some degree of agitation.

"I'm not late, am I? I should get a shave." Martin's top half emerged from the steaming bathwater as I entered the room. He blinked at me from under the fringe of wet hair, which the water had turned pale yellow rather than his usual white blond, and fingered his chin. "It must be at least twelve hours since I saw a razor. I swear this day's gone on forever."

"You need to be quick. Listen, I have to tell you something."

"I've got plenty to tell you too. I met an importer who—"

"*Martin.*" I put my hand on his arm as he made to disappear under the water again, feeling damp heat, hard muscle, and the wet, smooth texture of the hairs on his forearm. "It's important."

"Well, it's nothing too dreadful or you wouldn't be so calm." Martin soaped his face vigorously and rinsed it before speaking. "Couldn't it wait till dinner?"

"No. Elizabeth wrote me that Thea appeared in a theatrical entertainment at the Jewel Box. Teddy is going to have conniptions when he finds out."

"What kind of entertainment?" Martin pushed his wet hair back from his forehead, tousling it charmingly. I wanted to kiss him, but this was not the time for distractions.

"A pictorial piece," I explained. "Scenes from Shakespeare."

"But Mrs. Furmann would never allow her out in the evenings to perform in a theater."

"That's just it. She doesn't live in the residence anymore. She moved out to a boardinghouse on Taylor Street. Elizabeth had no idea until Madame told her. And Madame found out some three weeks after the event because it was only then that Mrs. Furmann mentioned it to her. I had a letter from Madame too. She's not happy."

Martin hauled himself out of the bathtub so precipitously that water splashed onto the marble tiles. "I'll be having a word with Mrs. Furmann when I get back."

"I don't think you should be too hard on her." I sighed. "It seems Thea convinced her that Teddy had given his permission for the change. She conveyed the impression that Teddy is going to live there too when he returns. Since Teddy's letter was so recent and he didn't mention it, I don't believe that's the case. And don't forget that she's sixteen now, one of the older girls in that residence. She's always behaved with Mrs. Furmann as if butter wouldn't melt in her mouth. I suspect she just completely fooled the poor woman."

I followed Martin as he, having vigorously applied a towel to his person, stalked into our adjoining bedroom. He began to dress with a rapidity and precision that suggested a certain degree of temper.

"Apparently, the boardinghouse is very respectable," I said to placate him. "And the theatrical piece in question was of the mildest sort. Elizabeth found out because one of the older ladies on that committee her mother has had her join— the one that's a breeding ground for future causes and the women to run them—told her that her own daughter was in the performance. I know that woman. She wouldn't let any child of hers be in anything that might reflect badly on her family."

Martin, halfway through donning his socks and garters, stopped and glared at me. "Is Miss Thea still working at Rutherford's?"

"Of course she is."

"Well then, you can stop making excuses for her." Martin reached for his trousers. "No shopgirl at Rutherford's can be an actress. I'll write to Joe and tell him to terminate Thea's employment immediately."

The warm day suddenly became chilly. "You'll *fire* her? You can't just do that—"

"Yes, I can. She's given us ample cause."

"But what will she do?"

"Go back to Teddy, of course. Or come back to us."

"But Teddy's planning to stay in Europe until sailings start up again in April."

"There's still time to recall him back to Chicago. As you

pointed out, he'll be fit to be tied, but there's nothing for it. He's the head of the family. Or, as I said, she comes to us."

"But—but—she hates living with us, and you said yourself —she was ruining our lives."

"You should have thought of that before, shouldn't you?" Martin crossed to the mirror, fastening his collar and tying his cravat with swift, expert movements before grabbing his hairbrush and the bottle of hair oil. "When you promised to do everything you could for them."

Indignation rendered me speechless for a few moments, and Martin had donned his evening pumps and cufflinks before I finally exploded.

"You're being unfair. *You* were the one that offered them a place in our home."

"Because *you* wanted it. And moderate your voice; we're in a hotel. I'm going to get a shave."

A CLEAN CHIN AND AN EXCELLENT DINNER DID MUCH TO CALM Martin's ire, although I sometimes caught him looking at me with an exasperated expression that suggested he was still somehow blaming *me* for the entire mess. I did my best to be the perfect wife and mother during the meal, ensuring that everyone had a generous portion of their favorite foods and that the conversation was bright and breezy, but all the while my mind was busy.

Traveling is a tiring business. By nine o'clock, even Miss Baker was ready to say good night and retire to her own chamber. Sarah and Tess had long gone to bed; the open window, fitted with screens against the night insects, brought in the sounds of passing carriages as Martin and I settled down in the parlor.

"Well?" Martin asked after we had spent a few minutes

indulging in the mundane chatter that married persons often use as a prelude to a healthy argument. "We didn't come to a conclusion about Thea."

"I thought *you had*," I said rather testily. "You're the senior partner at Rutherford's, so I don't suppose I can prevent you from firing her."

"But you'd rather I didn't."

"The idea makes my blood run cold," I admitted. "Thea working at the store was the perfect solution. Gainfully employed and out of everyone's hair but still under our supervision. If you give her the sack, might that not push her into Victor Canavan's arms? I've told you what I heard him say to her when we found her at the Jewel Box. The implication was clear that she'd asked him if he had a place in his theater for her. He was too sensible to make her any kind of offer—and I imagine he'd be even more reluctant to do so now he's a client of mine—but if you write to Joe and he fires her before we get back, I'm willing to bet Canavan's the first person she turns to. He seems to have a sympathetic nature; could he resist Thea if she's destitute? By the time we reach Chicago, she'll probably be a fully fledged actress."

Martin sighed heavily. "I see your point. She chose her moment carefully, didn't she? Perhaps I should wire Teddy and tell him to make his way to Liverpool at his earliest convenience. The steward on the *Germanic* told me they're planning November and December sailings this year. We might get him home for Christmas even if he misses the October embarkation."

"So do we wait to fire her till then? Months after the event? Or if we fire her as soon as we get back, what do you propose we do with her in the interval? Lock her in our house till Teddy gets back?"

Martin made a stifled sound of frustration, raising both fists to the ceiling like a man in manacles pleading for freedom. "How can one sixteen-year-old girl possibly be so much *trouble*?"

Our eyes met, and it was I who gave way first. Within moments, we were both wiping away tears of laughter.

"Heaven has revenged itself on me thoroughly," I said when I stopped gasping with mirth. "But what I did was far worse." I sobered, not seeing the luxurious hotel room, but the sun's hot rays through the gaps in a curtain of willow leaves. "I was so entirely heedless. I never even imagined the trouble I might cause for myself—for everyone. I just wanted to do what I wanted to do, and I considered that at sixteen I was quite old enough to make my own decisions. Now it shocks me I could have been so reckless."

"It's a reckless age." Martin dug his fingers into his hair, seeming to tear at it, and then spoke suddenly.

"When I was sixteen, I decided I was old enough to drink whiskey. I didn't like it one bit, but I was angry at the world. I thought this was a man's way of dealing with my anger, so I drank most of the bottle. The doctor said I could have died. Father whipped me raw the moment I was well enough to stand and informed me it was only Mother who stopped him from teaching me what a *real* beating felt like." His mouth twisted. "He waited two more years for the latter lesson."

I stared at him in astonishment. "You never told me that."

"No, well, I've always been ashamed of that day. Taught me to dislike liquor at least."

"You know, I was convinced *you* were the sensible one."

Martin smiled, his expression so tender that it lit a spark of joy in me. "It's the advantage of being so much older. I had more or less reached the age of reason before you were old enough to take notice of what I got up to. And I wasn't at all sensible when I passed up the opportunity to insist you marry me just because your particular brand of recklessness had visible consequences."

The warmth in Martin's eyes stoked a flame that prompted me to close the space between us and settle comfortably on his knees. The ensuing demonstrations of marital affection almost made me forget what we'd been arguing about, but Martin's threat to give Thea the sack had rattled me badly, and I knew I had to press my advantage.

"About Thea," I began after an interval.

Martin groaned. "And I hoped this evening was going to end so pleasantly."

"It will." I reinforced the promise with a kiss. "I just want you to swear to me we'll assess the situation first—together. That whatever we do, we'll do it as . . . well, as partners. Neither of us will go around dashing off letters to Joe about firing Thea until we've talked to her. And no writing to Teddy either. He'll be miserable if he has to come back to Chicago instead of spending the winter ministering to the poor of Ireland or whatever it is he's doing. To be honest, I'm worried he'll end up dragging the child back to Kansas and marrying her off to some rancher."

"Mmmm." Martin was clearly beginning to lose interest in the Lombardi children, but he did his best to rally. "We can hardly hide the fact from Teddy that his sister's doing precisely what he, and his parents, would regard as immoral."

"Teddy would regard more than half of Chicago society as immoral."

"And he'd be right. Darn it, Nell, stop using your womanly wiles to get your own way. You're far too good at it."

"I just want us to give Thea a fair hearing before we act. We could still write to Teddy—in time for him to be on the November sailing if necessary."

"All right. Now we are going to stop talking about anybody else but us until tomorrow morning."

30

CHARITY

$\mathcal{I}$ had purchased no end of fripperies and furbelows for Thea while we were in Paris. She had declined our earlier offer of a dress allowance, explaining that she feared it would cause trouble with the other girls, but I was convinced no miss of sixteen could resist the allure of a Parisian hat. So I'd bought two funnel-shaped creations in the very latest style, with the matching jabots that were currently all the rage. I'd had them packed in the prettiest of boxes. It would not be easy tackling Thea about the theater, but surely a hat or two would calm the storm.

I could hear Martin's voice in the corridor outside my office; he had undertaken to escort Thea to the fourth floor. We had decided that talking to Thea during working hours would be much easier than visiting her at her boardinghouse or summoning her to Calumet Avenue. I curled my fingers into my palms, trying to gauge Thea's mood from her brief replies to Martin's jovial—overly jovial—remarks.

"Here she is," Martin said unnecessarily. He pulled out a chair for Thea and seated himself, as was his wont, on the corner of my desk, facing her.

"I'm happy to see you, Thea." I was determined to *be* happy to see her. Why should I be nervous about a sixteen-year-old girl? "Have you been well?"

I had not yet lowered the awning above my window. The bright sun of a fine September morning intensified the golden center of Thea's eyes and brightened the glossy sheen on her thick auburn hair. The Rutherford's uniform of dark gray with touches of peacock blue seemed to have been designed especially for her. She was so nicely proportioned that almost any well-made gown would look marvelous on her.

"I'm quite well, thank you, Mrs. Rutherford," Thea replied formally. The poise that had been lacking when she arrived in Chicago was now abundantly at her disposal; the Kansas air that had clung around her had vanished like the dew on the prairie. Her features were entirely under her control; a woman of thirty would not have done better.

I drew breath to speak, but Thea forestalled me.

"I suppose you want to talk to me about living out?" She sounded calm, composed, as if we were discussing a minor matter.

I was taken aback. "Well, first I just wanted to find out how you were doing and give you a few little things I bought for you in Paris." I waved my hand at the packages stacked in front of my desk. "I'll have one of our delivery drays drop them off at your—your address."

I had been going to say, "your home," but those words implied a degree of acceptance I was not sure I was able to offer. "Peek inside the two hatboxes," I suggested with a smile. "The rest are just some small things I imagined you would like, and there are some items of lingerie you might not want to inspect in front of Martin." I grinned. "All suited to your age, of course."

I held my breath as Thea lifted the lids of the two hatboxes and inspected the pretty articles within. Would she throw them back at me with some stinging remark? But she showed neither excitement nor disdain, looking up at us after a moment with a pleasant smile.

"How nice of you. I'll be the envy of my friends."

I let the air out of my lungs slowly, unwilling to betray how nervous I'd been. I sensed Martin glance at me and knew we were thinking the same thing. Neither of us imagined for a second that her pleasure was genuine, but we were happy to take her reaction at face value.

Thea replaced the lids of the hatboxes and straightened in her seat. "Thank you. Shall we talk about the boardinghouse now?"

"And the unexpected news that you took part in a theatrical performance," said Martin. "We've refrained so far from writing to Teddy about it, but he must be told."

Now Thea smiled an authentic smile, her eyes seeking Martin's in a carefree manner. "Oh, Teddy will be as hot as a kettle on the boil until he understands it was all in such a good cause. It came up quite suddenly, otherwise I'd have written to him myself to ask his permission."

The highly unladylike retort "in a pig's eye" hovered on my lips and I didn't dare look at Martin. "What cause?" I asked instead.

"Why, raising money to help the wives and children of the men who died in the riots last year." Thea's face was the picture of saintly innocence. "There've been private *tableaux vivants* at the houses of some of the best families in Chicago to raise funds, but Mr. Canavan thought it would be a fine thing if he put on a piece at the Jewel Box to attract respectable folk who might not be able to attend a high-society function. He has many friends, you understand, from all walks of life—such generous and true-hearted people. Mr. Canavan is a very compassionate man."

"But why you?" I asked. "Mr. Canavan has actresses enough, in my opinion."

"He had a doubt that it might seem too commercial if he simply cast his ladies in the piece." Thea fluttered her long eyelashes. "He invited four young ladies to play the *ingénue* parts." She pronounced the French word well. "The other three were the daughters of friends of his, awfully nice girls. Mr. Canavan said we brought a freshness to the venture that made it more likely people would give generously to the cause." She glanced up at Martin. "It was a scene from Shakespeare. I played Portia, discussing her suitors with her maid —of course we didn't speak, but it was *such* fun. We raised ever so much money."

"Were you chaperoned?" Martin asked, frowning.

"Of *course*. Dulcie Hignett's mama looked after us, and Mr. Canavan hired a cab to take us home after the performances."

"There were more than one?" I asked, surprised. Clearly, Elizabeth and Madame Belvoix didn't know the half of it.

"Five." Genuine delight flitted across Thea's carefully schooled face. "And I was never tired at work; ask any of the senior staff if I seemed sleepy. I have so little amusement in my life that this tiny chance to do something different was like a tonic to me."

She looked me straight in the eyes. "I declare I've done nothing that would bring a blush to my cheek or shame to my family, Mrs. Rutherford. I'm certain Mamma and Pa would have been proud of me for helping to provide food, clean clothes, and doctors and I don't know what else to those poor widows and children. I don't think even Pa would have objected once he'd known all the circumstances. Oh, Teddy will moan, but he's such a stick-in-the-mud these days. I don't see how one person in a thousand could even pretend to be as upright as he considers himself. It's so *dull* and quite unnatural."

"Your denomination disagrees with any kind of theatrical performance." I privately agreed with Thea about Teddy, but I had to put his case to her. "We shouldn't have taken you to the Jewel Box at all, but it seemed unfair to leave you out of a respectable outing to the theater. I'm afraid Teddy would consider actually being on stage a step too far."

Martin cleared his throat. "I was going to tell you that being on the stage was incompatible with the standards we impose on our shopgirls," he began. "But I'd never imagined a charitable *tableau*. I'm a little ashamed for not devising a way to raise funds myself. I must give the matter some thought."

"As for living out, would you care to inspect the boardinghouse?" Thea turned the full force of her eyes on us, her expression beseeching. "It was a tremendous stroke of luck that I happened to find it. I can't tell you how charming it is to be in a smaller house with just three couples and two single ladies. The residence is very pleasant, but there were so many girls, and some of the other sixteen-year-old young ladies had moved out, so I was one of the older ones. All those younger girls jabbering and competing with each other as to dresses and ribbons and which young gentleman looked their way at the store. Apprentices, while I'm already a proper shopgirl. They seem like such *juveniles* to me." She shrugged, a pretty movement that accentuated the finely wrought shape of her slim shoulders. "Perhaps my experiences in Kansas have made me old beyond my years. I prefer the company of steadier heads."

Actress, I thought. *She's playing a part.* Several feet above me, Martin looked down his large nose at Thea in a way that chimed in perfectly with my thoughts. *Well, at least he's not fooled by her.*

"We still must write Teddy about the changes you've made," I said. "After all, he's convinced he should be the one to decide what you do."

"And isn't that ridiculous?" Again, Thea looked directly at me. "Teddy is a mere two years older than I am. I'm a young woman, not a child, a *working* woman. Haven't I shown myself capable of making sensible decisions?"

Judge not, that ye be not judged. I shifted a little uncomfortably in my seat. Did I have the right to sit in judgment over Thea? Did Martin? We had both done foolish things. Had Thea done anything truly foolish? And she had suffered so much loss. I didn't see how we could insist on her returning to the residence. As for giving her the sack . . .

"Our letter won't reach Teddy for several weeks." I looked up at Martin, uncertain. There was no reason to send a wire —drag Teddy away from his own escape from drudgery. We were surely capable of keeping an eye on Thea now we were back.

"And in the meantime, may I please stay in the boarding-house?" Thea raised imploring eyes to Martin. "It would mean so much to me."

"I must inspect it." Martin had that unreadable expression on his face.

"Of course." Thea smiled sweetly. "You should both come meet Mrs. Batham. Mrs. Easter Batham—her papa was a Methodist minister. You'll see you have nothing to worry about."

"Mrs. Batham seems like a rather unworldly lady for a boardinghouse owner," Martin said after the visit.

"Hmmm." I waited as Capell opened the door of the

landau and let down the steps. "I suppose you're right, but I liked her. She had eyes just the color of Mama's."

"Yes, I noticed the resemblance too." Martin followed me into the carriage and settled into the bench next to me with a contented sigh. "I thought it somewhat colored your opinion of her."

"The boardinghouse was so clean and prettily appointed," I said defensively. "And the other boarders—those we met, anyhow—seemed like worthy people."

"If a little dull." Martin's grin was touched with cynicism.

"Worthy people are often dull. I feared I would scream if Mrs. Batham mentioned her dear late husband or her darling spinster daughter one more time. You know, if you're going to write Teddy, I will enclose a note."

"Singing the praises of Mrs. B? You're far too transparent, Nell. You're determined to be on Thea's side."

"In this case, yes." I settled the carriage rug more firmly over our knees; the evenings were becoming cool, a sure sign fall was on its way. "I honestly can't see she's done anything really wrong since Thanksgiving, and that's ten months. Yes, she's enamored of the stage, but girls so often are. Half the girls of my acquaintance in Victory indulged in amateur theatricals of some kind or the other. We have to be quite careful to reassure Teddy that there's no cause for alarm."

"From the point of view of worldly people like us."

"I shouldn't have told you Teddy said that. Not that I see anything wrong with being worldly. The pastor was sure he had to follow God's calling to the utmost, whatever the sacrifice, and remember how that ended. If being worldly means not being a martyr—not forcing your family to be martyrs—then I'm all in favor of worldliness. I dread the idea of Teddy pushing Thea into a life she hates."

"Do you really view marriage as a cage?"

"With anybody but you, it might have been."

"I'm flattered, my dear, but you *were* contemplating marriage to the execrable Poulton—for the sake of respectability."

"I would never have gone through with it."

Martin stared at my face for a moment, and a blush rose to my cheeks. I turned my head away. If Martin had not come to the Eternal Life Seminary when he did—

"Well, Nellie, I won't pursue that argument." Martin spoke softly, and when I turned back to him, he took my gloved hand and kissed my fingertips.

"Thank you," I said fervently. "I really do think you are the only man in existence who would truly allow me to be *me*, if you understand what I mean. And it's quite possible that in five years—or seven or ten—Thea will be the sort of woman for whom matrimony is not only conceivable, it's a happy expedient. She's so *young*. Perhaps my rebelliousness was caused by Mama's project to see me settled at an early age, with a declared fiancé if not a husband. I know she was sure she had my best interests at heart, but," I felt my shoulders slump, "being the stubborn person I was—am—I declare it had the opposite effect."

"So you propose to catch this particular fly with the sugar of freedom rather than the vinegar of constraint."

"Something like that." I couldn't help letting a grin escape at Martin's words, but then I sobered. "Mama probably guessed that her time on this earth was short. It was a blessing she lived to know her granddaughter, even under such inauspicious circumstances. Catherine didn't get that blessing." A lump rose in my throat at the thought.

"Ah, Nellie." Martin felt under the rug for my hand, which I'd slipped under it for warmth. "Your emotions are well and truly involved, aren't they?" His large hand enclosed mine. "You couldn't be impartial if you wanted to. I intend to just state the facts to Teddy and leave the decision to him, as the man of the family—but I hope he decides to let the matter rest. I agree Thea has done nothing wrong, in my eyes at least. Perhaps stepped a little off the path Teddy would prefer, but at her age we might expect a lot worse. Maybe this is the point at which we must begin to trust her."

31

GAME OF LIFE

"Thea wins again!" Sarah, as good-natured about losing games as I had been, watched as the teetotum stopped spinning and Thea advanced her Checkered Game of Life counter to "Happy Old Age." She turned to me with a smile. "May I be excused, Mama? I'd like to read my new book."

I nodded, and Sarah slid down from her seat, more slowly than she'd used to. Now that she was nearly eight, her skirts reached well below her knee. She skipped away neatly, festive in her gray-blue silk and plaid trimmings; the red cravat I'd added and her red stockings made a striking contrast with her hair, but I was learning to be more daring regarding colors.

"Would you like a little cherry cordial, Thea?" I lifted the tiny jug in invitation; it had been placed there by Beatrice just moments before, and by some miracle Sarah had been too full to beg for some of the dainty cookies that accompanied it. Either that or she had her eye on some better sweetmeat.

But it was Christmas, and so far it had been a remarkably

harmonious one. The only jarring note was that when Tess had learned that Thea would be present, she had decided to visit her parents for Christmas. She would return for our evening meal once Thea had left for home.

"A mere drop, please, Mrs. Rutherford. Oh, that's quite enough." Thea held up a slim hand as the level of the amber liquid in the crystal glass reached an inch. "Miss Dardenne says that a lady should imbibe the smallest amount compatible with politeness."

"Does she now?" I said, filling my own tiny glass with one-and-a-quarter inches of the sweet mixture. It was one of the few forms of alcohol I enjoyed; Grandmama and Mama had always served cordial on special occasions. "Well, I quite agree. It doesn't become a woman to drink."

Martin made a face. "Better nothing at all than that nasty sickly stuff. You women."

"I'd ring for whiskey, only I'm sure you won't want it in mixed company." I handed Thea her glass, explaining, "Martin will take a whiskey when he's in the company of other men. He makes it last for hours."

"You seem to think a lot of Miss Dardenne's advice." Martin regarded Thea as she sipped her cordial. "Do you spend much time with her?"

"She visits me sometimes when I have a free afternoon or evening." Thea sounded carefree. "It's nice of her to take an interest. She's so sophisticated."

That's what I'm afraid of was written right across Martin's face, but he merely said, "She's much older than you."

"Oh yes." Thea nibbled on one of the almond-flavored cookies. "She's almost thirty. But I do *like* mature women when they're sympathetic, and Miss Dardenne is so unaffected—she has the heart of someone much younger. I enjoy having a woman friend who never patronizes me for being young and yet who is a real woman, not a girl."

Elizabeth had told me that Paulina Dardenne was Victor Canavan's mistress. Even to my "worldly" ears, this did not seem like a proper friendship for a young girl. I looked at Martin, uncertain.

"I expect Teddy would think it most improper for me to be friends with an actress," Thea said airily. "But we're not *intimate*. We just sit in Mrs. Batham's parlor, and Mrs. Batham sits with us and knits while we talk. She says it must do Miss Dardenne good to be in *wholesome* company for a change."

Her gaze rested on us, her eyes lambent. "I suspect Miss Dardenne may be a sinner. Like so many of the women Mamma invited into our parlor in Kansas to talk and drink coffee. Mamma always said we mustn't shun sinners; first because we are all sinners ourselves: 'All have sinned, and come short of the glory of God.' And then because if we turn our backs on the sinners among us, who will lift them out of their sin? Our Lord went among sinners all the time."

I looked closely at Thea, wondering if I could detect the sly looks of the hypocrite or the crafty smile of the casuist. But her face was smooth, perfect, glorious in its youth and beauty.

"And Mr. Canavan?" I couldn't help asking. "Does he visit you too?"

"Oh *no*." Thea sounded shocked. "Mrs. Batham would never allow a gentleman to call. I only ever encounter Mr. Canavan at the store. He often stops for a minute or two at the jewelry counter to inspect a new item. He buys pieces frequently; you must know that."

Martin nodded. "He appears to be a connoisseur," he said to me. "A collector, even. He told me he sometimes lends a nice piece to one of his actresses for a particular part, although he often has to resort to paste when the character in question is supposed to be wearing something quite spectacular. Not that good paste is cheap. We have some paste diamond necklaces that look most convincing and are surprisingly expensive."

"Of course, when Mr. Canavan stops by, he says hello," Thea continued. "He's kind to me."

It occurred to me that Thea was being unusually forthcoming. Perhaps it was the cordial, in which case Miss Dardenne would be quite correct about avoiding it. I took another small sip from my own glass.

"He had me try on a pendant on Friday and bought it for Miss Dardenne," Thea continued. "Mr. Canavan thinks I am quite the best frame for seeing jewels as they should be seen, gracing a woman. Mr. McCombs agreed. He was pleased to make the sale as it was a costly piece, with a large garnet and a freshwater pearl drop."

"I remember that." Martin nodded. "Yes, a *very* pretty present for Miss Dardenne." His gaze flicked to me in sardonic amusement. "I had that one in mind for you and was disappointed to find it was gone."

I fingered my Christmas gift, a crystal pendant inlaid with diamonds and rubies. "I don't suppose I lost out." I noticed the corners of Martin's eyes crinkle and knew I hadn't.

"So really, I did what a house model does—I showed the merchandise to best advantage, and it made the sale." Thea sniffed. "I don't see how there could possibly be anything wrong in that. I've seen the house models working sometimes when I've been asked to take up a bracelet or earbobs or something to the fitting rooms, and they look entirely respectable."

"They are." I smiled. "I admit I was a little reluctant at first, but I concede that seeing the dresses on a real woman instead of a dress form has a favorable effect on our customers. And when I saw the way the House of Worth uses its models, I was quite convinced they were a good idea."

"I didn't think we'd get through the entire Christmas day without talking shop." Martin grinned. "So let me just adduce in evidence the increase in sales since Nell designed dresses for the Jewel Box. That is a fine example of how seeing a dress on another woman arouses the acquisitive instinct in the female of the species." His grin widened. "I'm looking forward to each new production."

"So you see, Teddy is quite wrong. He's trying to decide for me based on something he knows nothing about." Thea pouted prettily; however serious the sentiments that prompted her to speak were, her tone was lighthearted. "I hope that by the time he returns he will have to admit how *sensible* I've been and stop making a silly fuss."

PART III
1879

32

INNOVATION

February 1879

       Since returning to Chicago in September, I had lightened the burden of work a little. I now took the whole of Wednesday, and often Saturday afternoon, for myself and my family. I was making some of Sarah's dresses, and I'd begun one for Tess.

It felt good to hold a needle in my hand again, to bend over a sewing machine with the absolute concentration required to sew a seam correctly. I even resumed the long-neglected hobby of fabricating delicate handkerchiefs embroidered with lacy motifs. I took the occasional lesson from an embroiderer at the store to improve my skills.

To make this extra time, I hired a secretary to help with my correspondence and administrative tasks. I now found it much easier to find the paper I needed when I needed it. Mr. Pyle always seemed to remember where things were, which saved me a great deal of searching—and I never again forgot to send a letter.

And yet the days flew by as fast as ever, with few opportunities to be a lady of leisure. I was tired again—not as badly as before, but I found myself seeking my bed earlier in the dark winter evenings. Madame had not yet noticed, which was a blessing, and my dresses seemed more sought-after by the belles of Chicago than before.

Which made Madame ambitious, apparently. With eighteen house models now at her disposal, she often asked me for new designs, especially as January became February and we began to plan for summer.

"What do you think of this?"

I held the drawing that was my morning's work as close to the atelier window as possible, searching for the best light. A vain search; it was only two o'clock in the afternoon, but a February snowstorm had blown in to cast an odd, grayish tint over the world outside our windows. Behind me, I heard the faint pops of the gasoliers being lit and murmured imprecations about the poor light from the women engaged in cutting pattern pieces. A sudden gust of wind drove a renewed flurry of snowflakes against the glass, where they melted into icy streaks and dripped sullenly downward.

"Ah, the V-shaped bodice is a nice touch." Madame ran a small, sharp fingernail over the center of the sketch, careful not to smudge the lines. "It allows you to suggest *les paniers*. The eighteenth century was a far more *élégant* time than our own."

"It's a tiny suggestion of the last century." I grinned. "I'd hate to see wide skirts come back. If the bustle returns—I know you think it will—I could reconcile myself to it because at least we can get through a doorway facing forward. Of course, a ball gown like this will give the poor woman two yards of train to worry about. I will put the loop for holding the train *there*." I indicated a spot.

"Hmmm." Madame was only half listening, tapping her lips with a finger as she stared at the whirling snow. "Do you know," she said, narrowing her eyes, "we should hold a ball."

"We? Who?" I asked, startled.

But Madame did not appear to hear my interruption. "The snowflakes, they put me in mind of young girls in white dresses, *n'est-ce pas*? What if our house models could dance?"

"*Can* they dance?"

"I have never inquired." Madame frowned. "That was remiss of me. I find some of them a little *wooden*."

"They're supposed to look dignified, aren't they?"

"A ball gown is made for *movement*." Madame's eyes, usually so sharp, held a dreamy expression. "You have given me four ball gowns—*enfin*, four ideas that could be adapted in many ways. You can doubtless produce more. I picture perhaps ten ladies of different ages, say six ingénues and four older women, so as not to neglect the possibility of sales to the women of thirty or forty. I see musicians, nothing too extravagant, of course." She waved a small hand in a dismissive gesture. "A pianoforte, a violin. Let this not be just for the elite."

"But not *too* rowdy a dance." I grinned. "Although a nice lively polka would show off flounces." I was catching my mentor's enthusiasm, seeing a froth of pale colors—for the summer season, of course—the dancers whirling, the women's trains held clear of the floor, their small feet hardly touching the parquet—

"A demonstration ball in the store," I mused. "Using the house models."

"Precisely." Madame smiled. "The Rose Room has a good floor, does it not?"

"Well, yes. Martin meant it as a place to hold receptions if we should ever need it, and the floor is polished wood. If we took up the carpets . . ."

Madame turned to me and positively beamed. "You catch my vision, do you not? A true innovation—far more useful than the machines of which our gentlemen are so very enamored."

I compressed my mouth to stop myself from grinning. I had made my peace with the stock ticker and the telephone, although the shrill bell of the latter and the monotonous clacking of the former set my teeth on edge and made me glad my office was at the end of the corridor, far away from Martin's. Progress was progress. But Madame's feelings were stronger and more vehement; she hated the machines with a passion.

"I see merit in the idea," I said. "You must rehearse well, of course—and I must work on some more ball gowns."

"First, I must ask whether any of the house models can dance, and I need to recruit some gentlemen." Madame's forehead creased in consternation. "That may not be so easy."

"And ask Martin and Joe if they agree, perhaps?" I suggested.

"Hmph." A conscious expression stole over Madame's face. I knew her well enough by now to guess she had not intended to consult Martin or Joe until her project was so far advanced it would be hard to halt. Now I had mentioned the need for consultation, she had lost that advantage.

"I'll speak to them," I said and saw my mentor's expression lighten. "After all, I'm a partner, and I agree your idea is worth considering. When would we hold this demonstration? It would have to be quite early in spring, I imagine, to fill our order books for the summer balls."

"April." Madame's steely eyes held an avid gleam. "We will need time for rehearsals and for the confection of the gowns. Everything must be perfect."

A BALL WOULD NOT BE COMPLETE WITHOUT JEWELS, AND THAT was why only a month passed before I was standing with Joe in the store's safe room.

"I hadn't realized we carried quite so much jewelry," I confessed as I looked around me. "Is there something in every one of those drawers?"

"Those are all empty. Room for expansion." Joe waved his hand at the bank of cabinets on one side of the vault.

Each drawer and cupboard was numbered, the cards bearing the black-lettered designation sitting inside a brass card holder that formed part of the drawer pull. The room was about the size of a small parlor. Other than the banks of cabinets, whose brass fittings gleamed in the flare from two gaslights of plain glass, it held only a long table and two chairs. On the table sat a ledger, an inkstand with inkwell, a bottle of ink, three pens, and a lamp.

We had entered the room at eight o'clock in the morning, after the employees from the jewelry department had taken perhaps twenty items up to the sales floor under the eyes of two uniformed watchmen. Thea had been among them. Through the bars of the internal door drawn across the doorway while the massive vault door was open, I had seen her write the numbers one of the male employees called out in the ledger, which the senior assistant then signed. She had demurely followed the small procession of men, each carrying a stack of the shallow drawers, out of the safe room, and Joe and I had entered it in our turn.

"We're pretty circumspect about what we take out each morning given the number of burglaries that have taken place in other stores over the last few months." Joe pulled the inner door across the opening and locked it from the inside.

"But supposing a customer wants to view a wide range of pieces?" I asked.

Joe shrugged. "We're not a jewelry store. We sell our

pieces mainly as an adjunct to a gown, as you well know. We limit our choice to the customer deliberately; and the kind of prospect who wishes to buy this sort of jewelry rarely quibbles about prices." His thin face split in a grin. "Our expertise brings them to us. Of course, we get casual buyers—mostly men, some women—who like to stop by the department to check what we're displaying on any given day. It's surprising how the idea that the piece could disappear back into this room for days, even weeks, focuses their mind on a purchase."

"Rarity value." I nodded.

"*You* can only peruse our entire stock because you're a partner and because I'm with you. If anybody robs the jewelry department at gunpoint, they will get away with relatively little—still a fortune in the eyes of all but the very rich, but nothing that'll break us. Now, emeralds, you say? They'd be over here."

I flipped open the book as I moved toward Joe, seeing only dates and numbers. "Isn't there a list of all the pieces?"

"Elsewhere in the store, under lock and key." Joe began removing drawers and laying them on the other end of the table. "Be careful to replace each item before you pick up the next one—I'm not as familiar with the numbering system as the jewelry staff. I don't want to get into trouble for mixing things up. There, these are all the emerald necklaces we have at present."

I surveyed the velvet-lined drawers. "That," I said, pointing to a circle of square-cut emeralds within circular diamonds.

Joe looked. "Trust you to choose the expensive piece." The lines bracketing his mouth deepened into a smile as he unhooked the necklace from the pins holding it straight and handed it to me. It was surprisingly heavy. "Each of those stones is worth more than I could expect to earn in a year.

The diamonds are nothing compared to them, although they're costly jewels in themselves. We must take out extra insurance if you intend to use *that* one."

"It has the right look." I gave the necklace back to Joe. "I must make some alterations because of the diamonds, but I think the idea I've just had will enhance the design."

Joe was replacing the necklace so it sat perfectly on its black velvet setting. "The way you *see* things is quite remarkable," he said. "You never hesitate."

"Oh, I do, but sometimes I'm just sure what's right. I would prefer a darker gold for the setting, but beggars can't be choosers."

"Perhaps you can commission pieces next time," Joe suggested. "If this first trial is a success. What's next on your list?"

A half hour passed quickly as we reviewed various combinations of precious and semiprecious gems. I had to admit that having such jewels at my disposal was a heady experience. I said as much to Joe as he busied himself putting the last few drawers back into their places.

"I will also confess I enjoy looking at them." Joe straightened up, smiling. "Leah likes jewels—we'd never aspire to some of the pieces you've seen, but I've been able to make her as happy as a duchess occasionally. It helps when you can buy at cost. Haven't you seen anything you'd like for yourself?"

"I was never overfond of jewelry." I looked at the rings on my hands. "I'm getting used to it now. Martin loves giving me things. He gave me a rather splendid pendant for Christmas."

"The crystal piece." Joe nodded. "Quite unique. Martin has excellent taste, and he understands you completely."

"He's known me since I was three. Does he come down

here and look through the assorted riches? It's like Aladdin's cave."

Joe's smile was a little tight. "He selects from a few pieces I have brought up to him."

"You mean he never comes down here."

"Can you blame him?" Joe nodded at the bars that presumably protected us from a daylight raid. "We both remember only too well how he felt about being behind bars. And he's far more sensitive than he lets on."

"Does he know that you know?" I didn't have to elaborate further.

"Of course not. I keep up the pretense that he's far too grand to bother with coming down here. Now, Mrs. Rutherford, I'm going to ask you to step outside while I set the time locks."

I looked at the shiny silver box, chased with designs of peacock feathers, which held two complicated dials, like arcane clocks with strange hour and minute hands. "How does it work?"

"Do you imagine I'd tell you?" Joe looked steadily at me. "Even Martin's in the dark, although he and I came up with the formula for setting the opening and closing times. They vary daily—and you'd laugh if we told you how we did it." He turned a key to unlock the bars, sliding them into their recess. "Certain employees, not the obvious ones, are privy to the secret. People who have earned the trust we put in them."

"You're risking your life for this, aren't you?" I suddenly realized.

"No, I don't think so." Joe paused with his hand on the time lock box as I stepped outside the vault. "The days when criminals would kidnap employees from their beds and torture them until they revealed a combination are pretty much over, thanks to these time locks. I doubt they're as infallible as their manufacturers claim, but they do help." He looked at the vault's concrete ceiling. "They could use dynamite, I suppose, but they'd still have difficulty—there are steel bars all around us, encased in concrete mixed with metal shavings."

I sat in an armchair in the small antechamber as Joe pulled the bars across again. He was out of my sight for about three minutes, adjusting the locking mechanism, before he stepped outside and swung the massive outer door shut, setting the combination carefully. I heard a series of clicks.

"And now nobody can get back in until such a time as I have determined." Joe offered me his arm. "Are you absolutely *sure* you noticed nothing you liked? Martin would cover you with diamonds if you only let him."

I rolled my eyes. "Very well, the tourmaline bracelet with the heavy scrolled gold setting. I prefer semiprecious stones, truth be told. The others are so showy—or else one has to opt for small stones, and small stones just don't have the same effect." I pinched Joe's arm in a sisterly fashion. "But not until my birthday, mind you."

"Your wish is my command. I'll make sure the piece is removed to Martin's own safe. Is this ball gown demonstration going to go ahead, then? You must be quite certain about the gowns if you're already choosing the jewelry."

"Oh, the gowns are the straightforward part." I sighed.

"What, Madame's *still* not found ten men and ten women who can dance to her standards?"

"She's decided to be content with six. She says that quality is better than quantity." I grinned. "She's thrilled with Miss Dorrian as the lead dancer. It's a stroke of luck that quite the prettiest of the floor models turns out to be so light on her feet. She and handsome Mr. Mangan make a splendid couple on the dance floor."

"Madame Belvoix has given me a list of items she wants

in the Rose Room—potted palms and such. And a refreshment table."

"You'll be there, of course."

"Wouldn't miss it for the world. I'll send up the invitation list for you and Madame to peruse early next week. We're probably going to keep it intimate, depending on who says they'll come. If it's a success, we'll put the word around that people can apply for an invitation to the next one, and then perhaps we can put on more than one performance—if I may call it such."

"If it's a success. Martin believes it should be. I must admit I'm a little nervous."

"About it succeeding?"

"About my own . . . performance, I suppose. After all, these are *my* gowns. I'm perfectly comfortable dealing with clients one at a time, but those are women who have come to me because they want a dress. *This* is about creating the desire to buy, and it feels different."

Joe squeezed my arm. "Martin will take care of the selling. You know how much he enjoys that part of the job. All you will have to do is to answer questions about fit, fabrics, variations, and so on, and you have the requisite expertise. The jewelry department seniors will be there to provide information about the baubles, the shoemaker about the shoes, and of course the ladies who sell unmentionables will be in attendance. My guess is that we're all going to enjoy ourselves."

"I hope so." I smiled as Joe held open the door that led to the staircase.

"Oh, please sign out some pieces of paste jewelry to use for the final rehearsals." Joe stopped, turning to face me. "The dancers will have to get used to managing the full regalia. But please don't tell them which pieces are being used for the real thing—let them believe it'll all be paste. We can't be too careful at the moment."

33

LOVE

"*Good* morning."

Martin got to his feet as I entered the room, stepping forward to greet me with a kiss. He smelled of the coffee he'd been drinking, and the buttery aroma of eggs rose from his half-eaten breakfast. I took a deep breath.

"You've missed Sarah and Tess." Martin held out a chair for me; once I sat down, he poured my coffee. "I'll ring for them to bring your eggs."

"No, don't." I reached for a piece of toast. "This will do fine."

"Still under the weather?" Martin gathered up a sizeable amount of food onto his fork and transferred it to his mouth, following up with a healthy gulp of coffee. "You're a little white in the face. You were fast asleep when I came to bed."

I broke off a piece of dry toast and nibbled experimentally. Finding that nothing drastic happened, I ate a little more. I pushed my untouched coffee cup as far from me as I could manage.

"They were both too hungry to wait for you." Martin

pulled his watch out of his vest pocket and opened the case, then replaced it and began eating faster. "I won't be able to linger if you're going to eat that slowly. You know Fassbinder's here, and I've arranged for all the department managers to be in my office at eight, so I want to be there at half past seven. You don't have to be there till eight, of course."

I looked down unhappily at my hands, which were tearing the toast into small pieces. Above all else, I couldn't confide in Martin about the dark cloud of misery that had settled upon me when I had realized—and I was late to breakfast because I'd been bathing my eyes in cold water so Martin wouldn't suspect I'd been crying. I was holding myself so tensely my back ached. The discomfort was echoed by the tightness in my breasts, which tingled maddeningly under my corset. I didn't want to say anything—but I had to, didn't I? This was an excellent opportunity. I must try to smile.

I took a few more deep breaths, willing myself to remain calm. At last, I spoke.

"I think I'm with child."

I had timed the announcement well, making sure Martin hadn't just swallowed a mouthful of coffee or was holding anything breakable. I had expected a reaction. But the shout of joy that escaped my husband as he leapt to his feet, knocking over the chair and pulling the tablecloth askew, did at least bring an uncertain, wavering smile to my lips.

I stood and let Martin pull me into his arms, folding me close in a way that was quite different from his usual embrace. I allowed myself to melt into his warmth, closing my eyes for a few moments as broken words of delight and love babbled into my ear, accompanied by a rain of kisses on every available patch of skin.

"Is that why you've been so ill?" Martin asked when he

came to his senses. He put a little distance between us, cupping my cheek and running his thumb over my scar. The gentleness of that gesture made me want to weep again.

"I imagine so. And I've been quite exhausted in the evenings, as you're aware."

"But that's been for some weeks. Didn't you say—weren't you indisposed recently?"

"I believed I was, but I must have been mistaken." One did not make a man, even a beloved husband, privy to matters that were grossly physical; if he were a gentleman, the murmured word "indisposed" should be enough to render him less insistent than usual. So I didn't tell him I had bled a little, on and off, and assumed that was my monthly visitor. After all, when I had been carrying Sarah, I had never bled. But when I had been carrying Sarah, I had never been ill. I'd been sixteen—almost seventeen—in those early months, in the most robust health, bothered by nothing except an increase in appetite. Now I was twenty-five—almost twenty-six—and the intervening years obviously counted for much.

"I calculate I'm a good three months along." I looked up at Martin. "I've been dreadful in the mornings. When I get out of bed, it's as if I'm on a boat. But because I was mistaken over . . . being indisposed . . . I just assumed it was something I'd get over." I smiled tremulously. "I'll get over this."

"You must rest more," Martin said firmly. "No, don't you dare argue. You must reduce your working hours straightaway."

And there it was—exactly what I'd been expecting. It was when I'd been fastening my bodice, annoyed that it seemed tighter than usual, that the lightning bolt of sudden knowledge had flashed through my brain. It had immediately been followed by the realization that my life was about to change, and then by the realization that I was upset by that prospect.

The first time I'd been *enceinte*, I'd simply been afraid of discovery. I'd been furious at the notion I might have to marry Jack—then stubbornly determined I would *not* marry my cousin. This time my mind had flashed ahead to—October? What would I be doing in October? Of course, the atelier would be hard at work on gowns for the winter season. Rich materials for the wealthy women and cheerful reds and plaids for the more modestly situated. It was always such fun to choose the fabrics for a new season, to outdo last year's creations—

But I wouldn't be doing any of that. Perhaps it was the weakness inherent in my condition that had caused the tears to gush from my eyes. Alice had found me sobbing when she'd come in to put up my hair and help me finish dressing. She hadn't asked a question or ventured an opinion, but she'd put a firm, competent hand on my shoulder and handed me a handkerchief, then fetched a bowl of cold water so I could bathe my eyes while she finished my hair. She must have realized, of course. She laundered my most intimate linen—how would she not realize? But she was nothing if not discreet.

"Once I'm over the worst and begin to feel better, I will work as long as I am comfortable," I said firmly. "I don't have a wasting disease, Martin. I have a baby. I worked up to the day I gave birth to Sarah and came to no harm."

I saw the expression on his face and softened. "But I'll concede that while I'm feeling so horrible, I should take a little extra rest. To be frank, I'd welcome it."

"And we'll have the doctor come to see you."

"What do I need a doctor for?"

"To prescribe nourishing food and congratulate me on my good fortune." Martin whooped in elation again. "When may I inform people? Just our closest friends, of course. Joe, certainly. And what about telling Tess and Sarah?"

"Not just yet." I leaned into Martin's chest, hearing the loud, reassuring thump of his heartbeat. "I'm not ready."

Martin shook his head. "I don't know how I'm going to stop myself grinning from ear to ear and giving the whole game away. Perhaps I should leave you to take the carriage and ride Gentleman, just to use up some of this energy. I declare I could leap over a barn."

"As long as you don't come close to me smelling of horse." My stomach lurched. "I'm sorry I have to keep turning my head away. It's not personal; it's the food and coffee on your breath. In fact, if you're able to spare me from this meeting, I'd much rather stay at home. I generally improve around ten o'clock."

BY THE TIME TEN O'CLOCK STRUCK, I WAS REGRETTING MY decision not to go to work. As the nausea subsided a little, I became restless, unable to settle to anything, reluctant to set off for Rutherford's in case Martin had told anyone and yet longing for my familiar routine.

I surprised Sarah and Miss Baker with a visit to the schoolroom and joined in a geography lesson. Miss Baker did not force Sarah to learn facts and figures by rote as I had been taught; she had managed to convey to Sarah not just the names of countries and capitals, but a genuine sense of each different land, its peoples, its languages, and its customs. At eight years old, my daughter was better informed than some of my Prairie Avenue friends. Her visit to Europe had sharpened her interest in the world outside America.

"And now our lesson is *over*, Mama!" Sarah left her seat and came to put her arms around my neck as I sat on the schoolroom's comfortable settee. "Can you guess what we're going to do next?"

I slipped an arm over my daughter's skinny shoulders as she sat down next to me, wondering at the hardness of the muscle and the sheer vitality of the small body. "You're going to South Park to see the sheep?" I suggested.

"Wrong!" Sarah bounced in her seat, grinning. "Our scheduled outing for today is to observe the fast driving on Lake Shore Drive. And then we're going to the zoo, because it's Friday and I've been ever so good. Mama, did you know that some little children in England grow up in nasty places called workhouses? Because they don't have mamas and papas. And then they have to go out and work when they're no older than I am. Supposing I had to go out and work? Do you think I could be a cash boy—or a cash girl—in Rutherford's? I can run fast."

"Why were you learning about workhouses?" I asked. The image of the Women's House at the Poor Farm rose in my mind.

"We're reading *Oliver Twist* together." Miss Baker held up the green-and-gold illustrated edition she'd bought in London. "A little ambitious, perhaps, but I was sure Sarah would enjoy a story about a child. And that's what we're supposed to be doing now, Sarah. Up at the table with you."

"You're welcome to go to sleep on the settee while we're reading, Mama." Sarah bounded up from her place on the settee and vaulted into her chair at the schoolroom table. Given the chance, she rarely seemed to walk or sit in the normal fashion these days; she was always leaping, skipping, jumping, racing. And yet she was able to be still when it suited her, or when manners dictated that she was to be calm and not disturb the grown-ups.

"I don't want to fall asleep." I smiled, rising from the settee. "I'll go sit with Tess for a while; she should be back from the market by now. Then I'll go to the store."

"Listen to me read first." Sarah found the location in the

322

book marked by a bright green ribbon. "'In great families, when an ad-van-ta-geous place cannot be obtained, either in possession, re-ver-sion, remainder, or ex-pec-tan-cy . . .' Merciful heavens, what does that *mean*? I can't possibly go on till you tell me."

I burst out laughing at the indignation in Sarah's voice; Miss Baker and Sarah joined in. "I'm afraid we're not getting on very fast with the book," Miss Baker said. "There's so much to explain."

"Because Mr. Dickens forgets that he's supposed to be telling a story," Sarah informed me. "And he—what was it he does?"

"Editorializes." Miss Baker looked at the page. "Fetch a slate and we'll go over those words. It's all about inheriting money."

Sarah slid off her chair and ran to fetch slate and chalk. "Is Oliver going to inherit money? I thought he was a pauper. Will I inherit money?"

"I'm sure your papa will make an appropriate settlement." Miss Baker smiled as she took the slate. "Now, read the rest of the paragraph, and we'll look at all of it together."

"May I read it to Mama again later? I want to get better at it first." Sarah looked up at me and wrinkled her nose. "Perhaps you'd better go see Tess, Mama."

I made my way to the door accompanied by Sarah's attempts to do her best with the rest of the paragraph, which she punctuated with cries of astonishment or condemnation as she got to the parts about flogging and beating. *This is a child who questions everything*, I reflected. *Just like Papa*. I lingered, fascinated, watching my daughter striving to learn and understand.

And what lesson had I derived this morning? I wondered as I shut the door. Perhaps it was that babyhood was so quickly over. I ran my hand over the area below my waist. *I have to make room for this child in my life.*

Tess turned around in surprise as I knocked on the open door of her sitting room and entered what Martin called "the Pink Domain." It was fresh and pretty with its gauzy curtains, figured wallpaper, and contrasting white paint. Tess was struggling with the sash window; the temperature outdoors was climbing fast, as it often did in mid-April, and the room was warm.

"Why didn't you ring for help?" I opened the window easily, my greater height and longer arms giving me an immense advantage over Tess. A fresh breeze blew in, making the curtains billow and bringing the sound of the chickadee's two-note salute.

"I figured I could do it. Nell, I thought you were at the store. Don't you have a meeting with Mr. Fassbinder?"

"My presence wasn't strictly necessary, and I was under the weather. I'm all right now." I made my way to the armchair opposite the one that was Tess's habitual choice. "How was the market?"

"There were some very nice fresh chickens." Tess beamed. "Two to roast and one to make into soup. Mostly for you, Nell."

My stomach gave a tiny growl, followed by a faint wave of nausea. "Are you going to see Aileen today?" I asked to distract myself.

Tess wrinkled her nose. "She might have Father Doonan over again, and I don't like him. He smells of drink. And he never stops talking. I guess I'll stay right here this afternoon, or maybe I'll have Donny drive me around a little anyway." Her eyes brightened at the prospect. "I saw him on the way home from the market, and he said I looked very pretty. Sometimes I think he's growing fond of me, but I can't work out how to get him to say *that*."

"Don't ask me to solve that conundrum." I smiled. "I'm determined to leave well alone. Have you seen any more of Annie?"

"She's walking out with a tall boy who drives a scrap cart." Tess beamed. "That's what Donny says. I asked him straight out if he was sweet on her, and he said she's just a friend and she flirts with the stable hands anyway, and he doesn't hold with women who flirt."

My eyebrows rose. "If only it were always so easy to be rid of a rival. You could come to the store with me if you like. I'm lazy today and probably won't get much done."

Tess was silent for a few moments, her eyes on me.

"Are you making a baby, Nell?" she asked eventually.

"What makes you say that?"

Tess angled her head to one side, considering my person from head to toe. "You look different. Sort of softer all around the edges."

"I'm haggard."

"You look a little tired. Not quite as handsome as usual."

"I may just be losing my looks." Tess's remark had not helped my mood, I discovered.

"So *are* you?"

"Am I what?" I was not inclined to be helpful. I hadn't wanted to tell Tess, not yet.

"Having a baby." Tess sighed. "Martin would be so happy."

I felt the prick of tears behind my eyes and cursed inwardly. I had not been prone to crying when I was carrying Sarah—what was *wrong* with me? I seemed to weep at the drop of a hat now. I compressed my lips, trying to decide whether it would be better to tell Tess now or to wait until some future moment and make a formal announcement with

Martin at my side. And then I realized I wasn't even capable of thinking, let alone deciding on a course of action and sticking to it.

"He *is* happy," I said baldly. "I told him this morning. Yes, I'm with child."

I expected Tess to clap her hands or leap from her chair or bounce up and down, the way she usually did when she heard good news. But she stayed in her seat; a smile spread across her round face, but it was an oddly serene one.

"When we were at the Poor Farm together, you never seemed to care all that much for your baby inside you," she said. "If I asked you about the baby, you always changed the subject. But when Sarah was born, you liked her better."

"When we were at the Poor Farm, I had decided I was giving my child away," I said drily. "There didn't seem much point in getting attached. It wasn't until we found the bodies of poor Jo and especially little Benjamin that I began to fret over the idea of somebody else looking after my baby. Started to believe only I could keep her safe."

"So if we'd never found them, you would have been all right with giving Sary away?"

The tears threatened again, and this time I had to dash the water from my eyes. "I'm sorry." I fumbled for my handkerchief. "I seem to have turned sentimental."

"I don't think you would have, not really." That odd serenity again, an assured confidence that was a rare expression with Tess except when she was reading her Bible. "It's not like you. Oh, you're always rushing around fussing after your blessed gowns and worrying what Madame thinks of your sketches—and when you get an idea in your head for a dress, you might as well be on the moon for all the attention you pay to any of us. But we all know how much you love us. The dresses, well, that's just your special gift from God. You'd burn them all up in an instant if any of us needed you."

"Would I?" The notion startled me. "I don't imagine I'm a particularly good mother. Or wife."

"Only because you want to be perfect at everything. We're all happy, Nell, so you can't be *that* bad."

"There was a point where you were convinced you'd be better off with your family," I pointed out.

"Only because I listened to Mary and Aileen, silly." Tess chuckled. "Now I listen to Da and Billy. The men in my family have more sense than the women. And you won't keep reminding me of that, will you? *You're* my family, Nell." Her brow creased. "But if I can get Donny to want to marry me, supposing he wants to live somewhere else?"

"Then you'll go with him, with our blessing. Doesn't the Bible say you leave your family and cleave to your husband?"

Now Tess laughed. "You've got it wrong, Nell. You really should listen in church. But I guess it would be all right to cleave to Donny. Only I would be very sad to go away."

"So would I."

I leaned forward as Tess sprang out of her chair, and we indulged in a long hug that brought the easy tears to my eyes again. I wasn't at all myself; I was tired and sick and emotional, and somehow everything looked different, *wrong*, as if I had stepped into some kind of mirror world.

"I should go to the store," I said after I'd sniffed and applied my handkerchief to my ridiculously moist eyes. "We've less than two weeks until the ball gown demonstration and Madame will be wondering if I'm going to put in an appearance at rehearsals. If Martin asks, you'll tell him I had a good rest this morning, won't you?"

"No, I won't lie for you." Tess patted me on my shoulder. "You've been stalking around the house fretting, haven't you?" She drew back to look at me. "Are you unhappy because you don't imagine you'll be a good mother to this little baby?" She grinned and put a small hand on the lower part of my bodice.

Now the tears were falling in earnest, eluding all my efforts to stem them with my handkerchief. "Oh, Tess. Why do you always have to be so wise?" I snatched up the small hand and kissed it. "I'm sorry, now I've made your hand wet. I'm ashamed for not being as delighted about this child as Martin is, I guess."

I had to stop to blow my nose, which was surely quite red by now. I'd have to bathe my face all over again. My head ached, which made me as sick as I had been first thing in the morning.

"You'll get over it." Tess kissed my forehead. "You'll see. You knew when you married Martin that babies would follow."

"Do *you* want babies?" It occurred to me how selfish I was being. But to my surprise, Tess shook her head.

"Not really. I have quite enough to do with everyone else's. But if God wants me to have babies, I guess He'll give me enough love for them. Now you go up and bathe your face, and I'll get Beatrice to bring you a little something to eat and drink before you go to the store."

"I'm not very hungry."

Tess gave me a stern look. "You have to try. You can't faint with the hunger, Madame says. You'll see—I'll make you feel better."

34

SUBSTITUTE

*T*ess's ministrations had the desired effect. She ordered both lemonade and tea; I discovered that the sharp taste of lemon, which I had always loved, was even more palatable than usual. After a few sips, I could nibble on the plain shortbread cookies, which were fresh and not too sweet.

After another half an hour, I was ready to send round to the stables for the landau, enduring the ride to the store with something approaching cheerfulness. It helped that the bright sun and rising temperatures were greening up Chicago's trees and patches of grass and causing a fresh, verdant growth of weeds to sprout from any untended foot of dirt.

By the time I arrived at the store, I had shaken off my maudlin mood and was looking forward to seeing the latest rehearsal in the Rose Room. The sound of a piano assured me that a rehearsal was in progress. I pushed open the door quietly to see a dozen men and women revolving around the gleaming wood floor.

One of the women was entirely unexpected. I cast a sharp glance at Madame, but her expression of fierce concentration warned me comments would be unwelcome until she herself indicated readiness to hear them. I stood and watched, slightly bothered by the bobbing motions of the dancers but increasingly forgetful of my own troubles. An explanation would be forthcoming, I was sure.

"I didn't know you could dance," was my only, and very mild, remark as Thea Lombardi freed herself from her partner with an abruptness that produced a decidedly sulky expression on young Mr. Mangan's face. He was not used to shopgirls failing to gaze adoringly at his broad shoulders, neatly pomaded locks, and firm chin. Upon Madame's announcement that there would be a fifteen-minute break, he strode from the room, shrugging as if he wished to disassociate himself from every woman in his vicinity.

"I've been taking lessons in dancing and deportment." Thea curled her lip in disdain as she smoothed her uniform where it showed the imprint of Mr. Mangan's large hand. Soon the dancers would be rehearsing in full dress, including gloves.

"Really? I never thought you'd be interested. After all, we tried lessons when you first came here."

I attempted to sound lighthearted, but my words rang with a falsely jovial note. I suspected Thea remembered only too well, as did I, how egregiously rude she had been to the teachers I'd engaged for her during those first terrible weeks of her residence at the Palmer House.

"Miss Dardenne suggested I try." Thea's face gave nothing away. "My dancing master says I am extremely musical."

"You dance well."

"Not as well as Miss Dorrian, but you will do nicely, Miss Lombardi. Thank you for offering yourself as a substitute." Madame, who had been hovering at my elbow, spoke with quiet conviction. Thea received her remark without emotion, dipping her head politely at the two of us before moving away to speak to one of the house models.

"Is Miss Dorrian sick?" I asked as Madame Belvoix and I moved toward the back of the room.

"Not sick, no. Gone." The expression on Madame's face boded ill for Miss Dorrian if she ever came back.

"Gone?"

"Left. Absconded." Madame spoke evenly, but there was something about the tenor of her voice that betrayed rage. It was a tone that would have quickly cleared any room on the dressmaking floor. "Miss Dorrian was found last night in a *most* compromising position. A man, *in her bedroom*, and discovered in—well, let us say in a condition that left no doubt as to their activities."

I swallowed hard against the sudden desire to laugh. "Oh, glory."

"Mrs. Fontana told Miss Dorrian to be prepared to appear before Mr. Salazar in the morning." Mrs. Fontana was the current night supervisor of the single women's residence. "But in the morning, her room was empty. *How* any of this might have happened when the women are *supposed* to be supervised *day and night* is a question I mean to bring up as a matter of urgency." Madame positively vibrated with fury, tapping a small foot on the boards. "All that time wasted, and to lose the best dancer of them all—" She looked up at me with a hostile glare. "I hope you do not intend to object to Miss Lombardi taking part."

"Does Martin know?" was all I thought of to say.

"*Non*. He has been busy with Mr. Fassbinder, and in any case—" Madame's mouth pinched itself into an expression that suggested she would simply not *let* Martin or me object to the substitution.

"And there's nobody else suitable?"

Madame folded her arms, her gaze on the dancers as they

reassembled on the floor. Mr. Mangan was talking to one of the younger house models, a fatuous smile on his handsome face.

"Nobody as well suited. It has been difficult enough to find the right dancers. Miss Lombardi is dark while Miss Dorrian is fair, but they are of a similar height and size. I have sent a note that I require Miss Lombardi for a fitting this afternoon. There is simply too much *detail* in that gown to redo it completely, Mrs. Rutherford. The embroidery, the lace—" She waved her small hands in the air in an extremely French manner. It occurred to me that Madame was unusually nervous.

"I have no objection in principle to Miss Lombardi taking part," I said. "She is awfully young, of course—not yet seventeen."

"But she might easily pass for twenty, which is Miss Dorrian's age." I could hear Madame's teeth grinding. "I *hope* Miss Dorrian's lover will marry her because she will not find work in another department store in this town."

I saw Thea take some instructions from the dancing teacher Madame had hired. She listened carefully, then submitted herself to being held again by Mr. Mangan and executed a few steps with a fluidity that brought a smile to the teacher's face—and to Madame's.

"She learns fast." Madame's gaze slid to mine.

"The only objection that may arise is that of her brother. He's due to arrive in New York on the twentieth."

As luck would have it, the sequence of polka steps Thea was executing brought her close enough to hear what I was saying. She freed herself from Mr. Mangan once more and came toward me.

"Teddy's coming?"

"Yes, I was going to tell you as soon as I found you. We

had a letter, then a telegram to confirm his date of arrival. The twentieth. Next week on Sunday."

A fleeting, and rare, expression of vulnerability flashed into Thea's face. Her soft pink lower lip disappeared beneath two little white teeth. And then her mouth firmed, and an expression of defiance came into her eyes.

"Has he not written to you as well?" I asked.

"He probably guesses I wouldn't answer. I don't reply to many of his letters. They're more like lectures, as if he's certain I've embarked on a career of debauchery in his absence."

There was something about the way she pronounced the words, as if trying them on for the first time, that made me suspect they were not original to her. Was she also improving her mind by reading? Or was she simply parroting the words of an older, more sophisticated friend? But her remarks about the tone of Teddy's letters were no doubt accurate enough. Teddy would get nowhere with Thea by lecturing her, as I'd learned some time ago.

"It would be kind to write to him more often," I said. "I'm sure he only wants what is best for you."

Thea started to look thunderous, then changed her expression to one of supercilious disdain. "It's hard to find something to write in reply to his endless recommendations on how to be a godly woman, as Pa and Mamma would want me to be. As if I'm thinking up ways to do wrong every day." She looked across at the assembling dancers, a faint flush staining her cheeks, and then gave the merest toss of her pretty head before joining them, her movements precise and elegant.

"She would make a fine house model," Madame said quietly. "Such skin, such hair—and I believe she is learning to control her tongue and her temper." She sighed. "*Eh bien*, but she is very young yet. I am prepared to wait."

"SHE LOOKS LIKE A CHILD PLAYING DRESS-UP."

Teddy, a picture of sober respectability in a new black suit, stood as close as possible to the door of the Rose Room. He struck an odd note against the evening finery worn by all those present, including Martin, myself, and all the other staff members. Madame Belvoix was not in the room, having chosen to supervise the dressing of the dancers while Martin and I dealt with our guests.

It was doubtless to our credit that a good many members of Chicago's wealthiest, youngest elite were present. The ladies sat in delicate chairs; the men stood behind their wives or collected in small knots to talk stock prices, horses, guns, Europe, and politics under cover of the music.

"She looks like a pretty young girl at her first ball. A beautiful young girl." I noted how the light struck gleams from Thea's hair and the parure of garnets I had chosen to go with her dress as she revolved gracefully in Mr. Mangan's arms. The skirt of the gown was fashionably narrow; from the waist down, a panel folded back to reveal a cornucopia of silk roses and gold lace echoed by the deep red roses she wore in her hair. The gold lace trim on the petticoats and her delicate silk pumps peeped in charming glimpses from the hem of the dress as she moved. Golden gauze wafted around the skirt like smoke from a genie's lamp, giving Thea an almost ethereal appearance. To dance well in such an ensemble took considerable skill.

She could be a Prairie Avenue belle—might have been one, in fact, if she had decided to stay with Martin and me. Did she think of that? Had she spied the two Thuringer girls among the assembled ladies? Both were a little too plump for their age, but both definitely aspired to be young ladies of fashion now that Mr. Thuringer's fortune warranted a permanent house in Chicago. They had recognized Thea, but there was no malice in their faces, only admiration at her looks and gracefulness. They were a merchant's daughters and did not yet despise those who worked, as their children one day might.

"She's only dancing, Teddy." I stepped out of the room to follow Teddy as he withdrew to the antechamber, past the three burly men stationed by the door. They were detailed to guard against robbery, even though the store was locked to all but its visitors. Downstairs, Joe waited with several more men, keeping a close eye on all doors and windows. "The ballroom is an essential element of society, you know that. It's how young people are brought together when they are old enough to marry. You can't possibly be against marriage."

"She's dressed up to display goods, not to find a husband." Teddy frowned. "I should go in there and drag her out."

Cold horror assailed me, not the least at the thought of Madame's reaction should her demonstration ball be ruined. My head swam; I groped behind me, mercifully finding a chair onto which I dropped as Teddy darted to my aid.

"I'm all right." I swallowed, tasting bile. "You won't —please—"

"Not if it upsets you *that* much." I looked up into a face that was far more like the open, genial Teddy of old but upon which concern for me was plainly written. "You need help— some water—maybe I should fetch Mr. Rutherford—"

"No." I sensed the color returning to my cheeks and gave Teddy a reassuring smile. "It's just nerves. We've worked so hard on this demonstration, and then one of the dancers was indisposed and Thea saved the day by stepping in at the last minute. We're grateful to her." I stood up a little unsteadily; my condition seemed to cause occasional light-headedness, a fact I did not intend to reveal to Martin.

"I swear to you, Teddy, we didn't set out to put Thea on

display." I put as much sincerity into my voice as I could muster.

"I believe you." Teddy fidgeted with his hat, which was still in his hand. "I apologize for upsetting you, ma'am." He sighed. "But the sight of her dressed up like that . . ."

"I know." I tried to smile. "Thea has a real talent for show, doesn't she? That parure she's wearing has already been spoken for, and I think I'll have half a dozen commissions for gowns based on that dress by the end of the evening."

And we had sold the emeralds, which graced the neck of one of the older dancers. A silver platter stood on a corner table to receive the visiting cards of guests desiring to buy or commission goods; a clerk carefully recorded the details on each card as it was handed in. A clerk from the accounting department wrote out neat bills of sale if a direct purchase were involved. Money and goods would exchange hands the next day. The jewelry would be meticulously cleaned and mounted in a smart wooden box with mother-of-pearl inlay before being delivered to its purchaser.

"I must get back in. There's going to be an interval in a moment, and I need to be there to talk about the dresses." My moment of faintness was wearing off, and I smiled at Teddy. "We're holding a supper for the workers once we've all changed out of our finery. Would you like to join us? You can meet the other dancers and see that they're all quite ordinary, industrious men and women. It'll be a good supper too. Madame saw to it."

Teddy hesitated but then smiled back. "I guess it would be nice to spend a little time with my sister. Absence makes the heart grow fonder, as the saying goes, and I'm mighty glad to see her in such good health. Is there somewhere I could wait? I don't belong in this elevated company."

"You do, you know." I laid a hand on his arm. "There's nobody in there so exalted they wouldn't be happy to talk to a fine young man who wants to be a pastor." I looked over my shoulder at the glittering show beyond the door. "You should stay till the end. Martin was rehearsing a tidy little speech earlier today in his dressing room."

I couldn't linger now; the music was ending. Squeezing Teddy's arm, I moved away, patting my hair and ensuring that my evening dress of royal blue-and-gold brocade had no creases. I was going to stand beside Martin as he made his speech; the dancers would flank us, giving the audience one last chance for a good look at the dresses and jewelry.

I walked slowly into the glittering room, thanking Providence for my momentary indisposition. Perhaps Teddy would begin to reconcile himself to Thea's chosen career, and we could all find ourselves in calm waters for a time.

35

INCUBUS

*A*nd yet even calm waters were constantly on the move. They shifted in never-ceasing waves, ripples, eddies, lying in wait to throw the hapless sailor off balance.

By June, just the mention of moving water made me shudder. Even though my condition had entered its fifth month, I still suffered from nausea, faintness, and lack of appetite. The summer heat brought headaches to add to my suffering, and dark shadows marred the skin under my eyes. I sometimes sensed the baby move inside me, tiny flutters more akin to the wings of a trapped moth than to a child.

I was soon to travel to Lake Forest with Elizabeth, Sarah, and Tess to pass the worst of the hot, moist Chicago summer in the fresh air of the Parnells' house near the lake. I had promised Martin I would rest. Besides—I could spend some of my enforced idleness working on our fall designs.

I couldn't hide my poor health any more than I could hide the increasing girth of my normally slender frame, and I was not spending nearly enough time at the store for my liking. Yet even Madame had said nothing. She merely nodded when I announced my Lake Forest plans.

But before I retired from Chicago altogether, there was Thea's seventeenth birthday to celebrate.

"It's nothing grand. But I wanted to get you something you might wear often." I watched as Thea held up the pretty citrine pendant I'd had made for her. It glowed the same tawny gold as the depths of her hazel eyes, catching the light from the large windows of our front parlor and gathering it into itself like a small sun. Its gold setting made a fit match for our pale silk wall hangings, pastel colors on a cream background, and deep yellow heavy silk drapes. Through the window, Lake Michigan shone as an azure strip, busy with the dark towers of sailing ships, the white triangles of yachts, and the squat black dots of distant steamboats that trailed faint wisps of smoke.

"It's quite lovely." Thea held up the teardrop-shaped jewel on its gold chain. "Thank you. I will treasure it."

That was the nicest thing Thea had said to me in her entire lifetime. I didn't expect—and didn't get—a hug or kiss, but the small smile that accompanied her words was enough for me. Our other guests—Teddy, of course, and the Fletchers—moved in to examine the pendant and comment on the clarity and color of the stone. Elizabeth Fletcher fastened the jewel around Thea's graceful white neck while the young woman held her glossy ringlets out of the way.

"A costly gift," Teddy said quietly to me as we watched David hold up little Mabel to see the pendant. "I hope she'll take care of it." A worried frown marred his face.

"That's up to her," I remarked. "She's not a child. At her age . . . Well, to be frank, Teddy, on my seventeenth birthday I was already carrying Sarah and soon to be dispatched to the Poor Farm to hide my disgrace from the people of Victory."

I had celebrated my birthday back then in my usual care-free fashion, happy, as always, to be spoiled by Mama and our housekeeper, Bet. How would I have experienced that day if I had known the Poor Farm lay ahead of me? The reality of what I had done, what it meant, simply hadn't penetrated to my obtuse skull. At that age, I saw the world as a boundless well of adventures into which I longed to plunge. I wanted to escape the limits of life in a small town; I hadn't realized I had effectively narrowed my choices.

I shrugged, looking up at the young man. "Thea has shown herself to be far more sensible than I ever was. I wish you'd trust her a little more."

Teddy looked down at his boots. "I guess I wish I did too. I just worry about how she's gradually wormed her way into getting exactly what she wants, even though I've spoken up against it. You've admitted to me that she's worked as a house model twice since April."

"In strictly limited circumstances. She has professed herself quite happy to stay in the jewelry department for now, and that's as it should be. She's still a junior employee and will be for some time. But should we neglect to give an employee with her talent for sales suitable work just because she's a girl? We would hand a boy her age who showed such promise increasing responsibility. We'd probably train him as a future shop walker with a view to becoming a department head or other kind of manager by the time he was thirty. Of course, nobody would employ a woman as a shop walker—but she might be a head of department one day. Marriage isn't the only path, Teddy."

"Or she might wake up in ten years' time with her looks gone and wish she'd married instead of filling her head with thoughts of a career." Teddy's round gray eyes fixed themselves on me with a seriousness that seemed old beyond his years.

"I don't imagine she's going to be the sort of woman whose good looks fade quickly. Your mother was still beauti-

JANE STEEN

ful. Besides, she'll probably marry," I added. "She'll have many suitors. We lose most of our shopgirls to marriage—that's no doubt why the heads of department are slower to promote the women. It's only in the dressmaking atelier that a skilled woman can advance quickly, and *that's* mostly because of Madame Belvoix." I smiled at Teddy. "And *I'm* married and fulfilling my duty as a woman, aren't I?" I touched the swell of my bodice lightly. "There's hope for all of us yet."

Teddy flushed as I drew attention to my condition, but his embarrassment turned to laughter as Mabel gave a loud screech of frustration at not being allowed to play with the pretty bauble around Thea's neck. I was glad of the diversion. I found myself losing patience with Teddy's insistence on seeing the gloomy side of things. I missed the carefree boy of his prairie days. He was too young to be taking life so seriously all the time.

"I'll take her, Mr. Fletcher." Sarah held out her arms for Mabel. "We can go to the nursery, and I'll look after her ever so carefully. Mama can send one of the maids up to see we're all right, and I'll watch over her every minute. I'm nearly eight and a half, and Miss Baker says I'm very responsible."

There was another person who took life seriously, I mused as I watched Sarah working out the best way to hold a large and very wriggly baby. Mabel was over a year old, making strenuous attempts to master walking, and liable to put absolutely everything into her mouth. I crossed to the button to summon Beatrice as Sarah found the trick of settling the baby into the place where her hips would be one day. I followed as my daughter headed for the door, hitching her burden a little higher, and was relieved to see she really could carry the little girl.

A minute or two later, I had seen Sarah head upstairs with our maid bringing up the rear and had reassured Elizabeth as to Beatrice's competence. They would be all right in the nursery. I hoped to get Elizabeth to myself to talk about anything but babies. Elizabeth was in a delicate condition again, and our husbands had spent a moment teasing each other about their impending fatherhood, but it had only been a moment. Like all men, they appeared happy to drop the subject of children. I looked forward to doing the same.

Unfortunately, Teddy had decided to lecture Thea on taking good care of the pendant. Why could he not accept that she had left childhood behind?

"It'll be a terrible temptation to folks who can't afford such things," he was saying. "Can you trust the people in your boardinghouse? It's worth more than most folks earn in a month."

I saw Martin open his mouth to say something, no doubt to head off the quarrel presaged by Thea's expression, but Thea was too quick.

"If you're going to run on and *on* about how poor everyone is, I'll walk straight out of here." Thea narrowed her eyes at her brother. "And that would be a great insult to Mr. and Mrs. Rutherford after the nice things they've done for us, and it would be your fault. And it's insulting to me to imply I can't take care of my own possessions and don't know the value of things. *And* it's insulting to the people in my boardinghouse to suggest they might not be honest."

She was entirely in the right of it too. Awareness that his words were both clumsy and unfair was written on Teddy's face. He might have apologized if Thea hadn't decided to get one more word in.

"Your trouble is you always have your head in the mud. You want to drag me back down to your level. Here I am bettering myself, striving to realize my inner potential, while you're wallowing down in the dirt with the poor people just like Pa and Mamma. You can't stand it that I'm going to make something of myself."

"What does 'striving to realize your inner potential' *mean*?" retorted Teddy, the tips of his ears flushing red. "Pa would call that hogwash, and he'd be right. Our parents were worth ten of you."

Elizabeth stepped forward and laid a hand on Teddy's arm. "Do tell me about your classes for Polish immigrants," she said smoothly. "It's so good of Mrs. Nowak to let you use her back parlor. Do you teach mostly men, or do the women join in?"

She led Teddy away from his sister as Martin, taking his cue, made a remark to Thea about the latest fashion in earrings. I breathed a sigh of relief as I followed David to the piano mostly used by Sarah.

"Do sit down, Nell." David moved a chair close to the piano and waited until I seated myself before installing himself on the piano stool. "You look a little tired. Where's Miss O'Dugan?"

"With her family." I dropped my voice. "She's not over-fond of Thea."

"Is *anyone* overfond of her?" David left off sorting through the sheets of music kept near the instrument and gave me a rueful smile.

"To be fair, Teddy's not helping. It was unkind of him to say what he did." I shifted, trying to find a better position. I never seemed to be comfortable these days.

"What exactly *does* it mean to realize one's inner potential?" David, a good musician, had found a new song among the selection of music and was preparing to play. "Has Miss Lombardi become a great reader, full of advanced ideas?"

"If she has any advanced ideas, they're not hers." I shook my head wearily. "She listens to her friends and no doubt apes their opinions."

"Don't worry, Nell. No child of seventeen is ever truly original." David laughed as he turned to the instrument and struck the first lively chords of "*Oh, Dem Golden Slippers.*"

I welcomed the music at first, but before too long every note David played seemed to hit a sensitive place in my head. The chair was becoming more uncomfortable to sit on by the second. It was hot; the noise of insects had built up outside, sometimes audible over the music. A pity. I longed to step outside into cool greenness, but I knew from the hot bar of light that struck a marble statue in the foyer, lighting it as if from within, that there would be no respite out of doors.

The doors between our three connecting parlors were all open. In the front, Martin sat talking to Teddy. Elizabeth had tried to engage Thea in conversation but had given up, leaving the young woman to amuse herself in front of the mirror in the middle parlor. She was trying to pretend, in the way of pretty girls, that she was not lost in rapt appreciation of her own beauty, but nobody with any powers of observation would fail to notice that she was striking poses, watching herself move, as vain as any actress.

I rose to my feet as the music ended and David reached for another sheet.

"I'll visit the nursery," I said as brightly as I could manage. "Mabel's such an amusing little thing. I'll be back down in a while, and we'll play some parlor games before we eat."

ELIZABETH FOLLOWED ME OUT INTO OUR SPACIOUS HALLWAY. The bar of sunlight had moved; the statue was once more just a piece of marble, a woman in classical robes, seated with bowed head and clasped hands in eternal reflection.

"May I join you?" she asked. "It's about time I saw to my daughter. She's bound to need changing." She sighed. "I'm going to hire a permanent nursemaid when this one's born." She patted her abdomen. "They do take a lot of looking after."

"Of course you can join me." I smiled in welcome.

"I just wondered if you might not really be heading for the nursery." Since the staircase was wide enough for two people, Elizabeth caught up with me and we proceeded upward side by side, our fashionably narrow skirts barely touching. "You might have just wanted the lavatory or to lie down for twenty minutes."

"Both of those." I grinned at her. "But that's more or less a permanent condition these days."

"Yes, you're not at all well, are you?"

"That's an understatement. I can't remember Sarah being nearly such a nuisance. This one's like hatching an incubus." I walked slowly, holding tight to the handrail. "And it's so *hot*. I declare my feet are swelling; I can barely lift them."

"Poor you." Elizabeth looked sympathetic.

"Oh, I'll be as right as rain after a few weeks' rest in Lake Forest. What about you? How are you?"

"Not too bad. I don't get so sick in the mornings now. I get plenty of healthy exercise following Mabel around indoors and walking her in her baby carriage outdoors. When we're in Lake Forest, let's bathe in the lake, shall we? I know a secluded bit where hardly anyone goes, so we won't shock the townsfolk with your condition." The dimple showed in her smooth cheek. "Or mine, when I start to show."

"I'd like that." I imagined the cool waters of Lake Michigan lapping over my feet, not spoiled by the railroad as our own piece of shoreline was. "Perhaps not as healthy as the sea-bathing in Normandy, but close enough."

I pictured the sea, and my stomach roiled. I stopped,

doing my best to suppress a small belch, my hand on my bodice. "Don't make me think of moving water, please."

"As bad as that?" Elizabeth's blue eyes were dark with concern. "Have you seen a physician?"

"Once or twice, but there's not much to be done. If a medicine bottle is so much as in the same room as me, I have to have it taken out—it's the smell. I can't take any of the usual soothing mixtures."

Elizabeth continued upward to the nursery while I stopped to use the lavatory. By the time I'd joined her, I'd splashed my face and held my wrists under the cold water coming from the faucet. What a blessing modern life could be at times; it was astonishing how much better a little cool water made me feel.

Mabel *had* needed changing, but the efficient Beatrice had managed perfectly well by plundering the supplies I had already been making ready for my baby's arrival. Sarah had clearly been fascinated by the procedure of changing a baby. She made several observations about Mabel's anatomy that made me wonder if I shouldn't start talking to her soon about certain matters. No doubt the questions would only multiply if she were to have a brother.

I sat in an armchair, sighing with pleasure. Martin had provided for the nursery with as much care as he'd devoted to furnishing the rest of the house; the armchairs were soft and low with deep, wide seats and well-padded backs. Even the rocking chair was upholstered in a cheerful, vivid yellow print. The few toys Sarah still played with were arranged on low shelves. She had brought out a set of unused wooden blocks for Mabel, and the two of them had been having a fine time playing a game whereby Sarah built towers and Mabel knocked them down.

"And she walked all the way from the chair to the table by herself, just holding on to *one* of my fingers." Sarah held up the finger in demonstration. "She's so strong—aren't you, Mabel? No, you mustn't throw the blocks, remember? It's naughty. Can you say 'naughty'?"

"Na na naaa ma mama bam." Mabel scooted over to where her mother sat and pulled herself up with the help of the chair. She held out a block to Elizabeth, who took it gingerly. It was dripping with spittle.

"I gave her some milk and bread and butter when she started getting fussy." Sarah darted back and forth, retrieving blocks and building them into a tower again. "We had a picnic. When are we eating? Is there going to be ham? What's everybody doing?"

"Mr. Fletcher has been playing your piano, and the rest of us have been talking."

"Thea too?" Sarah shook back her hair, which had become somewhat disordered. Her normally pale face was flushed with heat, and tiny drops of moisture spangled the skin near her hairline.

"When I left the room, she was looking at my latest copies of the *Journal des Demoiselles* and the *Revue de la Mode.*" I half closed my eyes, my body heavy and listless. I wanted to rest before I went downstairs again and played the hostess, and I wasn't sure I'd have the stomach to eat. Everything seemed to be churning as restlessly as the sea—*no, don't think of the sea.*

"Is she being nice to everyone?" But Sarah forgot her question as Mabel caught sight of the new tower and toddled toward it, crowing in delight. Beatrice, who had been straightening and tidying various objects that the children's playing had disarranged, opened the high windows a little wider so that a light breeze blew in, flirting with the wisps of hair that kissed my temples. She disappeared out onto the landing, evidently to put away the unused linen.

Elizabeth rose to her feet, took Mabel in her arms, and went to inspect the books that sat on the higher shelves.

Sarah loved books so much that we'd kept every one she'd ever owned, even the little primers we had brought in a trunk from the Eternal Life Seminary. Sarah ran around behind Elizabeth, pointing out the titles and promising to lend books to Mabel when she was older, but after a few minutes she came back to me.

"Didn't you say we were going to eat at five? It's almost five now." She pointed at the nursery clock. "Come *on*, Mama. Our guests can't start without you."

She held out her hand. I took it, rising to my feet.

"I must stop by the lavatory again on the way down," I confessed. "I suspect something I've eaten has disagreed with me."

Sarah huffed with impatience, but just for show; she was looking cheerful at the prospect of festive food. And then I saw her face change. She froze in place, her mouth open, her eyes round with horror.

"Mama! Oh, Mama!"

The words came out in a high, thready squeak that made Elizabeth turn around. I did too, to see what Sarah was looking at. Behind me, the new upholstery of the armchair bore a round, glistening patch of deep crimson.

I looked at Elizabeth and watched *her* expression change too, to one of deep sadness. But when she spoke to Sarah, her voice was calm.

"Fetch Beatrice back, Sarah. Or no—tell her to go all the way downstairs and ask your housekeeper to come up here immediately. And then would you please come back and look after Mabel again for a few minutes? I'd like to help get your mother to her bedroom."

"Is she dying?" Sarah's voice was a thread of sound, her face parchment white. "That's blood—I know it is."

"No, sweetheart. I promise you she's not dying." Elizabeth's voice wasn't quite steady. "But go—quickly—please."

349

For a moment, Sarah still seemed frozen, and then she whipped round and charged for the door, screaming Beatrice's name. Mabel, still in her mother's arms, began to cry.

IT DIDN'T HURT, NOT MUCH. BUT IT SEEMED TO GO ON forever.

There was the chaos of the beginning, as Elizabeth tried to calm her screaming child and hold on to me—my knees had sagged a little, more from shock at seeing the blood than anything else—until eventually she had gotten me to hold her arm. We proceeded slowly downstairs toward my bedroom; aware only of the strength and smoothness of Elizabeth's arm, I lost track of what everyone else was doing.

There was the commotion downstairs—voices and Martin shouting. They were telling him, no doubt, that such matters were not for a man to meddle in. They failed, and I was more glad of it than I could say, although I wept at the look on his face when he finally gained entrance to the bedroom. He found Elizabeth getting me out of my blood-stained skirts and petticoats, unhooking my corset, unpinning my hair, doing everything in her power to make me comfortable for the ordeal ahead. She had been talking to me all the time, calm, sweet words, saying nothing and everything. It was only when Martin burst in that I saw tears track down her cheeks to match my own sudden sobs.

"Is Sarah all right?" I was desperate to reassure my child I would not die. I remembered only too well the night when my own mother had almost died in childbirth, and I summoned up every ounce of strength that I had in me because I would not leave her to grow up without me.

"I left her with Teddy. He'll look after her." Martin curled his fingers around my hand and tried to smile.

"Don't leave her on her own. Don't put her to bed on her own. Let her stay up as late as she wants so I can let her know I'm all right." I was panting in an effort to convey the importance of looking after Sarah.

"I've sent to Miss Baker's house in case she's able to come over. And Tess will be home in a little while." Martin kissed my fingers. "Worry about yourself."

"I'm all right. I'm not going to die."

I was quite sure of that. I was convinced, in a strangely clear-headed way, that I would be fine. My body was young and strong; the cramps and quick, pinching pains that assailed it were not weakening me. The loss of blood was alarming, but not so great that I felt my vitality drain away with each new gush. It was a slow process, like childbirth—it *was* childbirth but far, far too soon. I was not the one who mattered.

Someone else mattered above all things, someone who didn't have a name. I had called it a nuisance. I had called it an incubus. Now, lying propped up in my bed with Elizabeth bending over me and Martin's large, warm hand wrapped around mine, I thought of it at last as a baby. My baby. *Our* baby. Too late, I wanted to undo the past few weeks and cherish the tiny life I hadn't carried for long enough. What a fool I was.

Elizabeth ceded her place to the doctor when he arrived with a nurse but stayed with us. Time passed; blood flowed; my belly contracted and smoothed while I stared up at the canopy of our bed and the surrounding faces.

"The doctor says he sees no cause for alarm about you." Elizabeth appeared beside me, holding a cup to my lips. I sipped the cold water with pleasure.

"The baby?" I heard Martin ask and saw the quick shake of Elizabeth's head.

"I'm sorry, darling." The tears slid down my nose and

cheekbones, as unstoppable as the process happening in the rest of my body. I felt guilty—horribly guilty—as if I had wished the child away, as if I had done it actual harm. "I think I'm going to lose your son."

"*Our* son." Martin gave my hand a little shake. "And it's you I'm concerned for above all. Make no mistake about that, Nellie."

"Sarah. Go to her. Tell her from me I'm going to be all right—she'll believe it coming from you. She needs you, Martin."

I turned my head to see Martin's eyes squeezed tight shut. He breathed hard through his nostrils a few times and then opened his eyes again.

"I'm afraid to leave the room," he said rapidly.

"*I'll* tell her." Elizabeth's voice had something of her mother's tart briskness, but there was a catch in it. "If you absolutely insist on abandoning all sense and ignoring Dr. Walter's express request that you behave like a proper husband and wait downstairs, you can at least make yourself useful. See that she takes some sips of water. It's such a hot day."

She shoved the cup into Martin's free hand and exited the room rapidly, banging the door.

By the time Elizabeth returned, red-eyed but briskly cheerful, I was in the grip of an inexorable process I remembered well from the long-ago day of Sarah's birth. The pangs were almost constant; they were quite bearable, but I was glad I had Martin's hand to cling to.

"Miss Baker is here, and Tess has come home," Elizabeth informed me. "Sarah's all right. She's asking a lot of questions; we sent the men away, and I did my best to explain." She grimaced. "She's a little young, but . . ."

"She always wants to know everything." I blew out my cheeks as my belly squeezed, and I fumbled for the handkerchief to wipe my eyes for the thousandth time. "I'm sorry."

"No need." Elizabeth hesitated. "David says we should both take Mabel home. He's concerned for me. I told him it wasn't catching." She put her hand on her bodice, and Dr. Walter's eyebrows rose.

"If you are also *enceinte,* then you should definitely leave, Mrs. Fletcher. Shock and excitement will do you no good."

"Women have fought in battles and traveled hundreds of miles in my condition," Elizabeth said tartly. And then to me: "I'm beginning to think I should leave you alone since Martin won't go and you've got more help than you need now. But if you don't want me to go . . ."

"I do." I reached out a hand to my friend. "Look after your own health. Are you sure Sarah's fine?"

"Yes, goose, she's fine. Children are stronger than we imagine. I reassured her several times that you were wide awake and talking. There was just one question I couldn't answer . . . I hope you'll forgive me, Nell, but you know what your daughter's like. She made me promise to ask." She turned to the doctor. "How big is the baby?"

Dr. Walter coughed. "I've never known a more irregular household. Quite improper. But since you must know, about the size of a weaned kitten." He held out his hands, half-cupped, to illustrate. "Just a little manikin."

"Then I think I'm done for today." Elizabeth cleared her throat and sniffed, forcing away another access of emotion. She'd been crying quite a lot, if I were any judge. The doctor was right—it wasn't good for her to stay.

She hugged us both; Martin returned her hug with

considerable force. I heard her footsteps recede down the stairs, and we were left to ourselves again.

I was weary. In the hushed and purposeful silence, my eyelids drooped despite the now-familiar pains. I wasn't asleep; but Martin must have thought I was.

"I want to see him," I heard him say. "The child. Don't take him away. We'll bury him ourselves."

Yes. But I kept my eyes closed, oddly reluctant to make the effort to open them. Was I weaker than I realized? Or perhaps I just needed sleep. What time was it? It had been five o'clock when Elizabeth and I came down from the nursery, and I seemed to have been in this bed forever.

"I'd advise against it." The doctor's tone was dry. "It's not an easy sight. And the child could be deformed. That could be why—"

"I want to see him." Martin's grip on my hand had loosened. "My first wife, she was carrying a child when she . . . when she died. A boy. I never saw him, and it's haunted me ever since."

The doctor tutted. "I'm sorry. Rotten luck." He used a different tone of voice with Martin than with me, I noted through the haze of tiredness.

"I've been told—" Martin cleared his throat. "That it's better to face things. Not let them grow in my mind." He was silent for a long moment; I thought I could feel his breath on my face. I tried to open my eyes but couldn't. "Is my wife all right?"

I sensed a cool touch against my wrist. "Her pulse is tolerably strong for the circumstances." A long hesitation. "I think she's exhausted. She—" but his words were becoming garbled and I couldn't grasp the rest of what he said.

I want to see our son too, I decided. *Martin shouldn't do this alone.* And then I seemed to feel Mama's lips against my forehead and dropped into the soundless void below me.

36
LIGHTER

*O*ur daughter must have been born very late at night. I lost all sense of time, but I sensed the household asleep around us when I finally swam back to the surface of life. The urge to push had awakened me, and rest had strengthened me so that I was able to accomplish that part of the proceedings with relative ease. I had stopped crying too and insisted on seeing the baby with a forcefulness that overcame the doctor's objections.

We had seen her heart beat. For perhaps three minutes, we had witnessed the blood move beneath her transparent skin, seen a slight movement behind her sealed eyelids, and then it was over. There was no deformity, only perfection; a tiny chin, ears that seemed hardly to have separated from the skin covering her hairless skull, hands and feet that displayed every bone and blood vessel like an anatomical drawing. So small, so vulnerable. Within a minute or two of the ceasing of the butterfly beat in her chest, the lividity of death had become discernible. We both knew it was finished beyond all repair.

Mercifully, the doctor and nurse withdrew, and we wept

freely over our lost child. It was both the worst moment I had ever experienced and a time of utter peacefulness, made sweeter by Martin's gratitude that I had come to no harm.

We called her Ruth.

"What o'clock is it?" I asked as Martin returned from letting the doctor and nurse out.

"Three in the morning." Martin pushed his fingers through his disordered hair. "Can I get you anything? Are you feeling all right?"

"I'm fine." I was still aware of the slow leaking of blood, but I told the truth; I was certain I would recover in the physical sense. "Perhaps you should sleep though."

"Do *you* want to sleep?" Martin looked down at me from his considerable height.

"I'd rather talk. Come and lie next to me."

Martin bent to unlace his shoes. He had shed his coat long before; now he removed his waistcoat, unhooking his gold timepiece and placing it on a table with its chain wound around it. He unpinned his collar and cuffs, scratching at his neck as he freed himself from the starched cotton. He pulled off his socks and garters, throwing the whole bundle into a chair before coming to join me on the bed.

"That's better." Martin sighed with satisfaction as his head settled on the pillow. He must have been utterly exhausted, I realized. He shifted to place an arm under my shoulders; I moved so my head rested comfortably in the hollow of bone and muscle where his arm met his upper chest. The blood flowed again as I changed position in the bed, but the nurse had left me well provided for. In the morning, Alice would be there, and I needed no other assistance.

"Are you all right?"

I didn't grasp whether Martin was asking if I was comfortable or inquiring after the state of my spirits. I chose to respond to the latter.

"I'm sad."

I wanted to say, *and I feel guilty*, but I wasn't quite ready to confess how much I'd resented the child. Ruth. How much I had resented Ruth. When I remembered her tiny face, unfinished yet already perfect, I glimpsed the lost future. The little sister who would toddle about after Sarah, the child learning her lessons, the young woman dreaming of suitors or a destiny without a husband, the adult with whom I could have sat and talked one distant day, wondering at the changes in the world around us. Not a nuisance, not an incubus, but a being of infinite potential.

"I should have rested more," was the only expression I could give to the knowledge this was all my fault.

"Don't say that." Martin squeezed my shoulder. "You *did* rest. I've never seen you so idle. It worried me, you know. It didn't seem right that you should be so exhausted." He kissed the top of my eyebrow. "Dr. Walter agreed with me. He suspects there was something wrong from the start. Perhaps it's even a blessing that you lost her so early. Maybe your own life would have been in danger."

"Maybe." I paused, trying to read my body. "Do you know, I believe I'm already better somehow. Lighter." I scrubbed at my eyes with my free hand. "How is it possible to be lighter and yet so heavy in heart? You wanted a child so much, and I've let you down."

"If you imagine it was the baby I was afraid for when Mrs. Hartfield came to tell me what was happening—" Martin stopped and drew breath. "When I saw you with your face as white as your petticoat and saw the blood—all I thought of was you. When the doctor told me the baby was almost certainly lost but he had little reason to worry about *you*, I wanted to kiss his feet. I would pass up any number of sons to have you beside me, Nellie." He chuckled. "Dr. Walter said I didn't even really need him there, except for reassurance. He implied that I was being a fussy old hen. I expect he'll regale his friends with the story of the man who wouldn't leave his wife's side."

I turned so I could see him better. "I'm a lucky woman to have such a husband."

"The luck is all mine, my darling." Martin wriggled around so he too lay on his side, his face close to mine. The lamp burned so low that I was only aware of him as a vague shape, blurred by proximity.

"Do you think Sarah will be all right?" I asked. "She was so frightened when she noticed the blood. I didn't scream at all, did I? I don't think I did. Thank heaven I was never in enough pain to scream."

"I promise the first thing I'll do when I wake up is go find her and bring her to visit you. They put her to bed after she fell asleep on the settee. Miss Baker is sleeping in her room."

"Where's Ruth?"

Martin pushed himself up on one arm and reached over me to turn off the lamp. In the darkness, I detected the soft breeze from the open window, cooling at last, heard the distant clank of the railroad and the sleepy chirp of a bird in one of Calumet Avenue's young trees.

"Mrs. Hartfield sent for the undertaker. He'll make her comfortable in her little casket." Martin's fingers explored my face, brushed my heavy hair away so it didn't encroach upon my cheeks so much. "Mrs. Hartfield thinks the baby shouldn't be alone tonight. She's going to watch over her and go to bed once there's somebody else to replace her in the morning. Everyone else is asleep." He kissed me gently on the lips. "We should sleep too."

"Yes."

"And you're still going to Lake Forest, you understand?" He yawned. "I want you to have a good long rest."

"Yes, Martin."

Rest. Yes, I needed it. Martin's breathing was deepening; perhaps I could sleep with him beside me. I fumbled for his hand and smiled as his fingers curled around mine.

"I love you, Martin," I murmured into the darkness. But if he made a reply, I was asleep before I heard it.

I WOKE TO FIND ALICE BENDING OVER ME, HER SENSIBLE FACE sympathetic but smiling. Martin had been as good as his word, appearing downstairs in robe and slippers to fetch Sarah—but he had sent Alice up first to ensure I was, as he put it, "properly disposed to receive visitors."

Some practical steps had to be accomplished, but twenty-five minutes later I sat propped up amid fresh bed linen, my unruly hair braided, my face and hands washed. Freshly arranged flowers scented the air. A glance in my hand mirror showed me that my face was pale but reasonably like its usual appearance.

Sarah entered the room quietly, holding Martin's hand, but she let go of it when she realized I was sitting up and smiling at her. She climbed onto the bed in a fluid movement and gave me a careful hug, placing a soft kiss on one cheek and then the other with none of the boisterousness she occasionally displayed. She then sat back on her heels and gave me a long, thoughtful look while Martin made himself comfortable in an armchair.

"Tess is downstairs praying for Ruth," she said eventually. "She says she'll come up later, but it's my turn now. Miss Baker will come up later too. She was on the trundle in my bedroom, isn't that funny? I did laugh when I woke up. Miss

Baker says I don't have to do any schoolwork today, even though it's Monday." Her smooth brow furrowed. "Ruth is in a little white casket in the parlor like a casket for a doll, and Papa says she's *very* tiny. I picked four flowers from the garden and put them on the casket for you and Papa and me and Tess, and I told Ruth all about her family. Alice said she was born much too soon. Miss Baker said the proper word is 'miscarriage,' but I mustn't go chattering about it to everybody because it's private. Did it hurt, Mama?"

"Not very much." I folded her left hand in mine, noting the ink stains on forefinger and middle finger. Sarah had been practicing with the pen again, schoolwork or no. I placed my other hand on my heart. "It hurts here, in the sense of feelings, because I'd rather have Ruth here with us than in heaven." I swallowed to stop the easy tears welling. "I'm probably going to be sad for a while."

"Tess said God's will is hard to understand sometimes. She's sad too."

"And so is your Papa." It was Martin who spoke. "But he's grateful to have a beautiful daughter already. He's counting his blessings this morning."

"And so am I." I gathered Sarah into my arms. "It's all right, sweetheart, you won't hurt me by sitting on my lap. In a few days, I'll be ready to go to Lake Forest with you, and I'll soon be myself again." I hugged her tighter. "We'll all miss Ruth, but we'll be a happy family, as we've always been."

37
RECOVERY

*E*ight years before, I had jumped into a river to save Sarah. Now, with nothing to do but rest and brood in the Parnells' pleasant home in Lake Forest, I experienced the same sensation of my feet searching for some kind of solid ground but finding nothing but emptiness below me. I was lost; I was myself, but I was not myself. I didn't belong.

"It looks like Martin's finally found his piece of land for our summer residence."

I put down the sheets of paper covered in Martin's neat, sloping hand and reached for my glass of lemonade. The liquid was warm.

There was no respite from the heat. The strident, metallic song of the cicadas leaped from tree to tree as one colony took over from the other in an endless concert. The shade of the immense oak tree, a survivor from long before the small town of Lake Forest had put down its roots between lake and prairie, was as welcome as the gentle breeze that blew in from the water.

"*His* land? Your land, don't you mean? I presume you intend to live here occasionally." Elizabeth's eyes remained half-closed, her flushed face shaded by the brim of a wide straw hat. Her position, reclining on a wicker divan, made her condition more obvious. She shifted, resting her hand on the swelling of her belly in a protective gesture that brought a lump to my throat. I changed position on my own divan, gazing out through the trees to the blue lake beyond the small park. Not looking at Elizabeth.

"I mean, it's Martin's project, that's all. He likes houses."

My voice sounded sharp to my own ears, but Elizabeth didn't notice. I heard her muffled yawn and the creak of the divan as she sat up a little. I turned back to face her.

"I'm so happy you're really going to build a house in Lake Forest at last." Elizabeth *did* look happy, as if life were quite normal. "Will you be on the bluff and have a beach? That's what this place lacks. Father always says he wanted to be well back from the bluff's edge in case it crumbled, but it would be so nice not to have to get the pony cart out every time we want to bathe, wouldn't it? I hope you'll have a grand estate and invite us to stay every summer. Lots of room for the children to play."

After a few moments' silence, she lifted the brim of her hat and looked hard at me. "Sorry."

"Don't be silly. You can hardly avoid the subject of children around me, and it's unnecessary, anyhow. I'm merely refreshing my memory as to what Martin said." I waved the letter I'd been staring at in illustration, then decided it would be most useful to cool my face and began agitating it vigorously. "Yes, we'll be able to get down to the lake. It's the three lots nearest to the cemetery, about fourteen acres. Martin says he'll build the house on the southernmost lot and keep the acreage near the cemetery as wild as possible, with paths for riding and walking."

"Fourteen acres, my word. I suppose it'll be a simply enormous house."

"I hope not." Giving up on trying to cool the warm air by moving it around, I folded the letter and put it in my pocket. "Martin says he wants a country house rather than an estate. He says it's a mistake to build too large or too grand. You have to think of the upkeep over your entire lifetime, and we can't just assume we're always going to have the same income."

Elizabeth grinned. "Cautious beast. Just like David."

"I'm glad of it." I looked out at the lake again. "I don't like the thought of the three of us—and Tess, of course—rattling around in *another* vast mansion."

Elizabeth remained silent for a long moment. "There's no reason you shouldn't have more children, Nell dear," she said at last.

"Of course there isn't."

Of course there wasn't. In the bodily sense, I was making a good recovery. I could walk for miles with ease in the cool of early morning and play with Sarah for hours without tiring. The reflected light of the lake had penetrated under my broad hat, bringing a little color to my usually pale skin, and the dark shadows under my eyes were almost gone.

My spirits were low, as should be expected. I lacked the usual inner urgings to create sketches or to make something with my hands, but I'd been through this mood before and knew my energy and creative powers would return as they always did. I loved staying with the Parnells; Elizabeth was stimulating, pleasant company; Sarah and I seemed closer than ever and often sought out opportunities to be alone together, walking hand in hand around Lake Forest's curving streets.

Tess appeared a little distracted, to be sure, but that was because she had insisted we bring Donny with us on the pretext that the landaulet would be the most suitable conveyance for a summer by the lake. She was happy—mostly, it seemed, because of the times she and Donny, who always managed to find some work to do, would sit quietly talking after his day's tasks were accomplished. All was peace and harmony in this household as the long summer days and balmy nights slipped by.

In short, there was every hope I would make an excellent recovery. Yet the situation between Martin and me was . . . peculiar.

The sweet intimacy of that night of grief had ebbed away like an outgoing tide on a quiet shore, a gradual fading that left bleakness behind it. It seemed natural, in the days following our loss, that Martin would sleep in the chamber adjoining his dressing room, which held a narrow bed and a small desk. He used that room when he worked late at night and didn't want to disturb me when retiring. In the first days after Ruth's too-early entry into the world, my nights had frequently been disturbed by troubled dreams and bodily discomforts. I had not been a good sleeping companion, so I didn't blame Martin when he retreated to his single bed and left me to fidget.

And then we'd come to Lake Forest, and Martin and I had once more been in the same bed for one night. Martin had kissed me good night, a swift peck on the forehead, as if I were once more his childhood friend, turned his back on me and gone to sleep immediately. He'd been tired, of course; we all were after a riotous dinner when Sarah, allowed to stay up late, had shown off with a determination that caused Mrs. Parnell's generous mouth to tuck in at the corners.

And yet my hostess had said nothing, either to me or to Sarah, and I knew she understood. We were all, Martin,

Sarah, and I, trying too hard. We were trying to put our family back onto its normal footing, back where it had been since I married Martin: the three of us and Tess. But it had been the four of us and Tess for a while, and none of us succeeded in forgetting it.

Martin had left me with the same gentle kiss, the jovial, affectionate cheerfulness that seemed so forced and unnatural. Left me with my guilt. Now he was writing to me in the most practical terms possible of the piece of land on which he intended to build us a summer home. It would keep him very busy, he said, and in those words, I saw a warning that he would be absent more often.

I picked up my glass again and considered the sweet liquid into which two flies had strayed and drowned. I swirled the glass a little to detach the victims from its smooth sides and rose to tip the remains of my drink into the roots of the oak tree.

"It'll be time to bathe soon," I said cheerfully to Elizabeth's hat, which hid most of her face. She couldn't see my face, so I didn't have to try too hard to *look* cheerful.

"Mmmm, cool water." Elizabeth stretched; I heard another yawn from under the hat as she swung her legs to the ground and stood up in a flutter of gauzy flounces. She had lost her taste for sweet things again, and her glass contained plain unsweetened tea, far less likely to attract insects than my lemonade. She held out her hand for my glass, which she put on the small table that held the now-empty jugs.

"Let's go over to the paddock," she suggested. "Sarah might be there if she hasn't gone off with the Ogilvie children. She's running quite wild with Miss Baker away."

"She is." I grinned, genuinely cheerful for a moment. "Those children seem to know a lot of *other* children. Do you know, this is the first time I've seen Sarah enjoying the company of other children in such an informal way. She seems to have learned not to boss them about and to hide her cleverness, and that's helping her make friends."

"It's also because they're from all walks of life." Turning her back on the cushion-strewn divans, the various journals with which she had been amusing herself, and the empty drinking vessels, Elizabeth reached out for my arm and steered me toward the small paddock at the rear of the Parnells' two-acre plot. "The Ogilvie children are the most democratic little urchins I've ever encountered, and that despite their father bringing in a small fortune in meat-packing. They've picked up half the servants' children in Lake Forest, to the despair of some of the mothers. But *they*—the mothers—shouldn't be such snobbish cats. Do you know, I've already been *lectured* by some of Mother's friends on not letting Mabel keep bad company, and she's not even two."

"I hope you'll be every bit as democratic as the Ogilvies," I said.

"Oh, I will. Feminism is all about equality. Once I've had this little one and hired a proper nursemaid, I intend to *plunge* back into the Cause. I'm sure I only have a short time before I'm having another, and I plan to make the most of my freedom."

It was so simple for Elizabeth, I thought. She had given in to David's desire for children easily and without a fuss; and easily and without a fuss, she would take up her own neglected interests at the earliest opportunity. Why could I not have done that? Why had I fretted myself into ill-health and lost my baby as a consequence?

"When is Martin coming to visit?" Elizabeth's voice interrupted my sour thoughts.

"He doesn't say." And I was determined not to ask him. If he needed time apart from me and the rest of his family, I wouldn't stand in his way.

"Men are always so *casual* about these things. How do they get away with it?"

Elizabeth waved, and I looked toward the paddock. Sarah *was* there, talking to Tess and Donny. She saw me and ran toward me. I saw she wore her oldest, shortest dress, which was now rather *too* short.

"Mama, I jumped a log!" Sarah wrapped her arms around me—she could reach higher and higher on my person every month. "Or at least Muffin jumped it, but the instructor says I've a good seat and I'm a fine horsewoman. When is Papa coming? I want to show him. One day I'll be able to go hunting with him, won't I? May I learn to play polo?"

"Goodness, no." Elizabeth laid a hand on my daughter's hair, which was tangled and full of dirt. "Girls don't play polo or hunt. You'll have to wait for a far more enlightened society for *that*."

"When is Papa coming here?" Sarah asked me.

"He doesn't say, sweetheart."

"I want to see him."

For a child who rarely whined, there was definitely something of a grumble in her voice. Fortunately, Sarah thought of another question before I worked out how to respond.

"Is it time to bathe in the lake?" She inspected the lines of dirt under her fingernails. "Can you come right into the water now, Mama?"

"Not yet."

"But you *said*—"

Sarah stopped abruptly and bit her lip, looking up at me. I suppressed a sudden urge to snap at my child in a way I almost never did and counted to twenty before I bent down so that her face was closer to mine.

"I said I would come in the water properly when I stopped bleeding, Sarah. I haven't. Now please don't embarrass me by asking again. There are things a lady doesn't talk about in public. This is why we don't normally tell children about such matters."

But Sarah had seen something children didn't usually see, and in our times alone together I perhaps said more than I should. I was surrounded by adults—people I liked—yet I had succumbed to the temptation to make a confidante of my eight-and-a-half-year-old child, because she was the only person in my immediate vicinity who asked specific and intimate questions and allowed me to talk about *everything*, to repeat myself a hundredfold, to describe endlessly the way it felt to lose—

I avoided overly unpleasant details, of course. She *was* only a child. But there were things I could say, needed to say, and Sarah wanted to know so much. She seemed fascinated by the entire process of being with child, of giving birth; she dredged every moment of her own birth out of my memory, although I had at least remembered to be vague about where she'd been born.

And she wanted absolutely every detail about Ruth. I should have felt badgered and upset, but there was so much relief in describing all the tiny things I remembered only too well that I gave in with little resistance to the small, expert interrogator with the jade-green, piercing gaze. How big were her hands? Her toes? Could we see her heart through her skin or just the movement? Did she open her mouth? Did I think she *could* open her eyes but didn't? What did her knees look like? Her shoulders?

"I'm sorry, Mama." Now Sarah's eyes met mine with a depth of understanding—and pity—that gave me a sudden glimpse of the woman she would one day become. She was grieving too, I remembered. I hugged her hard, the mingled scents of dirt, sweat, and horse in my nostrils, her tangled and matted hair scratching my face. Never since the day I had decided to keep Sarah had I felt such a need to cling to her, close as we had always been. And precisely at this age, she was learning to look outside our family circle for friendship. It was as if she was deliberately allowing me time with her too because she sensed my need. My loneliness.

"Don't pay me too much heed, darling." I finished with a quick kiss on a somewhat grimy forehead. "The heat's making me cross. I'll tell you what I'll do—after you've bathed yourself clean, I'm going to work every single knot out of your hair and braid it nice and tight. I'll be gentle, I promise. I know you're a big girl now and you can brush your own hair, but I think there are some spots you've forgotten."

"You can do it." Sarah put a hand into mine. "I don't mind."

In ordinary times, I would have made some remark about this concession since normally Sarah preferred anyone but me to brush and comb her thick, springy hair. I was deft enough with needle and pen, but I'd never learned the trick of hair—my own was so strong it had put up with considerable abuse before Alice tamed it. But these were not ordinary times. I tightened my grip on my daughter's hand, took a deep breath, and began to tell her about Martin's land purchase in Lake Forest.

38

TROUBLE

*R*eturning to our house in Chicago proved harder than I'd expected.

"It seems so strange. And so large," I remarked to Tess.

And so unlike a home. I looked around the spacious bedroom, trying to work out if anything had changed. Surely Martin would have made some mark on our shared space after nine weeks on his own? But there was an unlived-in look to the entire house somehow. Not dusty, nothing like that—in fact, it was immaculate, faultless, fragranced with beeswax polish and potpourri. I supposed Mrs. Hartfield had taken the opportunity to organize a thorough clean. I hadn't seen a grain of dirt anywhere.

"It's nice to have the extra room again." Tess's round face was rosy and shining with happiness, lightly freckled from the days spent out of doors in Lake Forest. "I like my sitting room more than ever, although I'm very grateful for the pretty bedroom I slept in at the Parnells'. But home's best, isn't it?"

"I suppose it is." I looked out of the window at the distant lake, blue under the September sunshine. Freshness tinged the air now as summer lost its grip. Something about the sharp, almost autumnal tang filled me with energy as we traveled back toward the city, but that enthusiasm had died when we entered the house. Still—

"I intend to go to the store," I announced. "I really must talk to Madame and find out what's happening."

"Now? I thought you didn't want to go back till tomorrow." Tess's scanty eyebrows rose above her spectacles. "What's the hurry?"

"Hurry? I've been absent for three months." *And I've barely seen Martin in all that time.* The thought made me irritable and restless.

I pulled open the dresser drawers, trying to remember what I kept in them—and then shut them again. Alice would take care of all that. I didn't need to know where things were stored any more. I suppressed a sigh and turned back to Tess.

"I don't want anybody making a fuss about my return. I'd far rather surprise them, and I'll get more of an impression of what's happening in the store if I just walk in like any other customer. People will be busy and won't feel obliged to treat me like the returning prodigal."

"You didn't mind last year when we came home from France."

Tess ran her hand over the small case that held my jewelry. It had been in Alice's possession all the way from Lake Forest, but she had left it on the bed while she supervised the unloading and disposition of our trunks and valises. The E.C.L.R. monogram gleamed bright gold against the dark blue leather, the R dominating the other letters cleverly woven into its sheltering strokes. Tess's stubby forefinger traced the swirls and lines in a way I suddenly found irritating, but I pushed down my feelings with determination. It wasn't Tess's fault that I was tetchy, and she'd reminded me of our happy return from France in all innocence.

"The trip to France was a much longer journey. It's of no moment to come back after a stay in Lake Forest." I resisted the temptation to pull the case away from Tess's hands and kept my tone carefully neutral. "You won't be too dull on your own, will you, after being used to so much company? I don't suppose we'll see Sarah and Miss Baker for the rest of the day. Sarah was in a lather of impatience to visit the zoo again."

"Of course I won't be dull." Tess grinned and left off touching my case, smoothing down the bedspread instead. It didn't need neatening. "And I'm not on my own. I'm going to do my own unpacking, go through all the household books with Mrs. Hartfield, and find out what they're planning for our meals for the rest of the month. But it'll be such a nice surprise for Martin if you turn up at the store, Nell. I think you should go. Or perhaps he's thinking of coming home to give us *all* a big surprise."

A brief spark of hope flared inside me at this notion, but I stamped on it. "I doubt he'll have the time." I looked down at my traveling dress. "I suppose I ought to change. Goodness, I can hardly remember what's in my closets. I'm sick of the gowns I wore in Lake Forest. I need something new."

I needed clothes that didn't remind me of the early summer. My figure had resumed its accustomed slenderness, was perhaps a little leaner than before. My appetite had not been good owing to the heat, and I'd done so much more walking than usual in Lake Forest. The dresses I had taken with me hung just a little loose, especially below the waist. That would not do at all; the clothes I wore constituted an advertisement for Rutherford & Co. and needed to fit perfectly. I would need to have a fitting done this afternoon and commission a dress or two. Ample excuse to turn up at Rutherford's half a day early.

Tess bustled off to see to her own room. I crossed to the bed, picking up the jewelry case. I spared a glance at the smooth coverlet and immaculately laundered linen, my treacherous memory taking me back to that night in June before turning resolutely away and putting the case down on a table. I owned a dark green day dress, I remembered, that I hadn't worn much because it had become tight across the hips—that might serve. I could kill two birds with one stone and please Martin by wearing the pendant he'd given me for my twenty-sixth birthday.

We had done our best that day, Martin and I. I had been genuinely pleased with the necklace, which was to my taste— unusual and exquisite without being in the least bit ostentatious. It was Indian, a delicate pattern of garnet flowers and peridot leaves and stems set in a minutely carved ivory base with four oval diamonds in the corners of the lozenge-shaped frame. They were the first diamonds I'd ever seen that didn't glitter; instead, they looked more like drops of water. Or teardrops. On the back of the pendant, the words *"Semper Idem"* were inscribed. Martin told me they meant "always the same," but he hadn't elaborated on why he had chosen that inscription.

We'd found little time to be alone and almost no time to talk. Martin had stayed up late discussing politics with Mr. Parnell, and I had been asleep when he'd come to bed. When I'd awoken, he was already up since he had an early appointment with the agent for the land he'd soon after purchased. He hadn't expected me to accompany him, returning only for a hasty meal before taking the train back to Chicago.

The last time I'd seen Martin was on the last day of August, and he hadn't stayed overnight. He'd arrived on a new horse, a spirited bay called Lightning, who, according to

Martin, liked to run and was therefore the perfect animal for the thirty-mile distance. He'd taken us to view the site of our new Lake Forest summer home, although there had been little to see as the only trails in and out of the property had been made by deer and were impassable to both the landaulet and the Parnells' carriage. Walking to the bluff would have meant struggling through mosquito-ridden brush invested with poison ivy, poison oak, and poison sumac, so we had admired what we could glimpse of the land and taken Martin's word for the rest.

I looked down at the jeweled pendant in my hand. It was like Martin; the more you studied it, the more it revealed of itself that was intricate and fine and interesting. And complicated. A small spark lit and smoldered inside my frame, and with it came a tiny surge of enthusiasm—at last—for my neglected profession.

My visit to the store wouldn't be just a matter of effort, I decided. Nor duty, nor avoidance of any kind of planned welcome. It wouldn't be about Martin, at least not about Martin in his role as my husband. I would go to the store because I wanted to be there, in the place where I had spent so many productive hours. I wanted to talk with Madame as a dressmaker and see the gleam of brisk, businesslike interest in her sharp eyes. I wanted to have a fitting done and then wander through the dress goods departments to pick out the most interesting new fabrics, obtain samples to consult as I came up with my first sketches since June.

I wanted to meet with Martin and Joe as a partner in the store and find out what had been happening over the summer. I wanted above all to see Martin in the environment where we had so much in common that was *not* directly personal, a place where change would only mean progress. Perhaps in that way I would begin to understand what had happened to us.

I opened doors until I found the dark green ensemble and pulled it out. Yes, it would serve. It followed the latest fashion by having no train at all, a style I always preferred for work; with its jacket-like overbodice it looked most businesslike. I could take the pendant off its heavy chain and pin it to where a modish fall of lace softened the high neckline.

"Time to look your best, Nellie Rutherford," I admonished myself. "Let everyone know you've fully recovered your health and are prepared to begin work again."

I turned and smiled as a soft cough and a bumping sound announced the arrival of Alice and the men carrying my trunks. Donny was one of them; he met my eyes with his shy smile as he lowered the large portmanteau he was balancing on a broad shoulder to the spot indicated by Alice. Suddenly, the room, so large and empty a few minutes before, took on some life and color. We would heap the bed with clothes waiting to be sorted, and by the time it was clean and clear again I would view it as just an ordinary piece of furniture.

"Yes, I *was* talking to myself." I grinned at Alice. "I'm going to the store, and I want to create a good impression. Let's get these things unpacked as quickly as possible, and then you can polish me up. I need to put the summer behind me and make a fresh start for fall."

I felt confident as Capell handed me down from the landau outside the main Rutherford's entrance. Its huge, ornate canopy spread above me, a riot of peacocks, fruit-laden branches, and exotic vines woven around the motto: *Dress Well*. The trunks and stems of the trees and vines were carved into the pillars that separated the three double doors; on the glass pane in every door was etched the legend "Rutherford & Co." and the peacock feather motif. The tingle of excitement in my belly at the thought that I belonged to this palatial enterprise was no less strong than on the day I first walked into the new store as a full partner.

A throng of customers, mostly women, passed in and out of the doors. The doormen were busy trying to acknowledge as many of them as possible, occasionally barking orders to the younger men whose job was to call for carriages or hired cabs. All of them tipped their hats to me with a swift murmur of "Mrs. Rutherford" that caused several patrons to crane their necks round with curiosity, seeking to catch a glimpse of me. I was glad the green dress became me well and especially pleased about the clever detailing on the cuffs that caught the eye as I folded my green-trimmed parasol. My hat was little more than a flexible oval on which were arrayed feathers and flowers in a sort of gladiator's crest, but it increased my height by three or four inches and showed off my thick hair in a way that had brought a beam to Alice's face as she inserted the pins needed to hold it on.

The doormen should smile more, I thought; they looked unusually grave. I stepped into the bustling entrance hall, which displayed the items women could not resist buying on impulse: hats, gloves, purses, parasols, lacy handkerchiefs, fans, hair combs, perfume bottles, and jewelry of the more modestly priced and ephemeral kind. Here, the atmosphere was one of febrile excitement, every counter an incitement to spend money on something frivolous before getting down to the serious business of the dress goods rooms. The customers were enticed into the latter by the tremendous displays of fabric over and around the doors, among which hung the large artists' representations of sample designs for which we were now so well-known. Not my designs, I realized. I had not, after all, come up with anything for the fall season. The thought lowered my mood for a second, but I remained determined not to give in to ennui anymore.

This part of the store was always busy. The employees who recognized me looked startled to see me but were too occupied with customers to say anything. I supposed they imagined I would stay at home—perhaps they thought I had lost interest in the store. They would know I'd been ill, but possibly not the nature of my indisposition; perhaps they imagined I would never come back.

I would have to spend some time speaking to all the sales staff. I decided to head straight to the atelier, where there were no customers, to prevent me from talking to the employees and see if I could speak for a while with Madame Belvoix. Perhaps on the way up I should stop by Martin's office. If he were there, I could arrange a time for a meeting between him, Joe, and me. I turned toward the doors leading to the staircase, threading my way through customers and around counters, automatically noting new items as I did so.

I had almost reached the stairwell entrance when I glanced toward the steam elevators and froze. Four men were approaching the elevators from the direction of the side entrance used only by employees; they were accompanied by a man whose dress suggested he was one of the Rutherford's managers, although at this distance I couldn't see which. The elevator's operator flung the inner and outer gates of the car open; the manager ushered the men in. They all wore the dark blue uniform of the Chicago police.

My breath caught in my throat. Three and a half years had passed since I had arrived for my first glimpse of Rutherford's and discovered the Chicago police had arrested Martin for the murder of his wife. Every second of that scene was preserved in my memory, indelible as if burnt in with a red-hot poker. The sight of the policemen brought it all back and set my heart thumping in an erratic, skipping rhythm that for a moment robbed me of all my sense.

Where had they gone? Should I make my way over to the

elevator and ask the operator to which floor they had been carried? I looked at the customers crisscrossing the sales floor, all intent on their errand. No, I shouldn't make a fuss. It was probably nothing. A petty theft, the discovery of a gang of pickpockets or purse-cutters—such things were not unknown on the streets of Chicago, even on State Street in the middle of the day. They were no doubt holding the miscreants upstairs on the third floor and had summoned the police to arrest them. It would not be Martin who had been arrested, not this time.

I yanked open the door to the stairway and started upward, moving rapidly, trying to calm my breath to make it easier to move. Even with its tiers of kick pleats my narrow skirt did not allow me to run upstairs, so I concentrated on taking small, fast steps. It would be all right, I kept telling myself. It would be nothing.

I heard a door above me open, and men's voices echoed through the air. One of them was Joe's, and they were coming downward, toward me. I stopped and waited.

"I certainly don't need the exercise." An Irish voice, accompanied by some laughter and humorous remarks from the other men.

"Mr. Storrar naturally assumed they'd be on the third floor," I heard Joe say. "Well, at least we're going downstairs —Nell!"

Joe had seen me, of course. He slowed his steps but did not halt his downward progress. To my relief, a half smile curved his lips.

"What's wrong?" My voice sounded a little breathless. "Where's Martin?"

"Down by the vault." Joe twisted to look behind him at the four policemen. "Gentlemen, this is Mrs. Rutherford, one of the other partners. I would like her to accompany us." He turned his attention back to me. "There was an attempt at robbery," he said shortly as he reached the point where I stood. "Of the safe room. In broad daylight, if you please. They knew the time at which the vault would be opened."

I began to head downstairs; it was much easier walking downward, and I was able to match the men's rapid descent. "I thought that was some kind of arcane secret," I protested.

"It is—normally. There's been a most unfortunate lapse in our precautions. Mr. McCombs is usually informed of the correct time at seven thirty a.m. via the speaking tube that runs from the third floor to the sales floor. But yesterday afternoon he sent a note to the third floor insisting he should know in advance whether the vault would be opened early or late within the usual four-hour period. He had a customer who was seriously interested in a diamond parure. A particularly expensive one."

"And they told him? Is Mr. McCombs under suspicion, then?"

"Naturally, yes, as a matter of routine, but he's been with us since we opened the store in '72. Before that he was one of Sol Bermann's most trusted employees, so it's unlikely he was in league with the robbers. He's certainly guilty of carelessness. It would have been a stupendous sale, and McCombs was eager to accommodate the buyer, who's a Cincinnati manufacturer—quite genuine and able to prove his bona fides—staying at the Grand Pacific. He ascertained the vault would be opened 'early,' meaning in the first hour of trading, and sent a note to the Grand Pacific arranging for the customer to visit the store at the end of that period. That was yesterday evening. The employee charged with delivering the note to the customer was supposed to put the note into his hand personally, and she did try to do so at first, at six p.m., only to be told that the customer had gone out. She returned at midnight, and being told that the customer had come in at ten and was now undoubtedly in bed—they wouldn't tell her the room number—she left the note there for him, and it was delivered to him with his breakfast. So there are a dozen different theories about how the note might have been read, although the customer swears it was in a sealed Rutherford's envelope. He burned the note, unfortunately, being himself a cautious party."

"Seems to me it'd be the lady who ran around Chicago with the envelope in her pocket we should talk to," one of the police officers said. "What kind of lady is out at midnight anyway?"

"Oh, she's down there with Mr. Rutherford. That's another whole set of problems," Joe said briefly. "In any case, Nell, when the customer arrived and was met by Mr. McCombs, the two of them got an unpleasant shock when two other men turned up and pulled pistols on them."

"In the store?" I could hear the astonishment in my voice. "How is that possible? Didn't it create a panic?"

"The miscreants played it very well." We had reached the basement, and Joe pulled open the door for me, then ushered the policemen through. "Pretended to have recognized the businessman from somewhere or the other, then once they were close enough, they threatened the two men and had them lead the way to the vault room. We've always told McCombs not to offer resistance to direct attack—to cooperate fully. No amount of money is worth a man's life."

"So were they caught? The robbers?"

Joe shook his head. "One of the men we hire to spot pickpockets and shoplifters became suspicious at the last moment and rounded up half a dozen men and sent the closest cash boys out to find a police officer. They found McCombs shaking like a leaf as he tried to work the combination, the unfortunate customer tied to a chair, and the two men with neckerchiefs around their faces like a scene from a penny dreadful. The robbers shot high to make the men back off and vamoosed right through the sales floor, which caused a certain amount of excitement, as you'd imagine. We'll be in the papers for sure. They ran off toward the Exposition Building. Three of the doormen gave chase as well as the policemen, but the robbers were fast, and once they made it to the railroad depot, they got clean away."

"So nobody's under arrest." We had reached the antechamber of the vault.

"Not this time."

It was Martin who answered me, but one of the policemen chimed in.

"We're just here to interview witnesses, ma'am. And check around, you know? There'll be a detective over later. We're taking this pretty seriously—there've been too many of these robberies in the last couple two, three years. You the owner?" he asked Martin.

At this point, various introductions were made, and I had time to look around. Not that I needed more than a fraction of a second to see who was present; the small room was now uncomfortably crowded. Martin, of course, looking formal and strange to my eyes in his immaculate tailoring, his white-blond hair bright in the light from the gas. Mr. McCombs, sitting in one of the armchairs, pale and uncomfortable. And Thea Lombardi.

39

STORY

*G*etting through even the preliminary inquiries was a lengthy business. The policemen seemed thoroughly familiar with the operation of a time lock; they entertained themselves by comparing the various makes and models available, which was all very well but had little to do with our own case. Martin explained that the opening time changed daily, going over much of the ground Joe had covered and declining to give precise details on how they chose and communicated the correct hour. His reluctance offended the officers of the law.

"You think we're corrupt, I guess," said the more senior of those gentlemen once the others were done blustering and trying to bully Martin into supplying further details. He had been silent so far, this officer, letting the other men talk. His eyes roved from Martin, to Joe, to the unhappy-looking Mr. McCombs, and to Thea's still, graceful form.

"I think it's a foolish man who says more than he needs to." Martin's tone was not unfriendly, but I saw by the tightness of his jaw and the carefully schooled expression on his face that this interview was dredging up some hard memories. He'd seen rather too much of the Chicago police in the year of Lucetta's death.

"Hmph." The senior officer turned to Mr. McCombs, who had been crossing and recrossing his legs and fidgeting so that he looked more guilty every second. "So we come to the matter of your arrangement with the gentleman from Cincinnati—who is where, by the way?"

"He wouldn't wait." Mr. McCombs bit the inside of his lip, speaking quickly. "He left all of his forwarding details and has promised to return to Chicago, but he had a train to catch." He hesitated. "I—may I—" He looked round wildly at the crowded room, the four officers, then at Thea, then at me. He flushed brick-red but drew a deep breath and faced the senior officer squarely. "I really *must* visit the washroom."

The admission of this all-too-human need seemed to release the tension that had been building in the room. Something that might almost have been a twinkle crept into the senior policeman's eyes. He nodded. "But two of my men will wait outside the door."

"You can all four stand and watch if you want." Mr. McCombs sprang to his feet and made rapidly for the exit, followed by two police officers. "Frankly, the alternative is too horrible to contemplate."

There was a moment of silence as we listened to the three sets of hurried footsteps. Once all the sounds died away, Joe spoke.

"Do we have to remain down here now you've seen the vault? I don't like keeping the ladies in this stuffy atmosphere. I don't see why we shouldn't continue our discussions over a cup of coffee." He looked at the two remaining officers. "Unless you have other ideas."

"We might want to take the two of them down to the precinct, at that." The senior man contemplated Thea, pulling at his mustache. "There's a couple of detectives been working on these jewel thefts, and I think they'll want to hear the details firsthand when they get back from Aurora. First time they've tried a daylight raid—*if* these are the same people and not some kind of imitator—and first time it might be possible to get some kind of description. I'll send for a police matron for the young lady."

"Is Miss Lombardi under suspicion?" I asked.

"We can't discount the possibility of an inside job." The police officer sighed. "Still, as Mr.—Salassi?—says, we don't need to all stay down here. Kind of stuffy, all right."

"Salazar. Our partner and general manager, in case you've forgotten. Does my wife need to remain?" Martin looked directly at me for almost the first time. "She's been unwell and only returned from the country today. She has nothing to do with this."

"If I can insist on staying, I *do* insist," I said quickly. "For Miss Lombardi's sake. I'm her—" I stopped. What was I? Not her guardian, certainly. I didn't think Thea would call me her friend. And she hadn't lived with us for almost two years. "I'm her employer in the sense that I'm a partner in this store." I made my voice as firm as I was able. "The only female partner and an intimate of her late mother. I think her brother would want me to stand beside her."

"A brother?" The officer made a quick note in the small book he carried with him. "Any other family?"

"None whatsoever." Thea spoke coolly, but there was a flicker of decision in her eyes. "There's no need to disturb my brother. I'd like Mrs. Rutherford to stay with me."

Mr. McCombs's embarrassment seemed to have overcome the shock he'd received from the robbery. By the time he and the two officers entered Joe's office, he had recovered much of his usual dignity. He declined the offer of coffee.

Joe had chairs brought in, so we were all seated in what resembled a reasonably congenial atmosphere. The police officers had not wanted to sit down, but their senior man indicated that they should. He placed himself directly opposite Thea, who continued to regard everyone with no sign of fear or emotion. I received the impression that the police officer considered her demeanor something of a challenge, although I didn't know why I thought so.

My attention was mostly on Martin. He had pulled a long piece of tape from the stock ticker and was studying it carefully, apparently deep in thought, as we waited for the senior officer to continue the discussion. Was he angry with me for insisting I stay? That impenetrable expression disguised some strong emotion, I understood that much, but I was unable to read him. Our nearly two and a half years of marriage might never have happened for all the notice he took of me. I was going to have to confront him later to find out what was wrong; the anticipation of that moment made it hard to concentrate on the present proceedings.

The senior officer, whose name, I finally discovered, was Culshaw, took Mr. McCombs carefully through every movement since he had broken with the normal procedure and insisted on being given an approximate time for the opening of the safe. Why did he make this exception? Because, said the head of the jewelry department, the customer was adamant he would be leaving on a train at midday and did not want to waste his time coming to the store if the vault wouldn't be open. He had been "quite rude," as Mr. McCombs put it, about the whole timed lock system, which he claimed was a ridiculous over precaution. If his wife's cousin, a regular customer, hadn't written her about the diamond parure she'd seen at the store, he'd never have come near Rutherford's—he didn't know why he'd even bothered to come to the store instead of writing—and so on.

"Do you remember the name of the wife's cousin?" one of the other policemen asked. Captain Culshaw looked annoyed, but his expression changed as Mr. McCombs gave the name of a very prominent Chicago family. "Easy enough to verify," he commented as he made a note in his small book. The bulk of the notetaking was performed by the youngest police officer, whose tongue stuck out of the side of his mouth in concentration as he scribbled.

"So after you spoke with the Cincinnati party, you sent a note to the third floor insisting that they tell you the exact time?"

Mr. McCombs's soft brown eyes widened in outrage. "Of course not. That would never do, or why have a system at all? I just wanted to see if my prospect could be here early enough to view the parure and, I hoped, give me the chance to conclude the sale. If he couldn't, I was going to suggest I arrange for the Chicago family to see it and try to negotiate the deal through them. I was sure I could persuade the third floor to hint if the opening time were early, middle, or late. It's been done before."

"Has it, now?" Joe looked at Martin, and I saw the same expression on both men's faces. "It won't be done again."

"No, sir." Mr. McCombs sighed deeply. "I can't tell you how dreadful I feel about all this. You will have my resignation—"

"Don't be foolish, man." It was Martin who spoke. "We all make mistakes."

I saw his gaze flick to me for just the fraction of a second, and something inside me turned to ice. *We all make mistakes.* He was having second thoughts about our marriage, wasn't he?

"What is the name of the employee on the third floor who

knows the correct time?" The police captain's tone was brisk and businesslike, but again Mr. McCombs's eyes widened.

"I don't know *that*," he snapped. "And what difference does that make to you? What would you do with the information? You're no doubt in someone's pocket—you all are." Martin's reassurance about his job seemed to have strengthened him, given him back his authority.

"Never mind that." Martin spoke again, looking hard at the policeman. "That information is never divulged, and any further attempt to elicit details of our security arrangements will not go down well with me."

At this point, one of the other policemen stepped forward and whispered in Captain Culshaw's ear for almost a minute. I could have sworn I caught the word "Gambarelli." Was he warning his superior that Martin was under the protection of his erstwhile in-laws, or was he reminding him of Martin's own brief spell in the shadow of the noose as a reason for his hostility? I sensed that Martin didn't trust these officers, and for good reason—the Chicago police were notoriously corrupt. But they had somehow become involved, and we could no longer handle the matter privately.

"We'll move on to the young lady, then," said the captain. He jerked his head at one of the other officers. "Did you send for a police matron?"

"I did. She probably got lost on the way, or maybe she's finding it hard to walk through a store without stopping to look at the pretty baubles."

There was some sniggering at this. The captain's mustache moved in a way that suggested a suppressed smile, but he merely said, "That's enough." He coughed. "So when you'd found out the vault would be open early, you wrote a note for the customer and gave it to the young lady. Name and address?" he asked Thea.

"Theadora Lombardi." Thea's voice was clear, soft, and

even. "I live at Mrs. Batham's boardinghouse on Taylor Street."

"Why'd you give it to her and not go yourself?" the man asked Mr. McCombs.

"I *am* the head of the department," said that personage testily. "Miss Lombardi volunteered her assistance. I allowed her to leave early, at five thirty p.m., and deliver the note before returning to her home."

"And he wasn't there."

"That's right," Thea said. "They had no idea when he'd be back."

"And so you went back home like a good little girl but at —what, eleven o'clock?—you took it into your head to walk all the way from Taylor Street, all those blocks of dark and dangerous streets, back to the Grand Pacific to do your duty." The captain, who had been looking down at his notebook, now glanced up so that his wide, cynical blue eyes met Thea's. She flushed a little.

"You know that's not true." Her voice had hardened.

"You tried to tell us you came back earlier, didn't you?" The blue eyes narrowed. "In a big hotel where the staff are changing all the time, it can be difficult to pin down the exact time when something was left or taken. But you didn't realize Mr. Rutherford was staying in the hotel, did you?"

My heart lurched.

"And he saw you from the staircase," the police captain finished. "You were there at midnight, in the company of a lady he also recognized."

"Lady," muttered one of the police officers under his breath before rising to his feet as the door opened to admit a woman who could only be the police matron. Her skirt, jacket, and bodice were of the severest cut, her only ornament a small metal star pinned to the jacket. She took in the scene as all the men rose to their feet and then accepted the seat they offered her. I was glad I didn't have to get up; my pulse was drumming in my ears, and I could not have sworn that my legs would support me.

No wonder our house had seemed so empty. Martin hadn't been there—and he hadn't told me. The Grand Pacific was where he lived after he'd concluded he couldn't stay in his marriage with Lucetta any longer. I felt sick.

Thea had said something—what was it? A name?

"A friend of yours?" the captain asked.

"Yes, an intimate friend."

"A friend you'd spent the evening with? And others?" The policeman stared hard at Thea. "Come now, Miss Lombardi. You know it's going to take us no time at all to ask at your boardinghouse whether you were there for dinner. A little escapade, was it? Or did you run to your friends and give them the note?"

"I didn't show it to them." Now there was a hint of anxiety in Thea's voice. "I forgot about it. There was a party —we were reading a new play—and I was so interested I forgot. It was Miss Dardenne who reminded me and even said she'd take me to the Grand Pacific on the way home. She took me in her carriage." She looked straight at me for the first time. "It must have been the hotel people who read the note. They had all night, didn't they? My friends only care about art, not jewels. Mr. McCombs didn't actually tell me I had to put the note into the customer's hands. I thought it would be all right."

"It sounds more like an escapade to me." It surprised me how normal my voice sounded, given the state of my heart. I saw Martin's gaze fixed on me and wondered how much of my distress had shown on my face. I must say something to help Thea. What would her mother have done? What was I going to do now?

"Hmph." The captain pulled at his mustache again, looking hard at Thea. "How old are you, young lady?"

"You asked me before." Thea drew herself up and tried to sound mature but couldn't quite keep a note of sulkiness out of her voice.

"And I'm asking you again, Miss. How old?"

"I'm seventeen years old."

"And when did you turn seventeen, Miss?"

"In June."

"Just seventeen, then." Captain Culshaw made a note. "And your brother? Where does he live? What does he do?"

Thea looked puzzled. "Is it relevant? He lives on Washington Street near the horsecar stables. He works at the stables as a yard supervisor. He's studying to be a pastor."

"And how old is *he*?"

"He'll be twenty in February," I said. I was also wondering where the captain's questions were leading.

"No parents? Guardian?" The officer directed the question to me.

I looked at Martin, uncertain. Martin shook his head.

"If anyone has authority over them in the legal sense, I suppose it's their denomination." He named it to the captain, who inscribed the name carefully in his notebook along with the address of the Chicago office. "That's under the terms of their parents' will, which is held at the denominational office. We assumed Miss Lombardi's care for a while after their parents died, but we've never considered ourselves her guardians. We're simply friends of the family."

"Huh." The captain frowned. "See, I think *you*"—he pointed at Mr. McCombs— "probably had nothing to do with the whole thing, except for providing the opportunity by mistake. But the little lady," he nodded at Thea, whose color had risen as we discussed her family, "I'm not so sure about. We're going to go for a little jaunt, you and me and the police matron here. You're going to introduce me to your friends, and then we'll go back to your boardinghouse and have a bit of a talk. Thing is, I've got girls myself around your age and I know how easy they go wrong, girls. You're what I'd call the weak point in the argument, Miss. And matters aren't straightforward because you're a minor child till you're eighteen. Your brother's the head of your family, but *he's* a minor till he's twenty-one under the laws of this great state of Illinois." His voice was sardonic.

"So he has no authority over me." Thea was quick to see that point. Spots of red now burned on her pale cheeks. "What I do in the evenings has nothing to do with him. Everyone lets him live his life the way *he* wants; why can't I live mine how I want? I'm doing nothing wrong or immoral."

"Why has an inquiry about an attempted robbery at our store suddenly become an inquiry into Miss Lombardi's morals?" I asked. "I'm prepared to vouch for her. She's worked at this store for a while now and has been an excellent employee."

"Oh, it's still an inquiry into the robbery," Captain Culshaw said gravely. "After we've had our little chats, we'll all go back to the precinct so the detectives can talk to the young lady. But she's a minor, and I'd be happier if she had a representative."

"I can be that representative." My voice sounded high. "Or if you won't accept a woman, how about my husband? We're her employers."

"You're a nice lady. It was your store they tried to rob, don't forget that. Like I say, I've got daughters, and I want to give this matter a little thought. For the young lady's benefit."

40

IDIOTS

"I don't understand why they wouldn't let us accompany Thea."

I watched in dismay as the hired carriage conveying Thea, Captain Culshaw, and the police matron maneuvered out into the slowly moving traffic, the driver shouting and waving his whip as he crossed in front of various vehicles proceeding in the other direction.

"They might be trying to make sure it wasn't a plan on my part to defraud the insurance company." Martin shrugged. "Although how I'd work such a scheme is currently beyond me. I'm having trouble thinking straight." His mouth set in a firm line as he looked down at me. "I was surprised to see you here, Nellie. What made you come to the store a day early?"

I stared at him blankly for a moment before I remembered why I had been there. "I wanted a fitting." I glanced down at the green dress. "I never thought of arranging for new clothes. And I wanted to talk to Madame, and to you and Joe if possible, about what's happening at the store. After all these weeks, I just needed to come here."

"You wish to resume work?"

I gaped in astonishment at my husband. "Of *course* I do. What did you imagine?"

I had spoken loudly. Martin seemed to realize we were on the sidewalk within earshot of the doormen, not to mention several dozen passersby. "Let's go inside, shall we?" He reached for my elbow.

I glared at him and jerked my arm away, my temper coming to my aid against the despair that threatened to overcome me. "Perhaps we should walk to the Grand Pacific since that's where you're living now. When were you going to tell me?"

Martin froze in place for a moment and then whipped round and raised a hand to one of the doormen. "Get us a cab, please." And then to me: "I'd be grateful if you could wait to start an argument until we're in my suite. It's clearly what you have in mind."

"I did not come—"

"*Please*, Nell." Martin's voice sounded strangled. His face was expressionless, but what I saw in his eyes made me fall dumb. I nodded.

The short ride to the Grand Pacific was painful. My throat was sore with unshed tears, a situation worsened by the fact that the man I loved more than any other seemed to be holding himself away from me, sitting stiffly so that his arm did not come into contact with my person. What had I done to deserve this treatment?

We took the elevator to the fourth floor of the hotel. Martin led me along the hushed corridors to his suite. When we entered, it was to the sight of trunks and bags piled in the center of the suite's parlor. It was the same one where he'd stayed after he'd been released from jail, I realized.

"As you can see, I was in the process of moving back home." Martin waved his hand at the luggage, sounding exasperated. "I'm behind schedule." He flung wide the bedroom door to reveal an open bag on the bed and a certain amount of disorder. "I intended to get the lot packed up by eight thirty and hoped to have it delivered to the house before you got there. In fact, I meant to leave yesterday, but I worked late. You know how it is."

Yes, I knew how it was. But I wasn't going to let him off the hook. "So you were trying to hide the fact that you'd been staying in the hotel from me?"

"Yes." Martin pronounced the word with a certain amount of temper. "Because I was sure you'd read something into it, especially as I was at the Grand Pacific, where I'd stayed after Lucetta and I—well, you remember. Women always make assumptions."

Well, of course, Martin was experienced in such matters. Had been married to one woman while in love with another. His wife had "read something into it" and drawn the correct conclusion.

"So why *are* you at the Grand Pacific?" I asked, trying to keep the shrewishness out of my voice.

Martin sighed. "Because I like their barber. The Palmer House barbers never shave me quite right." He rubbed his chin in illustration. "And I find this suite comfortable, even with the memories associated with it. Call me set in my ways if you want."

I made a noise indicative of frustration. "That's not what I mean, and you know it. Why are you here in the first place? Instead of in our home?"

All the air seemed to go out of Martin's body, and he slumped bonelessly onto the one spot on the bed clear of his belongings. "I stuck it out at home for two weeks." He inserted a finger behind his stiff collar as if it were irritating him, then swore mildly, pulled out his tiepin, untied his cravat, and fiddled with his collar studs until he'd removed the collar altogether. "I couldn't abide it any longer. Every moment I was there reminded me you were not, and that reminded me of *why* you were not. I couldn't bear the sight of our bed—the memory of you lying there with your face as white as the sheets and your tears running down into the pillow. So I was still sleeping in my dressing room, and I thought, why not get away from it altogether? Perhaps a few weeks elsewhere would take my mind off it all. Make me feel less guilty."

That puzzled me. "*You* feel guilty? Why?"

Martin looked up at me, his eyes wide, seemingly astonished that I didn't realize. "For wanting a son so much. For wishing and hoping and praying that I'd get you with child in the first place, as if that were the only reason for our marriage. I feel guilty that after you told me you were having our baby, all I could think about was the boy I wanted." He looked down at his polished shoes. "When it should have been *you—your* health—that mattered. When I should have been praying for a healthy child, not the right child."

His voice had become hoarse, and he cleared his throat noisily. I sank down into a chair, unable to hold my tears back any longer, and covered my face with my hands. I heard Martin take several deep breaths before he continued.

"When I saw her—Ruth—she was so beautiful, so perfect —" He choked again and coughed. "After the grief had worn off a bit, I was ashamed. I kept thinking of the daughter I—we—might have had. A little girl who'd have been a joy to us both, a sister for Sarah; I'm sure she'd love a sister—"

He stopped because my tears had become sobs that shook my entire body. I was gritting my teeth to stop myself from wailing and didn't realize he'd moved until his arms came around me and held me tight. I resisted for a moment, and then the last vestige of my anger dissipated. I leaned my head into the bare skin of his neck, my tears running down to soak his shirt.

We stayed like that for what seemed a long time before I was able to speak.

"I feel guilty too."

I had to say it three times. The first two tries were so incoherent that Martin didn't understand; I had to stop and get a grip on my emotions, wipe my face, and blow my nose. The process made me a little calmer, even though my head ached abominably.

"Why do you feel guilty, sweetheart?" asked Martin with such tenderness that I almost burst into tears again. "I told you, it wasn't your fault. You got enough rest."

"I feel guilty for not wanting to have another child." I gulped down air. "There, I've said it. I was afraid you'd trap me into staying at home when I wanted to be at the store. I feared I'd—I'd lose myself in being a mother." I heaved a sigh. "I know it doesn't make sense. I've been a good mother to Sarah, even while I've grown as a dressmaker. I'm surrounded by help—by kind women—and if I need more assistance, we can easily afford it." I blew my nose again. "But I never wanted to get married—never wanted children—and it's hard to shake off the old, self-centered Nell Lillington even after I realized I loved you so much I'd have to marry you anyway and to Hades with the consequences. And now you don't seem to want me anymore—"

"Don't *want* you?" Martin let go of me and rose to his feet, pacing swiftly as he spoke. "I haven't known what to do with myself for wanting you." He smote himself on the forehead. "Oh, perhaps that's not what you mean—the physical side—"

"Well, I can't imagine what I mean otherwise," I retorted, indignant. "The 'physical side,' as you call it, is part and parcel of marriage, after all."

"Exactly." Martin groaned. "I've hardly dared touch you

because I'd have wanted to put my hands on you, and I was scared of giving you another child and making you ill, and I was afraid you'd reject me and—well, if it weren't for Joe, I'd still be running around in those particular circles."

"Joe?" I was mildly amused at the sudden appearance of Joseph Salazar in our marital discussion, pleased to notice that my frame of mind had somehow shifted into a much better quarter.

Martin waved a hand. "That was part of what made me so late last night, if you must know. Joe forced me to talk to him. He's known me a long time, and men recognize that mood, where you want a woman and it makes you tense and irritable as a horse with a saddle sore. It makes life a particular hell for very young men at times." He grinned briefly. "So I fessed up, and he called me a damned fool."

"He did?" I was becoming more cheerful by the second.

"He sat me down and explained that every man whose wife has had a baby—or a miscarriage—is the same at first. We see our women as fragile when they're not. Well, some are, but anyway, he told me to just ask you. Or at least to ask you to let me know when you were ready. He told me I had to be honest and run the risk of rejection. And as for making you ill again, well—oh, I can't even tell you what he said. It contained rather a lot of personal history. And he ended up by pointing out I had proved I could father a child and should be eager to prove as much again."

"Hmph. How ridiculous that I hadn't even thought of that way of looking at things." I smiled at the thought. "You don't have to worry about not being able to father a child anymore."

I rose to my feet to face Martin, putting out a hand to stop his pacing. "I rather think we've both been complete idiots. I'm really going to have to learn to trust you."

"But do you still not want a baby? There are ways—it would be less dangerous—"

"Don't be absurd." I locked my arms around Martin's lean waist and pulled him to me. "Although if you start making babies on me one after the other as Elizabeth and David seem set on doing, I might ask you to read a certain book I could borrow. I—"

But whatever I was about to say was interrupted by a kiss that seemed to go on for an indecently long time. If I hadn't known it before, the warmth in my body told me I was most decidedly ready for a resumption of marital bliss. I believe that fact communicated itself to Martin in an entirely satisfactory manner.

The clock on the parlor mantelpiece struck the hour, its clear chime only too audible through the open door. Martin stopped kissing me and groaned loudly.

"Dear heaven, why do I afflict myself with responsibilities when I could be taking my wife to bed for the rest of the day?" He kissed my neck, nuzzling into the base of my hair. "I still have an attempted robbery to deal with. I suppose I should send for word of Thea and see if I need to consult an attorney for her sake. Blast the girl."

"And I should get a fitting done at the very least. I can't possibly appear at the store in last year's modes." I pulled away from Martin, ignoring his grimace of frustration. "Are my eyes horribly red?"

"You look beautiful."

He moved forward to kiss me, but I dodged around him, picking up his collar from where he'd thrown it onto the bed. I supposed it *was* a good thing the bed was covered with bags . . .

"Here." I held out the collar to him. "Resume the yoke of oppression while I do something about my face and hair. We can pack the rest of your things in ten minutes and have it all

399

sent off home, then get to the store in time to get some work done."

"I'll put on a fresh collar." Martin wrinkled his nose at a tiny crease on the one I'd handed him. "I suppose you're right." He sighed. "But promise me that when we get home . . ."

"I promise you that if I'm still able to stand . . ." I laughed as Martin made a grab at me, skipping away from him. "Or lie down . . . we'll exorcize the bad memories from our bed." I sobered a little. "Or at least we'll remember them as a sad moment in a long and happy marriage."

"WHAT NEWS?"

Martin spotted Joe immediately as we walked through Rutherford's main doors. Our general manager was busy talking to one of the night watchmen, who had clearly just arrived. I saw him disguise his indelicate grin at the sight of the two of us arm in arm with a quick series of coughs. I *hoped* he didn't imagine that we . . . and in the middle of a police inquiry too . . . but his demeanor quickly switched from that of a friend to that of a business partner, with just a hint of the friend remaining as a glint in his dark eyes.

"All serene here." He nodded at the watchman, who tipped his cap to the two of us and moved purposefully toward the rear of the store. "There've been some reporters. The man from the *Tribune* is going to keep coming back till he gets a statement out of you. You recall how enthusiastic they've been about writing up the robberies."

Martin nodded. "I'll talk to him tomorrow morning, not before. Until then, nobody in the store is to speak to the press. We'll need a meeting tomorrow morning to discuss the timing system."

"Already arranged. It'll have to be at seven, of course." Joe looked hard at Martin. "Are you going to fire anyone?"

"Probably not. But it's going to be unpleasant for all concerned." He pulled his watch out of his vest pocket and looked at it. "I intend to be home in time to see my daughter before she goes to bed. What should we do about Miss Lombardi?"

"My advice is to do nothing." The lines at the corners of Joe's expressive mouth deepened. "If the police charge her, she'll spend the night in a cell, but I doubt it'll come to that. They'll probably give her a hard time and eventually have Teddy take her home. Or perhaps they'll decide she's entirely innocent. I imagine she can talk her own way out if she is."

"That's a little harsh, isn't it?" I asked. "She's so young. Perhaps I should—"

"No, you shouldn't." Martin gave me what my mother would have called an old-fashioned look. "You're here to get a fitting, remember? Running after Thea won't solve anything. In any event, I had no intention of just abandoning her to the police." He looked apologetically at Joe Salazar. "Joe, do you think you could get someone from Isaacson's to run over and see what's happening? It's a bit late in the day, but a firm of attorneys should be used to that. They certainly had to work some strange hours for my case."

It wasn't often that Martin referred to his own months of tribulation in the grasp of the law, but he sounded quite unconcerned, as if the memory were of no moment. A sign of healing, perhaps. We *did* heal, I realized. Sobbing in Martin's arms had calmed and refreshed me. My wits revived and, along with them, my interest in work.

"You're right," I said. "I don't suppose I can do much for Thea by worrying."

"Nor should you." Joe frowned. "You've done enough for that child as it is." His expression softened. "Don't worry,

Nell, none of us have any intention of leaving an employee—
a young girl—at the mercy of the police. Go get your fitting.
I'll take care of Miss Lombardi. Martin, go with her and
forget you're the owner for a while. Heaven knows the two
of you could do with some time together."

WISCONSIN

*D*awn had not quite broken when we sat down to breakfast as a family. Martin was with us briefly; after ingesting an impressive number of sausages and buttered biscuits, he dispensed kisses and hugs with many expressions of how glad he was to have us home. His lips lingered on mine longer than usual before he remembered where he was and hurried off to his meeting at the store.

"He's in a very good mood." Tess reached for another biscuit, which she split and smothered with grape jelly. "You look happy too, Nell. Your face is all pretty and your cheeks are pink."

I took a sip of my black coffee. "It's warm in here. What are your plans for today?"

Sarah was the first to reply because she thought so much faster than Tess and could always start speaking before my friend had drawn breath to begin.

"We're going to begin the day with the *Eclectic Reader*," she announced. "That usually takes up a lot of time, Mama, because there are so many things to ponder when you read a story. And then I always do some penmanship lessons, which is so hard because I like to write with my left hand. Miss Baker says I have to try with my right hand as well because that's the normal way to write and I won't smear the ink, and she's right because in Lake Forest, Orton the Third called me a chickie paw when he saw me write something, and I don't want to be called a chickie paw. And then we're going to do mental arithmetic, and then we're going to do *real* mental arithmetic, not just from a book, because we're going to go to the cake shop and spend the four dimes Papa gave me, and I have to get my sums right before I can buy anything. And then, oh, I don't know, we'll learn something else."

"Don't put your thumb in your mouth, Sary," Tess said as Sarah ended her speech by inserting that digit in her mouth with a frown. "Babies do that."

"It's just because my mole is loose, Tessie. It annoys me so. My big teeth are pushing out my baby teeth and now it's my mole's turn, and it slips while I'm eating and hurts a bit."

"Your molar. Let me see." I held out my hand.

Sarah obligingly jumped out of her chair and stood beside me, her mouth wide open so that sausage-and-milk-scented breath filled my nostrils. I winced, but only slightly, remembering when such a fragrance would have sent me bolting for the washroom.

"It's all right. Don't wiggle it and it'll stop hurting in a bit. Now sit down again and let Tess tell us what she's going to do."

"I want to write some lists, Nell. I want to hold a dinner party for my family."

"What a good idea. We don't use that huge table often enough. Do you mean to invite everybody?"

"All the grown-ups, even Deirdre and Joseph." Tess beamed. "And Mary's and Aileen's husbands, and Billy's Kathleen." Billy had begun walking out with a young lady over the summer, and we hadn't met her yet. "But we'll tell

Mary to get one of our cousins to mind the boys because they'll spoil the party. You can come of course, Sary, because you live here."

"I might." Sarah pushed her springy curls back from where they'd fallen forward over her shoulders. "I mean, I'll come and say hello to everybody and meet Kathleen and especially talk to Grandpa O'Dugan." Sarah had a soft spot for Tess's father, who told her endless stories about Ireland. "But if Mama and Papa let me have a little picnic in my room, I promise *faithfully* I won't hide any candy for later this time." She gave me her most winsome smile, then spoiled the effect by absentmindedly wiggling her loose molar with her tongue. "May I be excused now? Miss Baker won't be here for a whole *hour,* and I want to play for a while. I like early breakfasts."

She kissed me in a careless, distracted manner and drifted out, humming tunelessly.

"She's changing, Tess." I sighed as I looked at the empty doorway, but I was too happy this morning to regret Sarah's growing independence. "It's as if she's realized that her grown-ups are just people, not some kind of magical authority for everything. Oh well. When do you want to have this party? Do you even want us there? Perhaps you should simply enjoy being the hostess. After all, this is your home as much as ours."

"I *will* be the hostess." Tess looked pleased. "And sit at the head of the table, and Da can sit at the other end. Or perhaps Donny should sit at the other end? But it would be nice if you were there in case Aileen says her sharp little things to Donny. I can sit you *right* next to Aileen."

That wasn't the most pleasing prospect; I tried hard not to react. I opened my mouth to reply, but for once Tess was quicker.

"And if you're going to say something about Donny not

being family and he shouldn't be invited, you can think again. You're probably right that he's not good enough for the likes of the Palmers and the Lindgrens and the Pullmans and the Deerings, but he's good enough for my family."

"I have never said *anything* about Donny being not good enough for society." My voice rose to an indignant squeak. "He's not comfortable in society, as you're very well aware. But as for good enough—who am I to judge anyone's suitability for good company? And I never have, Tess. It's unfair of you to say that."

Tess pushed back her chair and ran to hug me. "I didn't mean it like that, silly. Don't frown." She kissed my forehead. "I just figured out that was the best way to be sociable, that's all. We got to be such good friends in Lake Forest, and I want it to stay that way. Even if Donny never wants to kiss me."

"It's a wonderful notion. If you ever want to invite him to a family dinner, you must do so—or invite him along when we're hosting the Fletchers or the Parnells or the Salazars. They're all sensible people who would never think less of Donny for working in our stables, and I've noticed he likes their company. Then if he becomes less shy, we can introduce him to some other friends."

Tess's eyebrows rose. "I thought you might say, 'No, Tess, you can't invite him to dinner with your family.'"

"Why?" I smiled at my friend. "You can invite anyone you please to our house. *Your* house. Invite your family more often, for example."

Tess wrinkled her nose. "I mostly like seeing my family where they are, except for Billy. When I hadn't seen them for years and years, I used to dream they were like angels in heaven, always perfect. I told that to Donny, and he said he knows exactly what I mean. Sometimes he wonders if he might still have a ma or a da somewhere. When he was a boy, he used to think maybe they would come to the Poor Farm and find him, and his ma would be pretty and his da would be rich. But he says he's a man now, and if he were ever to meet them, he would meet them as just acquaintances, because he can be happy without them."

"That's sensible enough. Is Donny happy here, Tess?"

Tess beamed. "He's *very* happy here. He says he doesn't want anything more than what he's got, except maybe one day he'd like a sitting room. I told him about my sitting room. Nell, would you come up to my sitting room? It would be nice if you could help me plan my dinner. Were you going to rush off to the store again?"

"No-o-o-o." I *had* intended to go to the store, but one more day wouldn't make such a difference. "I want to find out what's happened to Thea, but Martin said he'd let me know, and he's coming home for luncheon anyway unless there's an emergency." Indeed, Martin had been as attentive that morning as if we'd only just gotten married. "Would you mind if I peruse the fashion journals Martin gave me yesterday while we talk and perhaps do some sketches? I must exercise my mind a little—I'm starting to see dresses in my head." I grinned, and Tess rolled her eyes.

"I suppose that means you're quite well again. All right, Nell, let's go upstairs. We can get lots done before Martin comes home."

THE MORNING PASSED PLEASANTLY. BY ELEVEN O'CLOCK, TESS and I had sent for more coffee and were taking a little refreshment before we returned to our occupations. At my elbow was a pile of sketches, although none of them were definitive ideas. I realized I needed to spend at least a day looking at the dress goods in the store and talk with Madame about which fabrics were the newest and most exciting. Or with Martin; my husband did not quite have Madame's encyclopedic knowledge, but he spent a great deal of time talking to the lady customers, and he was in constant touch with the buyers.

Alongside Tess's list of possible dishes for her family dinner lay my list of the features and embellishments that I intended to study closely in the coming days. Stripes, high necklines, little lace jabots—I smiled since I had anticipated their popularity as early as spring—and the perennial attraction of a long row of simple buttons that descended from the neckline, now almost to the knees, and required extremely good cutting and piecing not to produce gaping edges as the wearer moved. So deceptively easy to imagine when one looked at the tiny-waisted ladies in the fashion plates; so very difficult to execute well for real women. I needed to consider all the possibilities of the poufs and swags that were now just above the knee, making the waist appear even smaller and drawing attention to the lower half of the body in a way that would probably have made my own mother blush, so hidden were the nether limbs in her youth.

I was staring at the fashion plates spread in front of me and contemplating the intricacies of trains, half trains, and no trains at all when Martin entered. Tess, who had been sipping her cream-laced coffee and staring at the seating plan I had helped her draw, looked up with a beatific grin.

"You're early. You can answer some of Nell's questions. She's been *muttering*."

I stared blankly at my husband, momentarily seeing him clothed in a straight fall of wide pleats and wondering how to piece them so they gave the effect of a crystal vase. I should try that on myself—it was so interesting that I had gained an inch in my bust but lost an inch from my hips. Martin's hips were narrow . . . I shook myself mentally.

"You *are* early." The small clock on Tess's dainty little desk was striking the half hour. "Couldn't you bear to be away from me?"

I gave him a sweeping glance from under my eyelashes, knowing well how striking my large blue-green eyes could be when seen from that angle. I saw his face change from its business-day expression to one of irresistible amusement. He came forward to plant a hearty kiss on my lips.

"*You* are a disgraceful flirt. And yes, I looked forward to seeing you—but I'm afraid I have news, and I thought you'd better have it here rather than at the store. You're not going to like it."

"It's about Thea, isn't it?" asked Tess. "That girl is just trouble, Nell." She folded her arms, jutting out her chin in a way that reminded me strongly of her father.

Martin pulled out a small, dainty chair and sat down, looking incongruously tall and long-legged and male in the pink-and-white room. "The police do harbor some suspicions that the details were somehow passed on to Thea's thespian friends," he said. "By default, mainly; they can't think of any other way the trick was worked. But they can't prove a blessed thing. They're an incompetent lot at the best of times, although that Culshaw fellow is better than most. He should be in the detective force."

"So are they holding Thea?" I frowned. "That can't be right. You know better than anyone that a jail is no place for a decent person. Can't we do something?"

"We have done something, remember? Or were you too distracted?" Martin's smile was intimate but fleeting. "Joe arranged for an attorney to find out where Thea was and ensure she was properly treated. The attorney objected strongly to her being housed in a cell and won. She spent the night in a temperance hostel, a nice clean one, with the police matron sharing her room."

"She won't have liked that—oh, I'm having uncharitable

thoughts." Tess grimaced. "Didn't the detectives talk to her, Martin?"

"They did, this morning." Martin sighed. "They didn't think they had enough evidence to charge her—but here comes the bit you won't like, Nell. Culshaw sent for Teddy last night and took him to consult the denominational office this morning while the detectives and police matron were with Thea. The denomination naturally gave its full backing to whatever course of action Teddy might decide—"

"Why 'naturally'?" I interrupted.

"Because they extend the stipulation in Genesis that a husband rules over his wife to any close relationship between a man and a woman." Martin shrugged. "Are you surprised?"

"Genesis chapter three, verse sixteen." Tess had been listening intently. "Anyway, men rule the denomination, don't they? So they're bound to choose Teddy over Thea."

"And they have authority over her under the terms of the will, and that authority now devolves upon Teddy. Who is handicapped by the fact that Thea comes into her majority some months before Teddy comes into his under Illinois law. So, with encouragement from Captain Culshaw, he's taken her to Wisconsin, where the age of majority for a woman is twenty-one."

"What?" I pushed back my chair and stood up. "And you *let* him?"

Martin rose more slowly to his feet, resting a hand on my arm. "We've already established that you and I have no authority whatsoever, remember? Our man from Isaacson's did his best to follow his instructions, which were to act on Thea's behalf to have her released at the earliest opportunity. He protested such a conditional release into Teddy's custody, as it were, given that they were unable to prove anything against her."

He stroked his chin, looking through me into some imaginary distance. "But the denomination coming down so hard in Teddy's favor was an insurmountable obstacle, and Culshaw was clearly eager to make sure Thea had no further opportunities to get into any kind of trouble. Whether that was a sincere effort to protect her or simply the fellow-feeling of a man who knows what it's like to have wayward daughters is anyone's guess." He sighed heavily. "Apparently, those Galloway friends of Teddy's have moved to Wisconsin because Mr. Galloway inherited a farm. Teddy's taking her to stay with them."

"But we can stop them." I whisked away from the table, heading for the bell button. "Where are they now? I'm sure Teddy will see sense if we talk to him. Thea will just have to move back into the residence and undertake not to make any more attempts to go against her brother's wishes. I'm sure I can make her see she's being foolish. And that's all it is—girls of her age are foolish."

Martin shook his head. "Culshaw no doubt expected we'd intervene on her behalf again. He sent the lawyer packing, put the two of them into a hired carriage with the police matron for company, and gave orders to take them straight to the station and get them on the next train on the Milwaukee Road. They'll have gone to Clinton Street, and there are plenty of trains." He ran his fingers through his hair. "They had an hour's start on us before I heard the news, Nellie. I don't see the point of rushing after them hoping to stop them."

"But if they think Thea told her friends about your vault, why would they let her go?" Tess, still seated, looked at the two of us over the top of her spectacles.

"If I were looking for the bigger fish and thought I'd caught a sprat, I might want to get that sprat out of town before it warned the others that the police were casting a net." Martin considered what he'd said for a moment and then nodded emphatically, as if sure he had hit on the correct explanation. "If I were Culshaw, I'd probably have told Thea I'd arrest her if she gave Teddy any trouble. I wouldn't be surprised if the detectives were watching the Jewel Box carefully from now on."

He put his hand on my shoulder and squeezed it gently. "In any case, Nellie, she's gone—and she won't come to any actual harm in Wisconsin. Try to rein in your desire for instantaneous action and let's talk to Teddy when he returns. Perhaps we can change his mind."

MARTIN SENT A NOTE TO TEDDY'S BOARDINGHOUSE ON Washington Street asking for Teddy to contact us when he returned. He was right, of course, that rushing off to find Thea would be difficult without Teddy's cooperation.

And just how much did I want to find her? I asked myself that question as the days passed without news from Teddy. I caught myself thinking often of my own mother, who had let me be taken to the Prairie Haven Poor Farm with very little protest, convinced as she was of my stepfather's authority as head of our little household.

I had not protested either. Looking back, it seemed strange that I had unquestioningly trusted Hiram's assertion that the institution of which he was a governor was a good place. That puzzle gnawed at my brain as I went about my daily tasks. I found myself wondering why I had become so obsessed with my own past until the answer presented itself one morning while I was cutting a particularly fetching silk taffeta with narrow stripes, gold on gold.

"I see myself in Thea, I think," I said later to Martin as we reclined against the comfortable seats of the landau, which rocked in a smooth swaying motion as the matched pair of white carriage horses broke into a trot under Capell's expert hand. It was a glorious mid-September afternoon; the glass panes of the Exposition Building sent back blinding flashes of reflected sunlight, and its pennant flags fluttered bravely in the cool breeze.

"Have you only just realized that?" Martin gave me a sideways smile. "I'm certain I told you so myself some time ago, but you've forgotten. And now Thea's been dragged off to a remote location for misbehavior, just as you were." He glanced at the front of the carriage, where Capell and Donny sat side by side in matching maroon jackets and smart top hats; Donny was taking lessons in driving a pair. "Let's remember that according to you, that time of your life was the making of you."

"Yes, but don't forget I escaped from the Poor Farm, baby and all."

"Only because you had me to help you." Martin touched my gloved hand with the side of his. "Of course, it's highly possible that Thea will send word to her friends and arrange to abscond."

"Which is why Teddy has to see sense about letting her return to Chicago. He can't keep her locked up, and if she does escape—well, won't she go somewhere nobody can find her? That's what I'd do if my brother were trying to keep me away from my friends."

"It's harder than you imagine to just run away from everyone and everything you know." Martin raised a hand to return the greeting of an acquaintance who had twirled his cane in the air and shouted from the sidewalk. "You went back to the very people who might send you away again, didn't you? Because you couldn't imagine where else you could go."

"I returned to *you*," I said smugly. "I knew you'd protect me. I had no better friend, and that hasn't changed."

"That's as may be, my darling, but she'll also know I will get the Pinkertons looking for her if she disappears." Martin settled himself more firmly into his seat, crossing his arms. "For her own safety, of course. If I were Miss Thea, I'd wait out the months till I'm eighteen before trying anything."

"Would you not search for her if she were eighteen?" I asked, surprised.

"Of course I would, because you'd insist on it. But it'll be harder for Teddy to drag her back to Wisconsin once he's a minor and she's not, and I don't imagine she's missed that point."

42

A MAN'S CHOICE

*T*wo days later, we received a note from Teddy informing us he had returned. He would be happy to come to Calumet Avenue; but if we wanted to speak to him straightaway, he would welcome us at his place of employment. We set off within the hour.

We headed west under a crystalline blue sky, conversing idly as Capell guided the landau through the thronged streets. We slowed as we rounded Union Park and then picked up speed as we left the crowds behind.

The buildings thinned out around us as we reached the limit of the horsecar's western circuit, and the shop signs were less often in English. The shrieks of steam whistles close or distant marked Chicago's many railroad lines. We had to wait for a few minutes to let a clanking, noisome train pass before we turned toward the area where the tracks intersected.

We found Teddy in the small hut where he kept the records for the stable yard. His eyes were wary as he rose to greet us, but his handshake was welcoming. He still affected the dark, plain suit of a man who cared nothing for fashion, but his appearance contrasted sharply with the youth who had arrived in Chicago wearing clothes that were rusty-looking and frayed at the edges. He looked, if not exactly prosperous, eminently respectable, and in his workplace carried himself with an air of authority that gave the impression of a much older man.

"It does me good to see you looking so well, Mrs. Rutherford." He held my hand for a moment after shaking it. "Lake Forest is living up to its reputation for a healthy climate." He hesitated. "Thea is also in a beautiful, healthful spot. Lakes and rivers and low green hills; no ague, no bad air. I've truly tried to do my best for her." His look was beseeching. "With your money and all, I realize you could make trouble for me. Perhaps you might even force me to bring Thea back. I sure hope you won't."

"Don't imagine it hasn't crossed our minds." I gave his hand a squeeze before letting go. "Teddy, I'll say straight out that I think you're wrong to do this. In my opinion, forcing Thea into a life she doesn't want will just make things worse. If I'd known beforehand what you'd do, I expect I'd have done something drastic to prevent it. But I vowed I'd be a friend to *both* of Catherine's children. It's been borne in upon me that this is one of those times when I should step back and wait."

I watched the relief spread over the young man's countenance and continued before he became effusive; I didn't want him to be under any illusions about my feelings. "But in return, may I ask where these Galloway people are? I promise I won't try to bring Thea back," I said quickly as Teddy's expression changed. "But I'd like to write to her. I'd like her to know we haven't deserted her, and that I for one don't believe she was involved in the burglary."

"You for *one*?" Teddy looked hard at me and then at Martin.

"Call me a cynic." Martin adjusted his cuffs as he watched realization dawn on Teddy's face. "I'm not as sure as Nell is. We've agreed to disagree because neither of has proof."

"Just a strong suspicion." Teddy remembered where we were and brought his own chair round to my side of the small desk where he worked so I would have somewhere to sit. "A suspicion like the police captain said he had—he called it an instinct. He said he hoped it would be possible to keep Thea away from what he called valuable information."

Martin and I looked at one another, and I saw the same idea taking shape in his mind as I had in mine. "She *might* have been working as a spy," I said in answer to Martin's unspoken thought and then turned to Teddy. "The department stores in this town all spy on one another. I'll tell you about my own short career as a spy sometime."

"It was all in a very good cause." Martin laughed at Teddy's shocked expression but then sobered. "You do realize, Teddy, that you and I could be wrong and Nell right? Your sister might be entirely innocent of any connection with the robbery." He sighed. "And yet . . . you've spared me the painful choice between firing her for misconduct or condoning her being out at all hours. I saw her that night, you know. I should have summoned her to my office first thing in the morning, but I had something else on my mind." He looked at me for an instant but continued. "She'd have put me in a difficult position all right. I've more or less concluded that I'd have fired her, although I'd have tried to do it in such a way that she'd be able to find a job in another store."

And if Martin hadn't been at the Grand Pacific that night, I wondered, would Thea have continued to visit the Jewel

Box Theater behind the backs of all who had her best interests at heart?

"I'M HEARTILY SICK OF THEA LOMBARDI." I STARED AT CAPELL'S back as he spoke to the horses, aware of the landau's dip-and-sway motion as he negotiated his way over the potholes in the yard but not really registering the external world. "I'm almost glad Teddy begged me to wait six weeks till I write her."

"Amen." Martin looked smug. "I've been waiting an eternity to hear you say that. I'll count it as a victory for common sense, even though I'm sure that within two days you'll be imagining yourself guilty again over not making life perfect for Catherine Lombardi's daughter. And yet you gave her every chance for that perfect life. That child could be a society belle by now, wearing your best designs, living in luxury in the wealthiest part of Chicago instead of stuck out in the middle of nowhere. I'll need a map of Wisconsin to see where Jefferson actually *is*." He frowned. "More to the point, she might have been a member of our family."

"It was what you said about being almost obliged to fire Thea that convinced me," I confessed. "It made me wonder just how long Thea would have let us imagine she was sitting innocently in Mrs. Batham's parlor every evening while leading quite a different life. Unless I can believe this was the one and only time she had been out at night—and somehow I don't." I ran a fingernail along the smooth silk of my skirt. "Really, I should go ask Mrs. Batham to assure me Thea wasn't going out, but I'm afraid to do it for fear that she'll tell me Thea claimed to be going to temperance meetings or something ridiculous like that every evening for the last six *months*."

Martin, whose grin had been growing wider as I spoke, crowed softly, tipping his head back so that his nose pointed skyward. "Oh, inestimable joy." He opened his eyes to look at me. "I shouldn't sound quite so triumphant, but that wretched girl has cast a shadow over almost our entire marriage."

I felt for his hand. "It took a tragedy to bring me to my senses, didn't it? I barely thought of Thea while I was in Lake Forest; I'm not even sure I wrote her. She didn't write *me*." I shook my head. "I mean nothing to her."

We continued in silence until we reached the river.

"Only . . ." I began, and Martin groaned.

"No, I won't change my mind." I squeezed his hand. "It's just what you said—that Thea could have lived in luxury. So might I if I'd simply named Jack as Sarah's father. I would have been spared the Poor Farm and Kansas. I might have grown to love my jeweled cage." I smiled at my husband. "After all, marriage to *you* is turning out all right. But with Jack, I wouldn't be free. I wouldn't be *me*. There's a part of me that understands Thea completely, realizes why she's been so difficult—has bitten our outstretched hands so often. It's a yearning to be who we really are, in my opinion. To take the troublesome road rather than the easy one because, on the rocky path, we find our true selves. Do I sound like I'm talking nonsense?"

"No." Martin shifted a little so he was under the shade of my parasol. "I'd much rather have taken the hard road to Shiloh and Gettysburg and died in the attempt than stay at home in Victory during the war. And it wasn't just that home meant Father and all he did to us. I'd have felt the same if it had just been Mother begging me to stay for her sake. Perhaps some of us possess an ingrained desire to put ourselves to the test."

"But you took the difficult road by staying home. You

made your choice out of love, which makes you better than me. I made my choice because I *didn't* love Jack. Marrying him would have been far harder for me than the Poor Farm and all that's happened since." I frowned, perplexed. "We'd have been tested either way."

I looked up at Martin's face, which was perspiring a little under the brim of his black hat. "I can't work it all out," I confessed. "I'll resort to doing what I always do, which is to concentrate on the matters directly in front of me."

"To borrow your metaphor, perhaps all paths are rocky." Martin shrugged. "Maybe you and I are just not destined for a quiet life. Or perhaps we all need to walk a rocky road until we've learned a few lessons along the way. But as you say, we can only see our way forward one step at a time—and in this moment, I'm happy, my dear, that you're giving us a chance for some respite from Miss Thea Lombardi."

We traveled an entire block before I spoke again.

"What will I do if she begs me to come fetch her?" I asked. "When I do eventually write, that is."

"What do you think you'd do?" Martin's eyes were shaded by the brim of his hat, but I was aware they were fixed on me.

"I won't go against Teddy anymore." I had reached a firm resolution. "I've been favoring one of Catherine's children over the other, and it's time I stopped—however unfair I find it that he should be able to take her away from the life she wants. He loves her and will do what he considers best, even if his choices may differ from mine."

THE NEXT DAY I HAD A VISIT FROM VICTOR CANAVAN. DURING my absence from Chicago, he had worked with another of our couturières and appeared satisfied with that arrangement, but when I received a note that he was in the store and asking for me, I picked up my sketching materials and notebook before making my way to the first-floor meeting room.

"I am delighted to see you in good health, Mrs. Rutherford." The theater owner bowed over my hand in his slightly quaint fashion and pulled out a chair for me. He seated himself, his eyes on my face but clearly waiting for me to speak. It struck me how controlled he was, even when not on the stage—but I supposed it was his training as an actor that enabled him to suppress any temptation to fill a silence with empty speech.

"I'm quite recovered, thank you." I set out my papers and pencils in front of me. "I'm sorry I was unable to fulfill the commission we had started to work on. I was in poor health for much of the spring and summer."

"I was grieved to hear it. But the charming French lady took care of me very well—quite a character, isn't she? She introduced me to your Miss Filbey and made some excellent suggestions." He raised his thick, expressive eyebrows. "In fact—I must be honest with you—I liked the arrangement so much I would prefer to continue it. To be brutally frank, Mrs. Rutherford, your ideas were so marvelous they had a tendency to outshine the performance. I am used to ladies coming to me with adoration in their eyes at the end of the evening, not with a gleam of acquisitiveness and questions about fabrics and trimmings."

His smile was irresistible, and I joined in his laughter. "Perhaps I tried too hard," I said. "I'll admit we've gained quite a few customers from the Jewel Box. Women come to the store with your playbill in their hands, folded to show our advertisement. I'm glad you've chosen to continue with Rutherford's."

"The quality is excellent. So you see, I wished to tell you about the new arrangement in person before approaching

Miss Filbey for some fresh designs. It would be impolite to do otherwise—especially as my desire is for a magnificent pair of ball gowns for Miss Dardenne and Miss Keogh, and I'm sure you would have enjoyed the commission."

"I would." I shrugged, smiling. "But we have several excellent couturières, and I'm not interested in getting all the glory. We could put my name on everything and allow the other ladies to contribute without taking any of the credit, but that tends to result in the really good couturières leaving to found their own enterprises sooner rather than later."

"Sensible." He paused, leaning back a little in his chair. "I also came here to ask for news of Miss Lombardi—if you are able to give it to me. Again, I thought a direct approach best. I was very alarmed when she disappeared. I went to her boardinghouse and learned that her brother had arranged for all her belongings to be collected and sent to a far-off destination. Her landlady did not reveal that destination, and I did not ask her."

"I can't tell you either," I said. "Teddy told me in confidence. Do you understand why he deemed it necessary to remove her from Chicago? I should imagine the police made their suspicions clear to you." The direct approach was indeed best, I reflected, even if the result was the loss of Mr. Canavan's custom. Not that I believed he let personal matters interfere with good business.

Canavan waved a hand, closing his eyes briefly. "Oh, endless questions—poor Miss Dardenne was badly rewarded for her kindness in taking Miss Lombardi to the Grand Pacific. But we actors are accustomed to so-called respectable people attaching their lurid imaginings to us. It's the danger inherent in a profession where we might play a prince one day and a pander the next. The bourgeois find it hard to see how we can appear to be someone and not actually *be* that someone. I'm quite tempted to write a play in which I appear as a notorious jewel thief. Wouldn't *that* rub their noses in it?"

I smiled, although I didn't find his remark particularly amusing. It was our store they'd tried to rob, after all. "I understand from Mr. Lombardi that his sister is well," I said. "Beyond that, I can tell you nothing. He has asked me not to write her for the time being."

"I will not ask you to tell me where she is." His voice was gentle. "If you can reassure me as to her well-being from time to time, I will be content. And when you write, assure her of the best wishes of all of us at the Jewel Box."

"If you wish to speak to her brother, perhaps I might be able to arrange a meeting," I said, but Canavan shook his head slowly.

"I don't consider that would be wise. The poor child— torn away from everyone she knows after all that has happened to her. We had become a refuge for her, where she might be happy after a hard day of work, and the young man has used us to punish her—for what? For not choosing the friends he would have chosen for her?" He spread his long-fingered hands wide. "I would be bound by my friendship with Miss Lombardi to ask her brother that and other troublesome questions, and I think we would have an argument. I so dislike such scenes."

"Are you fond of her?" I wasn't sure from where the question came or what I really meant, but Canavan nodded.

"We are all fond of her. She loves us. She is so happy in our company. And for me, she is a reminder of myself as a child of her age, never content, always seeking until I found the life in which I truly seemed to fit. I would have her be one of us when she is old enough." The large brown eyes widened, for once not hidden by their drooping lids but candid, revealing, looking directly into mine. "On the stage she would make the most of her good looks, her gift for display, as it were. She will need a great deal of training—the young are so conscious of how they might look to others, but we must learn the trick of making ourselves disappear while being visible to everyone. To be everybody and nobody."

"She has already learned to hide herself." I looked down at my hands. "If she's truly happy in the company of you and your friends, that's more than I've seen since she was a little girl. You know, Mr. Canavan, I told myself I would abide by Teddy's wishes, and I will. I can't keep favoring Thea over him, which is what I'm doing if I keep taking her side. But I feel for her terribly. I only ever wanted to help her."

"And one day she may come to realize that."

His voice had deepened, and as I looked up, I saw the knowledge in his eyes of how much Thea hated me.

"I just wish she had found her happiness in one of the solutions I offered to her," I said.

"In a respectable life?"

"I don't think women can be truly happy in any life where they are not received by the majority of their sisters."

"But it's *not* the majority. It's a narrow furrow of life that imagines itself superior because it has the arrogance to draw up a set of rules for itself." Canavan's long mouth curved up at one side; if there were such a thing as a benevolent sneer, that was his expression. "Most people don't *care*. They live how they like."

"I don't believe that."

Canavan regarded me for a long moment and then rose, holding out his hand.

"I do not doubt your sincerity, nor your innate kindness. It's time I went to see your Mr. McCombs about finding me some paste jewelry that looks like it belongs to royalty. Poor man; from the article in the *Tribune,* it sounds like he received a nasty shock."

"He's fine." I too stood and placed my hand into his. "It

was an unsuccessful robbery, after all, and we're on our guard now. We won't let it happen again."

"Of course not." He kissed my fingers lightly. "To be robbed once is the sort of thing that could happen to anybody; to be robbed twice would start to look like carelessness."

43

INTENTIONS

"*A*nd Thea has never written Nell back, not once. So she thinks she's done all she can, don't you, Nell?"

Tess took a bite of the chocolate torte that was becoming her favorite dessert and smiled round at the table. Her first attempt at inviting her family to dinner in Calumet Avenue had been such a success that it had now become a fixture. The O'Dugans viewed Donny as a necessary component of that arrangement simply because Tess wanted it so, Aileen's sour looks notwithstanding.

"I still wonder if I should try to visit her," I said.

A chorus of "No" echoed to the swagged plaster decorations of our breakfast room. We were in this more intimate space because today's party was small—only Mr. and Mrs. O'Dugan, Billy, and Donny besides Martin, Tess, and me. We were holding a luncheon rather than a dinner to allow our guests to get home before the December dark closed in.

"You won't want to be traveling north with the snow and the ice coming toward you." Billy frowned.

"And what about Elizabeth?" Tess asked. "You must stay

here for her. When we went to see little Rosa, Elizabeth made us promise to visit at least once a week."

Elizabeth had been safely delivered of her second daughter on the fifth of the month. She seemed to be taking this joyful event in her stride, especially now they had hired a permanent nursemaid she actually liked.

"I hope you're not serious about chasing around after that ungrateful girl," Billy continued. "She's safe and well, so young Teddy tells you—and he would not lie, sure to God. It's my opinion that you have to leave Miss Thea to Teddy and the good Lord. She'll no doubt grow to love Wisconsin."

"She didn't grow to love Kansas."

"Girls are so difficult at that age." Mrs. O'Dugan took a dainty bite of her cake. "Mary and Aileen were both quite impossible till they married and settled down." She heaved a sigh worthy of an actress in a tragedy. "Deirdre's a good girl, I suppose, but how would I be sure? She comes to see us twice a year, like a visit from royalty, and doesn't write above once a month."

"Neither does Joseph, Ma. It's a fair piece from where they live to Chicago and they both work hard," said Billy.

"Ah, but Joseph is a man." Mrs. O'Dugan nodded as if there were no more to be said about the matter and turned her huge-eyed gaze to Tess. "Thank the Lord for Tessie and her wanting to be with us so often. I tell you, Mrs. Rutherford, your young miss might turn out well enough given a few years. It's marriage that will steady her. And children, if the Almighty blesses the union." She made the sign of the cross over her lean breast. "Marriage is the proper destiny for a woman."

I took a fold of my lower lip between my teeth as a gentle reminder that I was not to argue with my guests—or rather Tess's guests. But to my surprise, it was Donny who spoke.

"I reckon it's work that's the making of *any* person, man or woman. Why do women have to get married if they don't want to?" He frowned. "But maybe a man should marry a woman so she can be 'an help meet.'" He pronounced the last three words carefully. "Is that right, Tess?"

I had noticed that "Miss O'Dugan" and even "Miss Tess" had gone by the wayside in Lake Forest despite Sarah's attempt to educate Donny. Tess had stopped blushing every time she looked at Donny, but her smile was both adoring and encouraging as she nodded.

It was Billy who spoke though.

"I guess 'help meet' means that man and wife should work together for the good of their household, and perhaps that's why flighty young girls shouldn't become wives." Billy, who was sitting next to Donny, clapped the other man on the shoulder. "Men shouldn't marry neither till they're old enough to learn some sense and to spot the right girl for them. But here's the question I've been waiting to put to the assembled company, and you've given me the opportunity to do it."

He hooked a thumb into his vest pocket and leaned back. "Supposing a man who has sworn he won't even *dream* of marrying till he's thirty and prosperous meets a girl who is the pearl of great price? It's a conundrum, it is, because that very man is yours truly." He made a slight bow. "I appeal to this excellent company for their advice—and it's a fortunate thing that all the ones who'd have made *remarks* have stayed at home."

"*What* did you say?" asked Tess. "I wish you wouldn't use so many words to say things."

Her confusion, and her frankness, gave rise to fond smiles on all sides, but Martin stepped in to explain. "I believe Billy wants to marry Kathleen and wonders if he should wait to pop the question. How old are you, Billy, if it's not too impertinent to ask?"

"He's twenty-seven," said Tess. "But only just. He told me not to make a fuss about his birthday, so I didn't."

Smiles became laughter, and Martin and I, who had not known, stood to wish Billy many happy returns. That ceremony over, we sat, and Martin took up the reins of the conversation again.

"Are you afraid you'll lose her if you don't declare yourself?" he asked Billy. "Because that would be my fear in your circumstances. If you love a woman enough to marry her, you should tell her so and make your promise fair and square before life's chances pull you apart." He glanced at me; I responded to his rueful grin with a shrug and a roll of the eyes, and he laughed as he returned his attention to Billy.

"Would you be in a hurry for the wedding, my boy?" his father asked. "Is there a reason why you shouldn't ask her now and settle in for a long engagement?"

"Of course not, Da." Billy's plain, honest face reddened, but he soldiered on. "My only reservation is that Kathleen might expect us to wed sooner than my thirtieth birthday. She's twenty-four and her mother says it's high time. Said it to my face, she did. All her sisters are married."

"Are you in a position to set up housekeeping?" Martin asked.

"I think so, sir." Billy drew himself up and looked Martin in the face with as much seriousness as if he had actually made the proposal on the spot. "I hope her father agrees, as sure I'll have to ask him for her hand in a fitting manner."

"Perhaps we should have a little rehearsal before you leave." Martin, always interested in questions of finance, leaned forward. "You can make a speech to me about your salary, your savings, and your prospects, and I'll see if I can put a hard question or two to you. For my part, I think she's a lovely young woman and will be good for you. I can picture you as a family man."

"She's a very sweet girl," I agreed. The round-faced young lady with glossy dark curls and lips curved in a perfect Cupid's bow had endeared herself to me. She was sensible and thoughtful and seemed to have a mind of her own.

"I agree you *should* marry," said Tess. "Don't you, Ma? And, Da, you like Kathleen a lot."

"I do that." Mr. O'Dugan nodded emphatically. "Perhaps you'll let me sit in on your little rehearsal, eh, my lad? I might have something to add."

"I didn't mean to leave you out, Da." Billy turned his frank gaze on his father. "You're most welcome—it's just that Mr. Rutherford offered."

"Perhaps we ladies should retire and leave the men to talk?" I suggested. "If that's all right with you, Tess? You wanted coffee served—the three of us could go to the library."

As I walked out into the hallway, I could see snow falling outside. Thinking of our guests' return journey, I went to the window to get a better idea of the weather as Tess and her mother headed into the library. The temperature had not yet fallen much below freezing even at night; it reassured me to see fat, wet flakes that would mostly melt and not make traveling difficult.

I heard the door open and shut behind me and turned.

"Can I talk to you about something, Miss Nell?" Donny's shy smile lit his face. "If you don't mind leaving off joining the other ladies for a few minutes."

"Of course I don't." I led the way to the back parlor where we kept the piano. A fire was burning; through the French windows, I could see the snow settling in a sparkling crust on grass and hedges, melting into the flag-stones under the wrought iron pergola and onto the roof of the annex that Martin had claimed as a billiard room and hardly used.

"I'm going to be twenty-seven in April," was Donny's surprising opening. "April the twenty-seventh, so the number of the day will be the number of my years. Only I don't think it's my real birthday because nobody knows it. They just guessed a birthday for me."

"Three days after Tess's birthday." I smiled. "Perhaps we should hold a celebration for you too."

I motioned for him to sit down, and he sank cautiously onto a chair. He always had the air of moving gingerly indoors, as if afraid to break something, constantly looking up at door lintels and down at pieces of furniture to ensure he could pass through, ducking or turning sideways if he was the least bit unsure. Outside, he was more confident, especially around horses or when carrying a load that would have buckled most men. In his plain suit and yellow vest, he might have been from almost any walk of life. Since the summer, he had begun shaving regularly, giving him an added air of maturity.

"Tess will be thirty on April the twenty-fourth," he continued. "And I don't mind at all that she's older than me. The thing is, Miss Nell—" He stopped, seemingly tongue-tied.

"I can guess what this is about." I fought to keep a smile off my face. "At least I hope I can—and I'm touched that you've come to me. Has Tess finally . . . that is, have you also got ideas about marrying?"

He didn't answer, and for a horrible moment it crossed my mind that he planned to marry somebody entirely different. How heartbroken Tess would be. When he looked up at me, his brow was so creased I feared the worst.

"I don't know how I'll do it, Miss Nell. It all seems like so much to think about. I know it costs a man a heap of money to marry, and I've been saving, but I don't even know what I'd need. How would I manage if I had to move out of my room and find a place to live? Nobody ever taught me about those things."

I held up a hand. "Before we go on, I need to be certain. Is it Tess you're hoping to marry or somebody else?"

Donny's eyes widened under his fair brows. "Why would I be thinking of anybody but Tess?" He sounded completely astonished. "She likes me more than anyone has ever liked me in my entire life. Nobody's ever set much store by me, but *she—*" He stopped, as if words failed him.

"She thinks you're everything wonderful," I said softly. "And when Tess thinks that of a person, she's loyal for life. If you've seen that, then you deserve her."

"I don't understand what she sees in me." Donny looked down at his work-roughened hands.

"Don't you?" I swallowed down the lump in my throat, not wanting to elaborate in case I burst into tears of joy. "Why don't you ask Martin about the financial side of things? He'd be as happy to help you as he is to help Billy."

Donny rubbed at his thick shock of blond hair. "I'm not sure I'd understand if he told me. I can figure out how to do things with my hands, but I'm not smart with numbers and reading and things like that. And . . . I guess he makes me a little nervous sometimes, the way he can talk business and not even look at a piece of paper. I wanted to speak to you because we're old friends from the Poor Farm, you and me and Tess. You'll figure out a way through for me. And maybe you're the person I should ask for her—for her hand—because you've known us longest. I don't have anybody else."

I leaned forward and put a hand on Donny's arm, feeling its breadth and strength under the wool of his jacket. "You have my full agreement and support," I said simply. "As for the rest, we'll all sit down together and puzzle out what should happen. What sort of work do you want to do?"

"Exactly what I do now." Donny sounded startled. "I wouldn't have to change, would I? I wake up every morning happy because I work here. I notice what needs doing each day and I do it, and that's a fine thing."

"It certainly is. Well, the first thing you should do is propose to Tess and make it all official. Then we can discuss your future. I expect she'll have her own opinions."

"What should I say?" An expression of panic crossed the young man's face. To some people, that might have seemed amusing, but I had my time at the Poor Farm to thank for making me understand that individuals were intelligent in different ways. Donny had a wonderfully practical mind and could work out how to mend or make things, or how to get an animal to do exactly what he needed it to, but he balked when it came to words. I reflected for a moment.

"Why not, 'Tess, will you be my wife?' That's direct and easy to remember. Or you might say, 'Tess, I love you. Will you marry me?' You do love her, don't you?"

"Of course I do. I like that last one." Donny said the little speech under his breath twice, staring at the fire as his lips moved, and then gave me a tremulous smile. "I can remember that." He took a huge breath, his chest expanding alarmingly. "Holy Moses, Miss Nell, I've gone all shaky inside."

"Then you'd better take the first opportunity to ask her and get it over with." I pressed my fingers to my lips to suppress a grin. "I suspect it's quite common for the prospective bridegroom to feel a little nervous."

GIVEN THAT TESS—*AND* SARAH—HAD WALKED IN ON MARTIN'S proposal to *me*, I was tempted to maneuver the situation so I could witness Donny's proposal to Tess. The imminence of that proposal occupied my mind so thoroughly I barely concentrated on what Tess and her mother were talking about once I'd sent Donny back to the breakfast room and joined the ladies. Fortunately, Mrs. O'Dugan took it upon herself to deliver a thorough analysis of Kathleen's demeanor, family background, and religious observances that lasted until Martin led the men into the front parlor to join the rest of us.

"We've concluded that Billy is able to risk marriage within the next year," said Martin cheerfully as he waved Mr. O'Dugan toward the large straight-backed chair that suited him best. "With some careful housekeeping, a thrifty wife— and a little help at the start."

"And it's a wonderful thing that my own Da is the one to help me." Billy was grinning from ear to ear.

"We wouldn't have lived through the bad years if you young ones hadn't been willing to work as hard as you did." Mr. O'Dugan thumped softly on the ground with his cane. "I can't give as much as I'd like, there being so many of you, but I'm proud to do it, and let's say no more about it. Margaret, no tears now."

Mrs. O'Dugan, who was showing signs of emotion, declared that she reserved the right to cry at the wedding, and the next half hour passed amid a great deal of gentle teasing. But soon it was time for our guests to depart; the snow was still falling lazily, and there was ice on the wind as Capell brought round the landau, its graceful lines obscured by the stout leather top that was collecting a dusting of white.

"I should go back to work," Donny said as soon as the carriage had rounded the corner onto Twentieth Street.

"Don't be in a hurry," I said quickly. "The weather's dreadful—and Capell won't be back for at least two hours."

"But there's always something to do, Miss Nell." Donny looked fidgety, and I felt sure he would make good his escape until Martin came to my aid.

"Nell's quite right—why spoil a pleasant afternoon? Come and give me your opinion about some advertisements I've collected. I'm considering getting a phaeton so I can drive myself around town." He grinned at me. "When we've built our house in Lake Forest, I'm going to get a ladies' driving carriage and give you lessons, Nellie. I've given up hope of ever putting you on a saddle, but you could learn to drive properly."

"Only under duress." I gave my husband what I hoped was a quelling look. "Aren't you going back to the store?"

"In this snow?" Martin yawned. "And after such an excellent lunch? Besides, Sarah will be down soon. I'm going to call the store on the telephone and make sure all is well, and then I'm going to play hooky for a change." He headed toward the niche at the back of the hall where the instrument resided.

"And I will be with you in just a few minutes." I smiled at Tess and Donny. "Why don't you go on into the library? It's nice and warm if you keep the door shut."

And if that didn't do the trick, I reflected as I headed upstairs, then we probably wouldn't be done with the matter till after Christmas. It would undoubtedly be too obvious if I invited Donny for Christmas Day—wouldn't Tess be suspicious? Surely with all the matrimonial talk in the air, he would seize his opportunity. How long should I give him? Twenty minutes? But Martin would no doubt be back in no fewer than ten minutes. As convenient as a telephone was, it was a trial to use, what with the crackling and the difficulty in hearing the other person. I sighed and hastened my steps.

I was back downstairs in time to intercept Martin just as he reached the library door.

"Don't go in yet." I grasped his hand and towed him toward the front parlor, shutting the door firmly. "While you were talking to Billy, Donny more or less asked me for Tess's hand in marriage."

"My eye." Martin's face lit up with amusement. "What did we put in the drinking water?"

"Billy's little announcement encouraged him—but he's shy, Martin."

"Ah, no wonder you were so eager to keep him in the house. Are you going to turn into one of those matchmaking women?"

"Probably. Once one's own romance is well settled, what other fun can a woman have?"

Martin answered that entirely rhetorical question by sweeping me into his arms and kissing me thoroughly. We only broke apart when we heard a door opening. We stared at each other.

"I expect that's Beatrice clearing away the coffee things," Martin said, his hands still on my waist. "Perhaps we should give them another five minutes."

"I'm going to peek around the door."

"Open it slowly or the latch will click. Here—" and Martin, looking just as eager as I was, eased the thick door open with a finger on the deadlatch so I could look round.

From my vantage point I saw nothing—and heard nothing except for the well-known pattering of light foot-steps on the stairs. Another pair of stockings about to be ruined, no doubt. Sarah always kicked off her slippers.

"Donny!" I heard a thump as Sarah jumped from the second stair across to the hallway rug, as she so often did. I deduced that the click of the door had been Donny emerging from the library.

"Look at my drawing," Sarah's voice continued. "It's the Confederate and Union flags, see? I have to learn all the names of the battles—don't you think that's boring? But it's Saturday, so Miss Baker let me draw instead." She paused. "Why are you holding Tess's hand?"

I turned and flew into Martin's arms, hiding my squeal of joy in his waistcoat.

PART IV
1880

44

ARRANGEMENTS

January 1880

A touch of romance made our Christmas all the merrier, and the absence of Thea ensured that harmony reigned in our small household. The one discordant note was the prospect of imminent separation. Martin had asked for a few weeks to think about the best arrangement for Tess and Donny before giving his advice; by the end of January, when he summoned Donny for a meeting, Tess and I were nervous.

"I don't want to lose you." Tess's hand curled around mine, her eyes serious and imploring behind their spectacles.

"You won't lose me." I put my arms around her, feeling the warmth from the back parlor's well-stacked fire bathe the two of us in its comforting rays. "You're not having second thoughts about marrying, are you?"

"No, silly."

Tess backed out of my embrace a little so she could look at the ring on her left hand. A single rose-cut diamond, prettily set, gathered the light of the fire in its facets; I knew it had "Donny to Tess" inscribed on the inside. There had been some discussion between Martin and Donny whether "Donald to Teresa" would be more appropriate, but Donny had come down in favor of informality and simplicity. The unostentatious piece of jewelry had pleased Tess more than a bushel of rubies would an empress.

"It's beautiful." I admired the jewel for the thousandth time. "An extraordinarily pretty stone." It had cost Donny quite a large portion of his savings, Martin had told me, even though he'd let the young man have it at cost. Donny, not being prone to any kind of temptation in the way of drink or amusements, had saved almost every cent he'd earned since we met him. Martin told me he had glowed with pride at being able to buy a ring.

"It *is* extraordinarily pretty." Tess gave a satisfied nod and crossed to the French windows, outside which the snow was falling fast; it was very cold. "Where *are* the men? Nell, I wish Martin wasn't so mysterious about this idea of his. Hasn't he told you anything?"

"He hasn't given me a clue. I'm certain he's enjoying himself. Isn't it ridiculous that we have to wait around like a pair of spare boots for the menfolk to decide on where you live?"

"Supposing we're a long way away?" Tess looked truly worried. "We can't afford to live on this street, can we, Nell?"

"I imagine not." I didn't want to give Tess—or myself—false hopes. Since she'd shown me her little book, I had a pretty good notion of what her total wealth amounted to, and it would not buy a house on Calumet Avenue or even close. Perhaps in the area nearer to the railroad where we had our stables? But that was hardly suitable. I had begun to resign myself to having Tess at a distance, in some comfortable but modest neighborhood, and the idea depressed me. Would she and Donny be all right on their own?

A noise in the hallway suggested Martin and Donny were

joining us at last. I opened the door, relieved to see the two of them with broad smiles on their faces. Donny looked most presentable in a tweed sack coat and checked waistcoat, the latter being our Christmas gift to him; he had made an effort to get his thick hair to lie down a little, and the new style suited him.

"Well!" Martin rubbed his hands together, approaching the fire to warm them. "I have the future groom's approval in principle, but he defers to his fiancée for the final decision. Let's go, shall we? Donny, you and Tess should lead the way."

I narrowed my eyes at my husband. "What have you dreamed up? And why has it taken you so many weeks? And why the mysterious airs *now*?"

Martin affected an air of utter candidness as he offered me his arm. "I am, as I know Joe has told you behind my back, a showman at heart. I'm afraid that as my wife you must indulge that side of me occasionally. The delay was due to the need to consider every possible solution, as I am also a cautious man. In the end, I adopted the most obvious scheme, the one that will make both of you ladies happy and afford the most convenience to Donny and myself. And to my relief, he agrees it's convenient. Lead on, Donny."

We followed the pair, who, as always, looked a little incongruous because of the considerable difference in height. I was becoming accustomed to seeing Tess's hand in Donny's, a habit they had adopted rather than proceeding arm-in-arm because Tess found it tiring to reach so far up.

We didn't have far to go. Donny took us down the short stub of corridor that led to Martin's billiard room, a large pavilion-like space that contained, unsurprisingly, a billiard table. There was also a spacious area closer to the fire that held a variety of leather-covered armchairs. Shelving displayed a few books and periodicals about horses and machines and sporting pursuits and other topics of masculine interest.

"We're going to live in the billiard room?" Tess wrinkled her brow in confusion.

"Above it." Martin grinned conspiratorially at Donny.

"But there's nothing above it except the roof." Tess looked upward in dismay, and I saw Martin swallow hard in an effort not to laugh out loud. He looked like a man who had invented a terrific joke and was waiting for everyone else to understand it. I did.

"You're going to build above the billiard room—or are you going to knock it down and start again? It's not as if you use this room all that much." I folded my arms and gave my husband what I hoped was a challenging stare.

"Oh, don't knock it down." Tess's eyes shone. "We could hold a dance in here or a big party—well, we could if you took that silly table out." She tipped her head back to look at the coffered ceiling. "Would we really have all that space just to ourselves?"

"It would be quite snug." Martin, whose eyebrows had risen when Tess called his billiard table silly, now looked anxious. "None of your rooms would be as large as the ones you occupy now in our house—but I would like it to be a complete little apartment in itself, and Donny agrees with me. You could eat your meals there by yourselves if you wish."

"You're very welcome to dine with us," I said quickly. "Heaven only knows we have enough room."

"But if you were entertaining, and I didn't want to sit and listen to you all talking about things I'm not interested in, I would hide away in my own house instead." Tess clapped her hands. "That sounds just fine. Am I going to pay for the building?"

Martin made a face. "You'd rent it, I suppose—or we'd

make an arrangement based on Donny continuing to work for us." He looked at Tess, his expression dubious. "I don't like the thought of making part of our house a separate property in the legal sense, if it's all right with you. And this way you can live on your income, yours from the investments I've made for you and Donny's from his work. You should save your capital for when you need it. If my estimates are right, you might afford a maid to do your cooking and cleaning. You won't be able to be grand."

"But we'll be standing on our own two feet, fair and square." Donny's face wore the expression he often had, a little puzzled at the way the world worked. "At least—holy smokes, when I asked Tess to marry me, I'd forgotten she was a rich lady. Are you *sure* this is all right?" he asked Martin.

"You'll more than make up for the unfortunate fact of Tess's money by your hard work." Martin clapped the younger man on one massive shoulder. "As for Nell and I, all the Prairie Avenue district will consider us dreadfully eccentric—but who cares? Every other solution I came up with involved splitting up my family, and I'm not prepared to do that. As long as it works for the five of us, I'll be a happy man."

"YOU DON'T HAVE TO GIVE UP YOUR BILLIARD TABLE," I SAID TO Martin once the two of us were alone again. "Not if you don't want to."

Martin shrugged. "I might want to—you never know." He reached out a hand to me, pulling me in close. "I realize there's far more to this house than I originally intended. Perhaps I should have kept the original stable block, although I do like the extra room for carriages in the one we have and the larger garden I put in because we didn't need a stable yard."

"Husband dear, you are what Grandmama would have called hopelessly nouveau riche." I raised myself up on my toes to kiss Martin's smoothly shaven cheek. "If you build a fancy estate in Lake Forest instead of the pretty country house you've promised me, I'll desert you and find myself a sensible man who keeps one carriage."

"And whose idea was the landaulet?" Martin nuzzled my neck but then pulled back, sighing. "I guess I was afraid of how much of a step backward I was taking after the Prairie Avenue house—imagining the other fellows would think less of me if I didn't at least have a sporting room."

"And whose idea was the phaeton you're planning to buy?" I teased him. "Perhaps you'll have to be content with impressing the 'fellows' with your superior horseflesh and your fine carriages. Thank you for resisting the temptation to build another palace like the one you built for Lucetta. I suppose this house is very plain compared to *that* symphony in marble."

"But it's still too big for you, isn't it?" Martin's large hand closed around mine, warm and comforting as we strolled toward the front of the house. "And you've never said a word against it. Why didn't you object?"

"Because I was a new bride and wanted my husband to be happy." I grinned up at Martin, the elation and excitement of knowing that Tess would still be near to me coursing through my body. "I know I try to do too much and take on too many responsibilities and then get cross and irritable, and that I underestimate you and fail to trust you and criticize when I should be telling you how wonderful you are. It's been hard for me to adjust to being a wife as well as a mother and dressmaker. So I guess it's a good thing I don't care enough about houses to make *that* topic into an argument. It just wasn't a fight I wanted to pick."

Martin smiled. "I rather enjoy it when we argue, in some respects. I like the way your eyes narrow and your hair seems to acquire an extra curl, and the way you stand there all ramrod-stiff, as if you're bracing yourself for battle. It reminds me of when you were the little girl who made my sad days so much brighter." He pulled me into the front parlor so he could shut the door and wrap his arms around my waist again. "Besides, making up after our disagreements is *such* fun."

He demonstrated his meaning with sufficient proof of marital affection that I was sure my hair *was* curling more than usual. But then he released me again and leaned his forehead against mine. "Of course, if you want, we could sell up and start again with a smaller house."

"Heavens, *no*—not just as you've settled things so nicely for Tess. Anyway, I'd be an ungrateful fool if I were to reject *such* a lovely house." I looked at the cream silk wall hangings and the deep yellow drapes, beyond which a blizzard was now hurling snow at our windows, blotting out our view of the lake. The green damask on the settees gleamed; polished wood reflected the flames of the fire that crackled under the mantelpiece, where a clock ticked with a muted yet decisive sound, pleasant on the ears. It had become familiar to me—it was home. Besides—

"We can't leave Ruth." Our tiny daughter rested in a sheltered corner of the garden beneath a simple square of buff-colored polished sandstone bearing her first name and the date 1879. A month after my return to Chicago, we had watched the planting of a redbud tree to shelter her. I would see neither plaque nor tree again until the snow melted; and with that thought I pictured a far-off spring when I could sit in the sunshine under a tree grown much larger, its heart-shaped leaves filtering the sunlight. It would, perhaps, shade a grown-up Sarah, her children, even some younger brothers and sisters playing on the cool grass. No, this house had earned its right to be called "home." Even its too-new smell had worn off, softened by a two-year patina of beeswax, potpourri, and all the scents of family life.

"This is the Rutherford house now." I leaned into my husband's arms again, our embrace becoming tender as we remembered the griefs and joys of 1879. "The Rutherford-Clark house, in fact—or at least it will be once Tess and Donny are married. Big enough for two families and a whole host of experiences. Build away, Martin Rutherford." I smoothed my palms down Martin's cheeks, just as I had when my hands were those of an innocent child. "We all trust you to create a home for us."

45

SONS AND DAUGHTERS

$\mathcal{T}$eddy Lombardi rose to his feet, holding his teacup aloft, and smiled round at the assembled company. A cry of, "Speech! Speech!" from Martin brought a boyish flush to his cheeks, but he drew himself up to his full, lanky height.

"I thank you for the birthday wishes." He made a slight bow toward all of us. "I would like to extend my own felicitations to my dear friend Sarah on the occasion of her ninth birthday. I am honored and proud to share this date with such a charming young lady." He laughed as Martin whistled and several of us said, "Hear, hear," and then continued. "But especially, I haven't yet wished the prospective bride and groom every happiness. So, ladies and gentlemen, I give you: the bride and groom."

"To the bride and groom!" Sarah stood up too, raising her teacup with unusual caution. Her new dress was of white pleated mousseline with a pale green princess-line bodice gathered into swags and finished with a bow at the level of her lower hip, and she was being extra careful not to stain the fine fabrics. Alice had arranged her hair into a style that pulled it well away from her face, allowing large ringlets to cascade down from the back of her head; I was beginning to glimpse what my daughter would look like when she was old enough to put her hair up. She took a careful sip of her tea, barely wincing. She did not enjoy tea much but was trying to get used to drinking it.

We all stood, of course, except a blushing Tess and a slightly bemused Donny, who remained sitting side by side looking just as shy and awkward as any young couple should. It was a small gathering—us three Rutherfords, Tess and Donny, Miss Baker, and Teddy. Sarah, whom we'd allowed to choose both the type of celebration and the guests, had insisted on an English afternoon tea. She had also ruled that both Miss Baker and Teddy were to attend our "family" celebration since, she said, she regarded Miss Baker as *almost* family and Teddy as a sort of cousin.

As we all resumed our places, Sarah, with a conspiratorial glance at me and Martin, put her cup and saucer down. She crossed to the cabinet, from which she extracted two small, velvet-covered boxes.

"We have presents for the gentlemen," she announced. "One for Teddy because it's his birthday, and one for Donny because—well, because I noticed it when we were looking for Teddy's present, and I just wanted to give it to you, Donny." She came to stand in front of the young man, who looked flustered at all the attention he was getting, with an anxious look on her face. "Tess is my best Tess, and I guess I shouldn't have been unfriendly to you."

"You never were." Donny took the box, the familiar small frown on his face. "You've always been most genteel to me, Miss Sarah—Miss Rutherford." His huge, work-roughened hand wrapped around her small, slim fingers. "When were you ever unfriendly?"

"I think I was." Sarah looked back at the rest of us. "Once

or twice." She leaned in and kissed Donny on the cheek. "This is for all the birthdays you've had and didn't know about. And *this*," she kissed him on the other cheek, "is for friendship forever more. You have to wait to open your box till I've given Teddy his because they're almost the same."

She ran lightly around to where Teddy was sitting, pressing the velvet box into his hand, and then stepped back, raising her hands in the air like the conductor of an orchestra. "Ready? One, two, three . . . *Now*."

We all waited as the two men removed a small gold object from the boxes. "What is it?" Donny asked.

"It's a watch fob." Sarah skipped back to stand beside Donny. "You'll have to save it till you have a watch, of course, but when you have one, you hang it from the chain. But it's even better than that—it's a seal for sealing letters, see? When you push it into the wax, you get a nice circle with a horse in the middle. I chose a horse for you because you like horses. Look—it's prancing."

"I never thought I'd own anything made of gold." Donny held the fob gingerly between thumb and finger, staring at it intently.

"It's from all of us, but I chose it." Sarah bounced on her toes. "The stone's called an agate—isn't it pretty?" She went back to Teddy again, bright ringlets bouncing. "Yours has writing, did you notice?"

"Forget Me Not." Teddy smiled in the way he reserved for Sarah alone these days.

"And a flower, which I suppose is a forget-me-not, although I guess I've never seen one." Sarah took the gold fob out of Teddy's hand and held it up, squinting at the reversed writing. "Goodness, Miss Baker, maybe you're right and I *do* need spectacles. I've noticed you already have a fob on your watch chain, Teddy, but gentlemen can have more than one. Just promise me you won't give it away to a poor person, won't you? And that you'll never ever forget us and you'll come to our house a lot, even though you're twenty now, and that's awfully old, and perhaps you'll get married soon."

"I have no intention of doing anything of the kind," Teddy said amid our laughter. "May I kiss you in thanks? I guess you're much too big to swing up onto my shoulder now. How did you get to be so grown-up so fast, Sarah? I've been thinking of you as a little girl, but here you are now, nine years old and looking like a young lady."

Sarah presented her cheek, and he kissed it. Something caught in my throat. For a moment, I saw myself and Martin in memory, he twenty and I nine—the difference in age between us was the same as that between Teddy and Sarah. Had he teased me about growing up too? Sarah was positively glowing with pleasure at Teddy's compliment. Supposing, one day, she and Teddy . . .

No, I was *not* going to turn into one of those matchmaking women. My daughter was only nine. I soon forgot my moment of maternal solicitude as Teddy took hold of Sarah's hand, much as Donny had done.

"I won't be able to come to your house again for quite a long while, as it happens," he said. "I'm leaving Chicago soon —it's not the best moment to announce it, I suppose, but I'm afraid of running out of time and having to send a letter instead. Better to break the news while we're all together, and I can tell you how much I'll miss you all."

He smiled briefly and chucked Sarah under the chin; her face had fallen when he'd spoken of leaving.

"Don't look glum, Sarah. Be happy for your friend. I'll only be gone a year or two, and that's the blink of an eye in the space of a lifetime. I'm going back to Ireland—I've been wanting to ever since I traveled to Europe with you two years ago. And then perhaps my friends and I will travel some more. I've been corresponding with the fellows I worked with, and we've got plenty of ideas." He grinned at Martin. "I got a taste for Europe, and there's a lot of good work to be done there. Three of us are heading to Boston in a few days to find our way onto an early sailing. One of the men has a maiden aunt there who'll give us a room while we're waiting."

Martin frowned. "And what of your plans to become a pastor? I thought you were keen to head back to the Eternal Life Seminary when you had the chance. Wandering around Europe won't get you a church."

Teddy shrugged. "The world will be my church, sir, for a while. I have money saved up in the bank for when I return to America. God will guide my footsteps while I'm overseas, just like he did when I was in Ireland."

Martin nodded but said nothing as the others chimed in with questions and comments. I too was silent, studying Sarah's face as she stood with one hand on Teddy's shoulder. She seemed more interested than upset—after all, traveling to Europe was not an unknown experience for her, and she still had a child's trust in an adult's ability to solve all problems. Nobody thought to ask the one question that was on my mind.

AT A QUIET WORD FROM MARTIN, TEDDY STAYED ON AFTER Donny and Miss Baker had left and Sarah and Tess had retired upstairs. We were all so full of food that—with the undoubted exception of Martin—nobody would be able to eat much supper. How on earth did the English get through their days if they stopped for sandwiches and cakes every afternoon?

With a prayer of gratitude that I could leave the clearing up to somebody else, I turned my back on the crumb-strewn parlor and led the way to the library, shivering a little as I caught glimpses of the piles of snow outside the window. A Chicago winter always seemed at its worst in February.

"That was quite an announcement, Teddy," Martin commented as we closed the door behind us. "So what about Thea? That's what Nell's been dying to ask. By the time you leave for Europe, she'll have been in Wisconsin for what, six months? All of fall and winter. How does she feel about you leaving?"

"I don't know." Teddy's expression hardened. "Just before Christmas I received a letter from Mrs. Galloway explaining that Thea did not want to correspond with me or receive visits from me anymore." He looked at me. "She hasn't answered your letters either, has she?"

"No, she hasn't," I admitted. There had also been no response to the parcel of fabrics and trimmings I'd sent to Thea for Christmas, thinking she would need something new to wear. It bothered me not to know if she'd even received it. I wasn't sure whether to be annoyed or worried, truth be told.

"Mrs. Galloway said she's settled in well," Teddy continued. "She hinted that Thea has shown a liking for her older son, Jacob, who came to build a house on their land after his wife died. He has two small children of whom Thea's quite fond."

I frowned. It seemed unlikely to me that prickly Thea would conceive a fondness for any children, let alone another woman's. "Do you trust these Galloway people?" I asked.

"Of course." An expression I couldn't read flitted across Teddy's face. "Mrs. Galloway is a true saint. She says she'll do everything she can to soften Thea's heart toward us all. She tells me it's only natural that Thea is bitter about what happened, but the peace and quiet of their land is gradually soothing her. When she's twenty-one, she can choose what she does—but in the meantime she's safe from the corruption of Chicago."

I pursed my lips. *And the corruption of the Rutherfords?* I wondered. But I wasn't about to argue with Teddy about the superior virtues of the life we'd helped shape for Thea. In retrospect, I wasn't even sure myself how we'd gone from providing a home for a child to somehow allowing her to run wild behind our backs. Perhaps we were just complete fools, Martin and I; smart at selling clothes but lacking in understanding in other important areas.

"Would you give the Galloways our address?" I asked. "In case there's trouble."

Teddy nodded. "I will." He sighed. "But I wish—I beg—that you'd leave well alone, Mrs. Rutherford. I will enclose a letter telling Thea she can always write to you if she needs anything—is that right?"

Martin shrugged. "Obviously."

"I knew I could depend on you. But please—unless she asks you to visit, could you wait another six months before seeing her? Mrs. Galloway advises that since Thea doesn't want to hear from me, I should give her some time to think before turning up on her doorstep. I suppose the same should apply to you."

"A whole *year*—" I began, but Teddy held up a hand to interrupt me.

"It's not that long, as I told Sarah. Not compared to a lifetime. And for me, going to Europe makes it easier. I will pray unceasingly that when I come back, she'll be settled, and we'll be friends again. After all, she'll be eighteen before long and I'm sure time will smooth her into a fine little woman."

"*There* you are."

We all turned at the sound of Sarah's clear voice as she entered the library.

"Teddy, you're still here!" she exclaimed. "I'm so glad. I didn't get to tell you nearly enough things because I was being polite and not chattering all the time." She rolled her eyes at me in a very droll fashion. "Did I say that I'm going to Lake Forest next week?"

She settled herself daintily on her favorite window seat—not, I noticed, curling her legs under her as she usually did. I also saw that, for a miracle, she was still wearing the smart heeled pumps we had bought to go with the dress. Her white silk stockings might survive the day without holes.

"You hadn't favored me with that piece of information," Teddy said. "Are you going too, Mrs. Rutherford?"

Sarah opened her mouth to interrupt and then closed it, clearly mindful of her manners. I grinned. "I'll let Sarah explain. She's been far too quiet this afternoon."

"I'm going on my *own*." Even with the light from the window behind her, I could discern the pleased expression on Sarah's face. "At least Miss Baker's going to take me down there on the train because it's too icy for horses, but I'll be staying with the Ogilvies on my *own*. Junie Ogilvie's my friend, and she has three brothers and three sisters, and we're going to have sleigh rides and go skating and ice fishing. Teddy, may I write to you in Europe? And can you write me back?"

Teddy frowned a little, but then his brow cleared. "I don't know where I'm going to be, that's the trouble—but I know where *you'll* be." He rose to his feet and went to Sarah, squatting down so she didn't have to crane her neck to see his face. "Here's a deal. I'll write you whenever I can, and if I have a fixed address or can find a convenient post office, I'll tell you where to send a letter so I can have your news." He twisted round, positioning himself on one knee so he could see me and Martin. "That is, ma'am, sir, if you don't mind me corresponding with your daughter."

Martin and I looked at one another, and I let Martin speak. "Of course not," he said, "although I expect Sarah to let us know what's in her letters now that she's begun to have correspondents."

"So make them exciting letters, Teddy." Sarah patted Teddy on the shoulder as she rose to her feet. "I'm going to have exciting things to tell you, I'm sure. I didn't get a chance to tell you about my dancing lessons either—can you dance?"

"I don't dance." Mercifully, Teddy did not elaborate, and Sarah was too eager to speak after her polite reticence of the tea party, where she had played the hostess's part of drawing conversation out of others rather than dominating it herself.

"I'm learning dancing *and* deportment." She executed some waltz steps, counting, "One two three, *one* two three," before breaking off with her next piece of news. "And I'm probably going to have to wear spectacles for reading because I'm getting headaches from reading so much." She wrinkled her nose. "I think Mama needs spectacles too because sometimes she squints, but she says she doesn't."

"You'll be a young lady when I see you again, then." Teddy's smile was a little rueful. "It's dawning on me how much I'll be missing in Chicago when I'm gone. Don't forget me, will you?"

"Never." Sarah twirled, her mind still on dancing. "We're friends for ever and ever."

46

WIVES AND MOTHERS

"*M*e *do* carry Baby."

Mabel Fletcher stood in the middle of the Fletchers' parlor, eyeing her mother with a mutinous expression. The bright blue eyes that so resembled Elizabeth's were rounded into a rebellious glare. One chubby hand curled into a fist, resting on her waist, while she brandished the other in the air as if Elizabeth were the small child who had to be corrected over a misdemeanor.

"Me is *two*." She held up a pair of fingers in illustration. It was the day of her birthday, and we had all been teaching her how to show her age. "Me *can* carry Wosa." She approached the baby's crib, looking hopeful.

"You're so big and strong." Sarah's skinny legs folded easily under her as she lowered herself to the rug. She had grown another inch since she had returned from her stay in Lake Forest, although she was still not tall for her age. She picked up the large doll Mabel had dropped in her eagerness to impress upon her mother that it was the live doll, four-month-old Rosa, that she was interested in. "Look, Mama, this doll can sit down properly—what a clever thing! She has joints in her arms and legs."

She worked the doll into a sitting position, ignoring Mabel, whose face turned crimson as her grandmother scooped the baby out of her crib and took her out of the room. It was a beautiful doll—a gift from her doting grandfather, who had ordered it from Paris, and to my mind far too grand for such a small girl. With its blue glass eyes and blond horsehair curls, dressed in the very latest Paris fashion for children, it looked eerily lifelike perched on Sarah's knee.

Mabel's gaze fixed on the closing door. As it shut with a firm click, she sat down on the floor, screamed, "ME *DO* CARRY BABY," at the top of her voice, and began roaring at a volume quite uncomfortable to the ears.

Elizabeth sighed and rolled her eyes. I sent her a sympathetic look, speech being impossible against the wails of fury emanating from the small, frustrated person on the rug. All the while Sarah ignored her, singing to the doll and smoothing her fingers over the velvet, silk and lace of its dress. She did not care much for dolls but was becoming more interested in matters of dress as she navigated the year between nine and ten, and the doll's ensemble was very fine. She still couldn't hold a tune; the song she was inventing on the spot was more like a one-sided conversation to which a drunken composer had hastily added a theme.

"You are a pretty girl, and today is your birthday, and your boots are so smart, and I will give Mabel a chair for you to sit in if I can find one in a shop, and then we can play school, and I like the color of your hair better than mine, and today is a happy day . . ."

And on and on in the same vein, the notes rising and falling and occasionally wobbling into a different key. I realized that, annoying as Sarah's song was to her elders, it was attracting Mabel's attention; I supposed that was Sarah's aim.

The last year had taught us that Elizabeth's oldest daughter had a firebrand nature. Her temper ignited easily but died down just as quickly if you didn't argue with her. Sarah was adept at handling her.

Mabel's face faded from an even, bright pink to a blotched ivory, her tear-red eyes gradually ceasing to produce the great fat drops that had cascaded down her round cheeks. After a minute or two, she began to spy on Sarah from under long, wet lashes. She boosted herself up into a standing position and toddled toward my daughter, lower lip well pushed out.

"*My* dolly."

"I was just holding her for you." Sarah briefly raised her eyes to the assembled adults to ensure they were noticing how subtle and clever she was being and cuddled the doll to her as she smoothed its legs straight inside its silk stockings. "She's *so* pretty."

"ME carry dolly." Mabel's arms shot out in front of her in a possessive motion, small hands making clutching movements as she neared her target.

"Why don't we show dolly to Fan-Fan?" Sarah relinquished the doll into Mabel's care. The little girl held it in a way that would endanger life or limb if it were an actual child but looked ready to follow Sarah.

My daughter rose in one fluid movement and headed toward the door, her hand outstretched behind her but otherwise looking quite unconcerned. When she had Mabel's hand firmly in hers, she opened the parlor door and ushered the little girl through. She made a theatrical bow in our direction with her free arm before closing the door slowly, a grin on her face. "Fan-Fan" was Mabel's nickname for her nursemaid, a nice young girl we all liked.

"Too much cake," Tess said as the door shut. "She's overexcited. Sary always used to be difficult when she had too many sweet things. But I *never* remember her screaming as loud as that."

"Let's hope it's worn Mabel out and Sarah or Fannie can get her to take a nap. I think she's had quite enough of being the birthday girl for the time being." I turned toward Elizabeth again. "Now, if I recall rightly, you were asking about Tess's wedding before the volcano erupted?"

"The date," Elizabeth said faintly, pressing at her temples to massage away a headache. "I suppose the prospective bride should be the one to tell me."

"We think it's going to be on the eighteenth of September." Tess's delighted grin warmed the room. "Even if our new home isn't ready, Nell and Martin say we can live in the main house until it is. And it *might* be ready. They've already taken the roof off the annex. It looks so very funny, and one side of the garden is *covered* with stacks of stone and tiles and I don't know what, so we can only walk on the other side. But Ruth's redbud tree has some tiny pink flowers, and that's on the side of the garden we can walk in."

"Martin had the foresight to insist on foundations strong enough for a taller building, so adding another story is quite easy," I informed our friend. "Just a little noisy during the day. Martin's in his element, running back and forth between Lake Forest and this house and the architects' offices. Now the weather's improving, he can ride Lightning or drive that blessed phaeton of his, which makes him all the happier. He's having a great deal of fun working on a small dwelling for a change. It'll be the best-appointed apartment in the whole of Chicago." I patted Tess's hand, delighted to see the rosy glow light up her face again.

"And we're going to have a little cottage in the grounds of the Lake Forest house, near the ravine." Tess put a hand to her mouth, looking sheepish. "At least it won't be *ours*. Martin says it's a guest cabin, but then he said we're the most important guests." She giggled and rose to her feet. "I'll be back soon."

"So your grand estate now has a guest cottage?" Elizabeth said as soon as the door closed behind Tess.

"It's really not that bad. Come and have luncheon with us soon and I'll show you the drawings. Martin's taken to calling it 'the farmhouse' because he and his architect have decided upon something that looks a bit like a gentleman's farm, but it truly is a summer home and not an estate, thank goodness. Definitely not a farm. At least the only thing that's farm-like is the dairy, but Martin promises me there will only be two or three cows."

"Cows." Elizabeth's fair eyebrows arched up nearly to her hairline.

"Like a tiny model dairy." I grimaced in answer to her deadpan stare. "Sarah thinks it's an awfully good idea. Martin says it's best to know where your milk comes from."

"Do you drink a lot of milk?"

"We hardly touch it," I admitted. "And Sarah's quite lost her taste for it. But there'll be some permanent staff—a gardener, a manager, and so on—and then, well, Martin's not the kind of man who gives up hope easily."

"Ah. More children." Elizabeth's expression was sympathetic.

I shrugged. "And you know what a worry milk is in the warm weather. Martin's been reading periodicals about wells too. He's having one sunk next month for the new house. Everything modern and safe. A kitchen garden as well, and glasshouses." I wrinkled my brow. "I think it'll all be quite interesting. I can't stop him from wanting to build things, Elizabeth. I can't stop him from hoping—and I don't want to. I hope too."

"My dear, of course you do." Elizabeth hesitated. "You make me feel ashamed of hoping the opposite. I don't want another baby again *quite* so quickly—I'm going to nurse Rosa as long as I can to prevent it. A lot of women swear by that, and David thinks it's safer for the baby, anyhow. Oh, hello, Mother."

"I heard you, plotting to deprive me of grandchildren." Mrs. Parnell's sharp blue eyes twinkled as she entered the room and ensconced herself in an armchair. "But inconvenient as a nursing regime is, I'll admit you and the children look well on it. I swear you're getting prettier with every child, my dear. They say one should strive to be plump, but losing a little off your face, arms, and bosom suits you marvelously. I, of course, have never tended to gain flesh, but you looked at one moment to be perilously close to inheriting your father's embonpoint." She smiled at me. "A mother can say such things to her daughter, of course. And all wrapped up in a compliment. My pretty Elizabeth is quite the most attractive of my daughters, although I am proud of all of them."

"You'd better not say that to Frances," said Elizabeth, grinning. "You used to tell her *she* was the prettiest. Don't try to deny it. Did you know Tess and Donny have set a date for their wedding? September the eighteenth. I do *like* a fall wedding."

"Does that mean you won't be coming to us in the summer?" Mrs. Parnell inquired of me. "You're always welcome."

"I couldn't let a summer go by without a visit." I grinned. "But it might have to be a short one. The Ogilvies have invited Sarah to stay over the summer, and Martin will no doubt insist I inspect our property so he can show off what's been done; so I'll be running up and down to Lake Forest anyway. And there's to be a winter Rutherford's Ball as well as the spring one. Madame wanted a winter ball last year but postponed it because of my illness. So we must start planning *that* by August."

"As long as you don't become too tired again." Mrs. Parnell sniffed. "Of course, I invariably think it's an excellent thing for a woman to keep busy. I always have, even when the children were young. I don't suppose there's any chance of tempting you onto one of my committees when you have a spare moment?"

"Not the slightest possibility." I laughed. "As soon as I've emerged from all the preparations for this month's ball, I have a very special task for the summer—the invention of a particularly pretty *pink* wedding dress."

THE BRIDE

"*I*t was fitting Elizabeth's wedding dress that made me late the day I met Donny."

I took Tess by the shoulders, turning her so she could view her reflection in the cheval glass. The sun was pouring in through the high windows of the fitting room, heating the air, but its rays did not reach down to where we stood. I stepped back to let Tess see the full effect of the pale pink satin bodice with its long central row of pearls as buttons. The skirt was also of satin, falling in a simple, straight line to the floor. It was unadorned as yet; the arms of the dress had already received their sprays of embroidery and small pink pearls, but otherwise the bodice was also still plain.

"To think that was three years ago." I watched as Tess turned from side to side, my attention on the way the long cuirass panels of the bodice moved. "A chance moment. If Elizabeth hadn't delayed me, Donny would have been one of thousands of people working in Chicago and you might be marrying someone else."

Tess shook her head. "If I hadn't met Donny, I wouldn't be marrying anybody. Will there be lace here, Nell?" She

JANE STEEN

indicated the area between the deep V of the bodice. "I think there was on the drawing. I'm sure my corset cover's not supposed to be showing."

"Of course. We're merely making doubly certain of how the bodice fits today. The toile was perfect, but I always like to make sure at this stage. There'll be lots of embroidery on the front and hem panels. We sew those onto the skirt later and add the pleats at the hem last. There'll be pearls here and there, just like on the arms, and a pearl fringe peeping out from under the bodice and repeating on the front panel. A few pearls on your train, too—larger ones. But we won't make the dress too heavy or the train too long. I want you to feel at your ease."

"I didn't realize you could get pearls in pink. Why didn't I know that?" Tess mused, fingering the buttons.

"I suppose you don't see them all that often." They were a costly item, but Tess didn't need to know. The dress was my gift to Tess; Martin's contribution was the wedding feast.

I smiled, remembering the very first dress fitting I had done for Tess at the Poor Farm. It had been my first attempt to sew a dress for someone other than myself. It was a simple spring dress for which I'd managed to cut some panels from a piece of double pink calico I'd found among a pile of scraps. I'd been proud of being able to make a cheap, plain cotton prettier for my new friend. Tess had been, in effect, my very first client.

"Let's get that off you now." I began to unbutton the bodice. "That's the problem of doing a July fitting; my clients perspire, and I always want to get the gown off them as quickly as possible. Now this part is done, you can go to Lake Forest to get away from the heat and smells. We'll do another fitting at the beginning of September once the dress is complete. All we have left to do today is to visit the shoe-maker, and then you can leave your trousseau to me. I can bring the toiles for your other gown to Lake Forest for a fitting easily enough, as well as your new lingerie to show you."

I was easing the bodice off Tess's shoulders as I spoke and now hung it on the form that stood in one corner of the room. I unfastened the skirt and put it to the side before untying the very small bustle pad I'd had made to support the weight of the train. I helped Tess out of the narrow hoopskirt and petticoat made specifically for her wedding dress. Freed from her new clothes, she yawned and stretched, displaying the sparse, damp hairs under her arms.

"I wish I could stay in my combinations all day." Tess regarded the pile of clothing on a nearby chair with distaste. "I can hardly bear the thought of putting my things on again. It's too hot, Nell."

"I'll help you dress." I sorted through the heap of cotton and muslin to find a petticoat. "Now, do come on. The bride needs shoes to walk in."

RUTHERFORD'S HAD ITS OWN SMALL SHOEMAKING WORKSHOP, as many of our customers preferred a handmade shoe to the ones we had in stock. The Lithuanian master shoemaker was a taciturn man but an excellent artisan. Tess pronounced her wedding shoes—little satin marvels with a row of bows, each surmounted by a pink pearl—a perfect fit.

"You promise to wear them in the house for a few days?" I asked as we walked through the sales floor arm in arm, having arranged for the shoes to be delivered to our residence.

"I will practice till I can dance a polka in them," Tess declared and giggled. "Except I can't dance the polka. If only

I'd learned it at the Poor Farm, Nell. But they never taught us to dance, except for the Virginia reel."

"Then we will dance the Virginia reel at your wedding feast." I grinned at my friend. "And the New York Lancers—I remember learning that one. I'll teach it to you. And Sarah can tell us what she's learned when we see her in Lake Forest. Isn't it nice that the Ogilvies include her in their dancing lessons?"

"I wonder if they taught the men at the Poor Farm the Virginia reel?" Tess looked up at me, frowning. "I hadn't thought about dancing at our wedding."

"It's just going to be family and our closest friends, Tess." I hugged her arm tight to my side. "We'll have a fiddler and a piano player, and if we all trip over each other's feet and fall in a heap, nobody will mind."

We were still laughing when we reached the elevators. Tess did not care for climbing stairs, and I cheerfully broke the rule about staff using the elevators during business hours when I had a customer with me. We had just stepped in when the operator, who had been about to pull the grille across, opened it again with a smile.

"It's good to find the two of you looking so cheerful." Martin removed his silk hat and whisked a pristine handkerchief from his pocket to wipe his brow. "Especially in weather like this. Is the dress perfect?"

"It's the most beautiful and unusual wedding dress that ever saw the light of day." Tess raised her chin proudly. "Or at least it's going to be. Perhaps Nell will start a new fashion for pink wedding dresses."

"Perhaps we should all wear pink," Martin suggested. "And invite the newspapermen."

"Don't you dare," I said. "It was bad enough that all the details of the spring ball gown demonstration got into the newspapers. Madame thought it made the event less exclusive. No doubt one of our high-society ladies earns pin money by sending them information."

"It's not a bad thing at all to get a little free publicity. All of Chicago society will want to come to the next one. The Rutherford's Ball will become a Chicago institution."

Martin's tone was lighthearted, but once we stepped out into the fourth-floor corridor, his expression sobered.

"Look, I need to tell you something. Come to my office." He held me lightly by my upper arm. "You too, Tess."

48

INEVITABLE

"I saw Thea," Martin said without preamble after he'd held our chairs while we seated ourselves. "Saw her? Where?" I asked.

"On Michigan Avenue, this morning. And she saw me looking at her." Martin ran a hand through his hair, which was limp from being under his hat on such a hot day. "I'm sure she recognized me—and I'm sure she knew I recognized *her*. I was on Gentleman, of course, and she'd recognize my horse. She was getting into a pretty smart little carriage—not a hired one."

I had been merely puzzled at first, disoriented by the mere idea of "seeing Thea," but at the picture Martin's words painted, my heart began skipping beats. I closed my eyes, the sensation that my worst imaginings were coming true swooping down over me like huge, dark wings.

It was Tess who voiced the question that was no doubt in all of our minds. "Nice carriages cost a lot of money. How did Thea get the money for a carriage? Do you suppose she's done something sinful?"

A list of sinful ways in which a young girl could acquire

wealth immediately formed in my imagination. I squeezed my eyes tighter shut to banish my thoughts. When I opened them again, Martin was watching me.

"When I spotted her, I admit I felt a sense of inevitability rather than surprise," he said. "She turned eighteen last month, didn't she? And Teddy has gone. Would *you* have stayed in Wisconsin?"

"I would not," I conceded. "Even after nearly a year. Not if I considered I had been wronged. It's quite possible Teddy was misled by the Galloways to imagine Thea had settled down there when she hadn't."

"Or that Teddy deceived us." Martin's eyes challenged me.

"But Teddy wouldn't lie to you," Tess said slowly. And then, in a far more doubtful tone, "Would he?"

I rubbed my forehead, trying to work my way through the maze of conflicting emotions. "Whatever Thea has done, and whatever part Teddy may have played in this—and I far prefer to think he imagined Thea happy in Jefferson—I believe our only option is to be quick to forgive and offer assistance if Thea needs it. She's so young." My gaze sought Martin, and I heard a beseeching note creeping into my voice. "She may have spent all the money she has to make a good impression on arriving in Chicago. It may not be too late to help her." I took a deep breath. "And if she has . . . fallen . . . in some way, I will not turn my back on her."

"The Prairie Avenue ladies will gossip about *that*," said Tess.

"Then let them. If you'd turned your backs on me—Tess, if you'd refused to be my friend because I was unwed and with child when I arrived at the Poor Farm, if Mama had shut her door to me, if you hadn't taken me under your protection, darling," I smiled at Martin, seeing the answering light in his eyes with a tiny prick of joy, "where would Sarah and I be now? Mama said there are worse things than disgrace, and she was right. Being friendless is the worst thing."

My voice caught, and I had to swallow and blink hard to conquer the tears that wanted to come at the memory of Mama. Her gracious kindness toward her disgraced child and illegitimate granddaughter had taught me all I needed to learn about love. I cleared my throat.

"I just want to write her a note offering whatever she's ready to accept from me. If she wants nothing from us, then so be it. At least I will have tried." I frowned. "But first we must find out where she is, mustn't we? How do we do that? The Pinkertons?"

"No need." Martin snorted. "Hired detectives aren't the only ones who can follow a carriage on horseback. I wouldn't tell you she was here without making sure first. I'll admit I was praying she'd be on her way to the station to get on a train." He made a grimace to show his disappointment. "No such luck though. She's staying at the Sherman House."

"Oh, but that's such a nice hotel!" Tess exclaimed. "I like the shops there."

"Are you sure?" I asked Martin.

"I waited a few minutes after Thea went inside, then inquired after her at the desk. She is staying there under her own name," Martin said. "That might be a sign that she has done nothing wrong."

"There's only one way to find out." I bit my lip. "I will write her a note—the same as I'd do for any female acquaintance whose arrival in Chicago had been announced in the society columns—and ask if I can call on her. She may not respond, of course."

I WAS WRONG.

"I hope you're not here to offer me a job." Thea's beautiful face wore a half smile as she turned away from me to lead me into her parlor. It was as opulently furnished as one would expect from the Sherman House Hotel. The anonymity of its plushes and satins was enhanced by the absence of personal touches.

It would seem you already have one, was the uncharitable thought that pushed its way into my mind, but I shoved it back out and smiled at Thea as she indicated a chair.

"I didn't come to say a thing to you." I sat down, observing Thea closely as she took her own seat. Now that I had a chance to stare, I realized there was something different about her. She was perhaps a little leaner, harder-looking, more like Catherine in the latter years. Her dress was good—sewn for her rather than bought ready-made—and if my knowledge of Chicago's stores was sound, it had probably come from Field & Leiter's within the past month.

"There's not much you can say, is there?" Thea smirked. "You can hardly throw stones from that glass house of yours. So is this a neighborly visit?"

"In a sense, yes. Although I like to consider it a meeting between family members."

"You're not my family. I'm sure I made that clear." Thea's tone was pleasant, but her face was quite immobile.

"Thea." I kept my voice soft. "My love for your mother binds me to you, even if you push me away. I simply wanted to see you, to find out how you came to be here, and to offer you my friendship—or anything else you might need."

"Money?" Thea raised her fine eyebrows, her hazel eyes almost iridescent in the sunlight filtering in through the gauzy curtains. Her pink lips were curved, as if she were listening intently to an amusing anecdote.

"Of course. How much do you want?"

Her smile faded. "If you imagine I would ask you for

anything, you don't understand me at all. I will not be beholden to you for one cent. Nobody will ever have me in their keeping, ever again."

I couldn't help glancing around the expensive hotel suite. A cynical twist appeared on Thea's lips as she noticed.

"This is mine, whether or not I choose to pay for it. As it happens, I'm happy to pay. I may as well tell you because you'll find out sooner or later. I'm Vic Canavan's mistress now."

Poor, poor Catherine. As I absorbed Thea's words, I remembered her mother and father, who had done everything they could to teach their children the godly principles they upheld. I pictured Thea as a happy little girl, giving out small gifts and tracts she had copied out herself to the inmates at the Poor Farm. I thought of her mother and father smiling as they watched their children; I remembered the dignified yet loving Nonna who had ensured the young Lombardis always had the love and care of family, even when their mother was working. I schooled my face not to reflect the pity and sadness that was in my heart.

"I was under the impression Miss Dardenne was Mr. Canavan's mistress," was what I found to say after a few seconds.

"They had an amicable parting of the ways. Paulina's accepted a position in a theater in New York. She said she always knew I would be the next. She never minded in the least." Thea looked hard at me. "If you imagine Vic has me in his keeping, think again. You have no idea what Vic and I are to each other. You don't understand him any more than you understand me."

"I don't pretend to know anything more about Mr. Canavan than I've seen on the surface," I said. "But I understand the disappointments and desperate hardships you endured, Thea. Hardships I tried so hard to ease. I would have given your mother anything she needed; don't you realize that? I understand that you were a child who needed much and had to make do with very little, and it's changed you. You've built a hard shell around yourself to drive away the people who have your true interests at heart. I think the more you've driven them away, the unhappier you've become. You pushed away your mother's love—"

"You didn't come to say a thing to me, remember?" There was a hard edge to Thea's voice. "If you're going to preach to me, you can get out. I had enough of that growing up."

"I wasn't preaching." Dismay seemed to be almost suffocating me, thickening my voice. "I—"

"You were presuming to know what was best for me, and that's the same thing." Thea leaned forward, looking directly into my face. "You look better than the last time I saw you, Mrs. Rutherford. Let's see, that was when I was being taken away by a police matron, wasn't it? And not a word from you since."

"I wrote to you several times." I heard the indignation in my voice. "I gave up because you never answered. I offered to visit you—well, after the six months Teddy asked for to help you settle in. But I kept asking if you needed or wanted anything." I bit my lip. "I should have done more, Thea. But Teddy—how could I keep on favoring one of your mother's children over the other? In the end, I had to accede to his wishes."

"Because he's a man."

"Because—oh, Thea, don't you understand that you would have had to leave Rutherford's anyway? Any girl who broke the rules the way you did would be sent away."

Thea shrugged. "I would have gone to the Jewel Box. Do you suppose I cared anything about your ridiculous store? Vic's going to take me to Paris. I will order my clothes straight from Worth when I'm established as an actress."

There was so much of the spiteful child in these last words that I lost any desire to argue my case with Thea. "I'm sorry my letters never reached you," I said softly. "I'm sure I addressed them properly."

"My jailers intercepted them, no doubt. I never once got to go into town. Jacob would ride in to pick up the mail twice a week, so for all I can tell you might have sent me a fortune in gold. They watched me all the time; can you imagine? Every minute." She scowled. "Except at night, and they let those vicious dogs loose at sundown. They wanted to marry me to Jacob once I'd learned to be a good little wife."

She held out a hand, turning a small palm up to me so I could witness the calluses along the top of her palm and the lower third of her fingers. "I didn't need to be taught any of my tasks, of course. Thanks to my dear parents, I already knew how to work a butter churn and boil linen and work a mangle and iron and peel vegetables and make pastry and feed chickens." Her voice grew louder and harder as she progressed through the list. "In the end, I just did everything they asked of me to make the day go faster, so I could get to the end of it and lie on my bed and tell myself it wouldn't last forever. I got sick of Ma Galloway's endless lectures about how wicked I was and how godly *they* were every time I argued with them." She withdrew her hand. "It'll be weeks before I can take my gloves off in public."

"Did they hurt you?" My stomach turned as I pictured Thea's life of drudgery and isolation.

"You mean, did they beat me? Or leave me alone with one of the men? No. That would have been a sin. Besides, I was careful never to provoke Ma Galloway too much. She had something in her eyes that warned me . . . But keeping me a prisoner was for the good of my soul, and therefore a commendable act of sacrifice on their part. They kept my money for me too, oh yes—wrote a nice letter to Mrs.

Batham and got all my things sent up to Jefferson. Ma Galloway patched and turned and lengthened my dresses so she didn't incur the extra expense of providing clothing. *So* saintly. My kind jailer for nearly a year."

"I'm so sorry." My lips were numb. I supposed that from Teddy's point of view Thea was being well looked after—but it *was* a jail, of sorts. "When did you leave? And how? Did Mr. Canavan fetch you away?"

"How? He didn't know where I was. You kept your promise to Teddy not to tell, and I guess my brother asked the same of Mrs. Batham because Vic didn't get a sensible word out of her. Not that anybody ever got a sensible word out of that poor silly woman. No, I left because Mr. Galloway died."

My face must have changed because Thea laughed, a soft rippling sound that chilled me. "No, I had nothing to do with it. What do you think I am? I hated them, but I've never wished anyone dead, not for one second. Jacob came over that morning to ask his pa's advice over cutting down a dying ash tree that was threatening to fall on a fence. An hour or so later he ran into the kitchen with such a look on his face as I've never seen."

She blew out her breath in a short sound of contempt. "His father climbed the tree to attach a rope, and I guess he stood on a rotten branch. Ma Galloway started screaming and ran, and I knew I had my chance. I took what money I found—not as much as I was owed—and hitched up the mule cart. It wasn't difficult to find the town, and it wasn't difficult to find the railroad station, and there was a train pulling in. It went in the wrong direction, but I had enough money on me to work my way around to Chicago and get to the Jewel Box. I didn't arrive till almost dawn, but my friends keep late hours. I've been here for five weeks."

"And in those five weeks you've set yourself up as Victor

Canavan's mistress." I looked once more around the room, remembering Martin's description of the neat little carriage into which he'd seen Thea climbing. "You're living in some style."

"Thank you." Thea's smile was real this time, even though I hadn't meant to compliment her. "I'll repay him by becoming a better actress than any of the others. He says I have the potential. It's a good arrangement."

"Do you love him?" I asked.

"I'm fond of him. I like him. We understand each other. Vic doesn't need love. In fact, he'd rather be free of a woman groveling at his feet for love of him. He treats me well, and he makes me happy. That's enough."

"And supposing there are children? Won't you need his love then?"

Thea's gaze took me in, slowly, from the top of my hat to the tips of my boots. "Let me explain something, Mrs. Rutherford." There was a sneer in her voice and on her pretty lips. "I will never be as stupid as you. I will never bring a bastard into this world, a child who clearly doesn't even know where she was born and what the world might do to her when she takes her first steps into it. I would kill myself first."

She smiled prettily then, in one of those sudden, dizzying changes of demeanor that made me wonder just how broken she might be inside. "But I won't need to because there are ways to avoid children. Actresses are as well versed in *that* subject as whores. They have even more need to keep their looks for as long as they can. I'm learning a lot."

"But you won't be received anywhere. You'll be outcast—" I stopped because I heard Judah Poulton's voice saying the same to me, years before.

"Do you think I care about that?" Thea smiled again, as if we were discussing some trivial subject. "Respectability." She sniffed, giving a small toss of her head. "Thanks to you, I've tried respectable society, and I despise it. I've tried the society of working girls too, and I could tell you much about what goes on behind the backs of you employers. Respectable women are either hypocrites or miserable dullards who don't possess the courage or the imagination to make the most of their short lives before they die in childbirth. In the theater, we're free of respectability and we're free from drudgery. And when an actress becomes successful enough, society fawns over her and loves her because she's dangerous. You'll see."

"And Teddy?" It was the last appeal I could make.

"Teddy can go hang. Teddy was ready to leave me with the Galloways till I gave in and spent the rest of my life wiping the noses of Jacob's brats. I hope Teddy disowns me because I disown him. Now, Mrs. Rutherford, do you think you've gotten what you came for? Because I really must get on with my day."

I rose to my feet and put out my hand. "I will always receive you, Thea. For your mother's sake. And if you need anything, please let me help."

I had expected her to refuse the handshake, but to my surprise she touched my fingers with hers. "We'll see each other again. By the way, I've lost that pretty pendant you gave me. A real shame because I liked it—but it either wasn't in the things sent from Mrs. Batham's or the Galloways took it. Don't worry though, I'll have plenty of jewels of my own."

"I'M AS TIRED AS IF I'VE WALKED ALL DAY AND ALL NIGHT." I moved closer to Martin, grateful for the solidity of his arm around me as we sat together on our bedroom settee. "I'm simply worn out just from talking to Thea. At least I probably won't need to do that again anytime soon." I looked up at him, seeing mostly his jawline—which was, to be sure, a little tight. "Am I a horrible person for being almost grateful she's under Victor Canavan's protection, if I must call it that? That if she gets into trouble of any kind, she'll be his problem, not ours?"

"You're not at all horrible." Martin's embrace tightened. "You've offered an olive branch, and she's spurned it. I don't see what else we can do except write to Teddy to tell him where she is. I will do that, Nellie." He kissed my forehead. "At least I'll write a draft of the letter pending such time as we know where to send it. If they're working their way down the west coast of Ireland as he told Sarah, he might stay for a while in Limerick." I felt his chest move as he laughed. "We own a fine set of atlases, thanks to our studious daughter. She and I had a fine time traveling through Ireland in our imaginations, and I know where the large towns are now."

"I hope he doesn't feel he needs to come back," I said. "I hate to think of what would happen. Would he kidnap Thea and put her in an asylum this time?" I shivered. "For moral turpitude. My stepfather told me he was treating me like any other 'moral imbecile' when he sent me to the Poor Farm. If it hadn't been for Catherine Lombardi and her enlightened ways, I might have been heading toward an utter nightmare. I've talked with Donny about the Poor Farm—the Institute for the FeebleMinded—and it sounds nothing like the place I remember."

"You'll give me nightmares if you continue in that vein." Martin kissed me again. "I sometimes reflect on those days and am horrified that they sent you away for . . . for depravity, and I didn't even know."

"You took it calmly when you came to rescue me." I closed my eyes in pleasure as a breeze wafted in through the open window. It was too warm to be so close to Martin, but I didn't want to move.

"Because whatever you'd done, you were my little friend and I wouldn't turn my back on you." He was silent for a few moments. "I will use that argument when I write to Teddy. He must still love his sister, so he must forgive her. Until seventy times seven." He sighed. "That verse from Scripture was with me a great deal when I was in Switzerland, before I came back home to marry you. Not that I felt I had to forgive *you* for anything—but I spoke the words "I forgive you, Father" many, many times while I was in the mountains. Perhaps I forgave him seventy times seven because, in the end, I became less angry. I don't lose my temper much these days, do I?"

"You've never lost it with me." I turned toward him and put an arm around his neck.

"I've come close to losing my temper with you." Martin's eyes crinkled at the outer corners in the way I loved to see. "Don't you think we should retire for the night? You're not just tired from Thea, are you? Tess's trousseau is keeping you busy, and I realize Arlette Belvoix has already begun to consult you about the winter ball; and you have plenty of other work."

"Mmmm." I stretched, deliciously aware of Martin in a way that presaged a delay in getting to sleep. "Don't worry, it's just ordinary fatigue from a long day; I'm quite well. Say —" I straightened up so I could see Martin's face better. "I've had a perfectly marvelous idea for a wedding present for Donny. A gold watch—just a plain one, with a chain so he can put his fob on it. And for Tess, I saw the prettiest brooch a few weeks back, and I've been dreaming of it ever since. A big pink topaz with diamonds around it. I asked Mr. McCombs yesterday if it was still in the vault, and he said it was. Won't you come down there and look at it with me? We can stay in the antechamber."

"Another gift for Tess? What about the dress and all those pearls?"

"I can afford it. Thanks to your care of my money, I have my own private fortune. I'd cover Tess in diamonds if I could." I grinned, happiness welling up in me. "What's the point of having money if I can't spoil my best friend? I'm convinced she'd love it, and it would look perfect on her new dinner gown." I moved closer to my husband.

"If you also promise to pick out something new for yourself to go with the dress you plan to wear at the wedding." Martin gave me a lingering kiss. "Something horribly expensive."

"And a watch for Donny?"

"*That* I'll order from my own watchmaker. Plain, yes, but I want one that keeps perfect time." Martin kissed me again. "Now, if you're quite finished putting the world to rights, isn't it time we went to bed?"

VAULT

"*A*re you sure you don't want this one?"

Joe Salazar picked up a pendant from its velvet tray and held it up to me. Diamonds flashed in the gaslight, and a massive royal blue sapphire shed its hues over the huge, silvery tear-shaped pearl that dangled below the mass of diamonds.

"Too many diamonds," I said firmly.

"It's worth a king's ransom," Joe teased. "Isn't that what you told me, McCombs?"

"It's one of our more costly pieces." Mr. McCombs nodded gravely, refusing to join in Joe's levity, consummately professional as the possibility of a very large sale beckoned. Even at cost, these sales would count to his personal credit.

"This one's perfect." I gazed at the piece I held in my hand.

"Twice as many sapphires." Martin looked pleased. "I never thought I'd get you to accept sapphires."

"And only one diamond." I smiled at my husband. "I never thought I'd like sapphires either, but I'll admit these are rather beautiful. It's the use of seed pearls that charms me;

and the flower motif will go perfectly with the embroidery on the bodice of my dress."

For Tess's wedding, I had chosen a heavily embroidered silk satin, pink roses and gold flourishes on a deep blue background, that we had imported from France. The tablier was of the same material, the skirt and train of plain deep blue satin. Madame had described the shade of blue as "sapphire," and I was almost certain it would be a close match for the stones. I had, as I so often did, opted for a V-necked bodice with a small ruff of white lace to show off my creamy skin and long neck. The elbow-length sleeves would be trimmed in the same lace with gold bows, which were repeated on the train. I had thought long and hard before deciding on this ensemble since I would stand beside Tess in her pink bridal gown. The pink roses would complement it, and the blue silk would make her own dress appear richer.

I picked up the pink topaz brooch I would give to Tess, smiling as I imagined her pleasure when she opened the box. The cushion-cut stone was large and clear, with a hint of purple in its depths. With my left hand, I draped my own pendant on my right palm, lost in contemplation of the colors of the huge stones as Martin and Joe talked about the day's trading and Mr. McCombs picked up two trays to return them to the safe room.

Mr. McCombs had gone straight to the drawer where the pink brooch resided and had not missed his chance to bring out a few other pink topaz pieces "in case Mrs. Rutherford might be tempted." He was not the head of department for nothing. He had obeyed Martin's instruction to show us a few outrageously expensive baubles that might suit me with such accuracy that I had spent some time exclaiming over his good taste. I had only succumbed to the one pendant in the end and was mightily pleased with it.

"You'll have to give them back, you know." Martin held

out a hand, indicating the pieces of jewelry I was doting on. "They need to go back in the vault." He seemed relaxed despite the nearby presence of the barred room. Indeed, after an exceedingly well-spent night, we were both in the best of moods.

"Can't I just put them in my pocket?" I teased, moving my hand toward the skirt of my dress. "After all, I *am* a partner."

"You'll get them when they're cleaned and mounted in their boxes, just like any other customer." Martin tried to look severe. "Give them up, Nell. It's time we closed this room."

I dodged away from his outstretched hand, laughing; and then I stopped, puzzled. All six of the watchmen who had been on duty in the corridor, guarding the vault while it was open and preventing anyone but the most trusted employees from getting near it, were coming into the room.

I DIDN'T KNOW WHY I PUT THE JEWELS INTO MY POCKET AT that moment. With the fashionable silhouette becoming ever narrower, it was getting harder than ever to incorporate a pocket, but like most experienced dressmakers, I prided myself on being able to find a way to hide a small pocket somewhere on my dresses and on those I designed for my clients. My work dresses always had them, usually more than one; I disliked carrying a reticule around the store, but I couldn't abide not having space for a handkerchief, a small pencil, a thimble, two nickels, two dimes, and a long piece of marked string I used for approximate measuring when I didn't have my tape measure on me.

I slipped Tess's brooch and my pendant into the tiny niche in the top of the overskirt, pushing them down behind my handkerchief as I smiled at the men, still laughing a little from my playfulness with Martin.

"We're almost finished," I said. "I'm sorry to keep you waiting."

I saw a glance pass between Martin and Joe, but then my attention was drawn again to the watchmen as two of them turned back toward the double doors through which they had just entered. Puzzled, I saw them slide the bolts into place, but it wasn't until I heard the click of the passkey in the lock that it dawned on me—something was wrong.

Martin and Joe had seen it though. They bolted toward the door in unison, only to be stopped by the other four men who were already moving toward them, two by two.

The next couple of minutes were a blur of shouts and blows as Martin and Joe struggled with the watchmen. I looked wildly around the room for something, anything, I might use as a weapon. The prints mounted in frames behind glass—would I be able to break the glass?

But the sickening thud of flesh on flesh diverted my attention back to the fighting men. As I hesitated, one of them detached himself from the fray—which had gone ominously quiet—and drew the large knife every watchman carried on his belt along with a pistol and a club. He pointed it at me. I saw, behind the closed grille across the door, Mr. McCombs staring, open-mouthed. But then my attention became riveted on the knife, the point of which was now far too close to my person for comfort. The blade was long, large, and looked wickedly sharp.

"Good, Mrs. Rutherford." The man had seen me freeze. "If your husband cooperates, I won't stab you. If you stand still, I won't stab you. If you make any move to escape or hurt us, I *will* stab you. Knives are so much better than guns, you know. A bullet can go astray and make a lot of noise, attract attention. A knife is quiet, and if you understand how to use it, it always does *some* damage."

As he spoke, he eyed the baubles still on the antechamber table, glittering on their black velvet trays; but any hope I might have had that they would distract his attention was extinguished as his gaze slid back to me.

I looked away from him, my gaze seeking Martin. My husband, whose normally neat appearance had suffered much as a result of being manhandled, seemed unharmed, although the expression on his face was thunderous. His arms were tightly pinioned behind his back by the two men who'd locked the door while a third extracted his own belt knife with an almost casual air and pointed it at Martin's face. The last two men were dragging Joe to his feet. A large welt on his left cheekbone indicated a blow; a trickle of blood ran down his chin from a gash in his lip.

"Are we quite clear on the importance of cooperating?" the man nearest to me said. "We're not killers. Don't try to turn us into murderers by doing something stupid. Don't make us responsible for the accidental death of Mrs. Rutherford."

He smiled, bringing the knife a little closer to my bodice. If only I could be sure of being able to grasp it . . . I noted incidentally that the man's voice was accented, but I couldn't even begin to guess at his nationality. There were so many new people coming to Chicago all the time, from every corner of the globe. The men all bore some slight resemblance to each other, but perhaps that was because they were all tall and well-made. All of them, of course, were dressed alike in our plain dark uniform with the Rutherford's badge, the letter R interwoven with a peacock's feather.

"Our own men," Joe said in disgust, his voice a little slurred from his injured lip. "Petrovic, isn't it? And—and

Latas? I'm having trouble remembering the others. But I *will* remember."

"Not *your* men." The leader, the man called Petrovic, grinned. "And not our true names, so don't bother trying to recall them."

"Did your people have something to do with the attempt last year?" Martin asked.

Petrovic shrugged. "How would I know? You were hiring a lot of watchmen afterward though, and we were told to get ourselves hired." He flexed his broad shoulders. "And wait. So we have waited."

"The other watchmen will stop you when you try to leave," Martin said. "The staff entrance is well guarded."

"Some of the other watchmen are ours. The rest will behave because we will have hostages." Petrovic smiled and then looked over at Mr. McCombs. "Open that door and come out."

"I will not." The older man firmed his jaw, although I saw the tremble in his legs.

"Yes, you will, McCombs." Martin sounded quite unemotional. "You'll do everything they say. It's only merchandise." He glared at the leader. "I'll vouch for our cooperation."

"Good, good." Petrovic nodded at his men. "The Rutherfords on this side of the room; Salazar on the other. Come to think of it, McCombs, you'll be useful. I have a shopping list. And let's get going." He glanced at the clock on the antechamber wall. "We're on a schedule."

THE SHOPPING LIST WAS SURPRISINGLY SHORT. WITHIN FIVE minutes, Petrovic and Mr. McCombs emerged from the vault, a small pouch in Petrovic's hand.

"Doesn't look like much," Martin said derisively.

"Oh, it'll do a lot of damage." Mr. McCombs's soft brown eyes were less frightened now, even world weary. "Our insurers will put up a fight against paying such a large sum. These men are well informed."

He picked up the sapphire-and-diamond pendant I had examined earlier. "This is the one you wanted." He handed it to Petrovic, who dropped it into the bag. The men standing guard over us—three for Martin and me and two for Joe—all grinned with the pleased air of men who had done a good day's work.

"The jewels are just a little extra." Petrovic shrugged a shoulder. "We were told to keep an eye open for a specific opportunity." He raised his eyebrows at Martin. "Now, boys, let's get on with the rest of it."

"Right then—everybody standing." One of the other men spoke. Martin and I rose to our feet. Joe seemed a little more reluctant but was quickly dragged into an upright position by the two men guarding him.

"McCombs by the door." Petrovic brought his knife near to me again. "The rest of you, into the vault."

I saw by Martin's face that he didn't like the sound of that command any more than I did. Probably far less. Was he afraid? I wondered. But when he spoke, his voice was even.

"If you're thinking of killing us, spare my wife. I don't care what you do to me."

"I'm not thinking of anything except what I've been told." Petrovic's voice was just as neutral, the tone of a professional man discussing a day's work. "Salazar, you'll be setting the time lock. Ten hours."

Horror threaded its way through my veins, squeezing my heart as Martin and Joe shouted in unison. One of the men grabbed me, half-dragging me into the vault, the heels of my shoes sliding on the polished floor.

It was ridiculous how little I could do against his

strength. In a few seconds, he was forcing me to sit down in the chair. Truth be told, I was glad to sit; my legs were trembling now, as much as Mr. McCombs's had been. We were going to be forced to lock ourselves in. Would Joe be able to override the lock and let us out again?

With me inside the safe room, Martin soon followed. He was accompanied by two men, one of whom produced a set of handcuffs. He slipped one end over Martin's left hand and instructed Martin to bend down near the table. He then brought the handcuffs behind the stout table leg and slipped the other cuff over Martin's right hand. The effect was to fasten Martin to the table leg so he stood in a highly uncomfortable-looking stooped position, unable to make any effective movements.

We couldn't see Joe, but we could hear. It sounded as if they were trying to drag him into the vault, and he was resisting with all his might. To my horror, the noises ended in an agonized shout.

"Joe!" Martin tried to move so he was able to see out of the doorway. "Joe! Don't be a fool." He straightened up, perhaps in an attempt to tip the table over. One man foiled him by simply sitting on the middle of the table, shoving the ledgers to one side.

"Mind the lamp. Don't want to spill oil all over the floor. You might start a fire and roast them." Petrovic entered the vault. Behind him, two of the men flanked a white-faced Joe, the back of one of his hands bleeding freely from what looked like a shallow cut.

"Now then." Petrovic turned to Joe, looking down at him from his considerably superior height. "I don't like Jews. I'll be quite happy to cut some more lines into you if you don't get a move on and set the lock. No mistakes, now—ten hours. You don't want to end up killing your partners, and if you set it for less, I'll put a hole in your belly." He drew out a pocket watch and looked at it, then turned to me. "You'll get a good night's sleep."

"You can't make me do this." Joe's voice was unsteady. "There's no guarantee the air will last that long. I refuse to let you make a murderer of me."

Petrovic's only answer was to pull viciously at Joe's shirt cuff. Ripping it away, he pushed up shirt and jacket, and I watched, aghast, as a line of red appeared on Joe's forearm. Joe screamed.

Martin and I yelled in unison, formless sounds of sheer horror, and then Martin spoke. "Joe, for God's sake, do it." His face was as pale as Joe's. "We'll be all right."

But would we? My mind went back to what Petrovic had said: Joe might kill us if he got the time wrong. Neither Martin nor I knew anything about opening the safe.

And yet I added my voice to Martin's anyway. Martin had said we would be all right. I had faced danger before and survived. I wouldn't stand by and watch Joe being tortured, even if it meant we would be locked in a vault for ten agonizingly long hours.

DARKNESS

*T*he worst thing was the silence. Once the bogus watchmen had swung the massive door shut, the only sounds were the hiss of the gaslights, our ragged breathing, and the beating of my own heart. Not a sound penetrated through from the outside world. No voices, no rumble of traffic from the street, so familiar to me I'd hardly registered it while we were in the antechamber. The stillness was that of the tomb; we were entombed. Panic rose in my gorge.

"Take that lamp off the table." Martin's voice sounded clipped, furious. "Everything off. At least I'll be able to stand up straight."

I jumped up from my chair and complied with his instructions, stacking the materials in one corner of the room. I had meant to help him with the table, which appeared fairly heavy, but in a couple of heaves he had sent the thing crashing to the ground. The walls of the vault absorbed the sound in an ominous fashion, but at least the moment of violent action seemed to calm the temper I saw in Martin's eyes. He stretched to his full height, rolling his shoulders and flexing his long back before giving me a smile that had more of determination than mirth in it.

"Well, here's a to-do." He turned in a circle, surveying the vault. "They've got it neatly arranged, haven't they? I should have come in here before."

"You don't have to be brave with me," I said briskly. "I understand how you feel about this room. And I don't mind telling you, I was about to launch into a fit of the vapors."

"If you weren't in here with me, I'd probably be having conniptions myself." Martin's grin seemed more genuine now. "And yet the last thing I want is for you to be here. Can you help me move the table?" He held his manacled hands aloft. "I'd do it myself, but I'm somewhat inconvenienced." He looked around again. "I'd like to shift it so it's on its side with the top facing toward the door. Just in case they try dynamite to get us out."

We worked for a couple of minutes to get the table positioned the way Martin wanted it, with enough room for us to get in and out.

"We'll lie down in there once we turn the lights out." He contemplated the gas lamps. "They'll have to go out, Nellie. The air will be bad enough in here after ten hours without the gas suffocating us." He looked steadily at me. "You realize it's going to be a difficult ten hours, don't you?"

"I'm trying not to think about it too much, to be honest," I admitted. "Do you suppose they'll try dynamite?"

"I'm not at all sure that's a good idea." Martin hunkered down on his heels, staring at the door.

"Couldn't we work out how to open the door from the inside?" I moved close to the massive assembly of metal parts, looking at the array of boxes. Behind its etched glass, the timer dial looked like some arcane instrument to measure the tides and the seasons. I noticed, for the first time, that the looping swirls etched into the glass read "Cooper's Infallible Time Lock."

As I turned to look at him, Martin's face gave the answer away; but he let me wait for a long moment before he spoke.

"Would you like the bad news now?"

"I've just seen the word 'infallible,' so I'm getting the idea. Explain it to me." I looked back at the case. "And weren't there two dials before? Have you changed the lock?"

"Did you see any matches anywhere near that lamp?" Martin turned around, frowning instead of answering me.

"No."

"Then while we're talking, we need to be searching for some. Once we put the gaslights out, we'll have no means of making light if we do require it. You start that side of the room and I'll work on this. Open every drawer and look absolutely everywhere you can."

We had each opened a dozen drawers before Martin began speaking again. "The trouble with most time locks has been a tendency to fail on occasion. There's always a bypass method or failsafe of some kind, generally a second dial. That was the first kind of time lock we had fitted. But then, of course, they invented a better method—and I bought it. I wanted to make absolutely sure nobody could get in. It never occurred to me that anyone would want to get *out*."

"How careless of you." I shut yet another drawer full of fabulous jewels that now seemed like so many pieces of glass since what I really wanted to see was matches.

Martin snorted with laughter. "That's my Nellie. Thank heaven I married a woman who's braver than I am." He sighed. "The new contraption *can* be bypassed if it fails by obtaining a secret code from Cooper's and using it to hold the time lock open while you dial the usual combination for the door. But if it were possible to do that while the timer was running, a determined thief would simply get his hands on both codes—and there are plenty of ways of doing that. Collusion with a Cooper's employee would be where I'd start."

I sighed. "I'd say the solution is to hire honest employees, but I've learned too much about the department store business to imagine you can trust everyone."

"Precisely. The point is you can't open the blessed thing until the timer runs out or stops because it has failed. If you try, there's a lever inside that simply moves sideways and blocks the opening mechanism."

"And dynamite?" I asked. "If you don't mind mentioning it again."

We had come close to meeting in the middle of the drawers now. Martin stopped his search to look directly at me.

"Quite apart from the danger of dynamiting a vault with people inside it, the lock might jam—by accident or design— if it's subjected to a severe shock. We already realized that if, say, we had an earthquake in Chicago, we might have to take drastic action to get the door open. But no earthquakes have been recorded in Chicago." He shrugged. "It seemed like an acceptable risk. I just hope Joe remembers that using dynamite might make things worse." He began opening drawers again, and I followed suit.

"*My* prayer is that Joe's all right." I reached the last drawer on my side a few seconds after Martin had finished his. "I'll never forget the look on his face as they dragged him out of the vault. That second cut was bleeding badly, but he was in such anguish about shutting us in I don't suppose he even noticed it."

"I won't forget it either." Martin spoke the words quietly and then, on a rising note, burst out: "How can there *possibly* be no matches?"

"Don't kick or hit out in frustration." I put a hand on his

arm. "You might break or cut something, and then where would you be?" I waited a few seconds, my gaze on his rigid white face before it relaxed and he nodded. "You are perfectly well aware why we never allow our employees to be careless about leaving matches around. We can do without light for a few hours." I ran my tongue over my lips. "What I'd really like would be a bucket full of water. It's hot in here."

"We're lucky it's a lot cooler underground than upstairs." Martin brought his manacled hands up to my face, stroking my cheek. "Will taking off some of those layers of clothing help?"

"Turning the gaslights off and laying still will probably do the most good. What about you? I don't suppose we can get your jacket off without ripping it to pieces—"

"—and I'm hanged if I'm going to remove my trousers." Martin rolled his eyes. "If the worst happens, I'd far rather be found with my clothes on." He raised his hands to his neck. "I'll take this blasted collar off though."

Some twenty minutes later, we had both made ourselves somewhat more comfortable. I had torn a page from the back of the ledger—"McCombs will hate that," said Martin—and we had written brief notes to Sarah, Tess, and Joe "just in case" with my stub of pencil. They were not sentimental. It seemed somehow impossible to *be* sentimental in the circumstances. I said as much to Martin.

"I sometimes think what you call bravery on my part is simply lack of imagination," I confessed. "Or cowardice—refusing to face what might happen." I ran my hands through my hair, which Martin had helped me to free from its pins and comb, and watched as Martin stood to turn off the gas lamps.

"Not at all. It's just that in our heart of hearts, we're sure that what's going to happen will merely be a long and uncomfortable night."

Martin reached up with his bound hands, and I saw my useful piece of string grow taut. He'd tied it firmly around the table leg at one end and looped it over his hand at the other so he would be able to find his way back to me in the dark. The hissing of the gas jet died into nothing, its mantle still glowing; Martin moved to the other light.

Darkness replaced light. I was still able to see the two glowing mantles. I stared hungrily at those dimming points of red light, sensing Martin's movements as he carefully made his way back to our upturned table. The faint lights winked in and out as Martin moved between them and me; in a few moments, he took his place at my side. I had sacrificed my overskirt to use as a pillow, folding it inside out so that the fine lining would be beneath our heads.

"Are you comfortable?" Martin asked.

"Tolerable." My voice sounded somehow louder than it had when the lights burned. "Are you?"

"I'd be happier if my hands were free." Martin yawned. "But it's good to lie down. Try to sleep, Nellie. It will help."

I stared into the dark as the tiny red glow of the cooling gas mantles died into nothing, aware of Martin shifting as he tried to make himself comfortable. "I'll try." I said. "It won't be easy though."

I DID SLEEP, ON AND OFF. IT WAS OFTEN THIRST THAT KEPT ME awake; it wasn't unbearable, but it was a constant torment. At times I had to make a deliberate effort to distract myself from thoughts of cool water, rivers, pools . . .

Occasionally, there came moments of panic, convincing me that I would lose my mind if we stayed in this utter darkness for a moment longer. I would have to fight to calm my breathing. I didn't even know how I managed to free myself from the grip of fear time after time, but eventually my heart would somehow stop pounding. Out of complete exhaustion I would drift, slowly, into semiconsciousness again.

At another time, I found myself analyzing, quite dispassionately, the words "utter" and "darkness" and deciding that neither word was adequate to convey the sense of presence, as if the darkness were a *thing* that stood in opposition to light rather than the mere absence of light. How to describe true darkness? I didn't have the words. I had fallen asleep in the end and dreamed I lay in a sunlit field, knowing all the while that when I opened my eyes again, I would be as blind as a worm, that I had never been able to see and the sunlight was the product of my imagination.

When I was quite sure Martin was asleep, I gave in occasionally to a few tears, especially when I found myself thinking of Sarah. But at other times, I was certain he lay awake, still and silent as I; did he too weep when he knew I had at last gone to sleep again? I hoped not, and anxiety about him somehow, eventually, cast me adrift into another sea of oblivion from which I emerged only slowly and reluctantly, more slowly and reluctantly each time.

I was awake again. Somewhere in the darkness, Martin's pocket watch ticked frenetically. My own timepiece had stopped. I had no idea what o'clock it might be. Were we minutes from being released from our tomb, or had we only been here for an hour or two? Was it even Martin's watch that was ticking or the mechanism of the time lock, counting down the moments of our imprisonment?

A movement beside me signaled the sudden absence of Martin from my side. After a few moments, I realized he was relieving himself and that, in spite of my thirst, I needed to do the same if I were to have any hope of getting back to sleep. I confessed as much to Martin when he returned, and he helped me put the loop of string over my hand and set off in a different direction to the one he had taken.

The whole business was remarkably difficult; as soon as I stood up, I became confused and weak, and only the prospect of disgracing myself kept me on my feet for long enough to do what was required. I fumbled my way back along the length of the string and collapsed gratefully onto the floor between the legs of the table.

"I wish I could put my arms around you," Martin's voice whispered out of the darkness. It was odd, but since we had awoken this time, we had spoken in whispers as if there were another sleeper in the room we were afraid of disturbing.

"Couldn't you?" I forced my sluggish mind to find a solution that would not involve having Martin's arm trapped uncomfortably under my body, a difficulty we had already encountered as we shifted and turned through the endless night. "If you lay on your back and I put my head on your shoulder . . ."

It took a little while and the removal of Martin's pocketbook and various other masculine necessities from his inner pockets before I was finally comfortable, my head pillowed so I heard the thump of my husband's heart and the faint sound of his breathing. "That's better," he said.

"Yes." I was more fully awake now, a little clearer in my mind despite the trembling in my legs and the overall lethargy that was surely the result of my raging thirst. I remembered the other fact that had tormented me at intervals and decided the time had come to share it.

"I believe I might be with child again."

I heard Martin's sharp intake of breath, but he didn't speak, so I did. "I wasn't going to say anything yet, but I missed my monthly time last month."

"I thought you had. I didn't want to mention it either."

Martin's mouth pushed aside my heavy curtain of hair to

find the skin of my forehead, and his kiss lingered. I tilted my head back so that his lips found mine. Our breath was sour, our lips dry, and the darkness smelled of our own bodily waste, but it didn't seem to matter.

"It occurred to me last night," Martin said after a few moments. "When we were in bed. I worried that you might be carrying a child and I would hurt it." His arms tightened around me. "But you urged me on, and I couldn't help myself."

"I was similarly affected." There was laughter in my voice, faint as it was. "If that were our last night together in our bed, I'm glad it was such a good one." I swallowed, trying to bring some moisture into my mouth. "I love being married to you. I love *you*. I admit it wasn't easy for me at first, being married, after all the struggles within myself. But whatever happens to the two of us, I want you to know that I now think marrying you was the most splendid thing I've ever done. Better than becoming one of the best couturières in Chicago. Better than being a partner in Rutherford & Co., although that in itself is very splendid. I'm starting to feel *our* story is the bedrock on which all my other stories are built."

"Only starting?" Martin's mouth moved against my forehead. "I've felt like that ever since the day you said you'd be mine." He laughed, a little burst of hot breath against my skin. "And what do you mean, *one* of the best couturières in Chicago? You're the best in America, in my opinion." He moved a little, so my head nestled more snugly into his shoulder. "Don't doubt yourself."

I was clammy, as if I were covered with blankets and beginning a fever, but I didn't want to leave Martin's arms. Closing my eyes wouldn't make much difference in this darkness, but I closed them anyway, and my other senses seemed to sharpen. I shifted again, just a little, so I could find

Martin's hands and press them to my belly, keeping them there with my own fingers.

I was surrounded by Martin—his heartbeat, his breath, his touch, his smell, the strength of his muscles—and if I concentrated hard, I sensed his child inside me, a presence I could neither feel nor see in any concrete way but that I knew to be there, a tiny spark of life far within my body, unreachable as the outside world. It too was in the darkness, I realized, and needed to stay there until the time was right. I forced all anxiety from my mind and made my breathing as even as I could, relaxing into the soft velvet of the dark.

5 1

LIGHT

I was dreaming of the sunlight again, and I wanted to be sick. It was no wonder the way the floor swayed under me. I opened my eyes to protest, and instead of darkness a yellow light stabbed me, causing me to sit up precipitously. My hand encountered empty air—I fell forward—

"Mrs. Rutherford, no!" The floor beneath me stopped moving and hands steadied me, preventing me from plunging into the abyss below. "Lower the stretcher," the same voice said.

The familiar hardness of the ground under my torso allowed the wave of nausea to pass, and I opened my eyes. I lay on the floor again—but it was the floor of the antechamber, not the vault. I had survived; surely the ten hours must be over. Unless I was still dreaming.

"Martin?" I croaked.

"I'm here."

I blinked furiously against the light, seeking the source of the voice. Martin sat on the floor of the antechamber, his back against the wall. He was barefoot and in shirtsleeves.

There was something strange about that, and then I realized his handcuffs had been taken off. His chest heaving, he began making the effort to rise and then fell forward onto hands and knees.

I sensed the touch of liquid against my lips and tried to grab greedily at the water, succeeding only in slopping a good deal of it down my front. A hand guided the glass to my mouth again, and I gulped desperately.

"More."

"You need to wait a few minutes, Nellie." Martin accepted the help of two men and rose to his feet, staggering toward me like a drunken man. "I wouldn't listen and drank too much, and now I've been sick all over the floor." He sank to his knees before me, pulling the blanket tighter around my shoulders. I realized I was wearing far less clothing than I expected but had no memory of taking it off.

"I'm sorry I wasn't next to you just now." Martin stroked my hair. "As soon as we made sure you were breathing, I had to get out of there." He glanced back at the opening through which I had evidently just been carried and then looked around at the various men milling around us. The antechamber was very full, I realized, and I tensed as I saw the dark watchmen's uniforms among the crowd.

"Joe?" Martin called.

"Right here." Joe Salazar squatted down on his heels so he was on our level. He looked terrible; one eye was entirely closed and very swollen, his lip so distended that it made his entire face look lopsided. The skin of his face was bright yellow in places where iodine had been applied, as were the tips of the fingers on his uninjured hand. One hand and the other arm were heavily bandaged.

"You're a mess." Martin stared at his partner. "Any more injuries than the ones I already know about? What about McCombs?"

"No injuries," Joe said briefly. "They had a carriage ready. Two of them drove us to the north end of Government Pier, blocked the carriage doors with a couple of iron bars and left us there. McCombs did a pretty good job of getting us out and raising the alarm. I wasn't much use."

He grinned, showing his uninjured hand. "I did a nifty bit of field dressing with plenty of Lugol's Solution once we got back to the store. Nell, can we try to get you upstairs? The store's closed, of course; it's one in the morning." He shook his head ruefully. "You should start feeling better with some rest and sustenance, and then the two of you are going home. No arguments. I'll send the detectives to you if they insist on interviewing you straightaway."

"I'm not arguing." Martin pressed his hands to his temples. "I think my head's about to drop off."

"It'll get better." Joe sounded weary. "We'll all need our strength. We're going to have the devil of a time with police, insurance, and the newspapers. As soon as I can, I'm going home to Leah and the children. I'll never hear the end of it when she sees what they did to me."

He laid a hand on Martin's shoulder. "I hoped the worst nights of my life were behind me when I took off my soldier's uniform, but I've never felt worse than when I was on one side of that door and you two were on the other. Ah." He rose to his feet and in a moment presented Martin and me with glasses half-filled with fresh water. "Sip this. The only thing you should worry about right now is yourselves. We'll deal with all the rest later."

"Except for one thing I need to say," said Martin after he'd taken a cautious sip. "We are going out of the jewelry business—or at least out of the business of selling the costly pieces. Joe, as soon as you're better I want you to arrange for our stock to be liquidated—I don't care what I lose on it— and you're going to ensure that damned door is disabled and left open. Use the room for what you want. I'm done with that particular venture."

A MOVEMENT IN MY BOUDOIR WOKE ME. I HAD BEEN DOZING, half sitting on a chaise longue near the window with a light blanket over my knees. Outside, rain lashed the sidewalk, the wind tearing the leaves from the small trees that bent sideways under its fury; in short, a good Chicago storm was in progress. It must have been midafternoon, but it was twilight beyond our windows.

"Hello, Nell." Tess's round face and sweetly plump form emerged from the armchair where she'd been sitting, no doubt waiting for sounds of my awakening. "Do you want anything? Let me give you some lemonade."

I accepted the beverage with pleasure and sipped it slowly, reveling in the cool air that stroked my skin with gentle fingers. The French windows to the balcony stood open a crack; the eaves of the house protected us sufficiently from the rain. Refreshed, I remembered what my first thought had been upon waking.

"Do you know where my overskirt is from yesterday?" I set down my glass. "I've recalled something that I put in the pocket."

"The pretty jewels!" Tess exclaimed. "Alice found them. They bundled all your clothes and things into a big Rutherford's box and sent it home with you."

She bustled off into the next room and returned with a porcelain dish on which sat my little watch, my thimble, and the two pieces I picked out the evening before. *A century ago.* It didn't seem possible that it was less than twenty-four hours since my only concern was to find a present for Tess. I had been sleeping on and off all day, rising only for the basic necessities; Martin had slept until ten and had since then been closeted with either the police or the insurance men.

Lightning flashed across the sky, hurting my eyes because I'd been looking directly at the spot where it appeared. The rain intensified as the thunder answered with a low growl. The lights had been lit to counter the unnatural darkness.

"They're so pretty." Tess picked up the pink brooch, holding it up to catch what light there was. "I like the color of this one."

"It's yours." I grinned. "We'd just chosen it for you as a wedding present when it all happened. We were going to have it cleaned and put in a box for you, of course, but I put it in my pocket by accident."

"Mine." A pleased smile spread across Tess's face as she breathed the word. "Can I pin it on my dress *now*?"

"Of course you can." I took up the sapphire-and-pearl pendant. "And this is for me to wear with my blue gown."

I held the bauble up to the light, watching dreamily as the two sapphires reflected the glimmer of the gas lamps and a fresh stab of lightning, yellow against a dark gray sky. "I'm going to have a baby," I said.

Tess looked up from pinning her new brooch to her bodice. "Oh, *Nell*." Her smile was tender. "When?"

I counted in my head for a moment. "February, I suppose. Another winter's child, like Sarah. As long as our stay in the vault didn't do him—or her—any harm." I laid the sapphire pendant along the base of the ruffles that decorated the upper part of the peignoir I wore. "But somehow I don't think so. I had such a strong conviction during those hours that our baby was safe."

"I hope so." Tess raised my hand, the one that bore my wedding and engagement rings, to where she could kiss it. The fourth finger of my right hand bore the incised gold ring I received from Hiram to promote the lie of widowhood, and which for me had become the symbol of my love for Sarah. Next to it shone the peridot ring Martin had given me for my twenty-fourth birthday. *So many jewels.* I sat up, pleased that my head was clearer than it had been earlier, and gave Tess a long, hard hug.

"Would you go down and see if Martin's overexerting himself? Tell him he's not supposed to. And if you can find Sarah, let her know I'm awake. She can come talk to me."

Tess stood, looking down at me. "I wish you wouldn't keep getting into danger, Nell. It was so horrid when they told me what had happened."

"I know." I grinned at her. "And such a waste of time when life's already so full. I'm going to sit quietly tomorrow and work on the details of your wedding. What do you think of that? And then I might sketch some ball gown ideas." I drew my knees up to my chin, enjoying the freedom of being in such light clothing at this time of the afternoon. "But your wedding comes first. I want it to be an absolutely glorious day."

52

CONTENTMENT

"I've gotten my wish about the weather."

I raised my face to the September sun. Its warm, mellow orb had risen above a calm lake, and its autumn-gold rays were burning away the early fall mists.

"The lull before the storm." My husband, an expression of mirth on his countenance, tipped his head up to scan the blue heavens. "And by storm, I refer to the guests rather than the weather."

Our garden was once more neat and orderly. Tess and Donny's new home looked incongruously tall to my eyes, but I knew that was just because I wasn't used to it yet. Below it, we had festooned the space that Martin still insisted on calling his billiard room with ropes of flowers and ribbons. Cleared of anything remotely connected with sporting pursuits, it was elegantly furnished for a large wedding meal.

Given that Tess's family were Catholic while she had adopted the Protestant faith, and that Donny had not stepped foot in a church for most of his life, we had settled for a short, old-fashioned, thoroughly American ceremony at home. A clergyman would officiate, but it would lack much of the fuss that seemed to plague wedding ceremonies these days. "Five minutes of talk and the rest of the day to celebrate," as Martin said; and we all agreed that celebrating was better than talking.

It was an arrangement that well suited Tess and Donny, both alarmed at the prospect of a large public wedding where they would be the center of attention for an entire long service. We had arranged for a blessing to be given at St. James as part of the normal Sunday service instead.

I still thought our house too big, but at that moment it did not seem quite so capacious. We were about to fit in *all* of Tess's brothers and sisters with their husbands, betrothed, and children; all the Salazars; the growing Fletcher family; Mr. and Mrs. Parnell; Miss Baker and her housemates; and, to my delight, Madame Belvoix with her friend Madame Hélouïse. We had insisted that both Miss Baker and Madame brought guests if they wished rather than come alone, and they had accepted with enthusiasm. The children were to be present at the meal but at a separate table, well supervised by a bevy of nursemaids instructed to keep a special watch on the Sheehan boys and Mabel Fletcher, especially during the wedding ceremony. Our first truly big occasion in Calumet Avenue was going to be a riotous affair.

I tucked my arm under Martin's, relishing the bustle of activity. Mrs. Hartfield was in her element; after weeks of planning, I was happy to leave the actual day almost entirely to her.

"Do you feel all right?" Martin's grip on my arm tightened a little.

"I'm fine." I smoothed a hand over the slight swelling that was becoming apparent if I stood a certain way. "Or at least I'll be fine soon. Once we get to ten o'clock in the morning, I always feel well—it's just that until then, I have the sensation I'm on a boat. Do you imagine Mabel Fletcher or Frankie

Sheehan will make the most trouble this afternoon? I wish it were possible to just invite the other three of Mary's boys."

"Frankie is a fact of our lives, as is Mabel. We can't pick and choose, I suppose. How does Elizabeth feel about being *enceinte* again?"

"Not *entirely* pleased, although she's quite cheerful and stoical about it. She's glad we'll be having our children close together, and so am I. We can sit and gossip while they play."

I flipped up the timepiece on my bodice, squinting at the numbers. "Alice should have finished with Sarah's hair by now. I'd better run upstairs and subject myself to some hair-dressing. She has Tess's coiffure to do last of all, and then she'll want to get herself spruced up. At least her job is done before the ceremony starts. Still, the other staff seem quite happy about going back to work after they've seen Tess become Mrs. Clark."

"They're looking forward to their own celebration." Martin turned me round so we could see the iron pergola, which was being decorated with yet more flowers. It was here that the bride and groom would stand to say their vows, within sight of Ruth's tree. The latter had put on good growth during the summer and now reached almost to the top of Sarah's head.

"Tess is going to be an absolute picture." I sighed. "This is more exciting than my own wedding."

"What an admission, Mrs. Rutherford." Martin rolled his eyes at me as we turned and began walking back toward the house. "I recall that our wedding was *full* of incident."

"Well, yes—but I'm far less nervous. I *was* nervous, you know. I knew I loved you desperately, but I felt as if I were walking through a door that would slam shut forever."

"And what have you found on the other side of that door?" The corners of Martin's eyes crinkled in the way that always sent a dart of pleasure through me.

"Happiness, of course." I wrinkled my nose, trying to come up with something stronger than such a trite answer. "Perhaps contentment is a better word? I seem to have stopped fretting so much over the past and the future and just learned to take each moment as it comes. And you? You've seemed extraordinarily buoyant over the last couple of months. Is it the baby? Or getting rid of the responsibility of all those jewels? Or are you happy because you're working on building another house? You've certainly had plenty of healthy exercise riding to Lake Forest and back."

"All of those things." Martin's voice rang with a slight echo as we stepped into the hallway. "But most of all, I think, because I've solved a puzzle. I've always doubted I would face death with courage—I've never had the chance to try. I've seen you do it, more than once, and wondered. But now I know I can be calm even when faced with my worst fears. It almost makes being entombed in a vault worthwhile."

"I͟t͟'s͟ ͟a͟ ͟f͟i͟n͟e͟, ͟f͟i͟n͟e͟ ͟w͟e͟d͟d͟i͟n͟g͟, ͟M͟r͟s͟. ͟R͟u͟t͟h͟e͟r͟f͟o͟r͟d͟, ͟a͟n͟d͟ ͟I͟ ͟t͟h͟a͟n͟k͟ you for it. Whoever would have thought I'd see Tess married in such silks and jewels? And he *is* a nice-looking boy, when you take the time to really look at him. Gentle too, for all that he's as big as a prizefighter."

Mrs. O'Dugan applied her handkerchief to her huge, somewhat reddened eyes. "Ah, here I am crying like the Niagara Falls. Which I've never seen, of course, but now that Billy has been to Buffalo, he has described everything to me just like drawing a picture." She heaved a great sigh. "And him to travel to Florida next year as well. What a life these young people lead. Of course *you* have been to Europe."

"I don't set great store by traveling. Although it's good for Sarah to see a little of the world." I smiled at Tess's mother.

"You'll have Tess and Donny close at least. Not even a honeymoon for the two of them. They just want to start what Sarah calls 'playing house.'"

"I heard young Sarah asking those nice Salazar girls if they knew what happened on a honeymoon." Mrs. O'Dugan smiled through her tears. "You must keep an eye on that one. She's too clever by half. And so dainty. A darling little face and such beautifully shaped hands as I have never seen in my life. She looked so proud holding Tessie's bouquet during the ceremony. And her dress is almost as beautiful as my daughter's."

I smiled at Margaret O'Dugan. I had learned to like her better in the last few months as our families mingled more. She had told me much about the hard years of their lives, the anguish of giving Tess up to the Poor Farm, the deaths of two children, the poverty and grinding work, lightened only by her growing faith. In the O'Dugans, with their practical outlook on life and their entire acceptance of Sarah's illegitimacy, I had discovered friends to whom I could talk about the Poor Farm without reserve or shame, and I valued them for it.

A small cough behind us made me turn. I found myself under the watchful, yet uncharacteristically amused, eye of Madame Belvoix—who, like her friend Madame Hélouïse, was dressed in finery that almost eclipsed the bride. It was a side of her I'd never seen before.

"You are forgetting something, Mrs. Rutherford."

"I am?" I racked my brains. Having seen Tess and Donny married, I had allowed myself to relax for a little and talk to the other wedding guests without wondering every minute if something would go wrong.

"You are to give the signal for the procession to form." Madame nodded imperiously. "I do not think Monsieur and Madame Clark are up to the task. They are a very shy bride and groom. Madame Hélouïse finds them quite *charmant.*"

"Ah. Thank you, Madame. Excuse me, Mrs. O'Dugan."

She was right; I *had* taken that task on myself, in a moment of mistaken belief that I would know how to do it. I kissed my hand to Tess as I passed her, resplendent in her pink silk satin, her long veil crowned with a coronet of satin flowers and sprays of pearls on ribbon-covered wires. Beside her, Donny looked gentlemanlike in his dark blue cutaway coat, ivory waistcoat, and pale gray trousers. The pink rose in his lapel, brought especially from Mrs. Parnell's rose garden, had a sheen not even Rutherford's finest suppliers could match. The chain of his new gold watch shone in the sunshine. He was talking with Mr. Parnell, but every few seconds his gaze would stray back to Tess with a kind of baffled adoration.

For good measure, I kissed my hand to Martin, who was speaking to David, and saw both men grin broadly. I ducked under the flower sprays that decorated the pergola, smelling the sweet scent of hothouse lilies, and grabbed the small silver bell that sat in the middle of the table.

It took half a minute for the tinkling noise of the bell to produce the required level of hush. Elizabeth was still talking in a rapid undertone to Mabel, trying no doubt to head off another tantrum, when I began to speak.

"I'm not going to make a speech," I said and laughed as the younger men set up a ragged cheer. "I just want to give you the best news of all, that the wedding feast is served, and I hope you have all remembered the partners I assigned to you for our procession. Starting, of course, with Mr. and Mrs. Donald Clark."

More cheers followed. The guests assembled themselves and their children into a line that, when formed, ran right around the edges of the lawn and curled back in upon itself.

It was a more chaotic performance than I had planned, but eventually I set the newly wedded Clarks to walking into the billiard room through a double line of smiling household staff holding hoops festooned with flowers. I half-ran to join Martin, bringing up the rearguard of the adult party while the nursemaids and bigger girls kept the smaller children in position behind us.

Sarah, who had taken on the task of keeping Mabel happy, favored me with a tiny wink and a discreetly raised thumb to signal her approval of the proceedings. We had spent the last few weeks together in a whirl of activity, rehearsing both Tess and Donny until they could speak their vows without hesitation, practicing the Virginia reel with the bride and groom, talking over the wedding arrangements, chatting as I cut and sewed Sarah's ensemble, which was ivory and gold with touches of pink. The thought of the infant we would welcome into our home somewhere around my daughter's tenth birthday was shifting my perception of Sarah from child to companion, a change that both pleased and unnerved me.

"Well, here we are. And I've been far too busy to cry." I slipped my arm through Martin's and took a firm grip on the hard muscle of his forearm.

"You've never been a sentimental woman. Now, Nellie, your work is done; enjoy the fun before we go on to the next adventure."

"Thank you, but I'd be happier with a quiet life for a couple of years. I just want a well-born child and time to sit and draw dresses. Do you suppose we could manage that?"

"I'd like to think so." Martin's eyes were clear gray, serene. The weeks of fruitless investigation—and an unsuccessful attempt by the insurance company to suggest a fraud—had not seemed to disturb his equilibrium one jot. "But you're not a peaceful person, Nellie. Your strength and beauty and talent seem to draw trouble to you. Perhaps we just have to get used to having interesting lives."

"I could say the same about you, my handsome robber baron."

I smiled at Martin and then twisted round to see Sarah, who mercifully appeared to have placated Mabel and was performing a little dance with her as the line shuffled onward. "I wonder if Sarah's future will be quite so full of incident? I truly hope not."

"Don't worry about Sarah." Martin urged me forward; we had allowed rather a sizeable gap to open up in front of us. "She can take care of herself."

The Scott-De Quincy Mysteries

Lady Helena Investigates
Lady Odelia's Secret

A reluctant lady sleuth finds she's investigating her own family.

As the sixth daughter of an Earl, Lady Helena Whitcombe has grown up not to expect much from life. Yet widowhood leaves her with a fortune, a grand mansion in Sussex, and a friendship with French physician Armand Fortier—and her discoveries about her family's past ensure that her position as the baby of the Scott-De Quincy family will not remain her lot in life.

"I can't say enough in praise of Jane Steen's worldbuilding, the immersion into Helena's world, and her character"—Coffee and Ink book blog

FROM THE AUTHOR

Dear Reader,

I hope you enjoyed reading *The Jewel Cage* as much as I enjoyed writing it. I'm an indie author paying bills by doing what I love the most—creating entertainment for other people. So my most important assets are YOU, the readers, without whom I'd just be talking to myself. Again.

My promise to you is that I'll do my best. I'll research to make the historical background to my stories as accurate as I can. I'll edit and polish until the book's up to my (high) standards. I'll give you a great-looking cover to look at, and I'll make sure my books are available in as many formats and in as many places as possible. I'll keep my prices as low as is compatible with keeping my publishing business going.

What can you do for me? If you've loved this book, there are several ways you can help me out.

Let me know what you think. If you go to www.janes teen.com, you'll see a little envelope icon near the bottom of the page. That's how you contact me by email. Or you can use the Contact page on the website. I'd love to hear what you thought of the book. Or find me on Facebook, Twitter, or Goodreads.

Leave a review. An honest review—even if you just want to say you didn't like the book—is a huge help. Leave it on the site where you bought the book, or on a reader site like Goodreads.

Tell a friend. I love it when sales come through word of mouth. Better still, mention my book on social media and amplify your power to help my career.

Follow me on BookBub to be informed about deals on my books or new releases.

Sign up for my newsletter at www.janesteen.com/insider. That's a win-win: my newsletter is where I offer free copies, unpublished extras, insider info, and let you know when a new book's coming out.

And thanks again for reading.

AUTHOR'S NOTE

The Jewel Cage is a book I never intended to write. In the early days of writing the House of Closed Doors series I knew that there would be two trilogies, one for Nell and one for Sarah. It seemed like such a simple challenge when I first thought of it and has turned out to be incredibly difficult in a number of ways.

I knew that the point at which I wanted to start Sarah's story left a gap of several years after the close of *The Shadow Palace*, and naturally I had ideas about what happened in the intervening period. At the same time, I had plenty of readers clamoring for more Nell books. And I wanted to tell Tess's love story in a Nell book rather than a Sarah book. So I considered several ideas and eventually settled on writing a single book to bridge the gap.

In a sense, *The Jewel Cage* is the backstory for the Sarah trilogy, which is why it has to leave some questions unanswered. I'm sure you know what they are by now, and I apologize for not tying everything up in a neat bow at the end of *The Jewel Cage* (although if that's what you're looking for, why are you reading a Jane Steen book?) All I can say is that I will tie up those threads at the right time. I'm speaking, of course, to those of you reading the series before I've completed it; hopefully there are also people reading these words once the series is finished and wondering what the fuss was about.

The Jewel Cage has been a problem child for me for other reasons. I was working on the first draft when, one dark night in 2017, a drunk driver hit my car head-on when I was five minutes from home, at combined speeds of over 100mph. A well-designed car, a low grassy bank and my seatbelt allowed me to "walk away" from the crash with only a short visit to the local hospital but the trauma, the physical consequences of a high-speed impact, and the legal case went on for years. I eventually finished that first draft but had an aversion to working on it for some time; and when I got around to reading it again, the second half of the draft looked like someone else had written it. I had to rewrite the whole thing drastically, even though that meant adding far too many words.

Adding to my woes, the story as it developed simply would not combine with a "proper" mystery. I'm not a true mystery writer, anyway; as a reader, I'm quickly bored by the clues-detection-solution formula, so my stories always include other elements. As I wrote *The Jewel Cage* the other elements kept taking over, and it wasn't until I was nearing the final draft that I realized I'd written a many-faceted love story, with Nell and Martin at the center. Serves me right, I suppose, for venturing on beyond the Happily Ever After.

I keep the historical background to my stories fairly muted, but I couldn't ignore the Great Strike (also known as the

Great Upheaval) of 1877, which left its mark on Chicago through an event known as the Battle of the Viaduct.

Since the financial Panic of 1873, the United States had been enduring an economic depression that eventually lasted over five years. By 1877 its workers had had enough of seeing their wages fall while the rich merchants and industrialists—nicknamed "robber barons"—built enormous, ostentatious houses, traveled to Europe and back in luxury liners, and developed a lifestyle so lavish that the last part of the 1800s became known as the Gilded Age.

The growing gap between rich and poor led to a fermenting mass of societal unrest intensified by decades of socialist and communist theory, by the increasing importance of unions, and by a workforce swelled by mass immigration after the Civil War. The Feminists—capitalized in that era, which is why Nell capitalizes the word—were agitating for votes for women. Urban politics were increasingly dominated by corrupt authoritarians, while the people the parties claimed to represent were burdened by exorbitantly long working hours, terrible conditions, and child labor. And all this was happening after a presidential election in 1876 marred by allegations of voter fraud. It was only settled in 1877 by a highly dubious political compromise that destroyed America's fragile attempts at achieving some measure of racial equality.

Matters came to a head in Chicago at the end of July 1877. Thirty workers were killed at the Halsted Street viaduct during a fight between rioters and police that only ended when the cavalry arrived. The police, who minutes before had feared for their lives, turned on the mob in an exhibition of police brutality that restored "law and order" by intimidating and demoralizing the strikers. In the long run, the aftermath of the Great Strike strengthened the unions' resolve and brought about the beginnings of pension and sickness benefits, while on the side of authority it prompted the modernization of the police and the creation of the National Guard.

If you're seeing in my words some parallels with the fractured year 2020, you're probably right. I can't look into the future, but I always believe we can learn from history—and this particular slice of American history never seems to get the attention it deserves. As I've said before, in my opinion *1877: America's Year of Living Violently* by Michael Bellesiles is still the fastest route to getting a comprehensive picture of a pivotal moment.

The other facet of real-life history I couldn't help bringing in was the great couturier Charles Frederick Worth, who dominated the emerging haute couture industry to an extent I'm not sure has ever quite been matched. He was the first designer to put his own label in his clothing and the first to create a brand so recognizable that it eclipsed the women for whom the dresses were made. He made the word "chic" fashionable. He was a true innovator, for example inventing a system to track which gown was made for which occasion so that no two women would turn up at an event in a gown of the same style and color. There's not nearly enough written about him and I didn't have the space to do him justice; if you're interested, I recommend *Worth* by Diana de Marly as a starting point.

I haven't entirely done with Nell and Martin, of course. How could I? But I'm glad I struggled through all the challenges to write *The Jewel Cage*, because before I wrote it I didn't really feel ready to tackle Sarah's story. I do now.

ACKNOWLEDGMENTS

Author-publishers like myself are often dubbed "self-publishers", but like many of my breed I find that term falls far short of the reality. I don't write and publish my books by myself. I have a whole team of people without whom I couldn't offer you a polished finished article, and behind all of us there is an entire industry of app developers, service providers, and distributors who make it possible to run our businesses in ways I couldn't even have imagined when I started out with one book back in 2011.

My editor, Jenny Quinlan (historicaleditorial. blogspot.com), ensures that my manuscript is clean and consistent and invariably spots an anachronism or two along the way. My cover designer is Rachel Lawston (lawstonde sign.com), whose considerable talents grace books of all kinds and who is an author herself. For my audiobooks I turn to Elizabeth Klett (elizabethklettaudio.com) who narrates with aplomb and produces crystal clear, flawless audio. These three professionals are remarkably easy to work with, and I have complete confidence in their advice.

At the earlier stages of the book's development there have been advance readers, helping to make the story better by giving me their comments and advice on various drafts. My first readers were Sherri Gallagher and Maureen Lang, and as always their incisive observations were an immense help. Thank you, my writer friends.

Later in the process I recruited newsletter subscribers into my beta reading team, and what a team they were. I'm not an easy author to beta read for as my expectations of my beta readers are almost as high as my expectations for myself, but twelve wonderful readers stuck with me from beginning to end. Brandi Bartsma, Deena Nataf, Glenda Thompson, Hilarie Berzins, Jacomien Zwemstra, Jenna Matheson, Leslie McKinnon, Marta Tetzeli, Rebekah Witherspoon, Sharon Holt, and Shirley Stephens, you have my undying gratitude for all the hours you spent spotting my mistakes, analyzing my historical references, commenting on my Britishisms, and questioning my plot choices. *The Jewel Cage* is a much better book because of you.

If you noticed that I've only listed eleven names, you should probably be a beta reader. I've singled one out for a special thank-you. Kate Burgess was a member of the beta reading team, but she deserves a separate mention as a wonderful assistant on the reader services and publishing side of my business. Without Kate there probably wouldn't be a newsletter and certainly no giveaways. Asking her to put in extra time as a beta reader was perhaps a little cheeky of me, but she rose to the challenge magnificently and is finding more and more ways to help me become a better publisher.

I would also like to thank Susan Kings, Leander Couldridge, and Helen Turner at Kings Accounting for saving me hours and hours and hours and hours of work that I would be very bad at and ensuring that all my numbers add up and my paperwork is filed correctly and on time.

ABOUT THE AUTHOR

The most important fact you need to know about me is that I was (according to my mother, at least) named after Jane Eyre, which to this day remains one of my favorite books. I was clearly doomed to love all things Victorian, and ended up studying both English and French nineteenth-century writers in depth.

This was a pretty good grounding for launching myself into writing novels set in the nineteenth century. I was living in the small town of Libertyville, Illinois—part of the greater Chicago area—when I began writing the *House of Closed Doors* series, inspired by a photograph of the long-vanished County Poor Farm on Libertyville's main street.

Now back in my native England, I have the good fortune to live in an idyllic ancient town close to the sea. This location has sparked a new series about an aristocratic family with more secrets than most: *The Scott-De Quincy Mysteries*.

I write for readers who want a series you can't put down. I love to blend saga, mystery, adventure, and a touch of romance, set against the background of the real-life issues facing women in the late nineteenth century.

I am a member of the Alliance of Independent Authors, the Historical Novel Society, Novelists, Inc., and the Society of Authors.

To find out more about my books, join my insider list at www.janesteen.com/insider

- facebook.com/janesteenwriter
- twitter.com/JaneSteen
- bookbub.com/authors/jane-steen
- goodreads.com/janesteen
- pinterest.com/janesteen

Made in the USA
Columbia, SC
14 December 2022

73764330R00328